Radiance and Revenge
A Diamond of the Ton Regency Mystery
Book 3

Lynn Morrison

Anne Radcliffe

Marketing Chair Press

This novel's story and characters are fictitious. Certain long-standing institutions, agencies, and public offices are mentioned, but the story is wholly imaginary. Some of the characters were inspired by actual historical figures, and abide by the generally known facts about these individuals and their relevant time periods. However, their actions and conversations are strictly fiction. All other characters and events are the product of our own imaginations.

Cover design by The Killion Group, Inc

Published by The Marketing Chair Press, Oxford, England

LynnMorrisonWriter.com

ISBN (paperback): 978-1-917361-18-7

Contents

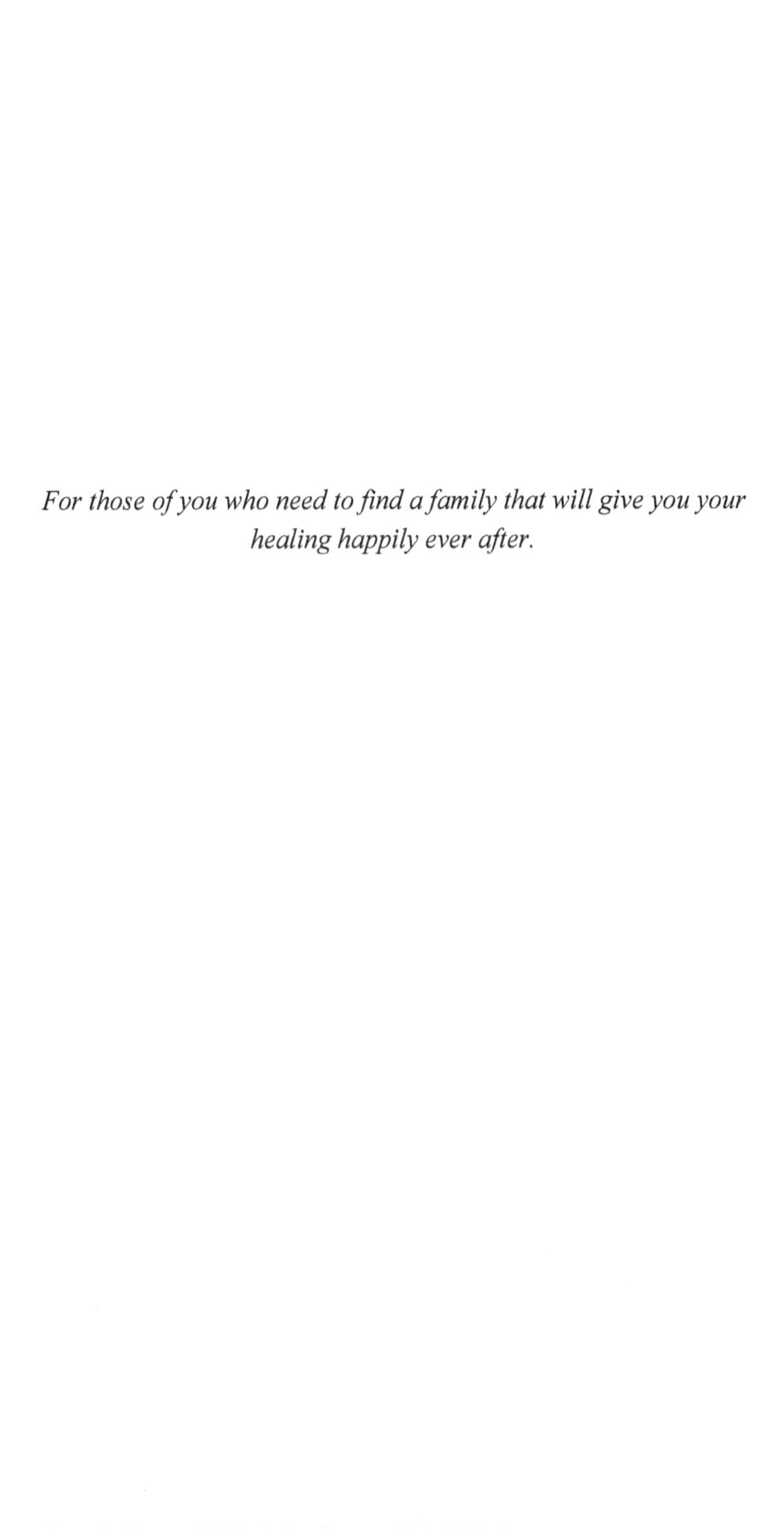

For those of you who need to find a family that will give you your healing happily ever after.

Characters of Note

<u>Main Characters and their Families / Households:</u>

- Lady Charity Cresswell – now the Dowager Duchess Atholl
  - Lady Vanessa Cresswell – Charity's mother
  - Lord Martyn Cresswell – Charity's father
  - Pritchard – Charity's butler
  - Miller – Charity's maid
- Lord Peregrine Fitzroy
  - Lady Marian Fitzroy – Peregrine's mother
  - Lord Robin Fitzroy – Peregrine's father, poisoned by Marian *(Deceased)*
  - Lady Lark Fitzroy – Peregrine's younger sister
  - Will Hodges – Peregrine's driver, former mercenary
  - Martha – Hodges's sister
  - Sammy – Hodges's nephew
  - Quinn – Peregrine's butler
  - Croft – Peregrine's valet and former batman of General Rowland Hill

- Edmunds – former Fitzroy family butler, last survivor of the old household staff
- Lincoln Frank – Peregrine's solicitor

British Royal Family and Major Government Officials:

- The Prince Regent – later George IV, also referred to as Prinny
- Queen Charlotte – Wife of the mad king, George III, and mother of Prinny
- Princess Charlotte of Wales – Prinny's daughter
- Princess Caroline of Brunswick – Spouse of Prinny, mother of Princess Charlotte
- Duke of Clarence – One of Prinny's younger brothers
- Lord Ravenscroft – Prinny's whisperer, the magpie
  - Antoine – Lord Ravenscroft's valet and lover
- Lord Sidmouth – Home Secretary, responsible for domestic security
- Lord Castlereagh – Secretary of State for Foreign Affairs, organizer of the Allied Sovereigns' visit
- Lord Liverpool – Prime Minister (Tory party)

Russian Royal Family and Court:

- Tsar Alexander I – Emperor of Russia
- Catherine Pavlovna, Grand Duchess of Oldenburg – Sister of the Tsar
- Constantine Pavlovich, Grand Duke of Russia – (Not present) Younger brother of the Tsar
- Nicholas Pavlovich, Grand Duke of Russia – Youngest brother of the Tsar
- Count von Lieven – Russian ambassador to London, accompanied by his wife

Other named visiting dignitaries:

- Prince William VI of Orange – The Dutch prince intended for Princess Charlotte
- Prince Klemens von Metternich – Austrian Foreign Minister
  - Baron Friedrich von Gentz – The Propagandist, Prince Metternich's right hand
- Prince Paul of Württemberg – Representative of King Frederick I of Württemberg
- Prince Leopold of Saxe-Coburg – Part of Alexander's entourage as a distinguished Russian general, but also unofficial representative of the duchy of Saxe-Coburg
- Frederick William III – The King of Prussia

Other allies and notables:

- Sir Nathaniel Thorne – the bastard brother of Duke Roland Percy
- Lady Selina, Marchioness of Normanby – The Order's former statesman
- Xavier – The Order's former spymaster
- Red Hand – An unaligned mercenary for hire
- Grace and Roland Percy, the Duchess and Duke of Northumberland – (not present) Charity's best friends and rescuers from the previous year
- Sir David Green – Accomplice in the theft of the ruby dagger, blackmailed by Marian Fitzroy *(Deceased)*
- Goldbourne – The Order's Financier, who managed a bank *(Deceased)*
- Duke Chandros – The Order's Strategist, with military contacts *(Deceased)*

- Godfrey Bellrose – (not present) Clerk from the Treasury who held Charity and Selina captive
- Grenville – The Fitzroy family lawyer Peregrine unknowingly poisoned *(Deceased)*
- McGrath – Marian Fitzroy's former hired killer *(Deceased)*

1

"Hell is empty and all the devils are here."
—Ariel, *The Tempest*

Lady Marian Fitzroy was many things—a mother, criminal, traitor. A murderer. She was a woman callous enough to attempt killing her own son.

And she was *here*.

The brush of heavy skirts across the throne room's polished wooden floors was the only warning Charity got before the woman struck at Perry. Marian Fitzroy leaned forward, embraced her son as he stood beside Charity, and pressed a kiss to his bloodless cheek. "Peregrine, love, how well you're looking!"

She straightened, fixing him with a predatory gaze. Lady Fitzroy possessed the same slatey irises as her son—but right now, hers circled reptilian voids, like those eyes belonged to something more dead than alive. The mask had slipped, showing that whatever spark of soul Marian might have possessed was... lacking.

Lady Fitzroy was unhappy to see her son alive.

The blood crawled backwards in Charity's veins. Never had she beheld anything so unnatural. And struck by his mother's deadly basilisk stare, the man who held her heart became as still as stone and just as ashen.

"How fortunate we arrived in time to wish you a happy birthday," his mother continued, radiating malevolence.

Not that the others nearby seemed to sense her uncanny *wrongness*. All they saw was a handsome, older woman wearing a slight, supercilious smile. She wore a silk dress overlaid with fine lace, and pearls dripped from her ears and neck. It was an ostentatious display of wealth that spoke of no hardship or privation this past year.

The watching members of the *ton* were not near enough to notice that her stare did not rightfully appear to belong to any human thing. But their whispers about other things swirled thickly.

"Did they invite her, or did she simply tell them she was coming?"

"Russia collects Fabergé eggs and fallen Englishwomen, it seems."

Peregrine had speculated his mother wouldn't dare to return to English soil—not short of having an army at her back. How terrifyingly right his supposition had been. She arrived in the train of the Tsar of Russia, the leader of the most powerful country, besides England, in the world.

The moment had an unreal feeling, like a nightmare. Charity might have thought she was trapped dreaming if the woman had not deliberately grazed her arm. The contact was brief—barely a brush—but it sent a shock of memory through her. The sensation of the silk binding her wrists skittered along her skin. The thick fog of laudanum, and many lost days. Strange voices that echoed in the cold chamber.

Charity held herself still, digging her nails into her palm to keep from reacting. And when she did nothing, Lady Fitzroy finally turned to regard Charity, narrowing her eyes in a direct challenge.

Peregrine's mother bore no guilt over kidnapping Charity during her last season. Revenge against Lord and Lady Cresswell —Charity's parents—had been the motive to ruin their daughter, and Marian had nursed this grudge against them for nearly thirty years.

Marian had gone unpunished. The woman had orchestrated her scheme so cleverly that charges would have cut both ways. She had been free to continue with her last intrigues until she had stolen from the Crown and escaped last year.

People continued to mutter. *"I wonder what the Cresswells think of their daughter standing next to the traitor's son now."*

Charity's back stiffened, hearing the insult to Peregrine. But Lady Fitzroy appeared unruffled. She smiled and patted Perry's cheek with a cruel familiarity, looking to all the world like a mother and son having a loving reunion. He stood stock-still beneath her hand, almost vibrating with tension as she whispered, "Smile, my dears. So many people are watching us."

With her parting remark, Lady Fitzroy pulled away.

Hundreds of candles shone in the candelabras, but the world seemed dim and spotty at the edges. In desperation, Charity turned towards the royal family, wondering if they noticed the Russian delegation housed a traitor.

Only the Queen's eyes met hers—the briefest, sternest flick— before Charlotte turned her attention back to a handful arriving from Saxony. The Queen knew. She *saw*. And she was ignoring Lady Fitzroy's presence here among all the gathered Sovereign Allies as though nothing untoward had happened.

Why hadn't they called the guards? Why weren't they doing anything?

The world began to turn on its axis, and an echo of Perry's voice snarled at her in her thoughts. *Breathe, Sparkles!*

Swooning. She was swooning. Her mouth opened in a gasp as her fingers shot out, looking for support and finding Peregrine's hand. His steadiness helped anchor her as she recovered her senses. Unfortunately, the act cost them their dignity.

"My word, she is holding Fitzroy's hand! Here!" Titters followed, and another susurrus of voices.

In a room with some of the highest-ranking titles in the world, the only name on everyone's lips was Fitzroy. She let him go the moment she heard the whisper, but the damage was already done.

Charity's chest tightened as the gossip battered them. In the short span of a few minutes, Lady Fitzroy had not only destroyed the progress Perry had made in separating his affairs from his mother's, she had shaken Charity enough to shame the both of them in front of the *ton*.

What couldn't this woman do, given a day? A week? Or a month?

And Lady Fitzroy was not even the limit of their problems, as she was abruptly reminded when Lord Ravenscroft, near Princess Charlotte, barked a sharp cough into his fist to draw Charity's attention. That tone demanded she *compose herself.*

She took in the room. Sir Nathaniel and Lady Normanby were waiting warily in their positions. But her eyes travelled past them to where her parents stood, side by side, glowering at her and Peregrine.

They had friends here, but they were beset by their worst enemies. Every single one of them was here in this room.

A despondent feeling began to crush Charity's chest. Had she and Peregrine been fools to dare to dream they might envision a future together?

Then, the Royal Chamberlain strode forward and banged his staff thrice, bringing order to the shuffling crowd. "Lady Fitzroy,

Dowager Countess of Fitzroy, and her daughter Lady Lark," he announced to the throne. "They have a gift to present, if you will allow it."

There. There was the Crown's chance to notice the viper in their midst. To send her away. Cool logic fought to halt Charity's descent into despair, offering a thread of hope. But it was about to be dashed again.

"Lady Fitzroy," the Queen murmured, her mien giving away nothing of her thoughts. "We were not expecting your return." Beside her, Prinny's eyes were hooded.

Peregrine's mother executed a facile, perfect curtsy. She was as graceful as one might expect from a season's Incomparable. Demure, almost pious in her guise, her shining eyes were upon her sovereign.

It was a flawless performance.

"My apologies, Your Majesty. What I brought, I hope, will make up for the messages that went astray," Lady Fitzroy replied, looking the Queen right in the eye as she rose up. "The Tsar was kind enough to offer us safe passage. Given the near priceless value of what I have brought, I dared not travel alone."

Lady Fitzroy turned around and motioned a footman to come forward, his arms holding a small wooden trunk.

All around Charity, people leaned forward to get a closer look at what might be inside. Charity braced herself, half fearing something dangerous might be inside. But surely even Marian Fitzroy was not brazen enough to commit regicide in front of an audience.

"Your Highness," Lady Fitzroy said, directing her words in Prinny's direction. "This is yours." She released the latch and opened the lid, revealing a weapon encrusted with blood-red rubies.

The British lords and ladies in the crowd gasped, hushed speculation flying along the receiving line yet again as people recognised the item in question. It was the ruby dagger that had been gifted by the Swedish ambassador last year. The one Lady Fitzroy had blackmailed Sir David Green, a former soldier, into taking from this very room before she had fled with Lark to the continent.

Peregrine gritted his teeth beside her, his hands balling into fists.

Charity darted a look at him, wondering if he was all right. Lady Fitzroy had intended for her son to take the fall for the crime. It had been one of Perry's weapons that had been left stabbed into the dead guard.

Now, here she was, presenting it back to the Crown as though it was a gift, and not the proof of her guilt.

"You dare arrive with that weapon!" Prinny looked thunderous.

"With respect, Your Highness, I only dare to restore your stolen property and clear my name." Lady Fitzroy's voice was steady and deferential. "I am afraid my dear son and I may be as much victims of Sir David as you have been. I found this dagger hidden in my trunks a while after I had been on the continent."

Lies rolled off her tongue with practised ease. "I dared not send so precious an item with someone else, and I was unsure when it would be safe for me to return. Then I heard my son performed such valiant services for England and was allowed to come home, a war hero. I beg you to accept my apology for the delay, and I wish you to understand how dear a friend Russia has been to England in this effort to bring it home."

"Indeed," Queen Charlotte murmured noncommittally as she glanced at the Tsar, who inclined his head. "It seems we owe you thanks for this small service."

Lady Fitzroy clasped her hands together, looking pleased. "I am so pleased to be of service to the Crown. I hope I might be able to reclaim my place in society if you are satisfied with my innocence?"

The Queen and the Regent were silent for a long moment. They were caught in a political trap, Charity realised.

They did not have to accept Lady Fitzroy's story—but if they didn't, there was a risk of offending the Tsar and embarrassing themselves. However, if they did accept it, they would be practically exonerating her in all but name. She would be free to go about her business in London.

They were beaten in this. Checkmate.

Charity watched in horror as the Queen pinched her mouth shut, biting back her true feelings. Her expression smoothed back into the unfeeling mask of an indifferent royal. She might as well have waved the white flag of defeat.

Queen Charlotte's lashes flickered. "We are satisfied no further inquiry is necessary at present. You may resume your place, Lady Fitzroy. That is, should society be inclined to receive you."

"You made quite an entrance, Lady Fitzroy. Let us hope your other activities here in London are... less eventful," Prinny said, earning a slanted glance from his mother. He motioned for the footmen to open the side doors, and the Royal Chamberlain banged his staff on the floor a final time before inviting everyone to proceed to the reception room for refreshments.

Prinny and Queen Charlotte led the way, followed by the princess and then the visiting delegates in order of importance. Charity fought against the tide, dashing for the doors to the terrace. Her stomach roiled with nausea. She could not be sick. Not here. Her lungs burned with the need for fresh air.

Perry was fast on her heels, refusing to let her escape without him. Charity's eyes stung with the threat of tears, blurring her vision. Her steps slowed enough for Perry to pull her to a stop.

"I am so sorry," he said. "This is my fault. I feel like somehow I should have foreseen this."

Charity blinked back her tears, fighting for control. "No one in England might have foreseen your mother's return. It is madness!"

"If only that were true, we might have a chance of defeating her," he muttered. "Sparkles, are you all right?"

Before she replied, a male voice growled, "Remove your hand from my daughter at once, Lord Fitzroy! Or I will remind you how gentlemen settle such disrespect."

It was her father, his face flushed as he strode up to them. She had not seen him this angry since the day she told him she had broken off her engagement with Roland Percy.

His ire, however, was not aimed solely at her. Lord Martyn Cresswell raised his finger and threatened to poke it into Perry's chest. "You have no place in this conversation. Take yourself elsewhere."

"Papa," Charity pleaded, "lower your voice. People are looking—"

"Lord Cresswell—" Peregrine began.

"People are staring at *your* brazen misbehaviour," Cresswell said, cutting them both off. He swung back to Perry. "I have given you no permission to court my daughter, nor will I. Take your leave before I call you out."

He met her father's glare head-on with a flat stare, refusing to heed the command. Crimson climbed up Lord Cresswell's neck, past his starched cravat.

"With respect, my lord, if the duchess wishes me gone, I shall go. But not before." Peregrine crossed his arms over his chest, waiting for her to decide.

Though she desperately needed his strength, she tipped her face up to meet Perry's searching gaze and nodded for him to go.

She did not want him to witness her father's tirade. Or to take the brunt of it.

Perry shook his head and stepped back, retreating out of earshot to a place where she was able to see and call him if she needed him.

Lord Cresswell wrapped a hand around Charity's upper arm and pushed her through the doorway onto the terrace, and then dragged her on until they reached the far edge away from the door. When she pulled free of his hold, he shifted position to block her escape.

From his youthful portraits, Charity knew her father had once been a handsome man. The years and his growing dissatisfaction had taken their toll, putting silver streaks in his light brown hair and a paunch on his midsection. Still, he towered over Charity, hot breath on her face.

"Is this why you wanted your mother and me to remain at the estate? Because you wanted to parade around London like some common street trollop?" Lord Cresswell's hands closed into fists, but he did not raise them.

"No, Papa, please, let me explain," Charity pleaded, begging him to lower his voice. She racked her mind for the right words to say. "We mean to marry… someday."

Or so she hoped. They had not discussed the future in such certain terms. Not while the threat of Lady Fitzroy hung over their heads. But she had to make him understand how serious she was about Peregrine.

"*Marry?*" Lord Cresswell goggled at his oldest child. "You cannot honestly expect me to approve of such a thing. To even contemplate it—dear God, you are a bigger fool than I thought."

His words took Charity by surprise. For all her life, he had held her up against Peregrine Fitzroy and found her wanting. Peregrine was the son he should have had, the heir he deserved. Thanks to Lady Cresswell's failure to bear an heir, the Cresswell title would pass to some distant cousin. There was nothing Charity could do to change that. But she had married well, risen above her station, and was able to open doors for them her father could not. Surely he would not begrudge her now.

"But I am happy, Papa," she said, trying again.

"Happiness counts for nothing in this society. I thought I made that clear when you stupidly broke off your engagement with the Duke of Northumberland. The only benefit you bring to our family is your station. In case you have failed to notice, Lord Fitzroy is an earl, and you are currently a duchess! A widowed duchess who provided no heir! You must cling to the Atholl title, not throw it away on foolish sentiment. How many times must we explain it to you?"

Lord Cresswell was so furious, he began gesticulating with his hands. Charity flinched as one hand swung too close unintentionally. He drew a deep breath and forced them back down to his side. "I should not expect more from you. A woman cannot be trusted to make the right decision," he said bitterly.

Charity dared not glance Perry's way. If he came to her aid, things would only get worse. And yet, she wanted him. She chose him. She was a grown woman. A widow. Was she never to be free?

Fate seemed determined to see otherwise. The wall of her father's anger was closing around her. He would drag her out, force her to retreat to the family estate. Lady Fitzroy would leash Perry. Ravenscroft and Selina would forget about her. And the Queen—the Queen would cast Charity from society for failure to obey her commands.

Her father shook his head in disappointment. "I suppose you must give some explanation to the Queen. Tell her you are unwell and cannot carry on as a lady-in-waiting this season. Have your maid pack your things. Your mother and I will come to collect you tomorrow."

She opened her mouth, but her father spun around and left. She steeled herself when he passed by Perry, who stood watching from the doorway to the throne room, but her father stalked past without a word.

There had to be some way to make her father see reason. She was depending on him to give Perry a chance to prove himself, so that her father might convince her mother to unbend. Now, however, her hopes for a grand reconciliation between Peregrine and her parents dimmed to almost none.

She and Peregrine had already been forced to overcome such odds to be together. And now a new worry now whispered into her ear. *You must face the possibility that you cannot have both your family's support and Perry's love. If you cannot, which one will you choose?*

2

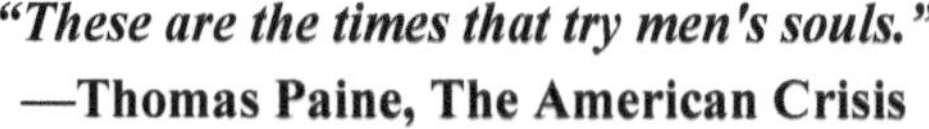

"These are the times that try men's souls."
—Thomas Paine, The American Crisis

Peregrine watched Charity and her father, trying to give them privacy for their conversation. But their postures spoke as loudly as words. Charity was ramrod straight, eyes downcast. Cresswell flung his hands about as he spoke.

There was little respect showing, and Peregrine considered interrupting.

Lord Cresswell's timing was terrible. Perry rather felt like a clock that had been over-wound. Or perhaps more like a row of buttons under strain, threatening to pop.

It had been only days since he had vowed to put himself on a path towards some sort of redemption. To be—for Charity's sake, if not his own—a better man. But while the monster had been staring from the mask of his mother's face, it forced him to ask himself whether he might be labouring under a delusion.

He was still a violent creature with questionable morals. How could he ever be more? Being a man worthy of Charity's affection seemed impossible.

His mother's soulless stare, devoid of anything light and human, had immediately torn the scales from his eyes. He was so naïve. He could not cleave to the idea that he had the ability to achieve moral righteousness. Not when all his paths lead into darkness.

Not when he had contemplated strangling his own mother in front of Charity and the entire assembly of Allied Sovereigns.

He had weighed the act of murder against the evil of keeping his hands at his sides. And in the end… he had chosen again to stay silent. To do nothing, which let his mother continue with her plans and put innocents at risk.

It had been an echo of the choice he had made before, when he had been torn between justice for Grenville and letting his mother bind him with the secret. If he struck down his mother that way—even if it was the right thing to do—he would lose everything. His sister. The respect of the *ton*. His life. And Charity.

He believed he had made the wrong choice before, when Grenville had died by his hand. He thought he had been prepared to pay the price if given a second chance to set things right. But again, he had shied away.

Perry had let his mother go—again—because this time, he did not want to give up all possibility of a life with Charity. He couldn't bear the idea that she would look at him and see another monster. One capable of murdering his own mother.

Why did he have to make this choice between two versions of damnation? Why did wanting to keep Charity's regard feel like such a *selfish* desire? It made him furious.

And left him blackly hopeless.

As if to further prove his unworthiness, he considered punishing Cresswell for his disrespect to his daughter. A parent shouldn't cause such pain to someone who loved them.

Perry held onto his temper as the man pushed past him without a word of acknowledgement. Even though the skin of his knuckles itched as though they demanded to be put to use on the lord's face.

Charity's father stalked back inside without a glance backwards, and though it was a struggle, Perry let him go, too. Physical harm to Cresswell would go as poorly as it would against his mother. Even if the man was being a colossal prig.

Peregrine turned his eyes back towards the duchess, noticing she had failed to mask her feelings. Seeing her struggle made it possible for him to slam the door shut on his own issues.

"Charity," he called to her, striding towards her and sweeping her into his arms once he checked to make sure her father was really gone.

She burrowed into his chest without even looking to see if others were nearby, which said a great deal about her state of mind. He could feel the way she trembled along the entire length of his body, which again made him want to set her aside and chase down Cresswell.

"Easy, Sparkles," he whispered in her ear. He slowed his breathing, hoping it would calm her. At least it would rein in his own racing pulse and cool his own savage temper. He hoped.

"Why must I choose?" Charity's voice was almost inaudible. "I do not want to have to choose this."

"What must you choose?" he asked softly, stroking his cheek against hers.

She was silent for so long, he began to wonder if she would answer. "Even if we did not have to contend with your mother... What if my parents will never let the past go? Or if they will never accept the idea of us together? What if they are never willing to set aside the fact that you are Lord Fitzroy and acknowledge we care for one another? Must I choose between having you in my life and having my family?"

He did not possess the answer to this dilemma either. "There must be a solution, Charity. Just breathe. It will be all right."

She said nothing. But there was something about her stiffness, the downward cast of her eyelashes.

Unspoken disagreement. A denial so plain, he could almost hear her unspoken words. *Will it?*

Perry swallowed. There was a sour taste of defeat on his tongue. A second sharp sense of loss.

This day's events had wounded them more brutally than he dared to admit. Their lives were in danger, again. His soul might be irredeemable. And Charity had fallen back into a confrontation with her own inner demon: Fate.

Even if Charity chose to fight against the forces tearing them apart, even if his mother was dealt with, it might be a pyrrhic victory if choosing each other cost her everything. She had been shaken so badly. Was she no longer sure they would keep themselves from being sundered?

She was already mourning their end. That was breaking his heart.

"Do not lose your faith, darling." Peregrine let his lips graze the glory of her hair, letting one hand slide down into the small of her back. "Don't give up on me already."

She shuddered, her breathing rough. "Do I have a choice not to? Why are we being punished, Perry?" She clung to him as though he were at risk of being ripped away. "Every time we find a moment of happiness, something snatches it from our grasp. Is it hubris? A curse?"

"Are there no other possibilities? Might there be a purpose to our pain? There is bad blood three generations deep between our families. What if we have been set to this task because only we can set this quarrel right?"

"It hurts to keep fighting to be here, with you," she admitted softly. "To keep believing that we can persevere when it seems like everything is against us. Sometimes I wonder if we will ever have peace."

Perry cupped her jaw with his spare hand, tipping her face to his. Her eyes were dull and rimmed with red, but she met his gaze. He buried his own pain deeply as he brought his lips down to rest against her brow, trying to quiet the dark whispers in her mind. Charity seemed unable to find her way free of hopelessness, and if they couldn't help one another, they would both be truly lost.

"Please always fight for me. Do not surrender to such shadowy thoughts when the sun may yet rise, Sparkles. And— don't be afraid of my mother. I will burn down the world to protect you. You know that."

She jerked her chin away, burrowing her face against his shoulder. "I'm not afraid for myself, Perry."

No, she was afraid she would lose him. He let his eyes close, his arm curling around her waist, fingers sinking into the silk. Orange and the scent of Charity's hair, the fading smell of joy, rose from the circle of his arms. She was pressed against him, head to ankle. The sound of her breathing, the tripping beat of her heart against his chest—it threatened to become his entire world.

The sound of conversation trickled outside through the window glass, a slow leak of poison that kept him from sinking fully into the dream.

"As long as we seek one another, nothing will keep us apart," he said softly, reminding her of her own words. "Not in this life, or the next."

Charity shivered. Granted, perhaps his reminder of the next

life was not a comforting thought right now. Not when Death herself had wished him a happy birthday.

"Question or command?" she asked, her voice muffled slightly.

His arms tightened. "Ask me your question."

"When we were in the townhouse, you asked me if things would stay the same if we went back a year. Do you regret this? Would you undo it if you could? It is one thing to face my unhappy parents. But your mother—"

"No, Sparkles. There are no regrets. Well, that might not be strictly true. I do regret the moments of unhappiness. But I would still let them happen over and over again, exactly the same as they happened before."

"...Really?" She sniffled. "Why not change the pain?"

Perry tucked her head beneath his chin and lifted her left hand in his right, folding their fingers together, palm pressing against palm. It was hard to find the right words. "When it comes to you, I cannot help but be selfish. I would walk the same steps, again and again, just to make sure that I will always find my way here. To you, and this moment."

Her fingers bit into his flesh through the clothing. "I am so sorry, Perry. I knew my parents were going to be displeased... but I thought they would relent once they saw I was happy."

Perry wondered if he should warn her now about the last family secret. His mother was not the only one who would have been happy to see him dead. Her mother had managed to bribe people, ensuring he was sent to the most dangerous fronts last year as little more than a common infantryman. Lady Cresswell had been the one who had him sent to the Nive.

"Question or command?" he asked her.

It took her a moment to decide. "Question."

"If I knew another secret about our families, would you want to be told?"

Charity seemed reluctant to hear it. "Would it cause a problem if it stayed a secret?"

The truth would come out sooner or later. But he did not want to burden Charity with unwanted knowledge. "No more than it already has," he hedged.

"Keep your secret, then—at least for today. I don't want to invite more trouble. Their being here is my fault," she whispered. "I should have written my mother back. But there was more gossip than there was time—"

"Yes. This is all your fault," Perry added in a lightly teasing voice. "There was all that time wasted between the riot and your kidnapping, after all."

Charity stiffened, her eyes hooding slightly in impudence. "What wasted time?" she asked bitingly. "Those hours I spent in —at Vauxhall?"

"Coward." He let his lip curl in gentle amusement. "Do not think I missed what you were going to say. I am rather confident you didn't consider the hours in my bed wasted at the time."

Charity flushed prettily, and she lifted her hands to cover her cheeks. It eased Perry to see her mood lift at least enough to chaff him back. "I may revise my opinion yet. Anyway, it was too late to write them by then."

"Ah. Then clearly you should have written them sometime while I was feverish in the next room. Can you imagine what your mama would have spluttered about that?"

"Oh, with perfect clarity. The priest would have been hauled in to marry us with you still lying in the bed." Charity dropped her hands, her slight smile fading. "That would have been especially awkward, given that within the day, you hated me."

"Not my finest hour. I was blinded by hurt, and I am not too proud to admit it. After everything we had been through, it was agony to believe you still did not trust me." Peregrine tucked a fallen strand of her hair over her ear, trailing his fingertips along her throat to rest on her collarbone. "I was so frustrated when I found someone else standing on my neck every time I earned my way free. And I was... humiliated by all these failings."

She moved in again to rest her forehead against his shoulder, leaning into his touch. "You are the only person I trust without reservation."

His stomach fluttered. "I'd wager you did not imagine you would ever say such a thing when you were glaring at me at Prinny's soiree last month, did you?"

"Absolutely not." Charity huffed. "I am sorry. You are comforting me when you are just as upset as I am."

His lips curved. "We're comforting each other, and only one of us is allowed to be beside themselves at a time."

"Is that a rule?" She laughed almost soundlessly, her shoulders shaking. "And you decided it was my turn? That was kind of you."

"A practical one," he corrected her. "Because if both of us are in a taking, you won't hold me by my cravat and prevent me from taking exception to your father's behaviour. And that would be regrettable. If I have to be thrown in gaol for anything I did at this event, I would ensure I earned it fairly with a better, more important target than your father."

Charity huffed agreement. "Don't get yourself thrown in gaol. Not for anything. What a disaster, and on a day that should be about you."

"My birthday has not been all bad," he murmured in her ear, inhaling her scent deeply. "The most beautiful woman in England asked me to stand beside her. I got to see the look upon my mother's face when she realised I was still alive despite her efforts. And while I might wish she were anywhere else right now, at least we now know *exactly* where she is."

"Practical." Charity's muffled word sounded more like

herself. "But why bother to bring back the dagger? Everyone important knows the truth."

"For the same reasons she destroyed all traces of her underworld empire. The Queen may try to investigate, but without evidence, it will be difficult to stop her. My mother will be able to resume her position, if that is what she wishes to do, and accuse truth-tellers of spreading slander. Duke Chandros said as much himself, right before he tried to bring the building down upon our heads. With the proof gone, the truth dies, and the false story left behind becomes the only one that matters. Now Marian is free to write whatever story she needs to suit."

Charity jerked in his arms, and she lifted her head again. "Do you suppose she would stay when Russia leaves? Would it suit her needs?"

He lowered his gaze, thinking. "Possibly? It muddies the waters, if nothing else. We don't have enough information to begin looking for her plot."

"But you think there *is* one."

Perry nodded reluctantly. "Of course. My mother has never done anything by half measures. The timing of everything that has happened is so clearly by design. But… why?"

The hesitant clearing of a throat behind him had Peregrine release Charity, whirling around.

"Duchess, Canary." Lord Ravenscroft stood there, looking uncertain. "I would like to make some crack about interrupting your dalliances, but wit is in thin supply this day."

Marian Fitzroy's sudden appearance, it seemed, wasn't only their own nightmare come to life. The older lord looked worn.

The magpie might be a collector of secrets, but Marian also knew the one that would destroy him utterly. Despite his reputation as a rake, Ravenscroft was also guilty of loving a man.

"The Regent, of course, is occupied with matters of state. So the Queen is convening a rather impromptu war council in her apartments for now," Ravenscroft told them. "Will you come?"

"Of course," Charity answered quickly, wiping at her face.

"Yes, well. Perry..." The man trailed off again, dithering. "Later, at your home, you will find a gift I sent you for your birthday. Now I think it might have been poorly chosen. Forgive me for that, will you?"

Abruptly, Ravenscroft turned to lead them upstairs, and Charity stared after him. "Goodness. I can't help but wonder. What did he send?"

3

"...men must either be caressed or else annihilated; they will revenge themselves for small injuries, but cannot do so for great ones; the injury therefore that we do to a man must be such that we need not fear his vengeance."
—Niccolò Machiavelli, The Prince

Selina, the Marchioness of Normanby, and Sir Nathaniel Thorne were waiting for them. The marchioness marched forward, eyes steely with intent, and stopped in front of Charity.

"Perry, I know she's precious, but must you hoard the duchess? Walk ahead with the men. The duchess and I need to chat." She offered Charity her arm and then shooed the men on. Charity's stomach churned; she had a good idea of what was on Lady Normanby's mind.

"You needn't chastise me. I am well aware of where I erred," Charity told her.

"I hope so." Selina gave Charity a fond pat on the arm. "It *was* a pleasure to see gossipmongers practically bursting at the seams when Perry took the space beside you. But was it necessary to take his hand before his mother, your parents, and half of London?"

"I was feeling faint."

"Understandably, Your Grace. Now you are leaning on my arm, and I will tell them your illness was the reason you clutched at him. They will grumble, but they will let the matter drop... unless, of course, you keep sneaking off together. Who *knows* what they will presume then?"

Charity's cheeks warmed.

"Much better," Selina said, satisfied. "You were looking positively bloodless. I thought I might be able to coax some colour back into those cheeks. Though why *I* should have to do that when you were just in the garden with Perry—"

"Might we change the subject, Lady Normanby?" Charity asked warningly, wishing her face weren't so traitorous.

"Are you vexed, darling? Irritation is good for the soul. Consider it polishing. Slough off what's dull and unimportant so the quality can finally shine through," Selina drawled. Her attention wandered to the backs of Peregrine and Sir Nathaniel, walking side by side. "There is great comfort in having the poise to be yourself."

For a moment, she seemed... uncertain and thoughtful. Perhaps sad. Charity wondered if she should ask the marchioness if she was all right. Lady Normanby had spoken no word of what had transpired between her and Bellrose after Charity's escape, and Lady Fitzroy's return had upset all of them. But she doubted the marchioness would answer such a direct question.

"Is it my turn to productively vex you?" Charity asked instead.

With a snap of her fan and a brief, enigmatic smile, Selina collected herself. "Do you see?" she evaded.

Charity did. At least, a little.

"I wish such tricks would work on my parents," Charity admitted, surprised by the sense she could confide such a thing to the older widow. "My father threatened to drag me from London."

"It will! Your father upset you, but do not forget the Queen no longer needs to intercede on your behalf. You are a widowed duchess, not a mewling debutante without a home or funds. Stand your ground. Imagine someone like your father trying to do that to me, and act accordingly."

Charity tried to imagine someone making Selina do anything against her will and almost laughed. But— "Do you think I shall lose them from my life if I do?" she blurted out in a whisper.

Selina understood, and squeezed her arm. "Only if they are unwilling to avoid losing *you*."

That was unexpectedly fortifying, and Charity felt a little better.

Queen Charlotte had laid claim to the velvet armchair in the centre of the room that had been appropriated for their meeting. Once the door was shut, she removed the heavy crown she had worn for the welcoming ceremony. The scowl she wore was terrifyingly regal even without it.

The room was disturbingly empty. Besides Charlotte and their little quintet, they had been joined only by the Home Secretary, Viscount Sidmouth.

Ravenscroft and Perry settled on a pair of silk-upholstered chairs near their sovereign, leaving the sofa for the women. Sir Nathaniel elected to remain standing out of the way, near the door.

"If anyone has an explanation as to how a traitor managed to return to Britain and gain entrance to the palace—under a Russian escort, no less—I suggest you provide it now." Charlotte's voice was iron, but her gaze was fixed on the Home Secretary.

Sidmouth flushed. Ultimately, he might be held responsible for this failure.

"Clearly, we miscalculated when we assumed she would stay in hiding," Sidmouth said, his voice clipped. "But we should have noticed when she arrived in Dover. I will investigate how she managed to conceal her identity, ma'am."

"A little late now," Charlotte remarked stiffly. "Not only did she flout the precautions and security of the palace, the Foreign Office, and the Home Office, she then had the audacity to parade the Prince Regent's stolen property through my throne room! We were forced to accept her ridiculous claim of innocence and *thank* that woman for its return!"

Sidmouth said nothing, weathering the Queen's ire.

"How did she end up in the Russian court, Lord Fitzroy?" Charlotte asked with narrowed eyes. "Were you aware that she was acquainted with Tsar Alexander?"

Peregrine shook his head. "No, Your Majesty. The Fitzroy family has no distant relations or acquaintances in Russia who could aid her. At least, not as far as I am aware."

"Well, it certainly was not the British diplomat to Russia," Sidmouth snarled. "She hardly would have sauntered right into the Russian court. Someone would have had to introduce her."

Selina's lips pressed tightly together. "Given her connections with the Order, she may have found someone to introduce her through us. I am sure Xavier would not have aided her deliberately, but his web of informants would stretch into the Ministry and the Tsar's court."

"Where is the princess?" Charity asked suddenly, concerned. Princess Charlotte had been a target of Lady Fitzroy's schemes, and it did not seem wise to leave her without supervision.

"At her father's side, with the suggestion she should not wander from him or the guards under any circumstances," the Queen said, rubbing a finger against her temple.

Charity slowed her breathing. Her worries did not disappear, but her nerves eased enough to focus.

"Lord Sidmouth," Queen Charlotte said, her words edged, "I trust you will have a word with the guards about the importance of tracking her movements."

"Yes, of course, Your Highness. I have confirmed already that she took rooms at the Pulteney, along with the rest of the Russian delegation."

Perry met her quick glance. He seemed to be relieved as she was to learn that his mother had no grand homecoming plans in store for them.

"So she is taking shelter in their midst," the Queen grumbled. "And doubtless there will be an outcry from the Russians if she is taken from their bosom as part of an inquiry."

Lord Sidmouth sighed. "Yes. But there is no point to an inquiry now. We could not prove her guilt even before she brought back the dagger. This was why we did not try her in absentia for her crimes."

"And what of the… other solution we previously discussed?" the Queen asked delicately, glancing at Perry out of the corner of her eye. "Elimination?"

Peregrine's hands tightened into fists again, but he betrayed no other sign that he had feelings about the matter. Charity felt badly about the fact that they were so casually discussing the murder of his mother in front of him. Again.

"No. She is too well protected at the Pulteney, in their midst." Sidmouth shook his head. "While she is under their hospitality, anything that happens to Lady Fitzroy will be as problematic as an arrest."

Lady Normanby scrubbed absently at her gloves. "Sidmouth is correct. Assassination will not be an option. We will have to figure out a way to remove her from the protection of the Russians."

"Prinny is furious," Ravenscroft muttered. "He believes the

Tsar knowingly aided a traitor just to embarrass him at this gathering of the sovereigns."

Selina looked annoyed. "I beg Your Majesty's pardon, but not everything is about making the Prince Regent look the fool. If the Tsar had any sense, he would see Lady Fitzroy as one of three things: a spy, an informant for the taking, or a weapon."

For the first time, Sir Nathaniel cleared his throat, looking apologetic. "Lady Normanby is right. It would not be wise to forget the fact that another ruler could employ Lady Fitzroy as a kind of weapon. Someone may have brought her to England for a purpose, and it may not even be the Russians. Or she has come back to do something she can only accomplish here."

"That counterfeiting ploy was focused on toppling the government," mused Sidmouth. "It would have weakened us for certain at the conferences in Vienna, as well as being a public disgrace. Another country would have stood to gain."

"But Vienna is far off." The Queen steepled her fingers together. "And the sovereigns will be gone by month's end. So it seems we must discover what tasks would require Lady Fitzroy's presence here—and now. Lord Fitzroy? Do you have any idea?"

Perry, grim-faced, shook his head. "At the moment, ma'am, I can hardly guess. Access to banks I did not find? Other resources? Just because Chandros and Goldbourne destroyed so much does not mean they did not move her funds elsewhere."

Poor Peregrine, Charity thought. For the entirety of the past month, he had been steps behind his mother's plans. Even though he successfully figured out every clue, they were often slightly too late. And he was likely blaming himself for not being clever or fast enough to prevent Chandros from destroying the evidence they needed.

"You stopped the counterfeiting scheme in time. You saved the government," Charity reminded him gently. "We will be able to figure out what she is up to again."

Peregrine met Charity's gaze bleakly. "A near-thing. And we only succeeded because you brought us the last piece of evidence in time that the treasury had been corrupted. I might have found the presses, but Bellrose was the key to Goldbourne's cypher and the list of men whose exchequer bills had been duplicated."

"A scheme we cannot at all tie to Lady Fitzroy, much less the Russians, and that is a problem. We cannot overlook the fact that we might be hosting an ally with duplicitous intentions," Ravenscroft growled. "At the very best, Russia might be causing mischief to skew negotiations in their favour. This might be far worse. So we are faced with the question: Is Russia the enemy of England? And if not them, whom?"

A little silence greeted that.

"They may not be," Selina said finally. "They may only be holding her, trying to gauge her value. Why would they not? If a member of Russia's court came to England outside of the usual diplomatic channels… would you not keep them in hand, Your Majesty? Especially if they were clever enough to have confounded your opponents?"

Queen Charlotte conceded she would.

Peregrine made an ugly noise in his throat. "You're right. The attack on the bank may have been condoned by the Tsar, but he would be too obvious the suspect. This is a great game for her. My mother gets no pleasure from making such boring moves."

"This way lies madness, Perry." Selina gave him a slightly feral grin. "If not the Tsar, what about her sponsor at the Russian court?"

"Or someone outside of it who benefits from Russia and England being at each other's throats?" Ravenscroft added.

"For heaven's sake! I do not like the thought of that *at all*," the Queen groused. "We cannot send Russia away, of course, without causing some grave offence. Which means that they will continue their stay, and Lady Fitzroy will be able to continue her stay with them. Oh, and also she may mingle freely with the *ton*, her movements completely unfettered, spreading sedition or who knows what manner of villainy. What must we do?"

"We should look for weaknesses within. Courts are full of jealous people." Lady Normanby ran the edge of her thumb over her lips. "If we ask around carefully, we may be able to locate a person in the Russian contingent who does not hold Marian in such high esteem. Who might be willing to trade information about what is going on inside the Pulteney? We might be able to find a thread we may pull."

"Do you think such a thing is even possible?" Charity asked before she considered the words. But Selina only smiled at her. Finding people willing to trade in information was how Selina had sunk her fingers so deeply into the Home Office.

"Lord Fitzroy," Selina continued more slowly, "there is one other person who may have information to trade about your mother. Unfortunately, I suspect only you might be able to exploit her."

Charity flinched at the word *exploit*. Queen Charlotte frowned at Charity before turning to Peregrine.

"Lark Fitzroy," the Queen murmured, pressing her chin to her fist as her elbow leaned upon the arm of the chair. "The first and best source of information on your mother is likely to be your sister, Lord Fitzroy, if you can press her for it. Besides, the question of her guilt or innocence remains unanswered."

Perry agreed. "I would reach out to Lark regardless. She is not safe where she is, especially if my mother's plans are threatened."

"We cannot count on success on either of those fronts. If we are to put a stop to Lady Fitzroy, we need to drive a wedge between her and her protectors." Sidmouth crossed his arms. "The Russians will rescind their protection if we have irrefutable proof of her misdeeds. Which means we must also allow her to continue with her plotting and attempt to catch her in the act."

Plotting which might include an attempt to kill one of them. Charity lifted her eyes from where they had fallen into her lap to see Perry staring at her, his expression anguished enough that she knew he had the same thought.

"We allow her to go about her business? Is this really the best of our options?" Lord Ravenscroft asked, his voice raising a pitch. "Can we afford to be on such unstable ground this close to the negotiations? Forgive me, allowing the woman who nearly forced the dissolution of Parliament to run loose does not seem like the most brilliant of plans."

Fortunately, Lord Sidmouth put a stop to that panic. "Not *loose*, Ravenscroft. We will make sure we follow the lady's movements. But we have to let her have space to act if we want to have any hope of guessing who or what the target of her next plan is going to be."

"This will be dangerous. To give the woman enough rope with which to hang herself also gives her enough space to enact those plans before we can catch wind of them," Thorne said in a soft voice, darting a quick look at Lady Normanby. "Such decisions are likely to come at a cost in lives."

Thoughts sprang into Charity's mind of her servants after the attack on her house. The many dead servants who had once served at the Fitzroy estate. The man from the Home Office, who had been murdered or driven to suicide. Goldbourne. Chandros.

Of Peregrine, with the collar of bruises from the hands around his neck and the healing scar on his abdomen. And Selina, trapped in a basement in Kensington with Bellrose standing guard.

How many dead and wounded had Lady Fitzroy left behind? Dozens, at least.

Lady Normanby was picking at an imaginary speck of dirt on her gloves again, not nearly as unaffected as she pretended to be. "Most of us are comfortable with the fact that we are on her black list already, Sir Nathaniel. There is a silver lining. If one of us falls, it may give the evidence necessary to convict her of murder. And that may be a price worth paying, given the stakes Russia may be playing for."

Thorne looked ill at that answer, but nodded. Sidmouth seemed regretful. Ravenscroft looked grim.

Peregrine, on the other hand, looked like the weight of the world was now on his shoulders. As if it were his responsibility alone to stop her before one of them fell.

Sidmouth sighed. "Of course, I will do what I can. But I think this will be a war fought in the shadows, and if so, you will be able to move more freely than those of my ilk. Find out why she is here. You must determine who is sheltering her. Someone introduced her at court and brought her to the Tsar's attention. I want their names. Use any means necessary to get it."

Lord Sidmouth bowed to the Queen. "If you will excuse me, I must return to the reception before my disappearance is noted. Lady Normanby, I trust you will keep me informed. My responsibility in the coming days is to meet with our potential allies, to see what they want in return for supporting us in Vienna. I do not want the Russians to hear what promises we make. It strikes me that if anyone is capable of building a web of spies for Russia, it is Lady Fitzroy."

Selina bobbed in confirmation. And with the Queen's approval, Lord Sidmouth took his leave.

No sooner had he gone than Lord Ravenscroft threw up his hands in frustration. "Find out why she is here, Sidmouth says. Isn't it obvious? Assist Russia, ruin England, and poison the punch on her way out the door, killing all of us."

Though Charity agreed with him, as Perry had said, his mother would never do anything for one reason alone. Marian had come back with Lark in tow.

"There is something else I think we should consider," Charity began, remembering the many minor princes and foreign aristocrats announced earlier. "This is Lark's second year out, and she is still unmarried. Lady Fitzroy will be pressured to make a match for her daughter, and there will never be a better opportunity to make a high-level match. Where could she marry more closely to a throne than at the meeting of the Allied Sovereigns?"

Perry's eyes narrowed. The Queen tapped her fingers on her armrest, mulling that over. "That may fit the pattern and explain why she returned the dagger as she did. Marian had little hope of getting anyone to offer for her daughter so long as there was a whiff of scandal attached to her name. But as a trusted confidante in the Russian court… both the mother and the daughter have something to offer."

"Who is likely to offer for Lark's hand?" Sir Nathaniel asked. "Pardon my question, but I am not familiar with the royal lines on the continent," he added, bowing his head to the Queen.

"Prince Leopold of Saxe-Coburg is of a similar age," Queen Charlotte ventured. "He is a younger son, and so might consent to wed outside of a noble family."

"There is also Prince Paul of Württemberg," Selina added. "Or perhaps Baron von Gentz. He is not in line for a throne, but he holds a significant amount of power as Metternich's man."

The Queen waved her hands irritably. "There are a hundred more options if we look outside of unwed princes. Lord Sidmouth issued his instructions. Now, I will add mine, and I cannot overturn all other plans simply because of Marian Fitzroy. Your Grace, you must encourage my granddaughter strongly to sign the betrothal contract. Prinny and I will push from our side, but a supportive word from you would not be amiss."

"Yes, Your Majesty," Charity agreed, even though it turned her stomach.

"Lord Fitzroy," the Queen continued, "it is doubly important to try to plumb your sister's mind. If her marriage is a key part of the scheme, surely she might have some sense of it."

"I will see if I can convince her to speak with me, Your Majesty."

"Lord Ravenscroft and Lady Normanby, I ask you to use your wiles and your connections to discover which of our allies are being courted by the Russians. Lord Sidmouth will pursue the official path. You two can be helpful in feeding him information."

"What of me, Your Majesty?" Sir Nathaniel asked. "I would like to be of aid to the cause."

"I have a suggestion," Selina spoke up. After the Queen nodded her approval, Selina said, "You are not as well-known as the rest of us. See if you can identify anyone of the lower orders whom Lady Fitzroy might have drafted to her cause. Courtiers or servants who are out of place, or more interested in eavesdropping than going their own way. We can ask my associate, Mr Xavier, to lend a hand as well."

"Take great care with whom you trust," the Queen counselled. "A mistake, even a small one, has incredible implications for the fate of this nation. And for you all."

4

"Which way I fly is Hell; myself am Hell;
And, in the lowest deep, a lower deep
Still threat'ning to devour me opens wide,
To which the Hell I suffer seems a Heav'n."
—Lucifer, Paradise Lost

Their merry little band of misfits had picked themselves up and dusted themselves off after his mother's surprise arrival, but there was still a marked sense of soldier's cheer. It was much like the martial stoicism that had driven his fellow soldiers towards the end of the terrible, bloody days of the Nive. Faith was faltering, though the others tried to hide it.

They were uncertain they could win this war against his mother.

Perry might be holding all of their lives in his hands. Though no one had said as much, he knew they were depending on him to see this through. They needed him to be better at this game than his mother—and he didn't know if he could be.

Bands of stress wrapped around his chest and along his throat, and absently, he set his hand against his stomach, focusing on his breathing while the others talked.

Selina stroked her lower lip with a finger, giving him a sidelong look at length. "I am loath to bring up such a barbaric topic, but our knight-errant wasn't wrong. People may be hurt. Even if it might help us trap the harpy, I am not keen to offer one of our lives to do so, and our enemy is willing to violate the boundaries of home. We need to safeguard ourselves."

"I agree with Lady Normanby, unfortunately," said Ravenscroft as he straightened his cuffs. He glanced at Peregrine. But swiftly, that look transferred itself to Thorne, standing to the side of the group. "The rest of us have some servants to guard the household. It isn't wise for you to stay in that empty townhouse of yours alone, Sir Nathaniel."

"You don't think so?" Thorne asked, his blue eyes creased with worry. "I doubt Lady Fitzroy has any idea who I am."

The raven-haired Lady Normanby ran her eyes over Thorne's tall figure. "You bear too strong a resemblance to the Duke of Northumberland to wager on that. If she has not figured out who you are yet, she will soon, and the moment she understands your relation to the Percy family, you will find yourself marked as an enemy. Perhaps you should become a guest of Perry's."

"He should stay with me," Ravenscroft countered. "Sir Nathaniel taking up residence at the Fitzroy estate will only mark him sooner. Besides," he said with a ghost of his toothy, wolfish grin, "Antoine will be overjoyed to continue to assist with his court wardrobe and dance lessons."

Peregrine could have sworn he saw the tiniest flicker of horror in Thorne's expression. The man's elevation from north-country-bred bastard to knighthood had been meteoric. Though he masked it well, clearly he was still vastly uncomfortable with his new position in society.

And dancing.

Selina and Ravenscroft's disagreement became idle banter, and Thorne's attention bounced between the two. Charity offered only a few words to the conversation. And while the others spoke, Peregrine's thoughts continued to tread into dark places.

The sense of time ticking pushed harder on his senses than ever. His mother had an appointment she was keeping; he was certain of it. If it relied at all on the events during the meeting of the Allied Sovereigns, then they had at most two weeks to thwart her plans. Likely less.

To allow his mother free rein in conducting her plans… God help them all. It did not matter that there was only two weeks for her to enact her scheme; it would be folly to assume that she hadn't left herself time to deal with the unexpected.

Like discovering her son was both still breathing *and* that he was consorting with the daughter of the Cresswells.

His gaze turned inwards, attention on the pieces of the riddle. Perry had the sense that the pattern was there, if only he could view it from the right angle. The pressure to see it quickly was punishing, because it was only a matter of time before his mother began to cut his allies down. She would, even if only to prevent their interference with her plans.

Charity would be in the most danger of all. Perry was still haunted by the vision of how she had looked when she had collapsed on her front walkway, covered with soot and scratches.

God, *how* could he protect Charity?

Would it be safer for her to stay in London, with him? Or would the right thing be to send her away to some hidden place? Wouldn't that be the cruellest irony—if he had begged her to keep fighting to stay together, and then he decided to send her away?

Occasionally his mother's voice surfaced in his head, pointedly reminding him that everything would have been simpler if he had found the strength to have put her down like the slavering beast she was. But he had not, and his circling, festering thoughts were making him feel ill. He swallowed reflexively, trying to settle his stomach.

Suddenly, a figure stepped fully into his field of view, forcing him to shift his attention to the golden-haired woman waiting in front of him. He lifted his eyebrows in inquiry.

Charity gave him a sad, knowing smile. "The others said I should talk with you. You are brooding most fiercely."

Peregrine glanced at Ravenscroft, Selina and Thorne, who had taken their conversations to a corner of the room. They were, all three, giving him furtive glances over their shoulders.

His first inclination was to get peevish. But now that Charity mentioned it, he realised he was grinding his teeth. He touched his fingers to his forehead, trying to relax the furrows forming.

"Apologies," he said to them shortly. "My thoughts are leagues away."

"You should *take yourself* leagues away, Canary," drawled the magpie. "There is nothing more to do here tonight at St James's. Duchess, drag him home. I trust you are a clever enough woman to figure out how to entice him."

A faint flush stained Charity's cheekbones at Ravenscroft's crass implication, and the words earned him a disbelieving look from Thorne. Thorne turned to see whether Selina would chastise the man, but she only hid a slight smile behind two fingers and turned her head away from the view.

Peregrine's mood grew a trifle blacker. "I do not require your mothering, Ravenscroft."

"Good. Then you may be duchess'ed. Don't worry; I will give all my tender affections to Sir Nathaniel instead."

Irritation flared, but Charity took his elbow, and the sensation ebbed abruptly. It left Perry drained, and he stumbled a little in her wake as she led him towards the door. "You do not have to help me toddle home either," he said.

"Perry, if I go to Atholl House, I am *sure* you can imagine who will be waiting." Charity's voice was so dry that Peregrine could envision the irate Lady Cresswell standing on her doorstep. "I do not mean to impose, but I rather hope you will not send me home to encounter my mother."

"If you can tolerate my poor company tonight—" He halted, realising he was being an ass. "Of course, Charity."

Quinn could prepare a guest room for her whether he was a broody bastard tonight or not, and her coming to the estate was for the best. Atholl House no longer had its guards. Even with only him and Will Hodges around, Charity would be safer than she would be at her home.

They focused on presenting a composed front as they exited the palace. Charity sent the Atholl carriage home and then waited serenely by his side for Hodges. "Don't mind Lord Ravenscroft. He and Lady Normanby were trying to be helpful," she added.

"In their way. The man should aim to be rather less helpful."

Charity tilted slightly to watch him out of the corner of her eye. "But Ravenscroft was right to suggest I take you home."

Will Hodges, worldly grizzled veteran that he was, seemed to be able to scent the trouble. He set both forearms on his knees and gave him a hard stare as Jack opened the carriage door and helped Charity in.

"Later. Not here," Peregrine told him firmly.

Hodges grunted an acknowledgement, but he settled back on the driver bench. And Perry climbed inside, taking the rear-facing seat even though Charity had left him space beside her.

The briefest flicker of pain crossed her face, but she hardened the set of her mouth. "You are pulling away from me again, rebuilding a wall between us. I wish you wouldn't."

He swallowed, gazing out the window. His thoughts ran like thorny brambles, every which way, menacingly sharp. "I am all right, Charity."

"That was almost convincing." She paused, and from the corner of his eye he could see how tightly her hands were clasped in her lap. "I think it is the first time you have ever lied to me. Or at least, I think it's the first time you've ever done it so directly."

He didn't bother to refute it. But it seemed that they were beyond polite boundaries now. She was stubborn enough to keep pushing. She spoke firmly, and without inflection.

"Look at me, Perry."

After taking a moment to steel himself, he turned his face in her direction, meeting her eyes. Those sky-striated irises, ringed with a darker, gentian blue.

"Talk to me. Please."

His throat hurt. "I don't want to," he said finally, the words coming out rougher than he meant them to. "Don't ask me to talk about this."

It would devastate her if she knew how slim he thought their chances were of capturing his mother without trouble. He didn't want to rob them of any sense of hope. And he most certainly did not want Charity to see he was desperately, terribly afraid she might be hurt.

This tension was a physical ache that ran from his lower spine to his teeth. Right now, it might be the only thing holding the broken pieces of himself together.

But she, too, had been afflicted by a fatalistic melancholy. A thought that time was slipping away from them. That these were wasted moments they would never be able to reclaim.

She began hesitantly, "I have been waiting for the right moment to say this…" And then she stopped there, as if gathering courage to finish her thoughts. After a deep breath, she lifted her gaze and looked him in the eye. "But should our days be numbered, then we must make every moment count for all it can. I love you, Perry. With all that I have."

Pain rippled through him, and the festering wound on his

heart was ripped open, draining its poison into his veins. Peregrine inhaled a sharp breath that only barely made it past the lump in his throat. And unexpectedly, tears welled and overflowed before he even felt them rise.

"No," he croaked.

It was unfair of her to say this to him now. To strip him so naked before her.

Parts of him threatened to unwind, spooling loose. And after another moment, Charity got up and moved across to his bench, pressing herself into the space beside him. She leaned against him, letting her left palm settle over his chest.

"You always push me away when you are afraid. Don't retreat from me; you have nothing you need to hide. I adore you, Perry, for exactly who you are. And I did not want to wait any longer to say this, especially when you so badly need to hear these words right now."

Peregrine stared at her hand lying over his sternum. He might have been struck by lightning, for all that his limbs would respond. He was rooted. Trapped, and unable to escape her touch. When he finally tore his gaze away from her hand and brought it back to her face, the corners of her eyes glimmered with tears.

"After speaking to my father, I was lost, and you brought me out of the shadows," she whispered. "I love you. Let me be the same light in the darkness for you."

"Charity—don't. Don't say such things," he gasped, swamped by grief. And elation and anger. A curious, light sense of freedom. And a thick line of dread. How could so many emotions spring from three little words?

"Why?" she asked him gently. "I know why you are afraid to say what you feel. But why does it hurt you so much when I am the one saying the words to you?"

His mother had been three steps ahead at every turn, even when she wasn't in England. And now the stakes were higher than ever. Could he prevent his mother from trying to ruin her socially? Hiring other killers? Stop every opportunity for poison or an accident?

In this, he stood truly on his own. He did not dare count on the Queen's ability to protect any of them.

Peregrine was lightheaded. "Because if you love me, and I fail you…"

I don't know if I will survive it, his thoughts finished.

And yet, somehow she still understood. He could see it in her eyes. She lifted his gloved hand, threading their fingers together and stroking his knuckles. "No matter how much it hurts to think about… I believe the only thing worse than loving you and losing you would be to live a life where I never had the chance to."

God. He knew that misery well.

The sharp pain faded into a soft twinge within his breast. A yearning. She was close enough he sensed the warmth of her skin along his arm. Their cheeks hovered only a few inches apart. He wasn't certain when he had begun to lean back into her like a flower seeking the face of the sun.

They were caught in the space between two star-crossed regrets, and the one thing Peregrine couldn't seem to make himself wish for was that Fate had never set their paths to cross. Even if it were possible, he couldn't wish he had forgotten the taste of her lips, or the feel of her hair sliding against his skin.

Or even just this—this quiet moment where his pulse began to slow, as his breathing found a rhythm with hers. The rawness of the moment eroded beneath the chastest of touches. The tender pressure of her living flesh against his, even through their gloves. The sound of horses' hooves and the bustle of the streets faded as they began to reach the quieter places of London.

And it was as though the world held its breath on the exhale, empty of crisis, an uncurling pause like the stillness following a physical release.

"Question or command?" Charity asked him after a time, breaking this temporary truce.

"Command," said Peregrine, reluctant to move.

He was a coward who did not want her to ask him if he wished he might undo the things between them. Or whether there was a chance he would ever say those three words in return.

But she did not seem discomposed by his reply. Instead, she reached for her reticule. "Close your eyes."

This was unexpected. He turned towards her, narrowing his gaze. "What are you doing?"

"I have your birthday gift with me," she said, loosening the drawstring. "Close your eyes."

Uncertainly, he did as she asked. He listened to the rustle of fabric as she reached into the bag, and a moment later, his senses were overwhelmed with the potently sweet, spicy smell of cloves and oranges.

Blinking open his eyes, he saw Charity holding a green silken bag close to his nose, her eyes twinkling slightly with mischief. He took the sachet from her fingers, confused by the odd choice of fabric. He turned it over, examining it, finding his initials embroidered into it boldly with a dark thread that stood out well against the light green. And then he brought it to his nose again.

Despite the bleakness of his thoughts earlier, the corner of his mouth turned up slightly. The scent reminded him of them together. The cloves in his soap; the orange in her perfume. He would treasure it for that reason alone.

But he couldn't help examining the bag again, wondering why the fabric was so naggingly familiar. "This bag. Is this…?"

Charity's mouth widened in a real smile, devilry sharpening the edges of it. "Do not tell me you don't recognise the colour, Lord Fitzroy."

A brief laugh was startled from his lips. "It is not."

But it was. He recognised it now. It had been sewn from the

old cabbage green dress she had worn in front of the Queen. The night that he had broken into her room. The night she had accused him of poisoning Prince William.

The night that she needed him, despite the fact that he was her enemy, to help her comb her hair.

"I assure you, it is! I cut up that dress myself," she retorted.

His melancholy faded as the memory took him. Almost from the beginning, they had seen each other at their very worst. But even then, even when they didn't trust one another… they had always needed one another. And they had always been there for each other in the end.

No, he wouldn't wish she did not love him, selfish though it might be. He wouldn't give or trade away a single second of it. And he was tired of his mother, her parents, Fortuna, and every other person in this godforsaken city attempting to pry the two of them apart.

"I adore it," he said, putting the sachet in his waistcoat pocket. "My turn. Question or command?"

She gave him a prim stare, but the corners of her mouth twitched slightly, and a wicked glitter lit her eyes. "Command, of course."

He lifted his eyebrow, his pulse picking up speed. "Are you quite sure, Sparkles? I won't allow you to change your choice, and I might ask you to do something terribly untoward."

"You will not!" she protested, but she had dimpled when he used her nickname, and her voice was amused. "You simply aren't that cruel to me. Go on then. Pose your demand."

Their time together might be so short. He didn't want to waste another second of it. He couldn't stand the thought of leaving her so unprotected to the world, should the worst happen.

He leaned in, their cheeks barely grazing as he brought his lips to her ear. She shivered, her breath speeding up and her throat tilting as though she expected his mouth to trace a path along the column of her neck.

But enticing as that thought was, that gratification wasn't what he was about to command.

"Marry me," he said instead. He pulled back to see her expression, and her face was a perfect, shocked blank. "As soon as we can procure a special licence. No banns, no invitations, no allowance for anyone's objection."

5

"We never live; we are always in the expectation of living."
—Voltaire

Charity's breath caught in her throat, her voice lost to shock. Had he heard the words she had spoken to her father? Was he calling her bluff? She searched his face for any flicker that this was in jest, but she found only hope shining in his eyes, so fragile and exposed that it made her heart ache.

He may have commanded it, but below his smile was just the barest trace of uncertainty, because he knew there were real reasons for her to decline. They had never discussed their future. And if she decided to marry him, she would have to give up her title. She would no longer be the Duchess Atholl.

Most people of their station wouldn't—or couldn't—sacrifice such things for love. Charity's marriage had bought her protection she had sorely needed last year. But the one thing that Selina and the Order had done was prove power could exist beyond a title.

As for her parents—

Her stomach soured as she remembered the expressions on their faces. There was a chance they would cut her dead if she married Perry. They might interpret an act of love as one of rebellion. But before her sat the man of her dreams, laying himself vulnerable, wrapping everything she wanted in the silk of a playful command.

A future of her own choosing. And he was waiting for an answer.

For once, there were no voices speaking in her head. All the words were coming from her heart—and that belonged to him. *I will always choose you. Over and over again.*

She had let her astonishment stretch a moment too long. The light in his eyes began to dull, and that more than anything forced the words from her lips.

"Perry," she whispered urgently. She crossed the space between them in a single, breathless rush, flinging her arms around his neck as she pressed her cheek to his. "Yes," she said, her voice cracking with the force of it. "Yes. A thousand times yes."

His arms reached around her, pulling her close. She felt the tremble in him as he shakily breathed her in. "I thought you might say no, because it would cause trouble with your parents."

It humbled her, this power he gave her over him and his happiness. She had not known it was possible for one's love to deepen, until this moment. It spread through her veins, growing and expanding until every inch of her soul overflowed with it.

"There must be some solution. We will figure out how to deal with them later," she murmured, her lips brushing the edge of his jaw. "I will fight to the end of days to stay with you."

"Let us hope we will find some peace before that," he whispered.

He tipped his gaze down, and his hands rose to cup her face, leaning back just enough that his wide eyes gazed upon her as if she were a priceless treasure—something he could hardly believe was real. His fingers skimmed over her cheeks, and with a tenderness that ate at her breastbone, he brushed away the tears she hadn't realised she was shedding.

Slowly, he kissed her brow, then the tip of her nose. His lips feathered over her cheeks and eyelids, worshiping her every feature. It mattered not that they were in a carriage riding through busy streets; every other consideration fell away. Everything, other than the burning exultation Perry elicited when his skin touched hers. His mouth. His fingertips.

She wanted to spend the rest of her life with the man, starting that very moment. The road, however, had other plans. The carriage wheel dipped into a deep rut, jostling the pair and nearly tossing Charity from her seat. Had Perry not been keeping such a tight hold on her, she would have found herself sprawled on the floor.

Then again... part of her wished she had tumbled down, so that he might have followed.

"Sparkles, you are blushing," Perry teased gently, helping her resettle on the cushioned seat. "I wonder what you were thinking."

"Take me on a honeymoon after all this is finished, and I will be happy to demonstrate exactly what I imagined," she replied cheekily.

Perry lifted his eyebrows, caught so unprepared by her comment that he burst out laughing—the full, unreserved sound she seldom heard.

"I want to make you do that again. Make you laugh like that," she murmured, finally feeling shy. "It would be nice to be someone who can make you forget your worries."

"You already are," he told her, pressing a gentle kiss to the point where her pulse fluttered in her throat. "When you look at me, the way you are right now, I cannot be bothered to remember that anyone else exists."

Charity sobered then, as the joy of his proposal waned and she allowed herself to remember that there was one person they could not afford to forget for very long.

"We could go to the Queen tomorrow, before we are required to attend the Drawing Room at St James's. I will send her a request for an audience." Charity's brow creased as she considered what else she needed to do. "I must send for Miller to come with appropriate clothing as well."

"Not the Queen," Perry said quickly.

"You cannot mean to ask the Archbishop. He will demand an explanation, and I rather doubt your mother will suffice. He'll think we've both taken leave of our senses. Queen Charlotte, at least, will understand the necessity."

"I am sure she would help us," Perry agreed, "but her assistance will come at a cost. The Queen would never miss such an excellent opportunity to bind our loyalty."

He made a fair point. "But then, who do we ask?"

"Truthfully, I had Prinny in mind." Perry had a faraway look on his face while he considered the options. "For all his other flaws, the Regent has always been willing to come to my aid."

That gave her pause. "Really?"

Charity rarely gave the Regent much concern, as closely tied to the Queen as she was. But Perry spoke the truth. Prinny had abandoned his evening plans at least three times at Peregrine's request. "Why is that?" she asked. "Why do you and Prinny have this strange camaraderie?"

Peregrine cocked his head, as though he had never given it much consideration. "I suppose we understand one another. We both live in the shadow of a ruthless mother."

She covered her mouth with her hand, almost laughing. "If the Queen finds out you compared her to Lady Fitzroy, she might also try to arrange your untimely death." Perry's eyes twinkled. "But… will you be able to have a word with him? The sovereigns will be keeping him occupied."

"Prinny makes time for things when he wishes to," was all he said. "And he will do this; he has a vested interest in keeping us on his side."

When they arrived at the estate, Perry's butler met them at the front door. "There have been… developments. I want to speak with all the staff in half an hour's time below stairs," Peregrine told Quinn.

Like Hodges, Quinn seemed to sense something was amiss. But his eyes only narrowed consideringly before he inclined his head. "Of course. And a package arrived for you from Lord Ravenscroft. I had it put in your study. Perhaps my lord will be able to advise on a… more permanent location."

Peregrine frowned; Quinn's voice was flat and almost censorious. But he escorted Charity towards his study. A study, Charity happened to notice, that had none of her love's personality. Had Lady Fitzroy controlled even what should have been his inner sanctum?

Given that his desk was tidy, it was easy to spot the thing out of place on the felt: a large, boxy thing covered with a cloth. Both of them stared at it for a moment, wondering what it could possibly be, and why the butler seemed so offended by it.

"Quinn wouldn't have left anything dangerous here," he finally declared, pulling the cloth off. The cloth fell away, revealing a shiny gilt birdcage with a little yellow taxidermied bird inside, forever perched on its golden swing.

A stuffed canary in a cage.

Perry goggled for a moment, and a shocked chuckle slipped from his lips as he picked up the cage, looking at the bird inside. It was such a ridiculous, tasteless gift. And to be fair to Lord Ravenscroft, it perfectly suited their thorny friendship. But given what had happened today… Well, now they knew why the dandy had apologised.

Fortunately, Peregrine wasn't insulted. On the contrary, his mirth increased the longer he looked at it. And when he finally looked at the card attached, he dissolved into a fit.

"What does the card say?" Charity asked, finally losing the battle to her burning curiosity.

The cream-coloured note dangled from a golden silk ribbon attached to the top of the cage. Unable to speak, Peregrine untied it and handed it to Charity.

You lived. This one didn't. Try not to get the two confused.

"Oh, good God. No wonder Quinn is in a huff," Charity murmured, embarrassed on Lord Ravenscroft's behalf.

Peregrine struggled to compose himself, wiping at his eyes with the back of his hand. "Perhaps it shouldn't be humorous— but somehow it is. I suspect I have grown on Maggie, and I think part of him absolutely hates that."

"Behaviour very much worthy of a brother," Charity murmured, thinking of the way she had seen her friend Grace and her brother Felix used to fight with one another. But despite the bickering, those two would do anything for one another.

She always envied the bond between Grace and her siblings. Charity didn't have a very close relationship with her sister, and given the age difference between them, possibly neither did Peregrine and Lark.

"Do you think so?" Perry's eyes crinkled in amusement. "Call him my elder brother and he might never speak to you again." His words were lightly cutting. Meant to be ironic. But there was a hint of furtive pleasure too, like the idea pleased him, but he thought it would be wrong to presume.

"Is that meant to be a threat of some sort?" She crossed her arms. "Ravenscroft will never cut me. Imagine the man attempting to stay silent for longer than five minutes."

The way he studied her with that amused, sultry look made her feel as though she were the most unexpected gift of all. "If the magpie is like a brother, does that make the marchioness my auntie?"

Charity choked. "Call Selina that at your peril. She threatened to add to the bounty on my head if I let a word out about Kensington, I'll have you know. Elder sister at worst."

"And Sir Nathaniel?" His slight smile widened.

Charity pretended to consider this. "He does have a rather lost-puppy feel to him, now that he's here on his own. We can take him into the 'family' as well."

This set Peregrine off again. Laughing, he pulled Charity into his arms, letting them wind around her so tightly it nearly squeezed the air from her lungs. But quickly, he loosened his grip, backing up enough to meet her eyes.

Amused by his friendly mauling, she brought her fingers to play along his jaw, glad that the shadow of worry had lightened. When he laughed, the planes of his cheekbones seemed sharper somehow. And when he smiled at her this way, he was... beautiful. Like a glimpse of something divine. He stole one's breath away.

"Could you imagine being related to the three of them?" Perry rallied her. "We would not have a moment's peace. Ever."

She could; the five of them being a peculiar sort of family wasn't nearly as unpleasant as one might think. In fact, it might be the only one she had after marrying Peregrine. "I think that is how a family is supposed to be, but in a happy way," she added dryly, and then she indicated the cage. "What will you do with it?"

Perry stepped back to survey the room, and then he walked over to a stand holding a small globe. He moved the globe over to his desk and put the gilded cage in its place. "This is likely as good a spot as any. Or do you have another idea?"

It was jarringly discordant. "It matches nothing. What would you like to wager that your maids will try to 'accidentally' knock it into the fireplace? When you speak to the staff about your mother, perhaps you should warn them about this dangerous thing also."

His smile slipped, and Charity regretted her flippant words. He had just stopped looking so tormented, and now he was back in a place of worry. "Go, update your household, and then come back and get me," she suggested quickly. "I need to write to Miller, to let her know to bring clothes tomorrow."

When he returned, Charity gave the letters to the footman, Jack. And once her hands were empty, Perry reached into his pocket and pulled a brass key out of it, putting it in her palm.

Charity stared at it, wondering why it seemed familiar. "Is this—?"

"The key I took from your bedroom at Atholl House." He gave her a chagrined smile. "I had thought about using it at some point to visit you. Or at least to annoy you. But the opportunity never presented itself, and… it seems you may not be in residence there much longer?"

Charity rose up on her toes and kissed the corner of his mouth. "As if a simple lock would keep you away from me. Especially in any room with a window."

Taking her hand, he led her over to the leather sofa near the fireplace. Peregrine settled on one end, tugging her down beside him. Feet up, and skirt tucked over her legs, she leaned in, resting her head on his shoulder.

Instinctively, she knew tonight was a night meant for comfort, not pleasure. She relished his warmth. The slowing rhythm of his breath. The steady beat within his chest. There were no others. Tonight, there was no one else in the world but the two of them.

"What are you thinking?" Perry whispered.

"About the night we first met on that balcony."

"You thought I was handsome, didn't you?" he asked teasingly, laughing again when she swatted him. "Lark told me once that all the girls did."

"Since your head is already swollen with conceit, yes. I considered you incredibly handsome," Charity said tartly. "I admit that I *may* have allowed myself to imagine marrying someone like you. Someday."

"*Like* me? You would lead me to believe you were dreaming of other men while I was standing in front of you?" The humour in his voice removed any sting from his chastisement.

"I did not know your name, remember?" Charity replied. "I could hardly imagine myself as your wife."

"My *wife*," Perry whispered, his voice adoring. Reverent. He stroked a finger down the side of her neck. "Can you bear to take on my name? To hear others address you as Lady Fitzroy?"

She smiled. "Not Lady Fitzroy. Lady *Peregrine* Fitzroy. Hearing your name will never bring me anything but pleasure. So no, I do not think I will mind it at all."

Near midnight, they crawled into his bed. Perry wrapped his arm around her waist and tugged her close against him. His hand did not stray from that position on her belly. After the trials of this day, he was in need of intimacy of a different sort that night.

With her fingernails, Charity traced gentle swirls over the top of his hand and wrist until his breathing slowed into the deep, steady cadence of sleep. Only then did she allow herself to drift off as well.

"Sparkles—" Perry's amused voice pulled Charity from the depths of sleep. "Help me. Your hair—"

Charity rolled over, freeing Perry's arm and moving her hair away at the same time. Without Miller there to help her get ready for bed, her braid had pulled free during the night, giving Peregrine a mouthful of loose hair. She pushed upright and scrambled to smooth her hair back in place.

Perry reclined on his pillows, plucking a stray strand from his nightshirt to hold aloft. "I wasn't lying to the Queen when I said this was a curse."

"Maybe you should offer that explanation to Prinny when he asks why we are in such desperate need of an exception." She put a hand to her mouth mockingly. "My wayward hairs could ruin my reputation if he doesn't help us wed straight away."

Perry lifted another hair from his pillow. "Then three days may be too long. We should leap into my carriage and ride straight for Gretna Green."

If only. Setting the scandal of an elopement aside, there was the matter of the guardianship of her ward, the young Duke of Atholl. The rumour mill might claim Perry was attempting to gain control over the heir and fortune.

Better not to risk it. "With our luck, our horse would go lame before we made it out of London. Proceed as planned and we shall begin our married life at least with Prinny's blessing." Charity leaned over and kissed Perry before crawling out of the bed and ringing for breakfast.

Miller had arrived with a few gowns, including her court dress. The Prince Regent's reply to Peregrine's request to meet arrived soon after. Prinny would see them in his private quarters at St James's shortly before the Queen's Drawing Room.

As they walked to the carriage that afternoon, Charity examined Peregrine's clothing. The touch of chiaroscuro in his appearance was a concession to vanity that even Brummell had publicly endorsed. His coat was so heavily embroidered with intricate patterns of silver thread and spangles along the cuffs and front that it shone like a night sky, subtly catching the light to complement his fair colouring.

On most, silver tended to fade beneath notice, but not everyone had Perry's nearly white blonde colouring. If he pushed up his cuffs, it would reveal forearms with a light dusting of hair that grew shades darker, the farther up his arm it went—

"Sparkles? Charity?" Perry called her name a second time before she blinked back to the present. "Are you having second thoughts?"

She cleared her throat, face growing hot. "Thoughts, yes. Help me into the carriage before I decide to act on them."

"Oh?" he drawled, looking interested. "Do tell."

"If I do, we will never make it to our audience with Prinny." Charity glanced down at the wide skirts of her Georgian court gown, measuring them against the doorframe. The Queen preferred the older fashion still. "You shall have to sit across from me, I am afraid; my hoops will be more effective than a chaperone."

Inside St James's, they found Prinny in the Regent's Closet. He was lounging in his chair, drinking from a glass of wine. The dark circles under his eyes suggested he had enjoyed another of his infamous late nights, and the near-empty bottle at his side suggested how he spent his day.

"Thank you for agreeing to see us, Your Highness," Perry said after rising from his bow.

"You provided me with the perfect excuse to stay hidden a while longer. My mother expects me to dance attendance at her Drawing Rooms, and from there I must endure another dinner with the Grand Duchess complaining about my every choice." The Regent sighed dramatically. "Whatever it is you want, you may have it, if you can rid me of that woman's eternal commentary."

"Your Highness, I have asked Her Grace to marry me, and she has agreed," said Peregrine formally. "I wish your aid in procuring a special licence from the Archbishop."

Prinny narrowed his gaze at the both of them and then frowned into his wine glass. When he looked up, he said the last thing Charity expected.

"Give us the room for a moment, Your Grace? I wish to speak with Lord Fitzroy on his own."

6

"Careful! There is war in women too, as you know by experience, I think."
— **Sophocles, Electra**

The door had barely shut behind Charity when the Prince Regent sprawled further, as if Perry's very presence exhausted him. "Really, Fitzroy," he exclaimed, waving a hand in the door's direction, "a special licence? For a widow?"

Peregrine blinked at him. "I beg your pardon?"

"Come on! We are speaking as one man to another. I will grant that the duchess is a lovely figure to get familiar with. But you cannot threaten to abandon London! Not now. Not when she's already been unwrapped, and you need no special permission to tup her."

That was why he didn't immediately say yes? Colour rose on his cheekbones. "There is rather more to it than that, Your Highness," he said stiffly.

The Prince Regent stared at him for a long moment. "*Oh?* Is there? I thought you and I both understood that there are enough problems in our lives without lighting a keg of powder under our mothers' arses. I suppose you cannot be persuaded to wait for things to settle down?"

"With my mother here in London?" Perry shifted on his feet. "No, sir. I do not wish to wait. And I will not offer her anything less than all that I am, freely and without condition."

It was the bare truth. If the Regent wasn't likely to grant his assistance, it did not matter how many flowery speeches or excuses Peregrine gave him. Prinny would either help him, or he would not.

"Less?" This time it was the Regent who blinked owlishly at him, even more confused. "Not one of my mistresses has ever complained about what I offered. And my methods have never threatened to take anything away from those I consorted with. But I imagine your pretty little duchess is smart enough to make the decision for herself."

She was. Even though it smarted to be reminded of the title Charity would give up to marry him.

"Then you will do it?" he asked the Regent.

"As long as you do not plan on disappearing for a honeymoon if I say yes, then who am I to say no?" he drawled, and waved his hand in dismissal. "But for the love of God—perhaps don't rush to rub it in either of our mothers' faces."

Outside the room, Peregrine shared only the good news with Charity, leaving out the more insulting parts of the discussion. Together they walked deeper into the palace, heading toward the state rooms where the Queen's Drawing Room was already underway. Anyone with power, wealth, or distinction who could gain admittance had come, but all Peregrine could think of was leaving.

"Surely no one will notice if I decide to spend an evening

instead with the woman who is going to be *my wife*," grumbled Peregrine quietly.

Charity bit her lip, though the corner turned up. "You are incorrigible. I still have a duty to the Queen and Princess Charlotte. And unfortunately, there will be no better chance to find a discreet word with your sister than tonight."

He exhaled, disgruntled.

"We have survived the past month. Three days will be nothing." Charity gave his arm a pat. "I should go; I am only being a distraction to you."

It was true. But still he watched as Charity slipped away into the crowd, missing her as soon as she had departed. Missing the way her buttercup yellow gown had appeared splendidly next to his black tailcoat and breeches. Like day and night, paired together.

He had barely stepped into the next room when another woman's gloved hand slipped around his forearm.

"Lord Fitzroy," Selina purred. "You seem better than yesterday. I trust the duchess's ministrations were effective?"

"You've got the look of a woman ready to dine out on my confidences, Sina," he said with a smirk. "We have tasks to accomplish besides gossip."

The marchioness gave him a wisp of a pout, but her attention was already elsewhere. "I do care about the two of you, you realise. At least be a gentleman and take me for a turn."

They manoeuvred through the crowd, Peregrine using their stroll to try to spot his sister's hair in the throng. "I appreciate the concern. Thank you for advising the duchess about her parents, as well; it seems to have helped settle her some," he ventured.

"She would have handled it herself if she had not been in a pother from Marian's unexpected arrival. The two of you needed a moment to recover your equilibrium after the shock, that is all."

"And how are you and the others?"

The marchioness paused before replying. "We are ready to rise to the challenge, Perry. Do we really have any other choice? Although speaking of challenges…"

Peregrine whipped his head up at the change in her voice. Lady Normanby's attention was on one of the far walls of the room where buttercup yellow skirts were hemmed in by an older couple. He resisted the urge to sigh. "The Cresswells have found her already? It has barely been a quarter of an hour since I left her."

The marchioness turned a sharp grin towards him. "Perhaps we might say good day?"

Selina had remembered that Lady Cresswell had interfered with her attempts to save Perry from the Home Office. "The duchess doesn't know," he told her softly. "Let sleeping dogs lie."

She huffed, but she subsided as they angled in that direction. Lady Cresswell was angry enough that even from ten feet away they could hear her fan snap shut like a pistol shot. "*Really*, Charity! I do not think your title entitles you to speak to me as if I were a servant in your household."

"It does," Lady Normanby muttered, for Peregrine's ears only.

"This is not the time nor the place," said Lord Cresswell cautiously to the both of them.

Because their backs were to the room, the Cresswells did not see Perry approaching. But Charity did, and relief clearly warred with the desire to warn them away. Before she could decide, Charity's mother saw her daughter's attention flicker, and she spun around, her mouth making an unsightly little pucker when she beheld Perry.

Really, Lady Cresswell should practice avoiding that face, Perry thought. It had the most unfortunate tendency to make her mouth resemble a dog's anus. That particular thought cheered him enough that it was easy to summon a mask of gaiety.

Otherwise, she said nothing to him. And after a delay long

enough it could be considered rude, Lady Cresswell looked at Selina and dipped her head, acknowledging the marchioness properly. "Lady Normanby."

"Lady Cresswell! Dearest, I haven't seen you in ages." Selina's smile was all teeth. "Not since sometime after that unfortunate incident with the Swedish gift of state, if I recall correctly."

Peregrine pinched the wrist of the marchioness discreetly as he dropped her arm, warning her to avoid antagonising yet another person who wanted him dead.

Without reacting, Selina turned to the earl and Charity. "Lord Cresswell. Your Grace, that is a rather fetching colour on you!"

Lady Normanby nattered on, but rather than have to converse with her and Peregrine, the Cresswells quickly decided there was somewhere else they urgently had to be. They made mumbled excuses and departed.

Lady Normanby watched their backs. "You seem to have the worst luck with mothers, darling," she said in an undertone to Perry. "No slight intended to you, of course, Charity."

Charity deflated slightly in fatigue, but quickly, she composed herself. "I believe my mother means well," she said without conviction.

Perry ignored the way Selina's glance swung to him at that. He also noted the way she neglected to mention her father's opinions at all. "I am sure she is only being protective of you after last year," he agreed neutrally.

Charity's eyes narrowed, and Peregrine wondered if perhaps he was starting to lose his touch with her, if even a polite half-truth had the sound of a lie. But before he could say anything further, Ravenscroft and Thorne descended upon them.

"Oh good, we found you," said the magpie. "Where have you been? It is almost as if you are under the impression that this is a party."

Charity began to look cross. "I was trying to find the princess." Making room in their circle for the new arrivals, Perry let his arm discreetly brush against Charity's, soothing her.

Sir Nathaniel was perspiring lightly due to the stuffy atmosphere. "If you are searching for the princess, we just left her vicinity. She and Prince William of Orange are surrounded five deep in a circle of well-wishers who are offering congratulations to their faces and contempt to the prince's back."

"Mmm," agreed Ravenscroft, producing a handkerchief with a flourish and indicating to Thorne he should blot his forehead. "I was rather hoping Prinny would reconsider Prince William. Obviously, public sentiment is not the foremost reason this match is a terrible idea."

Lady Normanby tilted her head. "How many of those well-wishers are from the Russian delegation, I wonder?"

"Some few—largely the ones who have no other choice." Ravenscroft gave her a knowing look. "But the Tsar has not been one of them. Nor his sister, the Grand Duchess."

Thorne made a noise into the handkerchief that sounded suspiciously like a laugh.

"What happened?" Charity asked him, frowning.

"Both the Grand Duchess and the Tsar seem to be playing the gadflies," Ravenscroft answered, his voice dry. "*He* is talking to people out of turn, mostly to the lower ranks. All the courtiers' noses are out of joint. And *she* is engaged in her favourite sport, which is trying to give Prinny an apoplexy. In short—chaos."

Which might be the worst of what they had planned, but Peregrine doubted it. Prince William was likely incompetent, but Russia didn't want England to strengthen its ties to the Dutch. And simply making the Prince Regent appear weak could help Russia's agenda in Vienna.

"And what is my mother doing?" Peregrine asked softly.

"Behaving herself, Lord Fitzroy. At least as best we can

judge," Thorne answered. "She is with the Russian delegation, and for now, she's content knowing she is causing a great deal of consternation."

Perry tapped his fingers against the sheath of his smallsword. Good behaviour surely wouldn't last.

"We mustn't linger together," said Ravenscroft. "I must get back to Prinny. Canary, your sister is catching up with some of last year's debutantes in the blue room. Lady Normanby, darling, would you like to keep the Regent from pulling his hair?"

"Not today, I think." Selina looked thoughtful. "It would be wiser if perhaps the Duchess and I paid a call at the Pulteney tomorrow. I managed to secure an invitation to visit from an old friend." She glanced at Charity for approval of this plan. And then her eyes lingered more speculatively on Sir Nathaniel. "I may have another idea."

"I like the way your mind works, Marchioness," Ravenscroft drawled in amusement. "Yes, that might be just the role for our budding spy."

Thorne blinked at them. "What exactly do you want me to do?"

"To flirt with the Grand Duchess, Sir Chivalrous." Selina took Thorne's forearm between both hands. "Let us go introduce you. I suspect she will like your company, and it will be *excellent* practice."

"Er," Thorne stammered, flushing a deep red. But he let Selina lead him away, and Ravenscroft wriggled his eyebrows suggestively as he, too, left.

Charity bit her lip to keep from laughing. "Do you suppose the knight might require rescuing this time?"

Perry pretended to consider, distracted by the sensation of Charity's smallest finger stroking along the side of his hand. "Hmmm. No. This will build character," he finally managed.

Then he winked at her and strode away, seeking the blue room and Lark.

Hopefully, the Cresswells would not track Charity down again immediately.

Lines of demarcation had formed despite the crowd. Middle-ranking British military men were clustered together, but to one side of that group, the allied generals from the visiting delegations were mingling, talking of war. The same had happened with the members of Parliament. Lower MPs grouped like sheep, and men like Liverpool and Castlereagh conversed with the London diplomats like the von Lievens.

The Austrians. The Prussians. The Russians. Great powers with the most present delegates, they formed islands in the swirling masses. The Germanic states made another. The smaller presences banded together in a more motley assortment—Spain, Portugal, Sweden, and the Dutch, mostly.

At last, Peregrine found what he was searching for. Lark was in a rather small knot of young women from the British peerage, chatting. Lark's expression was distracted, as if she was only half-listening, but her hazel eyes met Perry's, and she appraised her brother coolly as he approached them.

Lark turned to the other two ladies and politely excused herself before Perry got within speaking distance.

"Sister," Peregrine greeted her carefully.

"Brother." Lark tilted her chin, her face unreadable.

"I hope I did not interrupt your discussion."

"It was not much of a discussion. They were filling me in on gossip I missed." Lark fanned herself idly. "Was there something you wanted?"

Perry had a pang of regret. Their age difference kept them from being too close, but the gulf had, it seemed, widened in the past year. He had no idea what his mother would have told her.

What *had* Marian explained to her daughter about why the

two of them had packed and left without notice on the ship bound for Copenhagen, leaving him behind? Or of the ruby dagger that had been stolen and returned? What did his sister believe about Charity's kidnapping last year? Of his mother's former black empire?

Did Lark know that their mother tried to kill him? He couldn't tell.

"I wished to make sure you were... well," he said softly. To make sure she was safe. To see if there was something he might be able to do.

As if they both realised they had been staring, something ineffable showed on Lark's face, and she lifted the fan to disguise it. "This is hardly a place to talk, Perry."

Lark was only nineteen, and still so young. But he could see signs of his mother's hands on her, like the trace of unhappy nervousness that peeked through her calm. The attempt at studied nonchalance.

He gave her a ghost of a smile. "Perhaps I might persuade you to go for a ride with me tomorrow? It will give us the chance to catch up."

Whatever she had been told, Peregrine was sure she held him to blame for their situation now. Lark had left behind everyone she had ever known—even her lady's maid. They had been living in exile. Her friends had married and moved on with their lives.

"Mama did say you would likely try to talk to me alone," she admitted.

Perry closed his eyes briefly and wondered if the well was already poisoned. He would have to be careful in extracting information from his sister. So careful. "And? Did she say that you should not?"

"No." His sister looked unhappy. "She suggested that I ought to. But I don't know if I want to."

It made him nervous that his mother wanted them to speak;

that made it more likely that Marian intended to use her daughter against him. And it made it less likely that Lark knew anything of importance at all. If she knew little—and he told her the truth about their mother—it might put her in jeopardy.

Still, he had to try. To feel out whether she could be extracted from a dangerous situation. "Please." He gave her a beseeching look.

Lark's eyes dropped to the floor for a moment. "All right, Perry. I will tell Mama I have said yes."

Gooseflesh crawled on the back of Perry's neck. Marian would know exactly where to find him and when. But he nodded. "I will pick you up from the Pulteney at four o'clock?"

"Tomorrow, then," Lark said, showing him her back. The conversation was finished.

A preternatural prickling across his senses had him turning around. Another familiar bright-blonde head was weaving through the crowd purposefully, away from him. His mother was bound on some mission, paying him no mind.

Perry had a premonition of disaster, and that spurred him into following. When he spotted the entire Cresswell family in her path, he edged his way through the crowd as quickly as he could.

Marian Fitzroy bore down on them with the grace of a hungry predator before he could intercept her.

"—how very fine the pair of you look tonight," his mother said with a brilliant smile. "Vanessa, my dear, seeing the two of you side by side, it astonishes me how *uncanny* the resemblance is between your daughter and the way you looked at her age. I wonder if she inherited more than just your cheekbones."

"Mother," Peregrine began in a low, warning tone, and Marian Fitzroy lifted a finger in a bid for patience.

Charity's face was pale, but she stayed serene. Lord and Lady Cresswell, however, looked anything but.

"Yes, well, we all hope our children take the best of us, don't we, Marian?" Lady Cresswell said acidly, her eyes flicking towards Perry. "But the best of what some parents have to offer might still bear the stench of ruin. We should endeavour that our children have better lives than we do."

"It is quite all right," Marian murmured over her shoulder to him when he took a breath to object. "There is no need to make a scene. I couldn't agree more with Lady Charity's mother. Oh! Forgive me. It is *Her Grace* now, isn't it?"

That his mother knew Charity's status gave him pause. How much information had Cameron and her cronies given her over the year of her absence? But he bit his tongue, because Marian Fitzroy was right; they were already attracting a great deal of attention.

His mother met Vanessa Cresswell's eyes again. "Private feuds do not need to be aired in front of the *ton*—unless, of course, someone insists on hanging out laundry before them."

Lord Cresswell's jowls quivered slightly, and Charity's face creased in confusion. Cresswell bodily put his wife's hand upon his arm and began to tug her away, towards the door, leaving Charity rooted in place.

With a casual flick to open her fan, Lady Fitzroy followed them, her pace less of a saunter and more of a leisurely stalk.

With a glancing plea for assistance at Peregrine, Charity turned to hurry after them. "Do you know what is happening?" she asked him.

"She's forcing them to retreat to someplace more private," he gritted at her side, in as low a voice as he could. The Cresswells knew that Marian Fitzroy held an armoury of weapons to be wielded against them. They were armed with nothing save baseless accusations.

"Mother!" Perry barked again in a harsh whisper behind her, as the Cresswells huddled in the dubious privacy of a niche. "This is not the time or place."

Lady Fitzroy turned on a heel to study her son, rolling her head on her neck in a careless stretch. And she traced a line in the air over the very spot on his torso that he had been stabbed, which made his knees wobble.

"Perry, *my love*, not everything is about you." Lady Fitzroy turned to Charity and said in a playful voice, "I know a secret about your mother, Your Grace. Would you like to guess it?"

"Tell me that you wouldn't have done the same, if our places were reversed, you witch," Lady Cresswell hissed, half hiding behind her husband. "You nearly ruined my daughter!"

"Why would I steal another's betrothed by staging an attack on my own virtue, Lady Cresswell?" Marian asked, her eyes glittering. "Or, are we speaking of your own effort to ensure my son died in the muck like a common soldier?"

Charity and Cresswell's sharp intakes of breath were loud, and Perry resisted the urge to sigh.

"Was that not common knowledge?" Lady Fitzroy asked disingenuously. "Oh, Vanessa, I am so sorry. I thought you had told them already."

"What did you do?" Cresswell asked her in a low, furious tone, and Lady Cresswell blanched.

Charity, too, gave her mother a blank stare. "*You* were the one who made sure that Perry was sent to war?"

Lord Cresswell's face was a study of uncertainty, anger, and regret as he locked eyes with Peregrine. "Vanessa, we need to leave. *Now*." He dragged his wife past them, and Marian let them go, her face devoid of humanity once more.

Seeing Death wearing his mother's skin, Perry caught Charity around the waist and pulled her farther away from the woman. Gossip be damned; he would take no chances with Charity's life. Not when it came to his mother.

But Charity had been maddened enough by the exchange to attack the monster. "Why are you bothering us? It seems odd that you would care what my mother did, given what *you* did to your own son."

"Odd?" Lady Fitzroy echoed. "Why is it odd? I care because *he is mine.*" She took a menacing step closer to Charity, and Perry bared his teeth at his mother in an unspoken threat. Madness was dancing in her eyes. "Peregrine's love—his loyalty—his life. It is *mine* to break or burn, as I see fit. Not Vanessa Cresswell's. And most certainly not *yours.*"

Charity twitched in his arms. "That is *not* how you should treat someone you claim to love, Lady Fitzroy." His duchess was practically spitting, she was so angry. "He is a person! Not your possession."

The abrupt change from angry monster to amused mask was jolting. "How quaint. Love and marriage have always been tools of possession, Your Grace. You should know this. Or did the old duke decline to take your dowry before he took you to his bed?"

"The dowry, yes. For some, that may be the way they consider marriage, but—"

"I see. Tell me, Your Grace," Lady Fitzroy asked coquettishly, "how many rights do you have now without coverture?"

Charity sullenly didn't answer, and Lady Fitzroy continued. "My son was loved *exactly* as much as was necessary to mould him into what I needed him to be. Just as your parents did for you."

Perry could feel Charity shaking her head. The barest back and forth of disbelief. "Why will you not just leave us alone?" she whispered, resisting as Peregrine urged her backwards.

Lady Fitzroy was eerily still. "Because I do not wish to. Is that not enough?"

"We all know better. You never do things for one reason only, Mother," Perry fired at her.

"Are you casting the blame upon me? The trouble that has

happened to you these past two years is of your own making." She tilted her head, blinking slowly. "All of it."

Charity squirmed again, and he tightened his grip, sweat growing cold in the small of his back. "Don't," he murmured suddenly into Charity's ear. "Don't fight me, or her."

Their exchange had given him new clarity. A thought that he could barely even articulate to himself.

Somehow, somewhen, a year and more ago, he had met a girl and had been moved by the sound of her laugh. She gave him something for nothing. A moment of delight without expectation. Without demands. Without ill intentions or aspirations of what she would be able to extort from him. That had given him a reason to live. To fight. That had been what had made him defy Marian. To reclaim his dented soul for himself.

His mother was punishing them because Charity had set him *free*.

"You had best get back to the Drawing Room, Mother." His voice was steady, even if he was certain Charity could feel how rapidly his heart was beating against her back. Charity wove her fingers into his hand clasped around her waist.

He wasn't quite sure what expression was on his face, but whatever it was, Lady Fitzroy inclined her head and walked away.

"We will talk another day, Perry," she said as she passed them by.

7

"Let such as say our sex is void of reason,
Know it is slander now but once was treason."
—Anne Bradstreet

Peregrine wished Charity had come back to the estate, if only so he knew she was safe under his roof. But she had asked him to return her to Atholl House for that evening. She wanted to make preparations for the next two days, and they each had appointments to attend to.

The 9th of June dawned with the promise of good weather for an open-carriage drive. Charity would be going to the Pulteney with Selina to try their luck, and he would be going on his outing with Lark, so they would not see each other today. Later, he would begin his long trek towards Ascot, and tomorrow, the *ton* and the train of the Allied Sovereigns would arrive there. They might be able to get close enough to the Tsar to pose a few questions.

The day after that, they would have their licence to wed. And then, whatever else happened, at least they would face it together. A man and his wife.

His *wife.*

Peregrine had never imagined he would be the sort of man prone to fits of foolish grinning at odd times for no reason whatsoever, but it seems he was learning new things about himself every day.

Perry elected to make a show of this outing with Lark. They would take the sleek landau and both footmen. For the *ton*, it would send a message that the Fitzroy family was still a wealthy and powerful force to be reckoned with. To be seen with his sister, hopefully, would quiet the speculation about the extent of the family's discord.

To his mother, this was a show of force.

He had spent the morning testing the competency of Jack and Owens with smaller coach pistols, of which four had been stowed on the landau. It was enough to arm all of them, though Will Hodges kept his preferred carbine beside him. Both footmen had been country boys in the militia before coming to London, so they got a sense for the little firearm's aim quickly.

As Will Hodges pulled up the landau in front of the Pulteney, both of his footmen alighted. The Graves brothers looked both sharp and intimidating in the livery he had tailored for their burly six-foot frames. Owens headed inside to announce their arrival at the front desk. Jack assisted Peregrine down, then stood ready, waiting. Perry proceeded into the hotel to wait for Lark.

Lark—or his mother—had decided to make an unspoken statement also. Lark arrived alone.

His sister was not dressed in the usual pale palette of an unmarried young Englishwoman. Lark's gown was a shockingly deep, rich crimson that made her a vision of pale, ethereal beauty. The silk carriage dress cut open at the front to reveal a gold-embroidered ivory underdress, long sleeves cuffed in sable and high collar lending regal formality. Her pale blonde hair had been braided into an intricate coronet.

Had he not known who she was, he would have assumed her to be one of the Russians, or some other sophisticate of world travelling. The portrait he had held in his thoughts of his younger sister dissipated completely. After the past year, she was no longer who he remembered. But then again, neither was he.

"Lark." Peregrine greeted her simply with the truth. "That colour is stunning on you."

His sister blushed prettily—not immune, it seemed, to flattery. Then she silently took his arm and they made their way back to the carriage.

In silence, Perry watched her carefully as they rode for several minutes, considering and discarding the words he had thought he was going to say to her. His sister did not try to study him as he studied her. Her gaze was averted, only the tiniest wrinkle between her brows suggesting that the situation was... unpleasant.

"How does time feel to you, Lark?" he asked finally. "Does it feel like it has been a year? Or more like a lifetime?"

"A lifetime? More like a different life altogether." Her eyes finally flicked to his. "Like I am some Selkie creature who has been trapped too long on land and forgotten what it's like to return to the sea."

"I am sorry you got caught in the middle of what transpired last year," he said vaguely. "I'm not certain what you have been told."

She didn't enlighten him. Lark turned her head again. "I should not have come."

"To see me?" His stomach twisted. "Why not?"

"I do not know who you are. You are a stranger wearing a familiar face."

"Lark, I am still your brother. Still the person you've always known."

"No," she disagreed. "You are not. I haven't known you since you came home from Oxford. I adored you, Perry. You were so distant and untouchable but never cold. Not before. But then you came home. I thought we would be happy, but it was as though when you finally stepped into the title, everything had changed."

The impressions of a thirteen-year-old girl, standing outside of the events of that year, would be very different from his. Lark clearly didn't understand what had happened the year he had turned twenty-one, and he could not tell her. Though he had spent the next six years hiding the truth about Grenville's death, it seemed she hated him anyway.

Peregrine's lashes fell over his cheeks. "I am sorry you felt slighted by that. It is not your fault."

"No? And of the events that happened last year?"

"Those are not your fault either, Sister."

"That much," she said slowly, her voice cutting, "I already know. But what I *don't* understand is why you would so openly consort with Lady Cresswell and her daughter after everything they did to me and Mama!"

Peregrine lifted his chin defiantly. "What do you think they did to you, Lark? What do you believe happened? Go ahead. You can talk in front of my men. They won't say a word."

Lark's eyes flickered, her posture less certain. She did not know much; he could tell by her expression. There was only what she would have heard. Fragments of the truth and baseless speculation.

"Sir David Green, the man who put the dagger in our luggage, was a friend and the commanding officer once of the new Duke of Northumberland," she said suspiciously. "And Charity ended up engaged to the same duke."

A corner of his mouth lifted. "Is that all? Half the *ton* knew

Sir David Green well. And *all* of it knew about Percy's wager to marry the season's Diamond of the First Water."

"*Your* wager, Perry, not Percy's," she hissed. "They hate us. The Cresswells and the Percys. They blame us for what happened last year. And you are somehow involved in the why of all of it. Sir David Green killed that man with your knife. What you did is the reason we had to leave."

Peregrine exhaled softly. "The truth is more complicated than that."

"Is it, Perry? You were standing beside *Charity Cresswell*." Her voice snapped like the crack of a whip. "After what they did to our mother!"

"Her Grace, the Duchess of Atholl," he said with a warning rattle, "is as innocent of what has happened as you are. And if you don't suspect our mother has contributed to this feud, you certainly *don't* have the first idea about what happened last year. Edmunds can confirm Charity's drink was laced to sabotage her debut."

Lark blinked at him, stunned. "Edmunds would say such a thing about mother?"

The moment the words left his mouth, he regretted it. He had to be careful, lest his sister begin asking his mother dangerous questions. If Lark proved not biddable and ignorant enough to accept her mother's lies at face value, her mother would—at the least—bind Lark the way she had bound Perry's loyalties.

That would be the best-case scenario. At worst, she might decide her daughter's life was as dispensable as his.

"To make her clumsy. You have seen our mother do such things before."

When Lark's shoulders dropped, he knew that she learned that much already. But he could tell—she still did not believe her mother was capable of the evil he experienced. He had to get Lark away from the perilous position she was in.

"Come home to me," he said impulsively. "Come back to the estate."

"No," Lark repeated. "I am still furious with you."

"Why did you decide to come ride with me, then?"

"Because you asked. And it will look bad if we do not show a united front to society," Lark said stiffly. But these words clearly were more of an echo of Marian Fitzroy than Lark's personal feelings. "I do not want to be a pariah forever. I want to marry, to have a life of my own."

"Then I'll help you settle back into society and we will find you a husband."

"No, Perry," his sister said evenly. "I do not want to put my future in your hands. You barely even notice who I am. You will marry me off quietly and get me out of the way. But Mama reaches for greater things, and I have seen a year of proof that she is more than capable of taking care of us. I want more than a quiet life."

Peregrine stared at her silently. Separating her from his mother was going to be harder than he thought.

Selina greeted Charity with a warm smile and a pat on the seat beside her. "Good afternoon, Your Grace. I *do* like the colour of your dress."

Charity had chosen a gown of deep rose madder silk with a narrow band of gold embroidery that defined the high waist. The sleeves—cut just below the elbow—were finished with froths of sheer net and tiny, embroidered roses.

Selina had dressed in crimson taffeta. The bodice was sharply tailored, its squared neckline trimmed with a narrow ruffle of black Chantilly lace that echoed the jet beads threaded through her earrings.

"Your colours make you look ready for battle. Did you come armed as well?" Charity asked.

"With the rapier of my wit," Selina assured her. "And between the two of us, we are certainly dressed to launch a salvo at every man's heart."

Charity allowed herself a small smile. "On the subject of unconventional warfare... how did Thorne do with your assignment?"

"Better than I thought he would! Of course, with the fine figure he cuts, all he really had to do was stand there and allow himself to be admired—and the Grand Duchess did. Ravenscroft is half tempted to campaign for a barony for our knight errant at this rate, and if Prinny has any idea how much peace the man bought him yesterday, he might actually grant it."

Selina's thumb grazed the corner of her lip, fondly diverted by the memory. Coughing into her fist to cover a chuckle, Charity asked about their upcoming task.

"The Pulteney has spaces for guests to mingle. Yesterday, I sent a tendril of inquiry... and I received an invitation to pay a call," Lady Normanby explained.

"Your... 'old friend,'" Charity murmured, and received a nod of confirmation.

"Maximilian and I... we have some history. He is an attaché from Prussia who visits London occasionally. At any rate, he is here once more, and he will provide us with a convenient excuse to loiter in their coffee room, seeing what there is to see. Perhaps we can form a connection to someone else."

"Is this at all what you did for the Order, Lady Normanby?" Charity asked, fluttering her eyelashes at the older widow.

Selina gave Charity a small smirk. "Forming connections? Oh yes, Duchess. Granted, most of my efforts dealt with our politicians. But occasionally, there are foreign visitors in the area that require more of a... woman's touch."

The carriage slowed in front of the hotel, where Cossack guards stood at attention on either side of the front entrance.

"No matter what happens, keep your wits, and show respect where due," Selina reminded Charity while they waited for the footman to open the carriage door. "While I talk with Maximilian, keep an eye on the room. See who is talking with whom. There is more of a game afoot than simply Lady Fitzroy's presence in the court, but we have to catch it."

Informed of their appointment, the hotel footman led them to the coffee room, where clusters of individuals sat drinking the hot, bitter drink. "Your other guest will be here soon," they were informed. "I was instructed to ensure you were served while you wait."

"Prince Paul and Prince Leopold seem thick as thieves," Charity noted. The princes of Württemberg and Saxe-Coburg sat with their heads together, and she and Selina nodded respectfully in their direction, though they went unacknowledged. "Perhaps he's getting advice about playing cards. I heard that he lost a sum on his first evening here."

Selina bit her lip slightly, saying nothing until the footman who brought the pot of tea left. "More likely, he's looking for an ally in Württemberg's survival. In Vienna, the maps of Europe will be redrawn. And after spending so many years fighting for Napoleon, King Frederick of Württemberg has the task of proving he is worthy of retaining territory and title."

Charity considered that as she stirred her cup. "An ally in Saxe-Coburg?"

"More likely, in the Tsar," Selina corrected, lifting her chin in the direction of Leopold as she settled her fingers around the teacup in front of her. "Prince Leopold is one of the emperor's favourites. And it would be a subtle way to secure favour."

The marchioness may have preferred snooping in domestic matters, but it was clear she was rather well informed of what was happening on the continent. She had most likely worked more closely with Xavier, the Order's former spymaster, than she implied.

As they waited, Prince Paul got up and joined another table with some of the generals from the Alliance. She did not know their faces well enough to know who. But it was obvious that there was a great deal of political discussion afoot. Two men whom Charity recalled as being Russian ministers were joined by an older man with keen eyes that flickered over Charity and Selina, seated together.

He had a slightly knowing, intense expression.

"Is that Baron von Gentz staring at us?" Charity asked, keeping her lashes lowered. When she glanced up again, though, the older man's attention had turned towards the Russians.

"Mmm," Selina agreed, her voice very low. "Austria openly consorting? Interesting. It is almost as if they do not care if the English learn what they are about."

It did not feel like they were in English territory, despite the location of the Pulteney. Just one other Englishman was in the room, a rich industrialist Charity remembered from the ball at Burlington House.

And then, a group of people entered the room. The Grand Duchess of Oldenburg and Princess Charlotte stood at the front of it, causing Selina—and many other people present—to rise to their feet. Charity got up from her chair with alacrity, giving a respectful curtsy to the women, her eyes lowered.

"Her Royal Highness and Imperial Highness thank you," said another woman's voice as the princess and grand duchess continued on.

A familiar voice.

Charity straightened to see Marian Fitzroy standing before them. Marian gave Charity and Selina a saucy wink… and then proceeded to sit with the Grand Duchess and Princess Charlotte.

Horror and consternation crawled along Charity's throat. Marian Fitzroy was rubbing shoulders directly with the Princess of Wales. To what end? Was the princess safe?

Watch yourselves—something is happening. Peregrine's voice in her thoughts brought her to attention.

Marian Fitzroy was too canny a creature to do something that would endanger herself or her own plans, so the princess was likely in no immediate danger. But there was a sense that a stage was being set here, like an opera whose curtain was about to rise.

"Lady Normanby, I have a hunch something unpleasant is about to occur," Charity confessed in the lowest voice she could manage.

Selina's expression did not change, but she held so perfectly still that Charity saw that she, too, had a presentiment of disaster about to strike. And as Charity watched Lady Fitzroy, Marian leaned over the table beside her to whisper in the ear of someone sitting there.

The table beside them also had several women, some of whom were facing away. But the one Lady Fitzroy had whispered to glared over at Charity and Selina. Charity struggled to recall her name. Countess Orlova?

Selina held very still as Countess Orlova pointedly leaned forward to speak with the woman whose back was to them. Stiffly, that woman got up and crossed the room to speak with a man seated alone, reading a paper.

Folding the paper and setting it down with a sharp snap, the man stood to straighten his jacket. Then he marched over to both of them, according them slight bows. "Lady Normanby," he said crisply, his voice cold as winter. "I was told you wished to visit Herr von Steinbach. Alas, he cannot come—he is in a new role in Berlin, and I have taken his place."

The marchioness made her face wide and guileless. "That is

quite all right. I am sorry not to be able to renew our acquaintance, but—"

The man's bark of laughter cut off her words. Curious faces began to turn their way.

"I am sure you are sorry, Lady Normanby. Or should I say, *Fräulein* Normanby? For in my country, a title such as yours is not earned in a bedchamber."

Around the room, jaws dropped open. Charity dared to look directly at the table where Lady Fitzroy sat. Nothing could be trusted about Lady Fitzroy. She had orchestrated this somehow, for certain. Princess Charlotte's face was very pale. And the Grand Duchess... her face was... a study. Whatever this charade was, it was as surprising to the Grand Duchess as it was to Lady Normanby. But the Tsar's sister cloaked her expression quickly.

"I—I beg your pardon!" Selina finally stammered, outraged.

This nameless Prussian attaché, who had not bothered to introduce himself, clasped his hands neatly behind his back. "When he was here in London the spring before last, Maximilian made the acquaintance of an *extraordinary* woman. So extraordinary, in fact, that he was compelled to spill state secrets upon her pillow. We might never have known about his indiscretion... except it seems that somewhere along the way, the Home Secretary was sold those secrets too."

Selina's face was expressionless, but her countenance was pale. This man had named her as a spy, a manipulator, and a prostitute in front of all assembled in this room. Finally, Lady Normanby got to her feet, calmly collecting her gloves and lifting her chin.

"I deny these baseless accusations," Lady Normanby ground out, not looking down at Charity. "You, sir, use the moral outrage of an audience to replace the evidence you lack to prove this scandal. And in your cowardice, you attempt to smear the name of a good man who is not here to defend himself in the bargain.

Enjoy your coffee. I have better things to do than provide your afternoon entertainment."

She stalked out of the room without a backward glance, leaving a trail of rising whispers.

Stunned, Charity sat there for a long moment, the subject of some uncomfortable speculation. Selina left to protect her, she realised belatedly. A quick departure without explanation had made Charity's surprise real.

But this was terrible for Lady Normanby, and for them. Until Selina found a way free of this scandal—assuming she could—no one of standing would receive her. And any who risked it would likely suffer by association.

The rumour would spread, and Selina would be unable to show her face for the remainder of the sovereigns' visit. Peregrine's mother had ruined Lady Normanby so thoroughly, she would be unable to help them or Sidmouth. Perhaps Marian had done enough to ruin the woman completely.

For Charity, the scandal would likely pass her by. But for now, she could bear the stares and whispers no longer, and she got up from her seat to leave.

"Are you all right, Your Grace?" Lady Fitzroy asked. Butter wouldn't melt in her mouth. Peregrine's mother had stepped closer while Charity's thoughts had been whirling. "I am so sorry you were subjected to that awful woman's comeuppance."

Charity pulled away before Lady Fitzroy's outstretched hand could land on her arm. "Yes. I am well, thank you."

Lady Fitzroy stepped closer, the very picture of a concerned friend. "I could have told them why Lady Normanby did it, but I think it is more useful to keep that secret in reserve. Herr Krüger and the Prussians will wish to avoid sharing that Lady Normanby gave two of their spies to Lord Sidmouth in exchange for Peregrine's life."

Lady Fitzroy wanted her to see this: the terrifying reach of her web. From across an ocean, Lady Fitzroy had discovered who thwarted her attempts to have Peregrine charged and executed.

Marian also appeared to have her fingers within the Home Office, since she had discovered exactly what information had been traded to save Perry. The Home Secretary was going to be furious.

All works of genius require an audience to properly appreciate them, Sparkles, Perry's voice murmured in her thoughts.

"It must be terribly frustrating to you to see that your son is able to earn people's loyalty," Charity said, her lips stiff with anger. "Especially when the only way you can earn such things is through fear. Excuse me, Lady Fitzroy."

Peregrine would be furious that she kept baiting this monster, but she couldn't seem to stop doing it. The slightest flare of Marian's delicate nostrils was the only sign that betrayed the woman's ire. She did not stop Charity when she tried to leave.

Surely Selina would warn Sidmouth; this would affect him nearly as much as it did her. Charity had to get home and write to Ravenscroft. She wouldn't be able to get a note to Peregrine in time before he left for Ascot to warn him that one of their closest allies had already fallen.

8

*"Where secrecy or mystery begins, vice or roguery is not far
off."*
—Samuel Johnson

After he returned Lark to the Pulteney, Peregrine went back
to the estate to change carriages and set out for Ascot.

For someone leaving from St John's Wood, the trip would be
a long, dull carriage ride with an overnight stay. Charity would
not be obliged to leave London until the morning. He wished
there had been time to visit his duchess before they left town, to
make sure she and Selina had weathered their own mission all
right, but their schedules worked against him.

Will Hodges had been skeptically watching Perry pace at
every horse change, not accepting the guise of stretching his legs.
"You know," the man muttered, "if his lordship might be inclined
to stir hisself in good time tomorrow, we can intercept Her
Grace's carriage at Egham. You can ride the last leg with her an'
drive her to distraction instead of me."

Peregrine took a breath to issue a curt retort and then halted. "Hodges," he replied, "that's a brilliant idea. I could kiss you."

"*Don't,* my lord."

"I could. That does not mean that I *would*."

Hodges had issued one of his more expressive grunts, and Peregrine let the man be. He had an idea for mischief to plan for his duchess. Hodges could continue on with the carriage to Ascot without him. Since they would only have the races together—Charity would be obligated to attend the event at Frogmore—he would have to make his own way home anyhow.

Setting off in good time the next day, they arrived in Egham well in advance of most of the others travelling to the races. He located a spot to wait and found a spritely child willing to spy for him. Around luncheon, when the boy informed him that Her Grace's carriage was at The Red Lion, he made his move.

It wasn't easy or gentlemanly to wheedle the duchess's servants into assisting with his plot. Their willingness to comply came at a rather steep cost to both his honour and his purse. He had to swear to them that they would suffer no repercussions of his little stunt, plus a guinea each to buy their silence.

But the price was worth it, because her reaction was every bit as good as he hoped it would be.

Charity stifled a shriek and clutched her bosom as the footman threw open the carriage door, revealing him lounging inside, perfectly at ease. He gave her a bright, devilish grin, pleased with himself for the surprise. She put her hands on her hips and scowled at the footman for not warning her.

"Don't be mad at them, Sparkles," he waggled his finger at her. "I promised them you would be pleasantly surprised to find that I was here."

Finally, she lost the battle to maintain her stern expression, and she smiled. "I *am* very happy to see you," she agreed quickly, darting an apologetic glance back at her footman as she let him hand her inside. "But perhaps you might find a way to surprise me that doesn't scare me half out of my wits the next time?"

"I shall never make such a promise," he breathed, framing her face lovingly in his hands after the footman closed the door. "Surely you never imagined that marrying me meant I was going to stop irritating you."

"So I get to look forward to such antics on a daily basis for the rest of my life?" she asked, trying for archness. Instead, she sounded far too happy about it.

Her eyes sparkled at him the way that he adored. He would never confess to her that he had chosen her sobriquet for her eyes —not the title of the diamond. That secret was for him alone.

He tossed his hat across onto the other bench. "Well, possibly not *daily*..." he murmured against her lips. "I wouldn't want to lose the element of surprise."

They had perhaps an hour's journey before they reached Ascot. He didn't intend to waste a moment of this chance to show her how much he had missed her in their time apart.

Between languid caresses, Charity told him about what had happened at the Pulteney.

"Suddenly the reason she encouraged Lark to meet with me becomes clear," Peregrine exhaled, considering the consequences of this. "We were both neatly occupied and out of the way."

"I feel terrible about it. Again, the marchioness shielded me, and I couldn't think of a single thing I could do to help her that would not have made things worse."

Peregrine had shifted to stretch his frame along the squab, letting his knees press against the carriage wall so that his head lay in her lap while she uttered her confession. "I never should have told you that you were my fatal flaw," he said.

She blinked, looking down at him. "Why not? It was true," she murmured.

"Now you think it is your duty to prevent an incident if you are nearby when it happens. And you feel like it is your fault when we are hurt." Peregrine looked up at her through his lashes. "The game of intrigue has never been a safe one. Secrets are dangerous. In war, there are times when sometimes your *only* duty is to make certain that the others will be able to complete their mission, and that is true even if you are only fighting a battle of wits."

Charity's lips flattened together in rejection of his words, and Peregrine turned towards her, pressing his forehead against her stomach.

"The marchioness took the blow, but in a way she and Sidmouth will recover from it," he told her gently. "What my mother told you privately was information she could not allow the Prussian attaché to reveal, lest the blade bite both ways."

"Did you know she had given spies to Sidmouth for your favour?" asked Charity, combing her fingers idly through his hair.

"I knew my favour was expensive. Now I suppose I know why."

"Two spies, and then my mother—"

"Shhh. Not your fault," he said lazily. The heat and her fingers tracing circles on his scalp caused his eyes to drift shut. "I should have waylaid your carriage earlier."

She tweaked his nose. "So you could lay in my lap the entire journey like an oversized house cat?"

"I would be happy to trade positions, Sparkles." He slit an eye and found her blushing, so he grinned and turned the conversation. "My mother's sponsor within the Russian court is likely an accomplice to her plans. We should find them, if we can. She uses such connections hard and abandons them quickly, before they could use what they knew as leverage against her."

He had nicked her fan from her fingers earlier, and she had laughed at him for wielding it. So of course, he hadn't given it back. He was still stirring the air currents playfully, making the loose strands of her hair flutter around her neck.

"I should stay close to the princess at Ascot. I was nearly beside myself when I saw Lady Fitzroy with her and the Grand Duchess," Charity fretted. "With Selina unwelcome in society, it may come down to mostly you and me, unless Thorne and Ravenscroft manage to come across something useful. Who might we prod for more information besides the Grand Duchess?"

"We might try His Excellency, Count von Lieven, the Russian diplomat in London. Or his wife," Perry suggested. "We met them at the Barbour's salon, remember?"

"I remember," she said, the corner of her lips curling as she twined his hair around her finger. "Before we went to Vauxhall."

The look on her face was soft at the memory, despite being attacked in the dark walk and having to patch him up after he bled on her dress. But perhaps those things no longer troubled her.

"Stay close to the princess. I will see if I might corner at least one of Russia's royal family members," he told her. "And perhaps speak to the von Lievens."

"All right. Perhaps we can use Selina's misfortune to try to determine people's loyalties to Countess Orlova and your mother." Charity glanced outside through the curtain, and then down at him. "I do love having you in my lap, but you had best sit up. We are almost there."

Once Peregrine was upright and Charity had fixed his appearance, he reached over to pull aside the curtain. They had had a few extra, stolen minutes as her carriage had joined the line forming to disembark guests. The long approach had been full of carriages and curricles. The smell of sun-warmed broken grass, horse sweat, and dust was strong enough to coat the tongue.

It was a grand sight. Ascot spread in a broad, grassy sweep

under the open sky, racecourse marked out by rails and knots of spectators. Tents, colourful parasols, and snapping pennants gave everything a bright, festive atmosphere. They could hear the excited crowd even from where they waited in procession.

Perry pointed out the royal enclosure, gleaming with fresh white paint and gilt trim, flanked by a crowd of liveried footmen. They would join the sovereigns and the various dignitaries there.

Finally, it was their turn to alight. Charity opened her parasol to ward off the bright sunlight and some unfriendly speculation from the crowd. Together, they strolled towards the fenced area and were quickly escorted in.

Prussia's king was holding court with the Prince Regent, and together they became the focal point for many of the lesser sovereigns. However, the Tsar was conspicuously absent—nowhere to be seen within the enclosure at all.

Other members of the Russian royal family were there, so Alexander must be… somewhere. The Grand Duchess stood next to a stripling boy of seventeen. Peregrine had been rather distracted during the initial welcome ceremony, but he was fairly certain the young man was Nicholas, the younger brother of the Tsar.

The various royal women had gathered to themselves to gossip and watch the track. Queen Charlotte and her granddaughter had a small space around them, partially occupied by some of the higher-ranking British ladies.

"Lark and your mother are ahead and slightly to our left," Charity warned him.

Peregrine flicked his eyes lazily in that direction. Lark was looking down the field, holding onto her hat with one hand. But his mother—

Lady Fitzroy met his eyes squarely, making no attempt to be coy about it. Her lips widened slowly into a predatory smile.

Unconsciously, Perry's hand came up to rest over his scar, and as he did so, his fingers grazed his watch, tucked inside his fob pocket. The steady ticking of the timepiece beat beneath his glove like the rapid tattoo of a pulse, and unnerved, he dropped his hand again.

"Are you all right?" Charity asked him, her voice low.

"Yes," he ground out, his good mood from earlier all but spoiled. He pointedly looked away from his mother. "She will be trying to play games with our heads, Charity. Be on your guard, and be careful about what you drink here, especially if it has been unattended."

"You don't think she would try to poison everyone here, do you?"

"No. To do that would be suicide. But only you or me? I would not put it past her."

Charity nodded. "Promise me you will be careful as well."

She slipped away into the crowd. Peregrine glanced around again for the Tsar, spotting him where he least expected—outside of the fenced area and speaking to commoners. Then again, Peregrine reflected, perhaps that was exactly where he should have expected to find the emperor. Outside of Prinny's carefully established boundaries, giving the Regent a headache.

Thwarted, Peregrine considered his options and began to walk in the direction of Nicholas, who was now standing at the fence to see the next race, his sister talking with one of the ladies from Prussia.

"*Votre Altesse Impériale,*" Peregrine greeted Nicholas courteously in the lingua franca of diplomacy.

"You may speak English, Lord Fitzroy," the boy replied stiffly. "I wish to learn it better."

Peregrine supposed that it couldn't be helped; with the marked resemblance between him and his mother, of course it was likely the boy would know who he was. "Happily, sir. I hope you have been fortunate in picking winners."

"I have not placed..." he paused, looking for the right word. "Wagers?"

Perry nodded to confirm he had it right. "Your brother would not approve?" he asked, giving the boy an easy, conspiratorial grin.

Nicholas finally warmed up to the subject despite his halting English. "Alexander does not mind some gambling. Constantine —he hates it."

Constantine, Peregrine remembered, was the next eldest brother. He was also the Tsar's heir, since Alexander had no children of his own. Constantine had remained behind in Russia for this visit.

Perry elected to make a bit of a gamble of his own. "It is a shame your brother did not also make the trip. But perhaps since he is not here... you might be able to indulge the occasional wager. And if you wish to improve your English," he said casually, "my mother or sister, Lark, may be willing to help you. They made quite a journey last year. When were they introduced at court?"

The young man darted a glance out of the corner of his eye. "October, I believe it was."

That was some piece of information, at least. Depending on the route she and Lark had taken, there would not be little extra time to visit other courts. The odds were good, given the time of their departure, that she had headed there directly. She would have arrived with just enough time to situate herself. The Russian court began to resume its activities in October, and most events transpired over those winter months.

"Excuse me, Lord Fitzroy," Nicholas said suddenly, straightening to leave. "I enjoyed our talk."

Stymied, Perry prowled around the enclosure. Charity was still minding the princess. His mother alternated between watching the races and watching him, which made him twitchy.

And the Tsar was still speaking with everyone except for the people inside the enclosure. He was almost beginning to sympathise with Prinny's stance—that the Tsar's behaviour was rude.

"Where do you suppose might real power best be kept?" interrupted an exotic, cultivated Prussian accent behind Peregrine.

Peregrine turned, coming practically nose to nose with an immaculately dressed man of fifty.

"Not in the armoury, for weapons may rust. Not in the purse," Baron Friedrich von Gentz continued lightly, his face creasing in amusement, "for money is spent."

The man's eyes were shrewd, dancing with a trickster's mischief and a dangerous intellect as he waited for Perry to answer his riddle. Perry pretended to give it consideration. "A good secret is always valuable."

Von Gentz's eyebrows lifted. "True. But only for as long a time as one might wield it over the person the secret is about. And… people do tend to die," he said regretfully.

Peregrine considered the man carefully. He was the right hand of Austria's prince. The Propagandist was, by all accounts, as erratic as he was brilliant. Very few people that Perry met gave him the urge to proceed with caution, but Gentz was one.

"Ah. Well, if we are looking for immortal power… I believe a man like yourself, von Gentz, would put uncommon value in ideas."

The man grinned, pleased. "Not just ideas, clever friend." He clapped Perry on the shoulder, turning them both back to observe the cluster of Englishmen around the Tsar. "*Beliefs*. They are so much longer-lived. And harder to kill, yes?"

He wondered if von Gentz was being madcap, or if he had knowingly approached Perry for some other reason. It was impossible to be sure.

Peregrine nodded. "Although you do run the risk of their taking on a life of their own."

"Mmm," the man agreed vaguely, his eyes on the Tsar. "Alexander... he is a man of belief. People will flock even to a foreigner's banner if they see something in that belief that gives them power. So many of the rest only pretend.

"Treating with a man of beliefs might be difficult for England when they come to sit at the tables in Vienna. Sometimes it is harder to guess what they really want." Gentz gave him a sidelong glance.

Peregrine had the oddest sense that this was a test. Austria was one of the four most powerful countries in the alliance, so he dared not treat this encounter lightly. This fall, Austria was going to be the place the world sat down to divide Napoleon's spoils. Metternich—and this man, von Gentz—would be presiding.

"I imagine Alexander wants what everyone at Vienna will want," Peregrine finally replied. "Russia will want to think they got the best of any bargain."

Gentz tapped his fingers to his lips. "I am not certain Alexander seeks anything so straightforward. But then again, one who ascends by conspiring against his father probably rarely sits easily on the throne."

Alexander had become emperor after his father, Paul, had been assassinated in a coup. "I do not hold the view that the Tsar ordered the death of his father, von Gentz," Perry said. "As you said yourself, he is a man of belief."

The Propagandist's eyes crinkled with mirth. "And beliefs sometimes take on a life of their own," he added, echoing Perry's words.

This felt like playing chess against himself. Metternich's right hand might be almost as dangerous as his mother, if he were so inclined.

"You are prodding me about the Tsar," Perry finally hazarded, "because you are a clever man, and you know exactly who I am, even though you've yet to say my name. I suspect you are trying to determine my loyalties and capabilities. Perhaps you wish to guess at what I am about."

Von Gentz smiled broadly, and Peregrine knew he had guessed right. "Well thought, Lord Fitzroy, but you are not the only one I've prodded. We are all here to play a role. Some are sheep, others are wolves of intrigue and statecraft. All of us are jockeying to ensure that our 'horse' wins the race," he murmured, indicating the line forming at the post.

"Determining the capabilities of your opponents seems like the only intelligent thing to do. And a woman who I have never seen standing upon this field before seems to have gotten quite close to the Russians. Without any commonly accepted diplomatic pathway," he observed, lifting his chin in Lady Fitzroy's direction. "Her son plays for Russia's opponent. Or he appears to, at any rate. It is a most intriguing development when some of us are still deciding which horse to place our bets upon. Russia—" a flick in the direction of the Tsar— "or England."

"And?" Perry asked, curious. "Have you decided what to make of me?"

Von Gentz's smile was wicked, but he didn't answer the question. "When is a spy not a spy, Fitzroy?" he asked instead, and paused for a moment. Then leaned over to whisper in Perry's ear. "When he is a diplomat. Or she."

Perry's eyes narrowed, and Gentz straightened to leave. "Give my regards to Lady Normanby. She will be missed by some of us."

With a wink, the man strode away, leaving him bemused.

Peregrine marked Charity's position again—something he had been doing over and over. The princess was chatting politely with the Dutch prince and other people near her age. Charity had stepped a few lengths from her to give the princess a bit of privacy without abandoning her duties as chaperone.

A good time to reconnoiter. Perhaps Charity discovered what his mother had spoken to the princess about.

"Did I see you speaking with Metternich's man?" she asked him, and Peregrine nodded. "He seemed a popular figure in the thick of the Pulteney's intrigue."

"I believe he was trying to determine whether my mother and I were in league with one another," Perry told her.

"At least that makes it sound as though he is not in league with *her*. Perhaps he could be an ally?"

Perry shook his head, uncertain. "Gentz is most certainly playing for stakes of his own. Did you discover why my mother visited the princess?"

"No." Charity's shoulders sagged. "The princess met the Grand Duchess in the parlour, and Lady Fitzroy came upon them in the hallway outside the coffee room."

He sighed inwardly. Suspicious timing would be hard to prove. "Perhaps she was attempting to sway Charlotte against you. But look—" He pointed with his chin, because the Count and Countess von Lieven had come to a halt only about ten feet away. They moved in that direction.

"Count von Lieven, Countess von Lieven," Charity greeted the Russian diplomat and his wife. "It is good to see you again."

"I do hope that petty rumours haven't troubled you overmuch since your visit to the Pulteney, Duchess," the countess said with a polite moue of regret.

"Not so far," Charity agreed obliquely. "My involvement seems to be thought an unhappy coincidence."

"I greatly hope that continues to be the case," said the count calmly. "We consider what happened to be a private altercation between Englishmen. My foremost duty is to maintain the friendship between our sovereigns, and that must be kept separate from what belongs only to society pages. You understand… yes?"

The count held Peregrine's gaze, and Perry inclined his head, taking the man's meaning. The count was speaking to any who might be listening in on their conversation. By labelling it as an English affair, the diplomat was warning them that they would deny Russia's involvement in it and take no public position on the matter.

"Of course, Your Excellency." Peregrine opted for careful formality. "I laud your attitude. Not every man would find it within themselves to maintain such a fair perspective, especially if countrymen were involved."

"When one is given such a sacred charge, the interests of the state must come first, before my personal feelings, Lord Fitzroy."

At those words, Peregrine noticed Charity had shifted into the telltale posture that suggested she was thinking particularly hard —and troubled by the subject. It wasn't hard to guess what that subject was when she lifted her eyes, seeking the location of Princess Charlotte.

Sensing he was about to lose the Lievens, Peregrine decided to take the risk on a last question. "It must be interesting to see how someone from our society is received in yours. Has my mother made herself popular?"

They looked uneasy. "Unfortunately, I do not know the answer, Lord Fitzroy," the countess answered for her husband. "We made her acquaintance only once, when the entourage visited for a tour of our home."

"I understand. I was curious, that is all. Thank you," Perry said with a wide smile, and the von Lievens gave their farewells.

When he was alone with Charity, Peregrine followed the angle of her head to see where the princess was.

Princess Charlotte, it seemed, had found new male

companionship among the princes the moment both Charity and William had stepped away. And she looked entirely too happy about being the centre of their attention.

"A problem?" he asked Charity softly, and the duchess nodded, touching his arm with regret.

"Perry, I must go. I will see you back in London tomorrow."

9

"All the sacred rights of humanity are violated by insisting on blind obedience."
—**Mary Wollstonecraft**

C harity stared blankly at the mirror in her hotel room, but it was not her reflection that she saw. Instead, she watched the day play out in front of her.

After her arrival at Ascot, she had stepped away from Princess Charlotte only once. In the minutes she had spoken to Perry and the Lievens, the princess had wandered off.

Or perhaps wandered *towards* was a better way to put it. The princess had only gone a few feet away to approach Prince Nicholas and Prince Paul. And there she had stood with a bright smile while allowing the young men to pay her court.

Charity could hardly blame the princes; the princess had charm when she was free to wield it. Nicholas was handsome in their own way, and Paul was... not Prince William, at least. Not once, in all the time that William of Orange had spoken to the

98

princess, had he ever managed to coax more than a perfunctory half-smile from her. But these two had.

She covered her face with her hands, wanting to forget the memory, and the Queen's command weighed heavy. *Your Grace, you must encourage my granddaughter to sign the betrothal contract.*

Now her conscience was at war. Obeying meant encouraging the princess to enter an unhappy marriage to the Dutch prince. On the other hand, it was a wedding that the royal family felt was the best match.

She lifted her head and put her hands to work selecting her jewellery. *It doesn't matter what you believe is best for the princess*, she told herself. *We all must put England's interests first —me, Perry, and yes, even Charlotte.*

Charlotte and the House of Orange would solidify an alliance with a wedding, creating a kingdom that would suppress French expansion north. It would secure Britain's position against its own allies, too, keeping the balance of power in Europe in its favour.

The betrothal arrangement strengthened Britain, which is why Russia might be trying to see it stopped. It had to be done, and it had to be done now, before Marian or someone else found another way to exploit the princess's indecision.

But her heart did not agree.

If you do not have the fortitude to do what was asked, what is right for this country, you must go to the Queen tonight and tell her so she can take the princess to task herself, her mind reasoned.

No, she thought dully. *I will do this duty.*

Decision made, she departed for Frogmore House posthaste. As the carriage turned into the drive at the Queen's private estate, she was relieved to see no line outside the door. The other guests had not yet arrived.

"Good evening, Your Grace," the footman said, welcoming her as he helped her descend from her carriage.

"Could you see if Princess Charlotte is available?" she asked, steely with command. The footman bowed and hurried off. She barely had time to admire the chandelier before he returned.

The princess was dressed and ready, waiting until it was time to join the receiving line. Curls twisted prettily on either side of her face, framing her rosy cheeks and sparkling eyes. She seemed so young, and Charity felt worn and ancient.

"Oh, Your Grace, did you hear? Grandmama kept the guest list so short that the numbers are all off. You and I are to be seated at a table with the princes!"

And there it was again. That trill of delight lifting the princess's voice as she nattered on.

"I shall be forced to sit by William, of course, but Prince Leopold will be on my other side. You will be across the table. I know it isn't proper, but you will distract William with some sort of conversation, will you not? Surely you can find something he will discuss. Horses, yes! He does so go on about them…"

"I—that is…" Charity found her tongue twisted in knots. "Your Highness—"

"Yes? What is it?" The princess scrunched her brow. "Is my gown too frilly?"

"Your gown is divine," Charity said, reaching over to grab the young woman's hands. The princess had complained that everyone kept treating her like a child. Perhaps it was time to speak with her like an adult and the queen she would one day be. "I need to speak with you about another matter. A serious one."

"Can it not wait?" The princess wrinkled her nose.

"No, it cannot. Your Highness, I must speak with you about Prince William. He is still waiting for an answer from you. You must give him one."

The princess settled deeper into the sofa, her spirits deflating.

"I do not understand the insistence that he is the best choice, not now that I have made the acquaintance of other royal heirs. Why rush? I shall wait until the end of the visit to decide."

"I am sorry, but you cannot delay that long." Charity drew in a breath. "It is important that you resolve the matter right now."

"For the good of the nation," the princess parroted bitterly. "Or so my papa says. I cannot see how a few days will make any difference." The young woman was serious. She truly did not know why time was of the essence. She did not understand how her indecision gave England a yawning weakness.

"We must talk about how your marriage affects our country." Charity drew in a breath. "We must talk about Lady Fitzroy."

The princess stilled. She knew nothing, Charity realised. Despite the letters that had put a poison in her hand, she had not understood the woman. They had kept her ignorant, and that choice put them all in a position of harm.

"I told you already that I did not intend to meet with her. I could hardly give her the direct cut with the Grand Duchess there. A few words exchanged cannot be so dangerous."

Charity didn't laugh. "A few words were all it took for her to ruin the Marchioness of Normanby's reputation."

"You believe Lady Fitzroy orchestrated that? Why would she do such a thing?" the young woman asked, genuinely mystified.

How could one describe the way the woman's mind worked? "A thirst for power. And the lack of a conscience that would prevent her from doing evil," Charity replied. She told the princess about her kidnapping, the dark empire that she had hidden, and the attempts on her and Perry's life. And also how she bent her deeds to achieving her ambitions. "It was her efforts that saw the poison you used on William placed in your hands, in order to help prevent this alliance between Britain and the Netherlands."

The princess grew flustered. "I don't understand. Why are you telling me all of this only now? Why didn't you tell me when you realised she was behind the letters I received?"

"A desire to protect you—your family and me," Charity said with remorse. "I wish I did not know first-hand of her treachery; it fuels my nightmares. We thought you were safer in the dark, but that has only made it possible for Lady Fitzroy to exploit your ignorance.

"She does not care about your happiness. She cares only about her ends. If she is doing something—whether that is encouraging you to dismiss William, or to shame the Marchioness of Normanby into hiding away from court—she is the kind of creature that you must always be thinking forward to the reasons why. Perhaps there is some country or some person wanting to sabotage our capabilities or improve their own. Do not let your distaste for William cause you to shirk your duty. You must always consider first what is best for the people of Britain."

The princess rose from the sofa to pace along the carpet in front of the fireplace. Her brow was furrowed, her mouth pursed into a tight ball.

Charity's stomach was doing somersaults. The princess was starting to think more like a sovereign. Watching her mature this way was bittersweet, because she was stripping away the princess's innocence and freedom, forcing her to contend for the first time with the idea that this political marriage was the right choice for everything—except her happiness.

But at least Charity could give her some little reassurance that she would not necessarily spend the rest of her days in misery.

"Your Highness," Charity ventured, her voice gentle, and the princess stopped and turned around to face her. "Your grandmother and your father know what they ask of you. We *all* know. None of us had a real choice in our spouses. Neither did your friend, the Grand Duchess. But the Queen and King found great love together in time. I am seeking mine. Your father has found happiness of another sort. You will find your way to satisfaction too. I am sure of it."

"How can you know that?" Princess Charlotte asked in a whisper.

"Because you are smart, kind, and passionate. Because your spirit is full of light. Do not fight duty; you will find peace with yourself in it. Then, with a clear mind, the path to happiness will present itself when it is time."

The princess quickly brought her fist to her mouth, blinking away the shine of tears. Charity shifted forward to rise, but the princess waved for her to stay put.

"You are right, Your Grace. I have been selfish and let the obligation to our people go untended. I should not have dithered. I just… wanted a little more time."

Before Charity's eyes, the princess shed the last of her youth. She drew herself up, raised her head, and then she marched over to her travelling desk, opening the lid. From inside, she withdrew a roll of parchment. Charity did move then, hurrying over to see. Using a sharp quill and black ink, the princess signed her name to the betrothal agreement with a flourish. She lifted it into the air to blow on it and then handed it to Charity.

"Take this to my father. I will meet you downstairs shortly."

Charity longed to give the young woman a hug, to show some kind of softness. But the princess's voice made it plain there would be no such niceties. So, Charity bobbed a curtsy and let herself out of the room.

Despite the princess's command, Charity knew there was someone else who needed to be informed first. Out in the hall, Charity found a footman waiting to be of service and sought the Queen's ear, a part of herself withering inside.

The Queen was pleased with Charity's work. But there was

not a single iota of remorse from the Queen about what she had done to her granddaughter to get it.

"Well done," the Queen told her, holding the signed parchment. "How fortunate we are that I decided to sit the couple beside one another? Tonight will be the first of many they will spend presiding over a table together. Enjoy yourself at the dinner, Duchess. Tonight, England goes forth boldly into the future that our enemies would prevent."

Dinner was an intimate affair with a hundred attendees spread across three interconnected rooms. Charity was seated opposite Prince William and Princess Charlotte. The Queen, Prinny, the Tsar, and other higher-ranked guests sat nearby at another table.

The archbishop offered a blessing at the start of the meal, calling for an evening of celebration. Hope for allies bonded through shared interests, and future holy unions. Charity knew his words were aimed at the princess, but she could not help but imagine he also meant to include her. After all, he was due to preside over her wedding to Perry the day after next.

Prinny stood after the archbishop finished, raising his glass in a toast. "It is with a happy heart that I proclaim the betrothal of my beloved daughter, the Princess Charlotte Augusta, to the Illustrious Prince William of Orange. Let no man put asunder that which both God and country have blessed."

No man—*and hopefully no woman*, Charity thought.

As the footmen laid plates of oysters in front of each guest, Charity turned slightly toward her left-hand neighbour. "I do not believe we have been introduced, sir. I am the Duchess of Atholl."

The gentleman inclined his head with restrained politeness. "Von Hollenberg, Envoy Extraordinary to His Majesty the King of Prussia."

"A pleasure, Herr von Hollenberg," she said.

He regarded her with polite curiosity. "And may I ask—how are you connected to Her Majesty? Are you engaged to one of her sons?"

"No, sir," Charity replied evenly. "I have the honour of serving as one of her ladies-in-waiting."

"Ah." The syllable carried a soft but unmistakable drop in temperature. "I see."

He pointedly shifted his attention to the person seated on his other side of the table, toward a uniformed Prussian officer. Charity was left with nothing but the faint chill of being neatly and publicly set aside.

On her right, Prince Augustus, the youngest of Prinny's brothers, was deep in conversation with one of the visiting ladies from the Russian court. He was turned away enough that she hadn't a hope of joining in their discussion.

Charity caught herself fiddling with her napkin and stilled her hands. She stared instead at a painting on the wall. Even the portrait of a younger Queen Charlotte failed to offer her a smile. She was an invited guest, but not a welcome one in this space.

Needing a distraction from her thoughts, Charity raised her glass and studied the princess over the rim. Across the table, the young woman had her eyes focused on her plate, paying the empty oyster shells more attention than they warranted. Prince Leopold made a remark, too quiet for Charity to hear, and drew a smile from the princess. But just as fast, her face shifted back into a neutral mask. For once, Princess Charlotte displayed no interest in flirting with other men of her age.

So she had truly committed to her future, Charity sighed with some relief. If a thought followed about how subdued the princess was, Charity purposely ignored it.

The fish course followed next, Dover sole in a rich cream sauce. Again, Charity was left to eat in silence. The closest she came to a conversation was when Herr Von Hollenberg asked her to pass the salt.

By the time the first meat course arrived, Charity would have welcomed any word at all. A widow with no royal or political connections of note warranted no time and attention. For once, even her beauty was not enough to garner more than a brief look. *Selina would know what to say*, the voice in her head remarked, underscoring Charity's failures.

Just then, Prince Paul of Württemberg, seated on William's right, called the footman forward and asked for more of the red wine to be poured. When the glasses were full again, he walloped Prince William on the back and encouraged him to drink deep. "We must celebrate your forthcoming nuptials, now that they are certain."

If the princess was stoic, Prince William was jubilant. Prince Leopold, seated on the other side of the princess, expressed more reserved congratulations and then frowned into his glass, looking displeased.

Perhaps it had not been only polite conversation when he had spoken to Princess Charlotte at the races. Leopold was the Tsar's nephew. Had Lady Fitzroy been clearing the field as a favour for Russia? To put an ally on the throne at the princess's side?

If so, it was madness. Leopold was the fourth son, a far cry from the heir to a throne. Far away from what Prinny would want.

"What say you, Prince Augustus? Are you looking forward to your niece's wedding?" Paul asked, drawing the man at Charity's side into the conversation.

Prince Augustus flicked a glance at his niece, but she did not meet his eyes. He forced a smile onto his face and then replied, "It will be an unforgettable occasion, I am sure."

"We shall make it one for the ages!" Paul cheered and then walloped William again. Both men were swaying, already intoxicated.

"I am sure we have you to thank for getting the princess to agree to the match," Augustus said in a low voice. After so long in silence, it took Charity a moment to realise he was speaking to her.

"I did as Her Majesty asked of me," Charity demurred. "We must all do our duty."

"I suppose." Augustus's voice trailed off. "Particularly my niece. After being foiled so many times by me and my brothers, my mother was bound to do whatever it took to get her way in this match. The line of succession reigns supreme in her mind."

As the dinner progressed, Prince Paul seemed determined to turn the jubilation into a public spectacle.

Paul raised his glass high. "You Dutch are fine seamen," he boomed, "but I'll wager you cannot match a Württemberger for drinking!" He gave William's shoulder a thump that nearly upset his neighbour's wine, then waved a footman over before William's own glass was empty.

Charity averted her gaze, and then guiltily forced herself to look back. The princess pushed a slice of beef around her plate, giving the appearance of eating, but did not lift it to her mouth. She was like a marionette, and her strings were controlled by her father and grandmother.

On Charity's right, Prince Augustus sopped up the gravy from his plate with a piece of bread, all but licking the plate clean. He had escaped the bonds of marriage by joining the army. Seven royal sons, and only one legitimate child between them. Had they done their duty? Was service on the battlefield more important than their obligation to the family line?

Prince Paul, as if intuiting the direction of her mind, raised his voice and glass. "To our victory over the tyrant!"

William drank, and Paul was ready with the next toast. "To the fine ladies of England—and the even finer unions to be made here!"

Paul's own sips were moderate; William's were dutifully deep. His posture began to slacken, his laughter grew louder and less timed to the conversation, and his once-crisp coat now sat askew across one shoulder.

The other men at the table began to wise up around the third toast. Baron von Gentz was seated by Prince Paul, and he shifted forward to observe what impact Paul's efforts were having on the Dutch prince. His posture reminded Charity of both Perry and Lord Ravenscroft, and the way they would forage for information in their surroundings.

From her place, Charity could not tell whether Paul was acting out of sheer mischief or calculation. Perhaps he was following out a whispered instruction from some malicious party. Using an accomplice to cause William or the princess humiliation was something Lady Fitzroy might easily orchestrate.

She *was* humiliated. Princess Charlotte hunched, curving around herself as to protect herself from the drunken spectacle of her betrothed.

Charity had only one ally at the table. She bumped her elbow against Prince Augustus's arm. When he glanced her way, frowning at her faux pas, she murmured, "The toasts are more excessive than usual, are they not?"

Augustus scrunched his brow, not catching her meaning until she flicked a glance across the table, blanching at the state of Prince William. "Your Highness, perhaps we might give the toasts a rest," he suggested, leaning forward to catch Paul's attention. "The Queen—"

"The Queen," Paul interrupted, "she would surely not begrudge her future son-in-law another glass in honour of his good fortune!" With a smile that didn't reach his eyes, he turned back to William without missing a beat. "To a friendship so strong it will bind our nations for generations!"

William roared his agreement and lifted his glass, sloshing

half the pour down his cuff. Prince Augustus subsided with a sigh, his face tight with disapproval.

Paul was acting the scapegrace, and playing the part to perfection. But whether it was for his own amusement or another's purpose, Charity didn't know. And William, she noted with disgust, was playing right into his hands.

Gentz, The Propagandist, was also studying the scene—but he was watching the smirking Paul more than William. The look on his face was calculating, clearly wondering what Prince Paul of Württemberg's aim might be.

The badly behaved princes held their glasses out to the footman for another refill. Princess Charlotte, unable to take any more, reached over and laid a hand on her betrothed's arm.

"William, please," she said, loud enough to be heard over their noise. "We will need to stand soon."

Prince William was too far gone to see wisdom in her warning. Instead, her words added fuel to his fiery determination to celebrate.

"My dear, even when you are queen, you may not tell me when to sit and when to stand." His tone was not cruel so much as chastising, as though the princess was a naughty child. "I am the man who will be king, and *you* will be the wife who smiles beside him."

In the hush that followed, his words landed with an audible thud. Princess Charlotte's hand dropped from his arm as if scorched, her expression blanking. People at the table either busied themselves with their plates or pretended to fall into intense discussions with their neighbours, as disconcerted by the situation as the princess.

Charity was horrified and ashamed. But those feelings were leveled at herself, not William. This was the future to which she had consigned the princess. Embarrassed, belittled, silenced. It didn't matter whether Paul's actions had been dictated by Marian

Fitzroy. Prince William was easy to manipulate with nothing more than a wine glass and a few choice words.

I have to rescue her, Charity thought, but she, the lowest-ranked guest in attendance, surrounded by veritable strangers, could not move. Social constraints bound her tighter than any rope.

Charity glanced at Augustus seated beside her, praying he would understand her silent request and do something bolder. But Prinny's brother would not risk the Queen's wrath by calling William to order and offending the Dutch prince. Even if it was for his own good.

Charity glanced along the table and was disturbed to find that Gentz's assessing gaze had landed on her. Beggars could not be choosers, she supposed. Charity tilted her head towards William, silently pleading with Gentz to do something. Anything, to put them all out of their misery.

Von Gentz held still for a long moment, then he leaned back in his chair. "You have proven your skills at toasting, Prince Paul. But I wonder how you fare in other arenas. I have a deck of cards whispering temptation in my pocket, and a coin that dearly wants to change hands." His mouth took on a taunting slant. "Do you play as boldly as you flatter Prince William?"

Paul laughed and leapt from his seat, tugging William's sleeve. "What say you, my friend? Shall we show this diplomat what we can do with a few bits of pasteboard?"

"Lead the way to the game room, Baron. And prepare to lose." William grinned in boozy confidence.

Gentz's gaze flicked briefly at Charity, confirming she had seen his hook slide neatly into place. This was no mere act of gallantry. The Propagandist would use this opportunity for his own purposes. She could not find it in herself to care.

As the men left the table, the princess set her napkin on her plate and murmured her excuses to leave. Charity caught up with her before the young woman left the room.

"Your Highness," she called in as soothing a voice as she could manage. "Wait—"

The princess ignored her pleas, hurrying up the main staircase to her room.

10

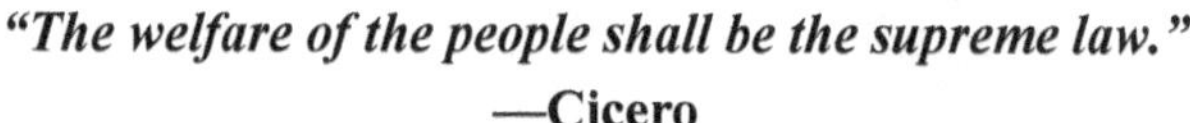

Against propriety, Charity followed the princess to her bedroom. She would not wait for an invitation. Not when the young woman remained in such dire need of consoling.

"Your Highness—Charlotte!" Charity breached the last barrier between the two, calling the young woman by her name.

The princess spun around then, revealing the tears leaving wet tracks on her cheeks, but her face remained expressionless. Without a conscious thought, Charity stepped forward, her arms reaching for the woman, but the princess raised a hand to halt her.

"No, Your Grace," the princess told her. "I will be all right."

Charity twisted her fingers together. "You are upset. Let me try to help."

The princess's teeth clenched. There was something so tired and hopeless about the young woman's expression. "I am not upset. I am… well, I suppose I am. But truly, I am not surprised,

Your Grace. After all, we have all seen him act this way before. Again, and again. It is high time to accept my life as a sovereign. Forging this alliance with the Dutch is what is most important in this arrangement for England, is it not?"

Was it? Suddenly, Charity felt unconvinced.

"Perhaps there is a way to encourage William to control his behaviour. I must think," Charity said to herself, pacing in a tight circle.

The princess let out a brief bark of laughter and shook her head again. "You may go. I needed a moment to—well, to breathe, that is all."

"Do you want me to stay here with you while you take a moment?" Charity asked.

The princess patted her eyes dry. "It would be better if we did not. We must return to the party. My grandmother expects me to be a gracious host. And William…"

Is a drunkard of the first water, Charity's mind suggested. *Worse than that.*

"It is the will of my father and grandmother. It will secure the line of succession. And it will prevent whatever designs Russia may have upon my marriage. You were right. I was too reluctant to accept that this is purely a state affair. William is to be my husband. And my troth is to stay at his side."

Silent and smiling? Charity gritted her teeth.

The princess's actions seemed wooden, but she did as a well-brought-up lady ought. The figure in front of her transformed into the perfect portrait of compliance. Beautiful, dutiful, quiet, and meek. It was a mask familiar to the Duchess Atholl, because she had worn it more than a time or two herself.

"Come, before our absence is noted." Charlotte carefully pinched her cheeks to give a healthier flush to her bloodless face. She beckoned to Charity, and together they walked down the stairs. The princess walked like a woman on her way to the gallows, but one who had scraped together her pride.

Princess Charlotte was no longer the vibrant English rose. She was empty.

And suddenly, Charity felt like she had made a terrible mistake.

Prince Leopold noted their return first, and his searching gaze asked the questions he could not raise. Princess Charlotte inclined her head in acknowledgement of him but did not stop to speak.

"Is she—" he asked Charity, the words slipping free before he could catch them.

She paused, unsure how to answer him. It would be inappropriate to discuss such personal details with a foreign prince, even if he and Princess Charlotte were friendly. Leopold might be a harmless well-wisher, but it would be foolhardy to forget he was also one of the Tsar's inner circle. His motives could be suspicious.

"The princess needed a moment to refresh herself," Charity finally murmured, and Leopold withdrew.

With William gone, a sense of normalcy had returned, though it was chilly and subdued. Perhaps some of that was for her station. Charity was overlooked and ignored, which gave the thoughts inside her head far too much time to talk with her instead.

You know this isn't right.

The rest of the evening, Her Royal Highness kept her hands clasped in front of her. And though her head stayed lifted, her eyes kept roaming downward towards the floor. She refused offers of a drink or of taking a turn around the room.

When her father invited her to speak with another group, Princess Charlotte went to him. She let the conversation flow about her and tried to maintain a posture of polite interest. Every now and again, a flash of irritation sparked in her gaze at some comment, but every time that ember in Princess Charlotte died out quickly.

The princess is being biddable, those whispers inside of her mocked, growing louder. *Is that not what you were tasked to accomplish?*

Not like this.

A memory of the rioters at Burlington House forced its way into her thoughts. The public loved their princess, and there was great sympathy for her. *They love the princess because she is a symbol of liberty,* Lady Holland had told her while they had clung to one another in the crush of bodies.

Princess Charlotte had been a defiant patriot willing to stand up against her father's excesses and repressive politics. Already Prinny's actions played in the columns and caricatures as those of a cruel, manipulative father. How much worse would it be for all of them if that symbol vanished?

Her own voice harangued her in a low tone. *Immoral. Unfair, unjust, unconscionable. Doomed.*

Charity had been afraid of the consequences of the princess failing to marry William. But did the benefits William offered now outweigh the faults of an undisciplined, drunken cur of a prince? Were they so focused on the Dutch that they were blinding themselves to the other problems that would arise from the marriage?

The princess had always been willing to shoulder the duty to her people. She had also been ignored when she had said William was the wrong choice. Of course, she was silent now. What else was a person to do when their disastrous course was inevitable?

What would become of Britain and its people with a fool for a king and a retiring queen?

Charity had a long time to mull. At the end of the evening, she circled the room until she arrived at the Queen's side. "Your Majesty, might I have a word with you?"

"Tomorrow," the Queen replied, brushing her off without looking.

"Tonight, please. It is urgent."

The Queen twisted to get a better look at Charity, raising a brow at her insistence. Charity let some of her anguish and determination show on her face.

"Very well. Meet me in my sitting room in half an hour."

"Looking at you is giving me a headache, Duchess Atholl," the Queen said with irritation. "You are wearing an expression that means there is trouble afoot. And since the only one here who could cause that trouble is the princess, I shall speak quite plainly. I shall not entertain the news that the princess has decided to tear up the marriage contract again mere hours after signing. I could see her sulking from across the room."

Charity took a deep breath, striving for calm—or at least courage. "No, Your Majesty. The princess has not sent me. I have come here on my own to ask you to be the one to tear it up."

There was a long silence.

"*What*?" Charlotte's voice cracked through the room like thunder. "We have been attempting to arrange this alliance between the Dutch and England for months. And *you*, in your great wisdom, would have us immediately cast it aside. Where, exactly, did you find such a store of audacity?"

Where indeed? And why had the audacity not rendered her knees immune to weakness? "Please, Your Majesty. I would explain my reasoning if you would give me a chance."

The Queen's face was alarmingly pale and tight at Charity's defection. "By all means, Duchess. Let us hear these pontifications of yours before *you* are the next thing I have thrown out."

Charity's jaw wobbled slightly when she parted her lips to answer. "Ma'am, today I have spent a great deal of time considering the nature of duty. Mine, yours, and that of Princess Charlotte. The burden of securing the line for the royal family has fallen to her, yes. She is ready to do that duty unquestioningly. And she is willing to do what she can to advance England's interests abroad.

"But what put the quill in her hand today was not that sense of familial duty or political machination—it was my doing. Because I told her about Lady Fitzroy, and that the woman wanted to prevent this alliance. I told her that her refusal to sign that agreement with William of Orange put the people of Britain at risk."

Queen Charlotte's expression was stony, waiting for Charity to continue.

"Your granddaughter needed no further convincing after that. She made the decision to set aside her chances for a happier marriage the moment she believed that it was the better choice *for the people*." Charity took a steadying breath, trying to keep from collapsing with nerves at what she was about to do.

"Your Majesty… a marriage to William might secure the throne and line of succession. It might create the bulwark that stands between France and its dynastic ambitions. But William will be a terrible king who can only weaken the country and hurt the people. It is what your granddaughter has been trying to tell us all along. We saw it clearly tonight. I was wrong to push her into this; I believe *we* were both wrong."

"You *dare*—" Queen Charlotte was nearly apoplectic. Her hands on the arms of her chair were like claws.

"Please, Your Majesty," Charity said quickly, bowing her head so she would not be forced to look upon her angry sovereign. "I understand you are angry, but I beg you, please. The princess was motivated enough to sicken him. If we force her to comply, she may lose the fire that makes her beloved by the people. Is it only to thwart Lady Fitzroy's decision to interfere that is making us stay this course?"

There was a long, hot silence. Charity was afraid to see whether Charlotte was having a conniption or whether she was agreeing. Even if the Queen was weighing her words seriously, Charity knew that this might well be the end of her welcome at court.

"What will the people do if the king is incapable of restraint, or perhaps even cruel, and the queen lacks the will to manage him? Will they be able to prosper?"

Charity finally lifted her gaze and knew that her words had struck home with the woman. Charlotte knew that William *would* have to be managed. The corners of her mouth were curled downward, as if she could taste the truth, and it was bitter.

"Your Majesty, this marriage to William does not have to be the only way forward. It may be difficult, but surely there are other matches that will serve Britain's people and its princess?"

Lady Cresswell was never going to recover from the indignity of this, that was for sure. Her own daughter telling her sovereign that she had made a mistake? They might never be able to show their faces in London again.

"You have more than overstepped, Duchess Atholl," the Queen finally ground out between her teeth. "You have *hurled* yourself beyond the pale. But considering your previous service to us, and the fact that you seem to be willing to sacrifice everything to make your feelings about the princess and the country's needs clear, I will think on your words. And I will speak with the princess."

With a hard swallow, Charity nodded, finally lifting her gaze. "Of course—thank you—"

"Do *not* thank me. We are not through. The Archbishop made sure to mention tonight that you had applied to my *son* for aid in obtaining a special licence, by the by. Let me make it abundantly clear, Duchess. Since you wish to make your opinion known about this wedding between the princess and William, then I will do the same regarding yours. You will not marry without my express permission."

"Yes, ma'am," Charity's voice was barely more than a whisper, her throat aching with misery. *Oh, Perry. I have ruined everything.*

The Queen got herself to her feet. "It is late, and I expect you will wish to leave early in the morning. You may consider yourself excused from attending the opera tomorrow evening. Now get out."

11

"Our greatest glory is not in never falling, but in rising every time we fall."
—Oliver Goldsmith

Between the good roads and an early start after a restless night at the inn, Peregrine was back at the estate an hour or so before noon. He managed a quick refresh and was still changing his clothing when Quinn came and found him with his valet.

"My lord, forgive the interruption, but the Duchess of Atholl is downstairs looking to speak with you."

"Already?" Peregrine was stunned. He hadn't expected her to return to London until the afternoon. For her to arrive practically on his heels from Windsor, she would have left very early. Whatever could have happened at the Frogmore dinner? "Is she…"

"Her Grace appears upset," Quinn confirmed, folding his hands together. "I took the liberty of settling her in the drawing room."

Silently, Croft decided on the simplest knot for his cravat and Peregrine strode out the door the moment it was tied. His flummoxed valet was left behind, still holding his coat.

Downstairs, Charity was hunched in on herself, almost like she was in pain. It made Perry angry enough to want to make someone bleed. "Charity?" he asked, holding onto his temper. "Did someone at Frogmore harm you?"

"No," she whispered, letting her head fall into her hands. "No one hurt me."

Peregrine closed the distance, holding out his hands to her. But she stared at them miserably, refusing to meet his eyes. "I have done something terrible. Something incredibly stupid."

Whatever it was that had happened, she needed bracing more than kindness. "Get to your feet, Sparkles. Or else I will get down on my knees to have this conversation. What will you?"

Finally she looked up, eyes puffy and shadowed as though she hadn't slept a wink. She had been crying. Cursing, he reached down and pulled her to her feet, taking her to the couch instead where they could sit together.

"Tell me what happened."

The dam broke, and she quietly confessed everything. From the moment she had left his side at Ascot onwards. Patiently, he listened, holding Charity's hand in his even though she tried at first to pull away.

Even before she got to the end of her story, it was easy to guess what happened.

"I shouldn't have said anything. It wasn't my place." Charity tried to get up—to pace, presumably. "I'm afraid I may have made the Queen our enemy."

"Charity." Peregrine held her fast, looking up at her. "She is wroth because she is wrong, and she knows that you spoke the truth. William *will* be a terrible king, and you were the only one who could tell her. It was more important that she hear the truth than be told flattering lies. It was a hard thing to do—but I agree with you. *It was the right thing.*"

"Well, the truth meant she asked the Archbishop to withhold the special licence." She looked drawn. Did she imagine he would be upset with her?

Perry gave her a gentle, wicked look. "Perhaps I should tell you why Prinny objected to the licence at first. *He* did not think marriage was a requirement for... delighting in each other's company."

"That man would think such a thing," Charity replied tartly, blushing. "Still, Perry... I ruined our wedding. I feel awful about it."

Peregrine pulled her down beside him again, pressing a kiss to her temple. And then he twined his arms around her tightly. Petulant sovereigns were not her fault.

"A delay, that is all. She may have blocked the licence, but she cannot stop us from getting married. You and I could leave for Gretna Green at any time we wanted to. Right now, even. Do you want to go?"

It was a jest more than an offer, but he felt the way Charity tensed. She wanted to throw her cap over the windmill and say yes. She really did. "We shouldn't," Charity admitted after a long pause. "We can't ignore our duties or your mother."

He smiled ruefully, and together they sat in stillness for a long moment, losing themselves in the sound of one another's breath. Until his mother was defeated, they were in limbo. Existing only for the moment.

This was no way to live. Hope required having something worth fighting for. So far, they had barely been able to think about life beyond 'tomorrow.'

It was time to change that.

Charity looked up in surprise when he stood, tugging her

hand. "Come on, Sparkles," he cajoled her. "Forget the Queen. She will either admit she made a mistake, or she won't. In the meantime, you and I have other things to do."

"We—we do?"

"It does not matter if we marry tomorrow. Sooner or later, you will be *my wife*," he murmured to her, drawing her close. His chest warmed at the thought of them bound together in every way. "All of this will be yours as well as mine. And you've not even had a proper tour of the house."

"Oh." She let out a small, shaky laugh, reluctant.

"I hate this place too," he confessed. There were a lot of unpleasant memories here—for both of them—but it was time to begin healing them together. "She left her mark on every room."

"Are there no happy recollections for you here?"

"A few, far distant ones, from before school. Catching fireflies with my father. A dog we used to have. My father fell sick the year I went away. I didn't know why, then, but I do now." He gave her a sideways look. "While I was away, my mother began slowly poisoning him to death, and that tainted a lot of what came after."

"Oh, Perry…" Charity turned to face him, resting her hand on his chest. "I should have guessed how you felt about this place. Why else take me to the townhouse?"

"Don't fret. I am just… tired of thinking that I sleep in the room where he died. I stare at the chairs my mother put in his study afterwards. I want to let the bad memories go. I want something for us. Let us transform this into a happy place. I cannot think of a more fitting revenge to have upon my mother."

The corners of her mouth turned up slightly. "All right. First… we should decide whether or not we should burn her things on the lawn."

He laughed.

It felt strange to talk about inanities like colours, furniture, and draperies. But it also felt good, like a slow stretch of cramped muscles. They had never had a chance to indulge in the chatter of courting couples before. This was… nice.

Perry slipped away to have a quiet word with Quinn while they made their way through the first floor. As they moved slowly from the maintained public spaces towards the family suite, a coil of tension began to grow in his stomach. A sense of nervous anticipation rising.

"You have already seen the adjoining rooms. But there is one other important place to show you here, I think," he said quickly, reaching around Charity to turn the knob.

Quinn had slipped inside long enough to remove the dust cloths from the furniture, opening the windows to let in fresh air. And the duchess stopped, stock-still in the doorway, looking into the nursery. A room that had been closed up since Lark had left it.

They had never discussed children. Not even in the casual way men and women usually discussed such things. He did not know whether she had given up all thought of having a family of her own when she tied herself to Atholl.

Peregrine certainly had, when he had gained his majority. He had denied even the possibility of marriage for so long that Charity was opening the sluice gates of his imagination.

The air was charged. And Charity was quiet so long that Perry wondered if perhaps she was unready for this discussion. Gingerly, he encircled her with his arms, hanging his chin over her shoulder. Unsure if his touch right now was welcome.

A strange, wistful yearning twisted in his breast. They looked at an empty room, but he saw the future. Charity carrying his child. Happiness on her face and bundled in her arms. A small legacy of a defiant *tendre* created by the both of them. The only true immortality that man was granted in this world.

Peregrine let his hand splay across her lower belly, imagining it swollen with life beneath his fingers. Daydreaming about feeling it quicken beneath his hands. "Not yet. But... maybe someday?"

"Someday," she finally agreed, her voice sounding thick with emotion. "Someday I would like this very much."

A drop of wetness fell on his hand. He pulled her tighter against his chest, content to be still. This day was theirs. They should seize this moment, and every other. Time was already cruelly fleeting.

And as the emotions tumbled through his breast, suddenly Peregrine thought of something else he had been wanting to do. "Will you let me try to paint you?"

For a while, art had been an outlet. A voice for the things he couldn't allow himself to say, or want, or think. But the pleasure in it had withered, and finally gone dormant last spring.

He had locked his work away to gather dust, and hadn't touched a brush since then. But Charity was rekindling that spark of desire. She reminded him that applying pigments to the canvas was more than just a hobby. For too long, painting had been the only place he was free to feel.

And perhaps she was a muse, after all. He was ready to experience that again.

"Paint me—now?"

He pressed his mouth against the back of her neck, smiling. "Unless you'll only sit for me once, in which case I had better practice more."

She prodded him smartly with her elbow, and then wiped at her face. "But, now? I must look like a disaster."

"I will be certain to have a word with the artist to make sure he only shows your best qualities," Peregrine teased her. "Although I have to warn you, he might be terrible at his work."

She huffed at him. "He is not."

"He appreciates your misplaced loyalty. Would you be loyal

still if you knew he also has the strangest urge to paint you when you've wrapped yourself up in all his blankets?"

"Goodness. You do *not*." Charity spun in his arms, scowling up at him.

Perry let his forehead press against hers, their noses touching. "I do, too."

"Why!"

"You are so beautiful, Sparkles. But never more so than during those moments where I see that vulnerability you show to me alone." He gave her a crooked grin. "Is there a greater feeling than knowing someone has found you worthy of that much trust?"

"As long as you know you are worthy. But I do not think I am ready to let you paint me in bed." Her mouth lifted to his in a sweet apology, giving him a sly wink. "Maybe someday for that, too."

"So, you will agree to a normal portrait sitting instead then?" he chaffed her. "In exchange for the ability to keep stealing my blankets?"

Charity disentangled herself neatly, giving him an arch look before she leaned in with blushing cheeks to whisper, "You will let me steal your blankets anyway, *Lord Fitzroy*."

He laughed again, cupping her face in both hands as he gave her a properly searing kiss that had them both gasping for breath when he released her lips. "You're right. And I will happily give them up for the rest of my life, you cover hog, just so you will always be the last thing I see when I fall asleep and the first thing I see when I greet the dawn."

They missed luncheon while indulging in leisurely pursuits. Peregrine did convince Charity to sit in the conservatory long enough to make several sketches, and she kindly said nothing when he ripped up several. It had been too long since he had done figure sketching.

Finally he had one worthy of a canvas. She had been inhaling the scent of a gardenia plucked from the glass-protected hot house, looking at him over the top of the blossom. While he had been sketching, Charity flayed him with savage repartee about the expressions on his face. (To be fair, he had been concentrating when his tongue poked out.)

When they grew peckish from missing lunch, they raided the neglected kitchen gardens. They found peas and a few strawberries that they fed one another, laughing like children. Or rather, Perry did most of the finding and feeding. Charity's cossetted girlhood meant she had no practical knowledge of any plants at all.

Peregrine's mother had ensured his knowledge of botany was both prodigious and practical. And he in turn introduced Charity to many plants like rosemary, chamomile, and rosehips. At one point she had opened her mouth to argue with him about his recitation, and he popped a mint leaf onto her tongue.

It was... nice to teach someone else. To turn that mostly ill-used knowledge into an experience of pleasure.

"No matter how it started... today was... unexpectedly perfect," she said to him as they sat nested together on a stone bench. "Thank you."

Perfect, yes. Perry let his head rest over her shoulder while she plucked the petals off a daisy. Charity smelled of the orange that he loved—but also there was a wild green scent to her, courtesy of their foraging. "I hope you won't be disappointed by our guests arriving for dinner."

Her hands stilled. "What guests?"

"The three people I invited to mark the occasion of our engagement." He grinned. "Assuming you will not cut the Marchioness of Normanby dead in the privacy of my home."

"Ravenscroft? And Thorne too?" she asked, and he nodded to each. "You consider them both friends?"

When he had considered who he had wanted to *tell*, all three had come to mind instantly. Thorne was, perhaps, the most perplexing of the set, but after the night of the fire and rescue, the man was as thoroughly entangled as any of them.

Peregrine didn't know if they were *friends*, exactly. But theirs were the only opinions that he cared about.

Jack went out to meet the carriage with a lantern. Peregrine and Charity hastened to greet their guests in the entry hall. Their *loud* guests. Even before Quinn opened the door, they could hear raucous laughter and conversation approach the steps.

Quinn opened the door to Selina arm-in-arm with both men, and Peregrine coughed a laugh into his fist. "Charity, the parade has arrived."

"Don't be catty just because I have two cavaliers for the price of one," Selina smirked. Ravenscroft thought this was hilarious, and even Thorne's teeth appeared briefly in a smile. She took her hands away from her escorts as Quinn began the process of collecting hats and coats, handing them off to Owens.

Then the marchioness swept over to Charity taking both of her hands with a firm squeeze. She gave Peregrine an affectionate pat on his arm, and then she reached into her reticule, withdrawing a drawstring bag for Charity.

Blinking in surprise, Charity loosened the drawstring, spilling an elegant but empty gold locket into her palm.

Selina split a sly look between them. "Forgive me for gifting you with an empty locket, Your Grace. But I thought perhaps you might like to commission the miniatures inside yourself. Perhaps from someone you know."

Charity looked up at Perry with a faint grin, letting the soft gold slither from her fingers back into its satchel. "That is a lovely idea, Lady Normanby. Thank you."

Ravenscroft bowed gallantly over Charity's hand, planting a kiss upon her knuckles. "Only you could have made an honest man out of the canary, Duchess." He clapped Peregrine hard on the shoulder, proffering the bottle of wine that had been tucked beneath his arm. "An 1811 Bordeaux to appreciate in good health —from my own cellar. *Do* make certain you appreciate it, you English heathen."

"A comet vintage?" And of a French wine, which would have likely had to have been acquired by illicit means during the blockades. Peregrine's eyebrows lifted. "A much better gift than my birthday present, Maggie."

"If you have some idea of what you got out of my collection, then be sure to thank Antoine. The grief I took from him over your birthday gift—that man has no appreciation for a joke, I swear."

Peregrine grinned at the magpie. He was willing to bet that the fussy French valet had his lord wrapped firmly around his little finger. "I do know—and I appreciate it. It is good to know who has the real taste in your household."

The old rake's eyes twinkled, and he cleared the hallway so that Sir Nathaniel no longer had an excuse to hang back. Thorne took Charity's hand respectfully, and when he turned to Peregrine, on a whim, Perry offered the man his arm. His blue eyes flared briefly with surprise and gratitude, and he clasped Peregrine's forearm in return.

"Your Grace, Lord Fitzroy. I am sorry I have little to offer of my own and not my brother's generosity—"

"Thorne," Charity told him gently. "You offered yourself when we needed your help."

Peregrine nodded. "That was more generous than anyone could wish."

The tall man ducked his head, clearly uncomfortable with praise. "Nevertheless. A... small token of a gift."

He placed a lumpy handkerchief into Charity's palms. She carefully unwrapped the two objects within, revealing two small whittled birds, about the length of his finger. A swan, reared up with wings half extended as if it was about to burst into flight. And a small, sleek peregrine falcon with its hooked beak and sharp eyes peering over its wing.

Charity found her voice first. "These are lovely. You're an artist."

"The duchess is right," Perry agreed, awestruck as he turned the little figures over to admire the detail on the birds' faces and feathers. "This is no simple token—especially in the short time you had. Well done."

"Ah. Well," Thorne said, brushing back his forelock, embarrassed. But then he gave them a roguish grin. "It gave me a reason to hide in Ravenscroft's gardens. Where I wouldn't make a mess."

Perry snickered. "Is that how you have been surviving in his household?"

"Aye." Thorne's voice was dry. "The way those two fight and flirt could drive a saint to the bottle."

With a laugh, Perry clapped Thorne on the shoulder and they joined the other two.

Dinner was a warm and relaxed affair. Eschewing tradition, they all retired immediately to the parlour to enjoy drinks and each other's companionship. Charity abandoned Perry to take Thorne's arm when they left the dining room, and amused, Peregrine watched Selina take Ravenscroft's. He brought up the rear.

"Aha!" Ravenscroft rubbed his hands together as they entered the room and he spied the pianoforte in the corner. "A chance to get Galahad on the dance floor for some practice."

Thorne immediately shot an appeal for help to Peregrine— something he hadn't expected. It was on the tip of his tongue to suggest that the magpie grant the man mercy and choose something simple and familiar like a Scottish reel. But the Marchioness of Normanby beat him to it.

"Play us something suitable for a country dance, Lord Ravenscroft," she said, releasing him and pulling Charity by her free arm towards the centre of the room. Charity let out a short laugh, holding onto Thorne's sleeve as she was tugged along, and Perry joined them in a square.

Thorne acquitted himself competently, if not with the flourish of an aristocrat. Selina murmured suggestions and encouragement, and Charity began to do the same. Soon all three were having a grand time, and by the third dance, Selina broached more complicated dances.

"The four of us cannot do a quadrille, but this is a good time to teach you the steps for some of the figures. Let's start with the ladies' chain." Selina's voice took on a commanding bark, pulling Thorne into formation like a soldier being ordered by his sergeant, and she directed all of them about as if they were all learning for the first time.

Charity had been right. This closeness was what a family was supposed to be. But a small ache of regret weighed heavily in his chest. He was finding a new family... but Lark was still alone with his mother.

Trapped in a situation, with no idea just how precarious it might be.

12

Charity gazed up at the glittering crystals on the chandelier, releasing the worries that had been building. Thorne was gaining confidence and grace as they practiced. And as Selina halted things to make another explanation, Perry wrapped an arm around her waist, spinning her around until she was dizzy and laughing.

"Am I to be chained to this instrument until dawn?" Ravenscroft finally complained. He made a show of stretching his hands. "If you intend to keep me slaving away for your pleasure, at least be a saint and fetch me a glass of claret."

Charity stifled a laugh, and everyone took a moment. "I am sure we can allow you a respite. Both you and Selina, since she has been teaching."

"I talked myself dry, but talking isn't required if I am playing.

How about a waltz?" the marchioness asked, walking over to the pianoforte and striking a chord.

Lord Ravenscroft set his drink aside and dipped into a deep, sarcastic bow in front of Thorne. "Will you do me the honour of this dance, Sir Nathaniel?"

"Er," Thorne said, looking down at the magpie.

"*Don't*, Nathaniel," Perry warned him. "Ravenscroft will try to lead just for the spectacle since you have a full head of height on him. Hardly an ideal way to learn."

Ravenscroft pouted, and then he pulled Charity away from Peregrine's side. "You are ruining my fun, Canary, so I will ruin yours and claim this one for a dance."

Peregrine glanced at Thorne, arching his eyebrow in a challenge. Thorne lifted his hands in a silent gesture for mercy, chuckling. That was all Charity had a chance to see before Ravenscroft swept her into a tight, anti-clockwise spin around the room.

"You and the falcon suit one another. I know it is not what I said to you early on, but I am happy to be incorrect, for your sake," the magpie admitted softly. "This path is hard—to love where others say it is wrong—but I daresay this group of ours understands a thing or two about adversity. Weather the challenges with grace, and have no regrets, Charity. You have all of us to lean on."

"Thank you. I am glad you have Antoine in your life, even if you must be together secretly. You deserve that."

Ravenscroft smirked, seriousness gone."And what have I done to you, darling, that I deserve a Frenchman's curse?"

"He... well, you are *not* a humble man. But at least he keeps you in line." Charity managed to primly arch her eyebrow for only a second before her expression cracked too. "Mostly."

"*Ugh*. Duchess, the canary is starting to rub off on you. I take back everything I have said in his favour. This development is intolerable."

"My turn," Peregrine informed the dandy as he swept in and caught Charity between forms. "Go away, Maggie. She's *mine*."

Ravenscroft pretended to huff indignantly, but he winked at Charity. Perry pulled her closer, until she was brushing against him at times. It made her feel daring, and yet safe.

"Thank you," she whispered loud enough for his ears alone. "For showing me today that I will never be entirely without family."

Peregrine gave her a smile, but there was a trace of pain in it. Charity closed her eyes with a wince. "I am sorry. That was callous of me, to remind you of your mother and Lark."

"You have nothing to apologise for, Sparkles. I have only been hoping Lark is all right."

Guilt stole some of Charity's happiness. Seeing his sister protected was important to him, and yet, Lark was still at the Pulteney. Charity came to a reluctant stop, reminding herself of the duty she owed to this man she loved. After a moment, Selina let the notes fade.

"I would like to pretend we have no worries, but there is news I should tell you." Charity fidgeted briefly. "The princess did agree to marry William… however, I believe I convinced the Queen last night that this alliance would not be the best for Britain."

Ravenscroft nearly dropped his glass, and flailed to catch it before it hit the floor. And reluctantly Charity recounted the series of events that happened at Frogmore.

"You told the *Queen* she made a mistake?" Selina asked with awe in her voice. "*Brava*, Your Grace."

"Looking at your face, that came with a price," Sir Nathaniel said softly.

Charity grimaced. "I was reminded that I live under her

control. But I think, in the end, she knew it would be a bad match."

"What happens now? If they break the agreement, will the Queen or Prinny attempt to negotiate a new match while the sovereigns are here?" Thorne asked.

"Likely. There are plenty of princes here vying for her attention," the rake said sourly.

"The Grand Duchess did seem intent on introducing the princess to all of her options," Thorne said, mouth cocked in amusement. "I have had a front row seat to more than one of those conversations."

"*That one*," Ravenscroft grumbled. "However, even the Grand Duchess's antics have paled in comparison with those of the Tsar. I can count on one hand the number of aristocrats he spoke to yesterday at Ascot. Prinny was furious that Alexander spent the day circulating among the commoners."

"Ah, aye, the lower orders," said Nathaniel. His voice was light, but he was feeling prickly enough to let his northern accent deepen.

Peregrine looked contemplative. "The Tsar is a man of beliefs —something I was told just yesterday. Von Gentz passes along his regards, by the way, Sina."

"Does he?" Selina's eyebrows lifted. "How interesting."

Ravenscroft looked confused. "Do you know The Propagandist?"

"By reputation. But he was present when Lady Fitzroy had my name sullied in front of a room full of high ranking nobility, however, so I am not surprised he knows who *I* am."

"He was testing my loyalties at Ascot, and he is of the opinion you are one of Sidmouth's spies," Perry told her. "I didn't bother to disabuse the notion. Gentz is paying close attention to all of the players on the board, my mother included. Have you spoken with Sidmouth lately?"

"Last night. I told him what happened at the Pulteney." Selina shifted, crossing her arms. "He was quite cross, actually, and I don't know which displeased him more—learning the Russian diplomats are openly courting potential allies on English soil, or that Lady Fitzroy is still working to discredit him."

"Him, and not you?" Charity searched Lady Normanby's face for a hint of how the woman felt about being cut from society.

Selina gave a small shrug of her shoulders. "Do not worry for me, Duchess. Krüger's story either makes me look powerful enough to outwit Maximilian, or it makes Prussia weak and foolish. By next season, the *ton* will have someone else to talk about. What does concern me is that I have been eliminated again by Marian," Selina added, discouraged. "I cannot be eyes and ears if I am allowed nowhere near society."

"You have one dubious honour," Charity pointed out. "Lady Fitzroy seems to consider you a capable threat."

"Far better if she thought I was no one of consequence." Lady Normanby sighed. "There is no one who can watch what the Russians are up to."

"My association with Prinny is too well-known," Ravenscroft said. "What about Sir Nathaniel?"

Selina shook her head. "Nathaniel does not know enough of the players to be able to make sense of what he sees."

"If rooks the Grand Duchess—"

Perry cut both of them off firmly, seeing Thorne's discomfort. "No. Look elsewhere for information."

"Countess Lieven?" Selina asked. "She will be well positioned. The Russian Orthodox Church services happen in their home. She will also likely be entertaining frequently—both as the count's wife and in her role as Patroness now with Almack's."

Peregrine considered that. "I don't think so. The Lievens warned us at Ascot that they did not wish to be involved in anything that would jeopardise their neutrality and his role in maintaining the relations between Britain and Russia."

"They might be persuaded to share information if we can prove your mother will interfere with what they consider their duty, Perry," Charity told him.

"Perhaps," he admitted. "But that would only work once, in dire need. We need an informer who will keep watching."

"What about Gentz himself? He has less of a direct view, but The Propagandist clearly keeps himself well informed," said Ravenscroft dryly.

Selina pushed at him when Peregrine hesitated. "You should test the waters. Even if he has no particulars on your mother's plans, he may know what Russia is offering to woo potential allies at Vienna. There is more than one concern for England."

"A fair point," he conceded, spreading his hands. "Let Sidmouth know we will try to befriend Gentz."

Charity looked at Sir Nathaniel, who had frozen halfway through running his hand through his hair. "What are you thinking, Thorne?" she asked him softly.

He smiled a little ruefully, the skin crinkling around his blue eyes. "Beyond that it's clear that I'm not much help to you four in matters of intrigue? I am wondering what Marian Fitzroy stands to gain. In these secret alliances, and in thwarting the marriage to William—Russia's benefits are clear. But not hers. What has she set her sights on?"

"What indeed, besides possibly marrying off her… daughter…" Charity began, but abruptly her words trailed off.

She could feel everyone staring at her, but Charity did not meet their eyes. She was too busy thinking, staring into space as the awful conversation with the Queen played again in her memory.

What will the people do if the king is incapable of restraint and the queen lacks the will to manage him?

"Now you are both gathering wool," Peregrine said, taking her arm. "Charity, what did you think of?"

"Something that might be lunatic," she confessed. "What if we have been thinking all the wrong things about why your mother wanted to prevent the princess from marrying Prince William?"

The marchioness put the pieces together first. "Good God," she laughed. And then she sobered. "*Could* she—?"

Peregrine's hands curled into fists as he, too, began to follow the drift of Charity's thoughts. "Lark has no royal blood."

"And the Netherlands is no real kingdom. *Yet*," said Ravenscroft. "But it will be. William is the son of last stadtholder of the old Dutch republic, and he has been in exile. He was only just proclaimed sovereign prince and the marriage to Princess Charlotte would have brought them legitimacy and Britain's support."

The lines on Ravenscroft's face etched deeper as he followed that thought through. "But Lark *could* be an attractive prospect despite her lack of blue blood if a marriage brought an alliance with Russia instead."

Perry nodded. "The Regent wanted the Dutch to hold France's border and give Britain more of a presence on the continent. Which Russia wouldn't want."

"But Lady Fitzroy could marry her daughter to William, put her daughter on the throne, and keep the useless king so sotted that he does most of his governing from the floor beneath his table." Thorne shook his head. "That might serve their ambitions nicely, if Lady Fitzroy could keep him under control."

"My mother would." Peregrine's voice sounded dead, and Charity set one hand upon his arm. "One way or another, she would be the one who really ruled the Netherlands."

"It fits," admitted Selina. "It matches everything we know. But if this was her plan all along…"

"Then I may have just helped her succeed in gaining a kingdom by asking the Queen to nullify the princess's agreement to marry William." Charity swallowed noisily. "And I certainly cannot go back now and tell the Queen I've changed my mind again!"

"Talk to your sister," Thorne told Peregrine firmly. "Surely she wouldn't be a party to this."

"Would she not, Galahad?" Ravenscroft asked him. "What young girl would not be thrilled to learn her mama could make her a princess?"

Charity shivered. "One who isn't safe wearing her mother's velvet leash. Lady Fitzroy will show her who holds the power the moment Lark decides not to obey."

"What should we do instead? Kidnap her?" Ravenscroft jested, drawing sharp looks. "Oh come on. It would thwart the marriage, for sure. And you must admit it would be faster than hoping the canary can convince her to change her allegiance."

Perry bent his head in frustration. "You are not wrong. My mother has poisoned her against me."

"I do believe the magpie may have given us the solution." Selina slanted a look at Ravenscroft from beneath her dark lashes. "Lark's guardianship—and her marriage prospects—are Peregrine's domain. Perry, the law would consider you within your rights to march into the Pulteney and take her."

Peregrine stiffened. "My mother would never allow me to take Lark from her that way. It would become a fight, and I fear my mother would hurt Lark rather than cede her. We cannot risk it."

"We could distract Lady Fitzroy, surely," Thorne suggested. "If we separate them, your sister will be safer. If your sister knows you are doing it because you love her—"

Thorne had chosen his words poorly. Peregrine silenced him by slicing his hand through the air. "No! I do not want to have to force her that way. I will not take my sister's choices from her!"

Seeing his upset, the others fell back. Charity moved to stand in front of Perry, cupping his cheek and bringing their foreheads together.

"Perry, it might be the only way to stop your mother's plans and protect your sister," she whispered into the space between them.

The breath he took was jagged. "My mother taught us that love's real purpose was control, Charity. I can't make my sister a princess. She will hate me for taking everything from her. And I will hate myself for doing to her what my mother did to me."

Charity settled Peregrine's hand over her heart, laying her own palm over the rapid thrum in his chest. "You know that is not what love is. Not between us, and not even for most people. We are not trying to hurt or control Lark. You are *not* your mother. You are her brother, and this keeps your sister from being used as a pawn."

He was listening to her, and she kept talking in a low voice. "Lark needs to be safe before she can know the truth. Until she knows the truth, how can she make choices for herself?"

Perry shuddered slightly, but then he nodded. "I won't force her to do anything else, Charity."

"Nothing else is needed. Although, it would be nice if she might give us some glimpse of any other parts of your mother's plans..."

"I do not think she will be inclined to share. At least not right away," Peregrine agreed. "We may have to be content with holding her."

They separated, and Charity glanced at the others. Their faces were sober, but not without compassion. Peregrine's fear reminded them this was a rather serious undertaking.

"So, we have to try to strike a bargain with an Austrian and extract a young woman from the claws of her mama. Do we have any ideas?" the marchioness asked brusquely.

"There may be an opportunity to do both tomorrow. Prinny and the sovereigns were planning a trip to Rotten Row," Ravenscroft offered, straightening his cuffs. "With crowds of people milling about and plenty of other things to watch, no one should be terribly interested in us."

Selina gave them a smile that was mostly teeth. She looked frighteningly pleased about this chance to deal a blow back to Lady Fitzroy. Charity couldn't blame the marchioness for wanting the chance to retaliate, given what had been done to her. "Well then, Duchess, gentlemen. Shall we plan a kidnapping?"

13

"For although the act condemns the doer, the end may justify him."
—Niccolò Machiavelli, Discourses

Hodges and Sir Nathaniel had left an hour before Perry to take the unmarked, closed carriage into London. So Peregrine was alone and on horseback when he traveled towards Hyde Park, the afternoon of June 12th.

It was a ride of some thirty minutes, and he used the time to let himself slip back into that role he kept hoping he never would have to assume again. He put aside all of his worries. Any semblance of softness. He needed to be a ruthless, Machiavellian man.

As Ravenscroft predicted, Rotten Row was filled to the brim with people from all walks of life—on foot, in open carriages, and on horseback. With the sovereigns informally parading for the gratification of the public, bodies were lined along the fence several deep.

While on horseback, he made a sweep of the occupants of the carriages parked along the drive. Ravenscroft had arrived by curricle, and Peregrine had marked his position close to a carriage of Prussian women. But when Perry went back to reconnoiter with the dandy, his carriage had been abandoned.

Ravenscroft had stepped out to stand a few lengths away. Peregrine slid down from the saddle, walking over, his horse following behind.

"Magpie," he said, wincing at the colour of the man's waistcoat in the sunshine. "Did you decide the sovereigns were not enough of a curiosity?"

"Did no one ever tell you that sarcasm is the lowest form of wit?" Ravenscroft looked down his nose at Peregrine.

"Spoken like a man who can't bring his wits to bear during banter." Perry's lazy smile took the sting out of his words. "Have you seen The Propagandist?"

What Perry and Ravenscroft had been uncertain about, during their late evening of planning, had been whether Gentz would join the procession. Most of the military men and highest ranking visitors had. Due to his importance, Gentz certainly merited a spot in the parade. However, Peregrine had made a private wager with himself that Gentz would not participate so directly in social peacocking.

He won that bet.

"The Swedish bigwigs entered his carriage some few minutes ago." Ravenscroft lifted his chin in the direction of the open conveyance, where Perry could only see the back of Gentz's hatted head. "We can waylay him when he is finished."

"And my mother?"

His co-conspirator scratched his nose in a nervous gesture. "I haven't spotted her yet. But they are not our concerns. Not right now."

Which was true. If they were to speak to Gentz at all, they

would need to before the second part of their plans were underway.

A military shout and the sound of many horses had Peregrine glancing over his right shoulder. The Household Cavalry were clearing the way for the front of the procession. The Tsar, Prinny, and Frederick William III, the King of Prussia, rode their horses in a tight, flattened triangular formation, surrounded by their guards.

These were the three most powerful men in Europe—or at least they were now. Prussia's King was a shy, indecisive man, but the changes his military commanders had wrought since the Treaty of Tilsit certainly captured people's attention. Within the span of a few years, Prussia had risen from their humiliating vassal status to possess one of the largest and most modern armies of the allied forces.

But Austria, despite Metternich's lack of title as sovereign, was not a country that a canny man should overlook. Armies wouldn't be the only force to be reckoned with at the diplomatic tables; Metternich and von Gentz played a more subtle game.

Peregrine looked back at the carriage holding Gentz and the Swedish gentlemen. "Gentz has some agenda of his own. Perhaps if we are lucky, we might even be able to glean a hint of it."

"For now, I will settle for what will help Castlereagh," grumbled the magpie. "With our luck, your mother will not show, and all those plans will be for naught."

"To be honest, a part of me would be relieved," Perry admitted.

The aftermath was the most dangerous part of their plans. One of them—not Peregrine, it had been unanimously agreed—had to let Lady Fitzroy know they were responsible for Lark's disappearance.

"It must be done. There is no reason to keep her location a secret," Ravenscroft reminded him. "Telling your mother where

Lark is will keep her from asking guards to do a search. She might rage, but you are Lark's guardian."

"That is not the part that concerns me; the part I don't like is having you deliver the letter."

"Ah, well. If you did it yourself, she's apt to gut you a second time—and this time she might well succeed." Ravenscroft looked disgruntled.

"Any child here would be willing to deliver the message for a shilling. And then you would not be standing there like an archery target, especially with that waistcoat of yours."

"Someone with fewer secrets?" Ravenscroft said, striking at the centre of the matter. He met Perry's gaze and did not let it drop. "It should be me. She needs the reminder that the Crown will not let her actions go unmarked, and Marian knows whom I represent unofficially. Now, put your mind to better use."

Peregrine nodded absently, shifting his attention as the parade continued. The milling crowd parted just enough that he noticed Charity in the back of it, waiting to catch his attention. When their eyes met, she smiled, and he could feel his spirits lift.

She didn't wait for a response, turning her head instead to look in another direction, and he followed the angle of her gaze, blessing that he had the height for a relatively clear view. He saw Thorne, who also stood inches above most.

Thorne had agreed to lead the kidnapping, ensuring Lark left the park in their company. He would also safeguard both Selina and Charity. Peregrine and Ravenscroft's role in that part would be to serve as a distraction and ensure that Lady Fitzroy did not look their way.

Thorne's gaze was fixed on a closed carriage ahead of them in the line, his focus complete. That could only mean one thing.

"My mother and Lark are here," Perry murmured.

Ravenscroft huffed an acknowledgement. "Thank God. Let us

see if we can hasten things and attract the attention of von Gentz. Mount up again."

Slowly manoeuvring around people, they walked down the line of carriages. When Peregrine passed near Gentz's conveyance, sitting slightly higher than the men inside, he tipped his hat in greeting.

"Lord Fitzroy!" Gentz hailed him, leaning on the side of the landau. "A pleasant day for a parade of kings, is it not?"

Perry gave a faint smile. "I would agree. Herr von Gentz, have you had an opportunity to meet my acquaintance, Lord Ravenscroft?"

The Swedes glanced at Perry and Ravenscroft, murmured polite excuses, and slid out of the far side of the carriage. Gentz ignored them, instead turning his keen eye on the magpie, his face amused. "I have not—although I know who you are, Lord Ravenscroft. Do you answer to 'Magpie' the way I do to my own nickname?"

"Only my dearest enemies are so bold, Herr von Gentz," Ravenscroft replied sardonically in Peregrine's direction. "I hope you are having an excellent visit to London."

"Sit with me. Else one of us will get a crick in our necks." Gentz opened the carriage door near him, inviting Ravenscroft to climb inside. Astride, with the horse standing next to The Propagandist, Peregrine stayed in the saddle.

"I have been thinking of our meeting at Ascot, Lord Fitzroy. You seem very devoted to your country," the Austrian said idly, fingering the ornate grip of the walking cane leaning against his leg. "It has been a shame to hear how your loyalty was repaid."

Peregrine could see from the corner of his eye that Gentz's attention was trained on Ravenscroft as he spoke.

"Yes, yes, we are all acquainted with his illustrious mama," Ravenscroft drawled. "And you, of all men, you wretched scribe, know the business of nations—how often it is wiser to strike first, and save the philosophy for after the dust settles."

Gentz laughed, his bright eyes glimmering. "So rare, a voice unadorned. It is rather refreshing. What do the two of you hope to draw from me, that you have so clearly sought me out?"

The Propagandist was baiting them to see who would negotiate first. Peregrine and Ravenscroft had agreed it was important for Ravenscroft to assert command, especially if he wished to keep communication going on with Austria.

"There are occasions it is worthwhile to spend one's time in a dance, and others it is better to cut to the chase. Half the diplomats in Europe are already here fluttering about like exotic birds, posturing and preening while they court alliances and deals. Not that I deny that there is a certain pleasure in the game, but sometimes the rest of us would rather get on with it. If we put our cards on the table, everyone may go home happy that much sooner." Ravenscroft waved his hand. "The Russians seem to have discovered the virtue of such brevity."

"I believe I see." Gentz wore an expression of enigmatic benevolence. "Strange that you harbour fears that your kinsman in Castlereagh stands at such a disadvantage in his own homeland. But I do understand there have been many... *distractions* lately. And Lady Normanby's disgrace has no doubt caused Viscount Sidmouth some trouble."

The man paused, glancing up at Peregrine. "Are you doing a favour for the magpie and the Regent, Fitzroy? Or is it somewhat the other way around? The whispers I've heard have been a muddle, but it is interesting that certain names come up time and time again."

"Do people have the luxury of such simple options?" Peregrine asked dryly.

Gentz's mouth cocked up on one side. "Unimportant people do."

"Come to whatever conclusion that you like. But I do not have the power to speak for the Regent," Perry told him, pointing at Ravenscroft with his chin. "He does."

Gentz leaned back against the squab, stretching out his legs comfortably. "We could talk about the wants of vain men. It is a nice afternoon, however, and I have the thought that if Castlereagh needs my help to find out the details anybody would know, perhaps you should replace him with a smarter politician? Or a few more spies."

"Does that mean you have no interest in potentially sharing details for concessions?" Ravenscroft asked, mirroring Gentz's posture. "I understand Austria would like to keep Italy."

Von Gentz inclined his head. "Metternich is always interested in discussions with powerful friends. But friends should be honest, and so it should probably also be mentioned that Nesslerode has also been willing to support our claims in Italy."

No surprise in that. Nesslerode was the most senior diplomat in Russia's foreign ministry.

"I do not mind trading such minor details for concessions, Lord Ravenscroft. But I would rather talk about the future of empires, my friends." Gentz leaned forward then, putting his elbows on his knees. "Lord Fitzroy will likely find that kind of discussion far more edifying."

Ravenscroft hesitated, thinking carefully and trying not to betray much. Perry felt some sympathy for him. The magpie was good, but he had always been more of a collector of gossip than an active participant in politics. The Propagandist had years of experience in this arena.

Finally, Ravenscroft glanced up at Perry, yielding the conversation to him.

Peregrine shifted, and the horse danced beneath him. "Again, you know I have no authority to negotiate things on behalf of England."

"Yes, I know," the baron nodded. "But when I see you, Lord Fitzroy, I see a man whose paramour is highly placed with the Queen. You possess the ear and the possible friendship of Prinny's court spy, a strange connection with Sidmouth, and—perhaps most interesting of all—there seems to be some naked aggression between this cohort of yours and a woman who was absolved of treason. So it makes little sense to pretend you have no influence over the Crown."

"Having an ear isn't at all the same as having influence," Perry said dismissively. "But put your offer on the table, such as it is, and we will pass it along."

Gentz quoted another riddle instead. "What is a banquet to which all come hungry, yet few will sample the fare? A place where a new map is drawn with old ink in a way where the final shape will please none, yet must satisfy all? What am I?"

"The talks in Vienna, I assume."

"Good. Your mother's route to Russia," Gentz told him, "if Britain promises to reject Russia and Prussia's demands for Poland and Saxony at the table."

Perry's eyes flickered as he considered what Gentz was really asking for. "You want an ally who will oppose the combined might of Russia and the Prussian armies on your doorstep. Especially now that Prussia has one of the most dangerous armies in all of Europe. In exchange for information on *one* woman." He let his voice take on a tinge of scorn.

The Propagandist grinned at him. "You have the price. Now we will find out how badly you want to know the answer."

As the waiting crowd of eager watchers came into view, a line of sweat snaked down Charity's back. She told herself that it was the heat of the summer sun baking down on her, and not nerves about her assignment. *We have planned every step of this*, she reminded herself.

Charity twined her fingers together to keep her hands from trembling. Glancing at the people walking along the path, she was delighted to see a face she recognised.

"Well met, Lady Barbour," Charity said, offering her hands in greeting. "Have you been well? I wanted to tell you again how very much I appreciated the salon you held for Perry and me."

Lady Barbour beamed. "It was my pleasure. I would love to have you both again—that is, assuming all is proceeding well between you two?" She cocked her chin genially in Charity's direction. "If it is not going *well enough*, let me know; I will throw another salon."

"Quite well, thank you," Charity said blushing as she tried to repress a smile. "Where is your dear husband, my lady? Is he here today?"

"Oh, somewhere," she replied, waving her hand. "As much as I would like to be, we cannot always be in one another's pockets. Come, tell me how you have been. Did you attend Ascot?"

Charity linked arms with the older woman and they strolled together, exchanging tidbits of gossip. A flash of pale blonde hair marked the presence of Marian Fitzroy standing near a group of diplomat wives, but Charity ignored her.

Right now, Marian Fitzroy induced less fear than the looming spectre of Queen Charlotte. Her Majesty sat under a canopy, glass of lemonade in hand, allowing her subjects to pay their respects. Lady Barbour's steps brought them closer to the line of aristocrats waiting.

Her stomach fluttered. What if the Queen cut her dead?

Charity stepped forward beside Lady Barbour, dropping into a curtsy, keeping her head bowed in a display of deference. Underneath the skirts of her walking dress, her legs shook.

"Your Grace, my lady," the Queen said, bidding them to rise.

She inclined her head in a single regal nod and then waved them on.

It seemed the Queen had found a middle ground. The terse acknowledgement was not a slight but a far cry from welcoming. Perhaps the Queen's anger would diminish in time. Even if it did not, however, it was a comfort to know she wouldn't be banished to the country.

The princess was a few feet away, speaking with a group of young British ladies. She glowed with such happiness that everyone around her hung on her every word. Men tipped their hats as they passed and the society dowagers seemed charmed.

She was so different from how she had been at Frogmore that could only be one explanation for her cheer. The Queen had heeded Charity's words.

The princess spotted Charity, and she excused herself from the others. After greeting Lady Barbour, she asked Charity to accompany her on a turn around the nearby fountain.

"Your highness, you are looking well," Charity said as they moved away from the crowd.

"I believe I have you to thank for that." The princess flicked a glance at Charity. "Who else would dare to tell Her Majesty that she was making a mistake? I am in your debt, Your Grace."

"You owe me nothing, Your Highness. Instead, I owe you an apology." Charity faced the princess. "You recognised he was unworthy, and you were right to resist. All I did was find the courage to insist on what you already told your father."

She dismissed that. "That may be, but you helped me be heard," the princess replied. "I was told my only duty was to provide heirs, to ensure the line. You helped me see that my duty is also to protect our people. I must find someone who shares those values."

It was far too soon to guess what kind of queen the young princess would eventually make, but Charity suspected

England's future monarch would not be anyone's pawn. Never again.

"It is my honour to serve you in that," Charity vowed. If she could defy the Queen to protect Charlotte, she could defy Marian too. Whatever the cost.

Charlotte clasped her hands briefly, sealing the promise. "Come. We begin the search for a new suitor today. I will not get a better opportunity to speak with Europe's heirs and see what they are truly like."

They debated the merits of each visiting prince as they resumed their walk. Charity cast her gaze over the faces of the crowd around while they talked, searching for one specific face. Hyde Park was as crowded as Almack's ballroom.

Finally, Charity spotted a glimpse of hair the same colour as Peregrine's blonde locks, peeking out amid a sea of darker heads. There, deep in conversation with the Grand Duchess of Oldenburg was Lark Fitzroy.

14

"All I insist on, and nothing else, is that you should show the whole world that you are not afraid. Be silent, if you choose; but when it is necessary, speak—and speak in such a way that people will remember it."
—Wolfgang Amadeus Mozart

Lady Lark with the Grand Duchess. Was this a simple conversation, or a meeting of the minds between two women bent on making trouble? Charity couldn't be certain.

It was strange to think that only last year, she and Lark had once been acquaintances—two young women launched into society together, sharing the same ballrooms, the same stilted conversations with prospective suitors.

A year had changed Lark almost beyond recognition. It was not merely a new hairstyle or fondness for Russian gowns. She carried herself differently now, taller, steadier, her expressions carefully schooled. The girl who had quaked before her presentation at court had been replaced by a young woman who had learned to mask her feelings.

When Lark noticed Charity approaching, she lifted her chin, feigning indifference. For all her hardening behaviour, Lark still lacked her mother's unflinching cruelty. The resemblance was there—but incomplete, as if the role were still a costume Lark was learning to wear.

There was still a chance to pull her away before her mother's influence consumed her entirely. And that task was falling to Charity.

Charity's part in the plan was to draw Lark away from the crowd and her mama. She needed to edge the young woman toward Peregrine's unmarked black carriage, which held Thorne and Selina inside. When Lark was close enough, they would seize her and spirit her to the Fitzroy estate.

Ironic. It was a plan not too dissimilar to Lady Fitzroy's, when she had her butler kidnap Charity. Charity had been taken to another Fitzroy property and held for days. The memory of how she felt that night—the thought that she would be a part of taking another woman and holding her against her will—made her pulse trip unevenly.

She found herself smoothing her glove over her wrist, willing the tightness around her chest to ease. *We are not doing this for revenge or to ruin Lark,* she reminded herself. *This is about protecting her and stopping Marian.*

The princess must have noticed her nervousness, for she drew up short. "Shall we wait a moment and see if Lady Lark moves on? I would not force you into an awkward conversation with Lord Fitzroy's sister, if that is what troubles you."

"You are kind, Your Highness. In fact, I am uneasy because I promised Perry that I would speak with her." Charity cleared her suddenly dry throat. "It would be… better if I could speak with her alone, perhaps."

"Of course. Leave it to me; it is the least I can do," the princess replied. She tugged Charity back into step and raised her voice, calling out to her fellow royal. "Catherine! There you are!"

The Grand Duchess swung around, at first searching to see who dared call her by her first name. When she saw it was the princess, Catherine practically cooed in delight. She held out her hands to welcome Princess Charlotte, greeting her with a kiss on each cheek.

"My dear, I have been looking everywhere for you!" The Grand Duchess held both of the princess's hands in hers, casting a look around. "Nicholas is keen to speak with you, and I promised I would bring you over to him as soon as our paths crossed."

The princess glanced over at Charity, fluttering her lashes. "Would you mind terribly if I left you here? You may keep Lady Lark company so I don't feel so guilty for letting the Grand Duchess steal me away. I believe you two are acquainted, are you not?"

Lark opened her mouth, and then thought better of whatever she had to say.

"Good! I am sure you two were fast friends when you debuted together last season," the princess exclaimed, her doe eyes daring Lark to deny it. "You must be looking forward to a chance to renew your friendship, are you not?"

"Of course we are," Charity agreed. She bobbed a curtsy and from the corner of her eye, she saw Lark doing the same.

Princess Charlotte's voice was too bright. The Grand Duchess's eyes narrowed briefly, sensing some hidden scheme. But she had no reason to suspect more than a catty prank afoot between members of the *ton*. Finally, Catherine smoothed her smile back into place and linked her arm through the princess's.

The royal pair swept off, leaving Charity and Lark alone. Not wishing to talk to Charity, Lark immediately began to make excuses to leave, but Charity held out a hand to stop her.

Charity had thought long and hard about how to best begin. Despite the feud between their families, they had not always viewed one another as enemies.

"Lady Lark… I was just thinking about last year. It seems like an age since we attended our first events together, so much has happened." Charity took a breath. "We used to speak more kindly of one another, once. Before our families intervened, and everything grew so tangled. I think back, and I wish things had been different."

"A year can change a great deal, Your Grace," Lark replied, making the honorary sound like an insult. "But I think my memories of last year differ from yours. Curiously, though—I do not recall you being particularly eager for my company then. Forgive me if I question what makes my company appealing now. Is it the absence of your other friend? Or is it simply your interest in my brother?"

Charity felt the sting of her words, but she vowed not to be easily defeated. "I do not blame you for wondering. It is true that I miss Grace; being her friend was easy to do, because she looked for so little from me. I was free to follow my plans for the season, and in my ambitions, I overlooked forming other friendships. Now, I would like the chance to get to know you better. To speak openly without… interference."

Lark whipped around, her cheeks bright pink with fury. "Interference? You mean my mother? *Or yours?*"

It was a fair enough question, for both mothers had done their part to encourage the family feud to continue. Lark's balled fists suggested she expected Charity to deny Lady Cresswell's part. Charity had no intention of doing so.

"Both of them," she admitted with candor. "I have no wish to be your enemy. I do not expect you to believe me, but I am not here to dredge up the past."

"It must be nice to have the past so neatly buried, when I am finding it is rather hard to forget it," Lark fired back. "You and your friends are the reason my mother had to flee London. The lies you told, those unfounded accusations, they nearly ruined us!"

A nearby gasp reminded the women they had an audience.

"Please, Lark, I would like to explain everything. The middle of Rotten Row is not the right place to talk, though. Will you walk with me?" Charity offered her arm, hardly daring to breathe.

Lark's hands were still balled. Charity knew then that she could beg the young woman until the sun went down, and this approach would bear no fruit. Peregrine's sister was so furious, she would not be willing to listen or cooperate.

She might still care about her brother, though. "Perry asked me to speak with you."

"Perry?" The name slipped out before Lark could stop herself, sharper than she intended. And then she cloaked her expression. "Well then, say what you must. But do not expect me to pretend you're here for my sake."

"We're attracting notice, and I would not speak about personal matters with an audience. Please, won't you come?" Charity held out her arm.

Lark looked around, her shoulders slumping. "Fine." She motioned for Charity to lead the way. "You are right; we should not give the *ton* more to talk about."

They had scarcely cleared the tight knots of promenaders when a sharp, furious voice rang out behind them.

"Charity! There you are! Do not dare walk away from me."

Charity stiffened. Lady Cresswell was bearing down upon them, skirts whipping about her ankles. Lord Cresswell trailed a pace behind. Her father's mouth was set in a grim line, and he looked as though he had long since abandoned any hope of restraining his furious wife.

Surprised, Charity stumbled. She threw a desperate glance at

Lark, hoping that Peregrine's sister would not take this opportunity to make an escape. But fortunately, Lark's animosity worked in Charity's favour.

A smile tugged at Lark's mouth. She was anticipating watching Charity being humiliated by her parents. That cut deep, and for an instant, shame pricked at Charity's eyes, hot and unbidden. Peregrine's sister clearly relished watching her stumble.

But so long as Lark stayed put, Charity would endure. She drew a slow breath, composing her features, and braced herself for her mother's onslaught.

"You stupid, stupid girl," her mother spat as she came to a halt in front of the pair. Lady Cresswell was so fixated on Charity, that she did not seem to even notice that Lark was there. "What did you do to anger the Queen?"

Since she had been expecting more lamentations about associating with the Fitzroy family, Charity was knocked off course by her mother's question. Had her mother been told what happened at Frogmore? She decided her best defence was to plead ignorance.

"I have no idea what you mean, Mama. I was just with the Princess of Wales."

Lady Cresswell lifted her right hand and pointed it in her daughter's face. "I had it on good authority that you were to be at the Opera last night, in the royal box. Instead, Lady Pelham was in your seat."

Charity's stomach soured at the mention of the woman dead set on being her nemesis. Of course the Queen would invite her in Charity's place, showing her diamond her displeasure in less direct ways.

"Lady Pelham," Charity's mama continued, "told everyone who asked that you were *under the weather*, but with such inflection that we understood it was a flimsy excuse. This is what happens when you spend time with the undesirables, Charity. You should have married the Duke of Northumberland. The Fitzroy stain is spreading across your name."

"*I beg your pardon*," Lark said, jutting in.

Lady Cresswell blinked and then glanced over, her eyes widening as she realised who was standing at Charity's side. Her face flushed in embarrassment, with more rising fury fast on its heels. "Lady Lark, I did not recognise you in those clothes. Then again, you and your mother barely escaped, what with the guard nipping at your heels. I imagine you had little chance to pack before you fled England."

Lark lifted her chin, hostile. "Your daughter's friends tarred us with their false accusations," she replied, trotting out the lines her mother had likely told her. "She never would have had the chance to marry Lord Percy. He likely realised your daughter is a liar, and that is why he ended the engagement."

"That is not what happened," Charity gasped, swinging round.

Lady Cresswell gave her daughter no room to continue. "The Duke of Northumberland is a family friend, and you should remember my daughter is a duchess. You are to refer to her as Your Grace if you must refer to her at all."

"Mama, that is not necessary," Charity murmured, though she did not know why she chose to focus on that point. She didn't have time to deal with her mother, not now, not when she still had to get Lark to the carriage. She cast a desperate glance at her father, silently pleading with him to intercede.

He did—but not in the way Charity had hoped.

He stepped around his wife, and latched onto Charity's arm. "Your behaviour is beyond the pale, Charity. We are taking you home right now, before you do something truly horrid, like ruining yourself with that rake Lord Fitzroy."

"My brother is *not* a rake," Lark growled. "He has never mistreated any woman—"

"He has forced my daughter to associate with his former mistress!" Lord Cresswell countered. He squeezed Charity's arm and pulled again. "The marchioness! Exposed as a lady of ill repute in front of half of Europe's royals, and with you sitting at her side. Yes, Charity, we heard about that too. This is all Peregrine Fitzroy's fault. He is dragging you into the muck."

"And now even the Queen wants nothing to do with you," Lady Cresswell spat, her eyes glittering with fiery anger.

"There is no ill will between myself and the Queen," Charity shot back. "Peregrine is a good man, one respected by the Crown, which you would see if you spent even a minute with him."

"You want me to spend time with the Fitzroys? After all they've done to us?" Lady Cresswell shifted her attention, pointing the burning orbs that were her eyes in Lark's direction. "Your mother kidnapped my daughter. Did you know that? Did you help her with that plan? I bet you thought you'd win the Duke's hand with Charity out of the way. Now your brother is trying to ruin her again."

Charity sucked in a breath, aghast at her mother's accusations. Lark was innocent, as innocent as Charity and Peregrine had been. Trapped all together in the maelstrom that was the feud between their mothers.

Charity caught Lark's eye and shook her head feverishly, making it clear she did not agree with her mother's words. "Lark was not involved at all. Nor Perry," she told her parents.

Lark scrunched her brow, concentrating on Charity's face as though she were trying to read the truth written in her soul. Did Charity truly care about her brother? Was Charity really taking a stand against her own family?

"I love him," Charity whispered, her words meant only for Lark. If her parents heard her confession, so be it.

Lark did not answer, but something in her gaze cooled, as though weighing which battle mattered more. In that instant, defending her brother outweighed sparring with Charity. She straightened, caught Lord Cresswell's hand, and pried it from Charity's arm with deliberate force.

Lord Cresswell shrank back. Lady Cresswell, however, was not to be denied her objective.

"There is something rotten in your family, Lark Fitzroy. I knew it the moment I first laid eyes on your mother."

"I am sure that is what you tell yourself, Lady Cresswell, but let us not forget. It was you who lured my mother's beau into that room, you who allowed him to take liberties, and you who threatened to blacken his name if he did not offer for your hand."

"I saved him from marrying a mad woman!" Lady Cresswell said. "Look at you and your brother. The bad blood has carried through to the next generation."

"At least my mother did her duty" Lark's voice was so cold that it burned Charity's ears. "Thanks to your actions, Lord Cresswell was left with a sad excuse for a wife, one unable to bear him a single heir."

Charity searched for some way out of this cycle of accusations, some way to get her mother to separate her hatred for Marian Fitzroy from tossing blame on Perry and Lark.

Lark, it seemed, had a simpler solution in mind. She drew herself up and announced, "I do not have to stand here while you sling mud upon my family name. In the future, please keep your distance, Lord and Lady Cresswell."

With that, Lark slipped her arm through Charity's, spun Charity around, and all but dragged her away.

"This is *not* an overture of friendship," Lark muttered. "But yes, I agree now that we should speak openly, without this interference colouring our opinions."

Charity bucked up and took control, angling their steps toward the line of waiting carriages. She spied Hodges sitting atop one not too far ahead. She coughed then, loud enough to draw his attention, and watched as he rapped on the roof of the carriage.

"Over here," Charity said, forcing her slippered feet to move even quicker along the dusty path. "That carriage there. They are waiting."

"They? Do you mean Perry?" Lark asked.

Thorne swung the door open and leapt to the ground. He wrapped his arms around Lark and bundled her forward, lifting her small form into the carriage with ease.

"Your brother wishes you to be safe," he said loud enough for Charity to hear.

Charity's last glimpse inside showed Selina and Lark sitting beside one another on the cushioned bench. Selina was rubbing Lark's arm, attempting to reassure her all was well.

Lark's mouth hung open, too shocked by the situation to think to shout for help. But when her gaze landed on Charity's face, her eyes narrowed into slits, promising retribution for this betrayal.

15

"Those who tell the stories rule society."
—Plato

Baron von Gentz was bold, Perry would give him that. Would Lords Castlereagh and Sidmouth want details on Marian Fitzroy's travels badly enough to agree to take Austria's side against the Russians and Prussians?

Mulling this possibility, Peregrine walked his horse away from the man's carriage, his eyes roving over the crowds. Ravenscroft had disappeared into the crowd to mark Charity's progress; Perry was now playing the bait.

He had gone to some lengths to make himself easy to spot in a crowd, especially with the height he had sitting atop his horse. So it was not surprising that Marian Fitzroy's eyes had found him long before he spotted her in return. He could practically *feel* the prickling weight of her malevolence, and he stopped, turning his head in her direction.

Marian Fitzroy was gloating, the tiniest smirk curling her lips as she fixated on him.

Go ahead, be smug. I know what your game is, Mother, Perry thought as he returned her stare. *Enjoy yourself now, because I am about to turn the tables on you.*

She caught the trace of confidence in his posture, even though he was attempting to conceal it. Even as her lips stayed fixed in that position of amusement, something changed in his mother's eyes. They became colder and more cunning.

His mother was studying him, trying to decide if he was engaged in a covert plan of his own.

That's right, watch me. You have never felt that my allies have been anything more than my eyes and ears, and you will fail to respect their capacity to act against you.

Her attention did flicker, but mostly to Sidmouth. The Home Secretary, trying not to be overly conspicuous following the incident with Selina, was watching the parade from the sidelines. Perry had passed him only a few moments ago.

Perry stopped looking in his mother's direction, waiting tensely. The minutes dragged on, especially since he was uncomfortably aware of Marian's attention spearing into his back.

Finally Ravenscroft slipped into the field of his gaze. The man looked relieved, which was enough to answer the question as to whether the gambit had been successful. But the magpie still scratched at his right ear. It had been the prearranged signal.

Perry scratched his ear in return, and then he turned to catch his mother's gaze again. Staring directly at her, he let satisfaction ooze to the surface. Marian's smile slipped.

And while she was fixed on Perry, Ravenscroft closed the distance to reach her side. He handed her the letter Peregrine had written. Then with a tip of his hat, Ravenscroft moved away.

Marian's eyes dropped to her hands. Perry knew what she would be seeing—the folded letter sealed with his stamp in red wax. The single sentence that would be inside, a written declaration of war.

I have taken Lark into my keeping, as is my right as her guardian.

The basilisk lifted its eyes to Peregrine in response.

Perry felt the exhilaration of the hunt rising in him. He had survived his mother's efforts to destroy him, and that had been a frustration to her. But she had maintained the upper hand in their battles.

Now—finally—the predator was sensing it had become the prey.

With a bob of his head, he turned and left, certain that his message had been received. Not caring about the rest of the parade, Perry took a ride through London's streets. He needed time to think. To settle himself. And to figure out what to say to his sister.

Lark would need a moment to herself as well. She was strongly under their mother's sway, plied with falsehoods. She would believe that the scandals their family had endured were the fault of others, and Marian would have fed her daughter steadily with vanity, flattery, and subtle threats.

When he was younger, his mother had plied him the same way. And when it had been no longer possible for him to ignore evidence of his mother's crimes, Marian had quickly traded that velvet noose for an iron collar.

An hour later, he turned northward, taking the path back to St John's Wood. He still didn't know what to say, but at least he was prepared to take the brunt of his sister's anger.

Quinn gave Perry a most expressive look when he greeted him at the door, taking Perry's things. "Lady Normanby and Sir Nathaniel are waiting for you in the library, my lord. I trust you had an eventful outing."

"You could say that. What of my sister?"

"She is safely confined to her room," his butler said, voice droll. "You may wish to visit the library first; it will give her a chance to finish breaking the heavy objects before you open the door."

Perry snorted softly. "Do you regret hiring on with me yet, Quinn? I daresay you did not expect your duties to encompass these sorts of… events."

"If you are trying to determine if my loyalty is being shaken by what has transpired lately, Lord Fitzroy, the answer is no." Quinn's posture was relaxed. "The challenges have been unexpected, but your morality is in good standing. Just think of the money I am saving by living in a chapbook instead of having to purchase them."

Quinn seldom showed such humour, but since it eased his black mood, Peregrine figured his butler had earned the leeway today. "Fairly said."

Perry began to turn towards the library but Quinn cleared his throat.

"One more thing, if I might suggest, my lord? I believe it might be wise to urgently consider hiring more staff."

Wincing, Perry nodded. "I suppose if nothing else, I need to hire a lady's maid or two."

"Lady Normanby has anticipated your need, at least for a time; she sent one ahead for Lady Lark, and that is who is minding your sister. But given the circumstances, there is more of a need now to ensure that the house remains… secure."

"I trust your judgement. See it done, carefully."

"Very good. Tea?"

Perry nodded and made his way to the library, pushing open the door. He expected them to be engaged and comfortable—judging by the cups sitting on the table, they had been served tea earlier—but he was surprised to find Thorne in a chair by the fire, a small book seated in his hand as he read to Selina.

"Perry," Selina greeted him serenely. "I was just introducing Sir Nathaniel to Walter Scott while we were waiting for you. I thought he might appreciate the words of another man of the north."

"You may borrow the book if you like," said Peregrine, curious.

Thorne had closed the book on his finger, flustered, rather than using the ribbon. "Thank you, Lord Fitzroy."

The man was stiffly formal, and Perry looked to Selina for guidance. Selina looked unbothered by Thorne's stilted behaviour, so he put it down to general nerves.

"I owe you both a thank you for bringing Lark here. I understand you sent a maid for her as well, Sina."

"Yes, well, I am rather glad I did. Saucy baggage, your sister is. I did not expect her to be a kicker, Perry." Selina's grin was mischievous.

Peregrine winced, wondering at the state of Thorne's shins. No wonder the man was out of joint. "Let me apologise for her behaviour—and any bruising—"

"She was upset." Thorne's unhappy grimace was telling. "We were as gentle as we could be, but putting someone in a carriage against their express wishes and making sure they don't jump back out again... involves a bit of unpleasantness all around."

Quinn interrupted them with fresh tea, and Selina played mother, fixing cups for everyone.

"I should add that she was also upset when she saw no familiar faces among the staff," Selina told him before Quinn exited, inclining her head in Quinn's direction.

"My mother had most of them silenced." Perry dragged a hand down his face. "The only one who survived was Edmunds. And that was because he came crawling to me for sanctuary, despite the fact I'd told him I never wanted to see him again."

"How did Lady Fitzroy react to the news, when you told her that you had Lady Lark?" Thorne asked.

Peregrine recalled the look on Marian's face. "We finally pierced my mother's scales and drew blood. But she will be thrice as dangerous now. Before, she seemed almost of the opinion that my allies were nuisances. I don't think she will ignore you any longer."

"Will Lord Ravenscroft be all right?" Thorne asked, concerned. "I can go back and ensure that there's another pair of hands to guard his household."

Peregrine shook his head slightly. "No need. When Ravenscroft insisted on representing the Crown, he told me he will take Antoine and ask to be a guest of Carlton house for the near future."

"You should take our knight errant here under your wing, Perry." Selina's voice was all business, but she was looking down, picking at a speck of dust on her skirts. Realising they were watching her hands, she smoothed everything and set them down. "If you managed to upset your mother, she might find another blade for hire. The more you can fortify yourself here, the better I will feel. Your house is too large and open to attack."

Thorne shifted uncomfortably, splitting a glance between Selina and Perry. "You are not wrong that Peregrine could use more help here. But you should not be left vulnerable either, Lady Normanby."

She gave him a small smile. "Your concern is appreciated. Do not fret, I have been dabbling in risky business a long time. Long enough to know the value of making my home a fortress. For now, I need to go and impose upon some royalty myself."

Selina stood up, shaking out her skirts.

She was supposed to take Charity and visit the Queen. "You are bound for Atholl House?" Peregrine asked, both he and Thorne standing up.

"Yes, everything is proceeding as we wished it to. Charity bringing the news about Lady Lark should mollify the Queen. But if it doesn't, I have one more card to play. Just before I left to meet everyone at Hyde Park, one of my gossips came flying to me with a very interesting piece of news."

Perry arched an eyebrow. "News that you intend to share with the rest of us?"

"Prince Nicholas was spotted visiting Rundell, Bridge & Rundell around noon." Selina's eyes danced maliciously. "Whatever do you suppose a young Russian prince might be doing, visiting the Principal Royal Goldsmiths and Jewellers? Especially without the escort of his brother?"

Letting out a long breath, Peregrine contemplated that. "You think the youngest brother of the Tsar might have been buying a token for Princess Charlotte?"

"It is certainly a possibility."

"A possibility that will give the Queen an apoplexy," he countered.

"Yes, but it should turn her ire nicely towards someone else," Selina said primly. "So I am off."

"I can escort you back," Thorne offered.

It was on the tip of his tongue to agree that Thorne should go, but Selina declined with a wave of her hands. "No, that is unnecessary. I will be safe enough in my carriage."

Relenting, Peregrine had Jack escort Selina out, and then he looked back at their displaced knight. "I am sorry, Sir Nathaniel. Perhaps we shouldn't have involved you in this plan. Not only have we compromised your honour, it puts you in a great deal of danger from my mother. If you like, I will pay your way back to Alnwick on the next post chaise, so you can take shelter with your brother."

"Have your jest." Thorne laughed briefly. "If you really have a concern for the state of my conscience, Fitzroy, you wouldn't even suggest this now. I did not relish playing the part of the kidnapper, it's true. But I agreed to do it because I liked the idea of leaving your sister in such a precarious place even less. I will admit, I did not care for you very much after the trouble your wager caused my brother, but even if that went unresolved, *my honour* certainly wouldn't tolerate leaving you and the Duchess to your mother over it."

Perry nodded. "For what it is worth, I didn't care for myself very much last year either, and I am glad Percy came out the better of that wager in the end. Shall we agree to let bygones be bygones?"

Thorne thrust his hand out immediately, and Perry clasped his forearm. "I will tell Owens and Quinn to get you anything you need. But for now, I should go speak with Lark."

"Please give my apologies to your sister, Fitzroy."

It was quiet in the hallway. Peregrine knocked softly on his sister's door, and a prim, strapping maid answered the door promptly. She looked vaguely familiar—he must have run into her at some point in Selina's household.

"My lord." She stepped out of the doorway promptly, making way for him to enter the sitting room.

"I was told that Lark has been… spirited. How is she now?"

The maid gave a small shake of her head. "Done breaking things, for the moment. I'll keep her in hand."

The bedroom door stood open, so Perry only gave a perfunctory knock before stepping through. Lark was curled on her side on top of the covers, facing away from the door.

"Lark, it's me," he announced when she made no effort to see who was there.

"Leave. I do not want to talk to you right now," she said, quietly furious.

"I know you are angry with me. But I wanted to talk with you. To explain, if nothing else."

"What is there to explain!" she snapped, turning over on the mattress and propping herself upright. "After our ride, you clearly decided that *I* must have been *lied* to. Tell me I am wrong."

"You *have* been lied to, Lark." Perry's chest hurt to admit it. "I know it will take some time to separate what is truth from falsehood. But try to be a little bit patient—"

"No!" Lark shouted at him, pushing herself off the bed. "You say *she* is the liar, but you are the one who had your friends snatch me from the park like common thieves. You knew I wouldn't come with you, so you simply *took* me like it was your right—"

"It *is* my right!" Peregrine roared back at her, stung. "And not just my right, my *duty*. I am trying to protect you!"

Lark stomped over to him, shoving him in the chest with both hands. Already regretting his words, Peregrine let her hit him, only rocked back slightly from the force of it.

"I didn't *ask* for protection! I don't *need* any protection! What do I need protection for? From whom? Our mother? The woman who has done nothing but care for me when it should have been *you* caring for *us*?" she hissed.

When Perry closed his eyes, she continued on the offensive. "You betrayed our mother, you've betrayed *me*. You've broken with everyone. You've sided with the Cresswells—against us. You fired all of our servants. You have no loyalty! Mama was right. You have betrayed everyone!"

There was little he could say to counter these words. "I did not side with the Cresswells! I objected to causing harm to someone who had nothing to do with her parents' actions. Charity is not your enemy."

"*Liar!*" Lark shouted in his face. "You used her to rob me of my freedom. That makes both of you my enemy."

You only thought you were free! Perry bit back the words He took a shuddering breath, struggling to rein in his temper.

"I don't want to do this—to hold you," he gritted out. "Unfortunately I don't know how I can make you understand now that I am only doing it because I have to!"

Seeing that he wasn't responding to her anger, Lark attempted reason. "Please, I would like to go back, now," Lark told him. "I want to be with everyone at the Pulteney."

"And I need you to stay," Perry replied.

"Why! And don't you *dare* say 'for your protection,' Perry!" she shouted.

Perry's breath escaped in a frustrated hiss. "Unfortunately, that is the truth. And right now, it is the only truth I can afford to give."

Tears overflowed. "I *hate* you," Lark informed him, swapping to guilt, her lower lip trembling. "If you really wanted to prove you were caring for me, you would be honest. You want to use me as a pawn against our mother. You want to force me to betray her the way you have used others to."

His heart bled a little more. She knew exactly where to strike him the hardest. It frustrated him so badly to know that the only course that might convince her—telling her the entire truth—was the one course he could not take.

Lark would lie, rage, plead, and scheme to go back to the Pulteney. There was a chance she could escape. There was a chance that he might be forced to give her back, especially if the Russians decided to involve themselves, and his act posed a threat to diplomatic discussions.

He could not tell her the truth, and as long as he kept her in the dark, she would believe what Marian had told her. There was no winning this battle. At least not this way.

"You aren't a pawn to me. I would not play a game with your life," he said softly, abandoning the fight for now. "If you believe nothing else, believe that. I really do want you to be safe, Sister, and happy. It grieves me to know it doesn't look that way, but your safety is the most important thing to me in the world right now."

Lark screamed, a single short high note of frustration. "Go away! I do not want to see you anymore."

Peregrine let her be. But as he left her room, he came to a decision, and went looking for Quinn. His sister would never soften towards him if he didn't show her that he was not their mother. And there was only one voice he could think of that she might heed.

Quinn knocked on Edmunds's door, unlocking it and opening it for Perry.

Peregrine made himself look at his mother's former butler, the only one of the former house staff who had survived, as far as he knew. Edmunds waited silently, as if knowing why Perry was studying him. Judging him.

"I have asked myself a hundred times since you came back here: can I really trust anything about you, and why you're here?" Perry told him bitterly. "And I still don't know. But I think I have to take the risk on you anyway."

"You can trust me, Lord Fitzroy," Edmunds told him, his jowls trembling. "If only because my life depends on your goodwill."

"All well and good, until I have to entrust you with another's. Tell me, Edmunds. Dare I trust you with my sister's life? Because she needs a friend and confidant, and I cannot be it for her."

"You have Lady Lark?" Edmunds breathed, his face lighting with joy. "I would never do anything to harm her, my lord."

"I expect you to understand the burden of too much knowledge, Edmunds. Though I very much wish this was not the case, Lark doesn't know what Marian is. It is not safe for either of us to tell her, yet. But I suppose at least your presence might prove to her that I haven't broken quite with *all* the old household staff."

Edmunds licked his lips, nodding his understanding. "I understand. Thank you, Lord Fitzroy. Thank you for giving me this chance to reclaim my honour."

16

"Just as women's bodies are softer than men's, so their understanding is sharper."
—**Christine de Pizan**

C harity's head was throbbing by the time she returned to Atholl House. She had stayed long enough to let Ravenscroft know her part of the plan was complete, and then left without another word. Finally safe at home, Charity handed her wrap and gloves to Pritchard and asked him to bring a cup of tea to her sitting room.

"No, make that a glass of lemonade, instead, please," she corrected herself before he strode off. "I will be in the bower."

Though she had spent the afternoon outdoors, she found herself still very much in need of air. She paused on the back terrace and squeezed her eyes shut, gripping the stone ledge, not caring that it scraped her hands.

It was no use. Even without the words, she would never forget the vile words dripping from her mother's mouth. Nor could she forget what Lark had said in reply. That Vanessa Cresswell had struck the first blow, stealing Marian's suitor using the worst of manipulations.

Would Lady Cresswell ever accept any blame for the bad blood between the families? Charity was sickened by the whole thing.

No wonder her mother's voice inside her head had been fading, a more loving one taking its place and soothing the broken edges of her soul. *Do not surrender to such shadowy thoughts when the sun may yet rise, Sparkles.*

Charity sucked in a breath, then another, holding out her arms until she could feel the warm rays of sunshine soaking into her skin. Then, she massaged her temples and let the weight of the fear that had plagued her since dawn slip from her shoulders.

When she could take a full breath, she opened her eyes and retreated to the place she loved most in the gardens. A simple iron bench like the one in her childhood home, nestled between rose-covered trellises, against a backdrop of thick hedge.

That was where Selina found her.

Charity slid over on the bench and patted the space beside her. Selina needed no further encouragement. For a moment, the pair sat in silence, listening to the birds.

At last Selina broke the quiet. "I expected to find you at the front door with your hat and gloves. Instead you are hiding out here as though hoping the world might pass you by. What ails you? Is it Lark? She will forgive you both, eventually. Though not without tormenting you first, I should think."

"Believe it or not, Lark's anger had entirely slipped my mind. It is something else."

"Oh?" Selina said, but did not pry further. Selina would not, for she knew better than most the importance of keeping secrets and worries close to the vest.

Charity needed counsel. Not from Perry, though he would be a willing ear. But from a woman, someone who could make sense of what Lady Cresswell had done. Someone who would understand the pressure to marry well, at any cost.

Her dearest friend Grace had always been far too independent to give such a thing any thought. But Selina—Selina would know.

"My mother and father," she trailed off, searching for the correct word. There was no way to pretty it up. "They accosted me today, while I was with Lark."

Selina listened without a word as Charity related the incident, though her expression hinted at amusement more than sympathy. When Charity finished, she tipped her head, lips curving faintly, and gave a single nod. "I think I see. It is not gaining Lark's forgiveness that troubles you—it's facing the idea that perhaps your mother does not deserve yours."

Charity flinched. How neatly Selina's sharp wits had cut to the very bloody centre of the matter.

Charity drew a slow breath. "If I refuse to forgive her, then what happens? Am I to cut my parents off as though they are nothing? The consequences of such an action are not small." She faced a loss of social standing, not to mention the loss of her family.

Selina turned her head and watched. "May I speak plainly?'

"You have not been before now?" Charity's eyebrows shot up her forehead.

"Plainer, then," Selina said, drolly. When Charity gave leave, she went on, "You are right; there will be consequences. But somehow I think you are strong enough and clever enough to find ways to circumvent the worst of it. You have a more powerful social circle of your own, and none of it will cut you because they harbour any special love for the Cresswells."

Charity turned to the rose-covered trellis and plucked a half-withered blossom. Each soft petal faded from deep red to a cracked brown edge, dried and crumbling. This was what her mother had become through hate. Once a perfect bloom, now halfway to a dried out husk that barely hinted at its former glory.

"My thoughts are chasing their own tails. I keep thinking how failing to forgive her might keep alive the same quarrel that poisoned our families. But my mother had Perry sent to the front lines because of her hatred for Marian. She meant for him to die, for no fault of his own. How can I forgive such a thing?" Charity cried, pain scourging her. She dashed a wayward tear from her face and took some deep breaths.

Selina took the dying blossom from her hand and set it aside. Then, with great gentleness, she folded Charity's hands in hers.

"Forgiveness is no duty, my dear. It is a luxury. No one has the right to claim it from you. You alone may bestow it, or withhold it." She tightened her grip on Charity's fingers until Charity's eyes lifted to meet hers. "And if you choose never to part with it, well, no one worth a farthing will think the worse of you."

"*I* might think worse of myself. Perry is tormented by the thought that sometimes when he acts, he is no better than his mother. After today, I finally understand that fear. What if refusing to forgive her makes me… unworthy?"

"That you are asking the question makes you worthy of it, Your Grace."

Charity made a choking nose.

"If life were simple, we should all manage virtue without effort," Selina said, gaze drifting outward. "Marian Fitzroy's villainy is gaudy and obvious. Your mother, though—she chose the weapons society so cheerfully permits. By law and custom, she is blameless. So tell me, do you mean to accept that fiction?"

Before Charity could form an answer, Selina cut her off with a wave of her hand. "Forget about your parents for a moment. Think about the future. About yourself, Perry, and the riotous brood you no doubt will one day have. How will you keep them from wearing the blame for their grandmothers' sins? How do you and Perry cut yourselves loose from the bloodied chains those women forged?"

The thought of a child of hers having to endure any of the suffering she and Perry had turned her stomach. The motherly need to protect her children, though not yet born, rose up fiercely. How strange, that one could love the idea of something that did not yet exist. Perry felt the same, she was sure of it.

That was the way love from a parent should be. And not only did Marian Fitzroy threaten that, her own mother did too. If Vanessa Cresswell could not let go and move on, well, there would be a price to pay.

Suddenly, the answer to her question became clear. She alone had the power to protect herself, Perry, and the family that would come next.

Charity's spirits did not exactly lighten, but her friend's gentle words banished some of the dark clouds filling her thoughts. She blinked to clear away the moisture in her eyes, and then pulled her hands free and stood.

"The Queen must be back from Hyde Park by now. We should go."

Selina smiled. "My carriage is out front. Come along, and I will tell you what else I pried loose today. With any luck, we will leave Buckingham House with you restored to the Queen's favour this very afternoon."

They made good time to Buckingham House and arrived to find an unmarked carriage waiting near the gates. The Queen's aide-de-camp came rushing outside, his hands flapping while a footman helped Charity and Selina descend the carriage steps.

"I cannot imagine how you got here so quickly, but thank

goodness you did," he murmured, wringing his hands. "I only sent the messengers off a few minutes ago."

"We did not get any message," said Charity. "What has happened? Is something wrong with Her Majesty?"

"Other than Lady Fitzroy sitting inside her home?" he squawked, pointing at the other carriage. "She showed up here not five minutes ago and demanded to see the Queen. She said, and I quote, 'the Queen's Diamond kidnapped my daughter from Hyde Park.'"

Charity and Selina exchanged concerned glances. They had feared that word might reach the Queen, but neither expected Lady Fitzroy to come in person with a message guaranteed to catch her attention.

But they should have expected it. Lady Fitzroy's arrival had undercut any advantage. They had been counting on telling the Queen first.

"We will explain it to her," Charity said, trying to soothe the man's nerves.

"*Explain*? You mean there is truth to Lady Fitzroy's accusations? You acted without first consulting the Queen? You will be lucky if she does not consign you to the Tower!"

Charity froze, the truth of his words, and the implications that followed, punching her in the gut. The Queen hated being the last to know. "We may as well order our coffins now," she whispered, turning to Selina in search of help.

Selina's eyes flickered, her nimble mind already at work, and she brought her thumb to her lip. "Courage, Duchess. I have an idea. Besides, we did not even know that Lady Fitzroy or Lady Lark would be there. Let us hope she appreciates our reasoning for being cautious, if not for the delay."

"It is your head either way. Follow me." The aide-de-camp set a brisk pace despite his short stature, navigating the corridors with ease.

He passed by the Queen's guards without a word, leading the two women into Her Majesty's private chambers. He knocked on a closed door, and after a muffled voice granted him permission, he strode into the room and announced their arrival. "The Duchess of Atholl and the Marchioness of Normanby are here, as you requested."

Charity and Selina entered, took one look at the Queen's expression, and dropped into curtsies so deep they nearly hit the floor.

"Get up." The Queen struck the floor with her cane with such force that the crack could be felt up Charity's legs and spine. Her face blazed crimson, her lips drawn back from her teeth in a snarl that was almost animal. The lace at her bosom trembled with her heaving breath. When she spoke to them, her words whipped through the air.

"What have you done, and why am I learning about it first from Marian Fitzroy?"

Charity composed her reply, carefully avoiding the words Lady Fitzroy had leveled in her accusation. "Lord Fitzroy has evoked his right as guardian and brought Lady Lark back to his home."

"I see." Queen Charlotte smiled at her then, but it was a hideous, terrifying spectre. "And I presume he came to this decision and acted upon it immediately afterwards? For I cannot imagine you would plot such a thing and *not tell me about it in advance.*"

"Your Majesty, if I may?" Selina interposed, neatly diverting the Queen's ire. "Lord Fitzroy's sole thought was for his sister's safety, and he seized the first moment that offered itself. In truth, it was little better than an improvisation, born of our uncertainty over when mother and daughter might be parted. Only those strictly necessary were informed. Any wider confidence would have been folly."

Queen Charlotte's grip on her cane tightened. "Are you suggesting *I* might have told Lady Fitzroy?"

Selina's lips curved in the faintest smile. "No, ma'am—never that. But the walls of Buckingham House and the Palace alike are not famed for their discretion. Eyes and ears abound where one least expects them." She flicked her eyes backwards, reminding the Queen of the footmen stationed at the doors behind her.

Charlotte's eyes narrowed. Then she banged her cane again to get everyone's attention and ordered her servants from the room.

"It would not be the first time I have heard that there is a rat or two living in my palace. But it does occur to me to ask, Lady Normanby, how you know that fact as well. One wonders if you may have availed yourself of those outlets of information."

The marchioness gave the Queen a cat's paw smile. "Long have I been of the opinion that in our world, information is the only currency that matters, Your Majesty, and I should like to do business with you."

Charity sucked in a short breath. Selina had said much the same to her, right before adding a warning not to let other people pick her pockets. Now she could see how that bargain played out. Because that was what Selina was offering the Queen—a chance to bargain.

And the canny queen Charlotte knew it too. "I would like the names of the servants pedalling my secrets."

"A list I could furnish, Your Majesty." Selina inclined her head, her tone silky. "Yet I might suggest that, in my experience, the names matter less than who is purchasing their information. Such knowledge might be turned to your advantage."

The Queen's brow smoothed out. "I am open to further discussion about how one might benefit the other, Lady Normanby. Let us delve into this matter later—after we have dealt with the problem you have created for me."

Selina looked surprisingly unruffled by her statement. Charity wondered what the marchioness was thinking. She held her tongue as the two of them sat in the indicated pair of chairs near the Queen.

"Tell me, what do you make of Lady Fitzroy's choice to parade herself here?" Charlotte speared them each with a glance. "She is far too shrewd not to grasp that she will find no champion in me. Which leaves the question of what mischief does she hope to stir by placing herself so boldly in my sight?"

"You mean, beyond the discord she intended to create?" were Selina's blithe words.

"She was not here to gain an ally, Your Majesty, but to strip us of one. You," Charity added. "She gambled that you did not know about Perry's intentions. Likely, she was hoping to make you angry enough with us that you would try to force us to give Lady Lark back."

And judging by the Queen's closed expression, had come close to succeeding. Recognition of that unspoken fact flitted across Charlotte's face.

Selina made a subtle gesture to Charity, and Charity held her tongue. "Time was of the essence, and it would have tipped our hand, ma'am, making the task far more difficult. Do you recall when we talked about Lark's marital prospects, back when the sovereigns arrived? Last night, the duchess came up with a rather disturbing theory about Lady Fitzroy's plans. It had the unfortunate reek of probability."

This time, the Queen's expression invited Charity to explain herself, and grateful for Selina's support, she did—everything they supposed about Lady Fitzroy, the interference with negotiations with the Crown, and a chance to make Lark a princess.

Charlotte's brows drew lower. "The audacity of that witch. Now I am doubly vexed that I did not know of your little ploy so I could not find a seat to watch the expression on Marian Fitzroy's face when she realised what you had done."

"For what it is worth, ma'am, we were also denied the spectacle. Perhaps we shall get Lord Fitzroy to recount the moment for all of us. All he told me before I hurried to get here was that the manoeuvre drew blood," Selina murmured, her drawl wandering towards that of gossiping confidence. "Is it not the most fitting end to strike back at Marian Fitzroy with her favourite weapon? Kidnapping?"

"Fine. Forgiveness for this stunt granted, if for no other reason than I refuse to hand that woman a victory." Charlotte pegged them both with a stern look. "Do *not* keep testing my patience. Is that understood?"

Charity and Selina both bobbed their heads, and Charity marvelled at Selina's deftness. Lady Normanby had both handled the Queen so adroitly she defused their sovereign's anger, and she had also managed to give Charity the credit needed to restore herself to the Queen's good graces.

"We may have an opportunity now. Lady Fitzroy will need Lady Lark returned. If I fail to assist her, what is her next move?" Charlotte asked.

"Would the Russians come to her aid?" Charity asked. She glanced at Selina. "This is more your area of expertise."

"I doubt it. The footing would be tricky," Selina murmured, rubbing her lower lip again. "It will be a bluffing tactic at best. They will not want to disrupt talks over an English girl, but they might use the opportunity to cry insult for some other concessions. It is far more likely that Lady Fitzroy will take Lark by force or intimidate Peregrine into giving her up.

"But putting Lady Lark aside," Selina continued, "I do have one other concerning piece of information. Before I left for Hyde Park, one of my gossips came to find me. It seems that a certain Prince Nicholas paid a visit to Rundell, Bridge & Rundell. He specifically asked for something that would appeal to English tastes, Your Majesty."

"The Russian prince visited the Royal Jewellers? Why would —" the Queen halted abruptly. "*No.* Surely not. You cannot possibly think he is attempting to court Princess Charlotte now that the negotiations with William are finished. Even his own people would be against it."

"Would Lady Fitzroy have a hand in that? Does she think she could somehow broker such a match?" Charity asked, aghast.

"Unlikely. But she certainly might whisper such nonsense in the Grand Duchess's ear," Charlotte snarled. "The Grand Duchess should know better. Marriage is impossible. Prinny and I will not allow the princess to convert, and neither will the Russians allow Nicholas to abandon his church."

Selina continued to look thoughtful. "But... perhaps marriage is not the prize at all. Let the princess entangle herself with some wholly unsuitable fancy, and suddenly she is loath to be bartered elsewhere again. England weakened, alliances delayed, two young hearts steered into folly for the sake of disorder? Now *that* is a game I can believe of those two."

Charity would believe that of Lady Fitzroy, but to do something so mean-spirited to the princess sounded unlike the Grand Duchess. They seemed to have something of a genuine fondness for one another. Perhaps such a match wasn't quite as impossible or as unsuitable as the Queen thought—at least not if the Grand Duchess was willing to throw her support behind it.

Or perhaps the clever Russian woman was more devious than she thought.

"The Grand Duchess was looking for Princess Charlotte today at Hyde Park. She said Nicholas was keen to speak with the princess," Charity said reluctantly.

The Queen pointed a ringed finger toward Charity. "See that my granddaughter remembers her duty. She will listen to you, out of all of us. If necessary, pay a visit to the Grand Duchess as well. I will not tolerate even a whiff of scandal between the English and Russian royal heirs."

Charity rose and then sunk into a curtsy, not rising until the Queen allowed her to do so.

"I must still speak with Lady Fitzroy, but I wish the two of you to listen in on the conversation." Queen Charlotte growled, pointing at the next room. "Unseen."

Charity went through the connecting doorway of the dimly lit room first, Selina right behind. Selina pulled the door shut, but caught the handle before it could latch, leaving a narrow slit through which they could see into the Queen's sitting room.

Charity took a quick glance around behind her, ensuring they were alone, and then lifted her skirts out of the way so she could lower down to the ground. Selina leaned over her, and both women peeked through the gap.

The Queen lifted a bell from a side table and rang it. A footman appeared almost at once.

"Bring Lady Fitzroy to me," she commanded.

A few minutes later, Marian entered, her curtsy carefully proper.

"I am very surprised by your accusations, Lady Fitzroy," the Queen said at once.

"Your Majesty, I would not trouble you were it not so grave. Yet today, before all London, my daughter was taken from me. She was spirited away as though we were in some lawless quarter, and not under the Crown's own eye. I cannot think it augurs well for your reign if such affronts may be carried out openly," Marian answered smoothly.

The Queen's cane rapped once against the floor. "The Crown is not to be dragged into every domestic squabble. Whatever befell your daughter is a matter between yourself and your kin. It touches neither my reign nor my honour."

Lady Fitzroy's smile was thin. "Ordinarily I would agree, Your Majesty. Yet it ceases to be a private quarrel when the hand that seized my daughter belonged to your Diamond. When a lady-in-waiting to the Crown aids in abducting a child of the nobility, it *cannot* be called a family matter. It is a stain upon your household."

"You speak boldly, Lady Fitzroy. But tell me, how is it that you know the name of any lady said to be involved? Because I have it on good authority that Lady Lark is in the hands of her legal guardian. Her brother—not the Duchess of Atholl."

Lady Fitzroy's eyes flickered slightly as she considered the Queen's awareness of the situation. "When I made inquiries, several people informed me that the last person they saw my daughter with was the duchess."

Charity took a slow breath.

"Were you there yourself, to see her kidnap Lady Lark with your own eyes? Or do you set the weight upon the whispers of the crowd? Because being seen *talking* to your daughter, Lady Fitzroy, is not the same as being complicit."

Lady Fitzroy knew that this course was futile. Charity watched as the woman trimmed her proverbial sails to catch a different wind. "I had hoped that if I sought you out, Your Majesty, you would see the sense in helping restore my daughter to me instead of waiting for a scandal to erupt unchecked. Because to be taken by force, from an event attended by the Allied Sovereigns—well, I am sure the Russian cohort will take notice. The Tsar may even ask questions."

The Queen's silence was deliberate, impenetrable.

Lady Fitzroy's smile was brittle, her eyes hard. "Would it not be simpler for all concerned," she pressed, "to avoid such questions altogether? Perry has had his little jest. If he returns Lark to me, I am prepared to forget this ever occurred."

"No." The Queen's single word cracked. "English law is quite clear. I see no reason why I, Prinny, or even the Tsar of Russia himself should presume to meddle."

Marian met Queen Charlotte's gaze directly. "The Russians will meddle, because they value us, Your Majesty. You would risk their ire over the interpretation of a law?"

"Lady Fitzroy, let me be plain. This is *my* nation. My laws. My people. If you expect me to bow before a foreign ruler, you will wait past your dying breath. I do not yield."

And then—Marian's mask slipped.

The polite, subservient lady vanished. Behind the lids of her eyes peered the monster.

"When one lacks the power to maintain their hold, they yield eventually," she whispered. "Even queens."

The Queen held her silence, the weight of it more crushing than any retort.

Marian's lips twisted into a grotesque parody of a smile. Then without a by your leave, she turned, and swept from the room, leaving the air thick with menace.

17

"All the darkness in the world cannot extinguish the light of a single candle."
— St Francis Of Assisi

Trouble came addressed, officially, to Peregrine late that evening, as the gloaming began to turn into full dark.

He had taken refuge in his study with a glass of brandy, when Quinn appeared with a sealed packet balanced on a silver salver. Peregrine rose and took the folded letter from Quinn. The red wax bore the heavy impression of the royal arms in it, and Perry cracked it open, reading the two lines quickly.

Earl Fitzroy is required to attend upon His Royal Highness the Prince Regent at Carlton House, at noon tomorrow, in the matter of representations made by the Russian Minister. — By command of Viscount Sidmouth.

After Charity's letter to him earlier about his mother's visit to the Queen, this wasn't too much of a surprise, but it was still unwelcome. Folding the page again, Perry let it fall to the desk, meeting Quinn's inquiring gaze.

"The messenger-at-arms is waiting in the front hall for your reply, my lord," his butler said without fuss. Quinn may as well have been describing the weather.

Perry gave him a slight smile and walked down the stairs to where the man waited, dressed in the dark blues of his government uniform. His bicorne was tucked beneath his arm, and he stood rigidly upright, waiting expectantly.

"Tell Lord Sidmouth I shall attend at the appointed hour," Peregrine informed him, and the man nodded, issuing a sharp military bow to Perry before placing his hat back on his head.

"Were you expecting this outcome?" Quinn asked him after closing the door, his curiosity apparently getting the best of him. Or perhaps he was only asking so that he could begin forming a strategy to deal with this predicament.

"I was, but not nearly this soon," Perry admitted, rubbing his hand absently over the scar tissue on his side. The wound was still itching, only just finally closed over. "And certainly not with this level of formality."

They had presumed a day or two would pass before a formal complaint might be lodged, but no moss was growing on Marian's stone.

"Shall I tell Hodges you will need the carriage tomorrow?"

Peregrine considered the options. "No. I think perhaps I will go alone on horseback. I can answer this one for myself, and tomorrow will be about maintaining the posture of someone confidently within his rights."

His thoughts wandered towards Charity, who had stayed in London after she and Selina met with the Queen. Her note ended with *I miss you.*

He missed her too, desperately. Perry sensed it was weighing in the back of her mind that today would have been the day they should have been getting married. What could one write about that in a letter?

The words I write can't seem to say what I want them to. But I will come find you tomorrow, he wrote back.

He would find some excuse to be near her after dealing with Sidmouth.

Stabling his horse at Carlton House the next day, he was escorted quickly to the audience chamber. There, he was greeted by the stony expressions of the Regent, Sidmouth, Castlereagh, Count von Lieven, and another official-looking Russian, plus a smattering of secretaries of both countries.

"Your Royal Highness," Lieven lifted his voice slightly, "may I introduce Pyotr Andreyevich Malenkov, Attaché of the Imperial Russian Mission? It is by his hand that a representation has been placed before us on behalf of Lady Fitzroy, who has for some time enjoyed the protection and hospitality of this embassy. The indignity she claims to have suffered touches not only her person but the honour of the mission itself, and Pyotr Andreyevich is therefore charged to speak in the matter."

Perry examined Malenkov. The Russian had the polish of a courtier, but not the air of one born to command. He was in his early thirties, smooth-faced, and his uniform was impeccably cut. Though he carried himself with the deference of a man used to opening doors for others, there was something watchful and tense about him.

Fully in his role as Russian diplomat, Lieven gave Peregrine a hard, meaningful look before bowing slightly to the Regent. "Your Royal Highness, it is my unhappy duty to convey a most serious concern. Lady Lark Fitzroy, who has for some time moved within the suite of His Imperial Majesty's household, was seized in a most public manner by Lord Fitzroy."

Lieven paused for effect. "Whatever claims of guardianship he may advance, the affront is plain. A British nobleman has torn

Lark Fitzroy, a young lady who had been received by the Russian court, from our protection at an occasion convened in peace."

"With Your Royal Highness's leave," Malenkov nodded, looking down his nose at Perry, "Lady Fitzroy's grievance is an injury to the dignity of Russia's mission. The lady's abduction, without recourse to His Majesty's ministers, cannot but be viewed as a slight to the Imperial household itself."

Calmly following protocol, Perry remained silent, observing the men. Prinny looked flushed. With wine or high emotion, it wasn't clear which. But all of the British men were grim.

Lord Castlereagh, the Foreign Minister, looked especially harassed. Clearly, he was angry at Peregrine for causing this trouble right now, catching him between the hammer and anvil when he had other things worrying his mind. "Your Royal Highness, Count von Lieven, the difficulty is this… Lady Lark Fitzroy is an English subject. However ill-judged the scene, Lord Fitzroy is her legal guardian within English law."

"Then the insult to Russia is allowed to stand?" Lieven asked, his voice tight.

"No. No," Castlereagh repeated quickly and firmly. "The complaint remains before us. When His Imperial Majesty departs, Lady Lark's wishes shall be ascertained. If she elects to remain under Russian protection and return with you, we will not oppose it."

"Malenkov," the Prince Regent declared, with a spread of jeweled fingers, "let us not allow a trifling domestic matter to cast a shadow upon the harmony of sovereigns. Let the young lady remain with her brother—just for the moment. She's in no danger with him, after all. Everything else shall be examined with the utmost gravity before His Imperial Majesty and his Court take their leave of us."

Von Lieven was masking his expressions stiffly, but he bowed fluidly. "As Your Royal Highness commands." He glanced over his shoulder at Peregrine again. "Russia places its confidence in your word, and awaits what you have promised."

"Your Royal Highness is most gracious." Malenkov's tone, as he stood a half step behind Count Lieven, clearly implied the opposite. "I shall convey to Lady Fitzroy that her complaint has been received. Hopefully, with due seriousness."

Von Lieven bowed again, withdrawing with Pyotr Andreyevich and their clerks.

Castlereagh turned to Peregrine. "What in the nine circles of *hell* were you thinking?" he hissed, his voice low enough that it wouldn't carry to the others. "Do we not have enough problems without embroiling two courts in a spat over your *sister*?"

"I have my reasons," Perry retorted loudly, flickering his eyes over the British secretaries and leveling a look at the Regent himself. "And as you pointed out, I was within my lawful rights."

"You may go. We will confer further in private." Prinny waved his hand carelessly at the secretaries along the wall, and they filed out.

"By all means, enlighten me on those reasons, Fitzroy. Especially since I am the person who has to look like a fool in front of the Russians," Castlereagh barked.

Sidmouth held up a hand in front of the angry Foreign Minister, cutting him off. "She is very likely a pawn in whatever games her traitorous mother is up to. This cuts her off at the pass, if so. Fitzroy did not act without warning, Castlereagh. I had wind of his intent—but only barely. I didn't even have a chance to warn you."

Castlereagh raked a hand through his hair, annoyed. Then he made his excuses to the Regent and left abruptly.

To Perry, the Home Secretary gave an unhappy look. "Neither I nor Lord Castlereagh will be able to shield you from further storms. If you would not see your sister carried back to St Petersburg, you had best convince her to stay or make your case before they depart. You have only a week, Fitzroy, maybe less. *Don't dawdle.* Do you understand me?"

Sidmouth didn't mean that there was only one week to sort the situation with his sister. He expected Lady Fitzroy to be taken in hand by then, too. Perry already knew that time was running out. He didn't believe—not for a single second—that Lark's marital prospects were the crowning achievement of his mother's scheme.

Perry's reply was clipped. "Perfectly, Lord Sidmouth."

Perry briefly considered looking for Ravenscroft. The magpie was likely a guest of the Regent here someplace, but there was nothing to tell Ravenscroft that the man wouldn't have already heard.

Besides, his thoughts had moved on to St James's. To his wife. He left Carlton House with long strides, eager to get into the saddle and be out of there. The forecourt was swarming with carriages and idling footmen, but a groom stepped forward at once.

"We had to move your lordship's horse to a quieter part of the yard. The noise was making him skittish," the groom told him, pointing with his arm to the side.

Perry gave a nod and followed the groom. But as the man led him past the open stable doors and through a narrow arch, they ran into another groom in the passageway, just before it opened into a small yard.

"I'll see to his lordship. You get back out front," the second groom offered.

There was the slightest hesitation, but the first groom gave a nod of understanding, dipping his head in farewell to Perry without meeting his eyes. Perry quickly dismissed the incident from his mind as they finished their circle to the back of the stables.

The lane was quiet. The noise from the activity out front was dulled by the narrow passage, and behind the stables, the straw scattered underfoot further hushed sound. As promised, his horse stood alone. The groom was moving towards the mounting block tucked against the wall.

"I do not need the assistance of the block; just hold him," Perry suggested.

"Aye, m'lord. I'll hold him steady." The man steadied the bridle and placed a hand to the stirrup, holding it.

The moment Perry lifted his leg to set his boot, the nagging hint of concern worrying in the back of his head exploded into a full-fledged apprehension. It slowed him, just enough.

The groom jerked his horse's bridle suddenly, and the horse skittered away from both of them. But because he hadn't yet set his foot, he avoided being trapped in the stirrup and being dragged. Bad enough, though, that he was unbalanced because he had been leaning on the horse. Perry threw out his arms, trying to avoid falling.

The man posing as a groom grabbed Perry's left arm, pulling Perry in towards him. Instinct had Perry shove himself forward with both feet on the ground, shoving himself away and ripping his left sleeve in the process of jerking his arm out of the man's grasp.

For that reason alone, he avoided the knife plunging toward his kidney. The point of the blade snagged only his coat instead of flesh.

Stumbling forward, Perry twisted. He was unarmed—disadvantaged. All he had on his side was momentum. So before this assassin could ready another attack, Perry threw himself into the man, slamming his shoulder into the man's chest hard enough that they staggered together into the shadowed wall of the stable.

The timbers cracked, and the assassin's head hit the stable wall, but not hard enough. He held onto both blade and wits, recovering with terrifying speed and grabbing Perry by the lapel of his jacket, trying to rake the knife across his midriff instead.

Again, Perry barely avoided the blade by throwing himself away from his attacker. It whispered along his waistcoat, cutting a rent in one side and barely kissing skin. The assassin snarled epithets, dragging Peregrine in once more.

"Hold still, m'lord," the killer hissed at him, smashing Peregrine in the side of the head with the butt of the knife.

Dark lights burst in Perry's vision, and he reeled, disoriented.

The groom's grin showed broken teeth, and he seized a fistful of Peregrine's cravat, dragging his head back for the killing strike. Perry drove forward with his elbow blindly, connecting with the man's ribs. They both crashed into the wall again, and the assassin had to turn to lift his knife arm.

Perry caught the man's wrist as he did so, preventing him from being able to bring the knife down. Both men were straining. Peregrine could feel the inside of his gloves slick with sweat, his arm trembling with the strain of keeping the point hovering a hand's breadth from his throat.

And then—the sharp crack of boot heels on stone. The thug's eyes flickered towards the passageway, and Peregrine heaved with all his strength, forcing the man's knifehand back against the stable wall and away from his neck.

A heavy fist swung between them, clouting the groom in the temple. He staggered, dropping to one knee, and released, Perry fell backwards, catching himself after a few steps. The newcomer loomed above the man pretending to be a groom. Without hesitation, his unexpected ally swung again, this time laying out the assassin on the stone.

The man's body twitched once before going still on the stable floor. Probably dead.

Breath ragged, Perry checked himself, finding several gashes in his clothing, but nothing worse than scratches lay beneath. The newcomer waited a few steps away for Peregrine to right himself, not coming closer.

"Yer in trouble, Lord Fitzroy," the man told him, his accent thick. "You an' yers. Red Hand sent me to let ye know."

"I figured that part out," Peregrine muttered, looking down at the body. "But your appearance was timely nonetheless."

The man grunted. "Last night marked an early grave fer Nibs."

It took a few seconds for Peregrine to recall why that name sounded familiar. "That was the record man who held the Duchess Atholl's bounty?"

He gave a nod. "Red reckons 'twas one o' yer ma's. Nibs was found with 'Thief' carved in his gut, an' the whole underbelly's up in arms. She's layin' waste to folk now, Fitzroy. Six new names marked last night. Bounties set on you, the duchess, Lady Normanby, Lord Ravenscroft, Sir Nathaniel, an' some bloke called Antoine. Red says if yer smart, you'd leave London today."

Peregrine let out a short puff of consternation. Thorne and Antoine too? And despite all of the deaths and searching in the last week, his mother still retained enough influence in London's underworld to access hired killers.

"Thank you," Peregrine told him sincerely. "I have to go. But I owe you—you and Red Hand both. And I won't forget my debts."

"Red counts on it, m'lord," the man said with a crooked grin.

So urgent was Perry to get back to Carlton House, he almost forgot his horse, who had backed itself as far away from the fight as possible. Clucking at the beast, Perry caught the reins and swung into the saddle, riding the short bit back to the front yard so he could give the mount to another groom.

"Hold him here," he said shortly to the man who took his horse. "Nowhere else. Where is the groom who was helping me earlier?"

"Digby, m'lord? He went down to the farrier's."

Perry filed that name away in his thoughts, marching back to the front door. The porter stared at Peregrine. Or rather, he stared at his clothing. One sleeve half ripped, a gash in his waistcoat. The porter probably thought he was lunatic.

"If you are done having a long look," said Perry dryly, "I need a private word with Lord Ravenscroft. *Now.*"

He was ushered quickly into a side room, and his request must have been sent at a run. Lord Ravenscroft trotted into the front hallway only a few minutes later, concern already writ across his face, and with someone else's coat in his hands.

"Ah. So things have taken a turn for the worse," he said in a hushed whisper, staring at Peregrine's clothing. Then he turned to the footman. "Mind your business! Preferably outside of the door," Ravenscroft barked at the footman who was openly staring at the two of them.

"For the worse, do you think? An assassin accosted me behind the Carlton House stables—his body is still there, by the by—and paid off one of Prinny's own groomsmen to bring me there. A man by the name of Digby, who I expect will never return from his 'errand' to the farrier's."

The magpie began to play valet, helping Peregrine out of his torn coat. "We can go see Prinny—"

"No. There is no time to spare for him. I have just learned that my mother has put out contracts on all of our lives. *All* of them." Perry leaned in until he was almost nose to nose with the dandy. "Antoine is on the list too."

Ravenscroft turned as white as a shroud, but to his credit, he gritted his teeth in determination. "What do you need me to do, Fitzroy?"

"I need you to play messenger. Warn Selina to leave London. Warn Thorne too; he is still at my estate. And… then perhaps it's time for you and your valet to find a safer harbour too, Maggie."

The lord took several deep breaths, staring Peregrine in the face. "You would want us to leave you to have to face your mother alone?"

"My mother will hurt Antoine to punish you. And she will most definitely harm you to hurt me." Peregrine laid his hand on Ravenscroft's arm.

"I may not be much of a fighter, but I shall not play the role of a coward, Canary. When I delivered the letter, I already knew that this was going to be the outcome. Don't ask me to turn tail and run now that the consequences of the actions I expected are here. I cannot leave, but perhaps Antoine—" Ravenscroft bit his thumb, thinking quickly.

"Whatever you decide to do, do it quickly, but know that I will not be disappointed if you decide to protect yourselves. Tell Prinny what has happened, and have someone deal with the body. I have to find Charity."

"The Queen and Princess are at St James's. You cannot go like that—" Ravenscroft ran his fingers down the front of Peregrine's waistcoat, bending to peer at the tear. "Good God, Fitzroy. You nearly got yourself gutted again!"

"He missed, Maggie."

Ravenscroft snarled, shaking him. "Not entirely, Lord Catastrophe. Fortunately, it's little more than a scratch, but for God's sake. You've somehow made us care about what side of the dirt you're laying on. So have the courtesy to keep your guts where they belong, will you?"

He thrust Perry into the spare coat, straightening his disordered cravat. "It is a bit large, but it will have to do."

It would. Perry spun on his heel the moment Ravenscroft's hands pulled away from him, hurrying back out the door and leaping on his horse, still being held in the front.

~

A footman attempted a hasty announcement, but Peregrine was already striding past him into the Queen's withdrawing room. Charity was indeed there, along with Queen Charlotte and the young princess. All three women turned to stare at him, the Queen's chin lifting as her expression sharpened.

"This chamber, Lord Fitzroy, is not White's. Explain yourself!" she blazoned.

"Perry? What happened?" Charity added, her eyes seeking his.

Peregrine held her gaze for a fraught moment, and then turned to the Queen.

Her lips turned downward. "Charlotte Augusta," the Queen instructed her granddaughter, "you may retire. All of you," she added, waving at the other ladies in waiting.

There was a silence as the others left, and in the rustle of their departure, Perry turned to Charity, taking her hands. Charity was looking at the ill-fitting coat that was clearly not his own, and she swallowed, licking her lips. "Were you hurt?" she whispered.

"Bruises. Not enough to stop me," he told her softly, squeezing her hands. "But Charity—it's time for you to leave. Take Thorne and Lark, and ride out for Northumberland. *Please*."

Her mouth parted, eyes glistening. "Are you mad? No. Absolutely not."

The Queen sharply cleared her throat, once the door shut behind the departing women and servants. "Do share with everyone, Lord Fitzroy."

"My mother is striking back with a vengeance, Your Majesty," he replied tersely. He told them both about the summons to Carlton House to meet with von Lieven and Pyotr Andreyevich Malenkov in a full diplomatic meeting. He ended with the news from Red Hand's messenger. "If she was able to have someone infiltrate the stableyard at Carlton House, the palace grounds are not necessarily safe."

The Queen looked as discomfited as he had ever seen her.

"Your Majesty," he continued. "I would like to send everyone on my mother's list away that we can. At the very least, my sister, the duchess, and Lady Normanby should depart London."

"No," repeated Charity, in a louder voice, calmly folding her arms over her stomach. "You cannot send me away, Perry. I will not leave; none of us will."

Perry turned to her, surprised by the amount of pain a man could feel even though he hadn't been dealt a physical wound.

He didn't want to say the words he had hurled at her, the last time he was so afraid about bringing the violence in his life to hers. But they were true. *Real.* They lay like stones in his thoughts. Poison on his lips. Broken glass in his chest, tearing his heart into pieces.

If she could not find a way to strike at Perry, Marian Fitzroy would attack the people that he had somehow unexpectedly grown attached to. Everyone who cared for him. He would grieve any of them, but one of those names had the power to utterly destroy him.

Peregrine sank to one knee, his knees too unsteady, and he took her hands, pressing them to the sides of his face, letting his lashes fall closed. "When I woke up in Atholl house, Sparkles, I believed beyond the shadow of a doubt that I was treading the path that would lead to my destiny. I am here because I must put a stop to my mother's evil. And I suspected it might come at a price."

He never imagined a cost that could be so high.

"You are the candle that was given to me to light up the darkest time in my life. Don't ask me to let you stay and face such danger." Perry finally looked up, his eyes stinging as he noticed the tears coursing down her cheeks. "I love you. *Please.*"

Smiling through the tears, she stooped down to drop a

lingering kiss on his brow. It was a benediction, of sorts. It felt sacred, like the whispered promise of redemption.

"And I love you. Don't you see? This move is meant to weaken you. Isolate you. She needs to divide our loyalties, because she will never have the strength that comes from any kind of love." She stroked his cheekbones with her thumbs. "Have courage. Have faith in all of us. Don't ask *me* to let you walk alone into the dark."

18

"Doubt thou the stars are fire; Doubt that the sun doth move;
Doubt truth to be a liar; But never doubt I love."
—William Shakespeare

Charity straightened, still holding Perry's head in her hands, only then remembering abruptly that they had an audience. The Queen was sitting stock-still and silent, watching them. The woman who so seldom showed any expressions besides boredom and annoyance wore a distant expression that hinted at the grief she carried.

It was as though she was remembering she, too, had once experienced love like this, before the King had gone mad and been locked away from the world.

Charity had never known this version of the Queen, and would not even have guessed that such softness existed within the woman. She wanted to turn her head away, to grant the woman privacy, but something compelled her to straighten, take Perry's hand in hers and face forward. To use this rare chance to forge an emotional connection that transcended rank and status.

After a moment, the Queen's eyes focused, meeting Charity's gaze. But she left her guard down, allowing the younger woman to see past the stony facade she wore so well, and blinked to clear her eyes. In a voice that bore a trace of hoarseness, she declared, "You shall wed. Today. I shall not stand in your way any longer."

"Ma'am?" Charity gasped, unable to believe her ears.

"Real love is not ribbons and sonnets, nor the foolish flutter of youth, Duchess. It is duty carried willingly, sorrow borne together, and the refusal to abandon one another when all reason counsels otherwise." Charlotte's eyes settled on Peregrine, telling him without words that this message was for him too. "Guard what you have, both of you, for such a thing is beautiful precisely because of the fact it is so difficult to find."

She paused, swallowing once. And then she let her expression close, becoming the Queen once more. "To go forward against Lady Fitzroy, you should armour yourselves with every method of protection. Arranging extra guards for your estate is only a temporary solution. Stronger is a legal binding. You must consolidate your households in the eyes of the law, so the duchess may intercede in the matters concerning Lady Lark, and afford her protection from the estate, should the worst happen, Lord Fitzroy. And I will smooth the way regarding the matter of guardianship of young Duke of Atholl."

Charity opened her mouth to speak, but Queen Charlotte held up her hand.

"The Archbishop can conduct the ceremony here in the chapel. It is the least I can do." The Queen looked at Charity. "I told myself it was your insolence I rebuked. But it was your honesty. You were right about Prince William. Love and duty—whether it is to a husband or a people—do not often permit the easier road."

"Your Majesty—" Peregrine began, but again, Queen Charlotte cut him off by rising from her chair abruptly.

"Time is something we do not have in abundance. Invite whom you wish; a pair of footmen will be at your disposal. You may remain here until the Archbishop arrives." With that, she gathered her skirts and swept quickly from the room.

As soon as the door shut behind the Queen, Charity threw herself into Perry's arms. He caught her and held her hard, as though he felt like he might lose her and never intended to let her go again. Tears blurred her sight, spilling hot and unchecked onto his shoulder. But they were tears of happiness—of wonder that the impossible had been granted.

"Charity," he murmured, her name breaking against her hair, reverent and unsteady.

Her sniffles must have startled him, for he pulled back just enough to see her face. Concern furrowed his brow until he saw the smile trembling on her lips. With infinite gentleness, he brushed away her tears, his thumb tracing her cheek as though to memorise her. Then he bent to her, pressing a kiss to one eyelid and then the other, before trailing down her cheeks, drying her tears with the warmth of his mouth.

When at last his lips found hers, it was no conquest. It was surrender. A kiss of devotion, of relief, of a love that had so far survived every trial set against it.

Charity drew him closer still, threading her fingers into his hair as if to anchor him, as if to prove he was real and hers at last. A laugh broke through her tears, soft and incredulous, brushing against his lips. "We are to be married," she whispered. "Finally."

He rested his brow on hers, and made a vow of his own, his tone lightly ironic. "We will survive this. We must because we already witnessed a miracle."

That the Queen had apologised, in a fashion, for halting their hasty wedding in retaliation against Charity, he meant. She muffled a laugh against his shoulder.

They stood in that fragile, perfect hush, the world outside forgotten, the Queen's drawing room transformed into the centre of their universe. For that moment, there was no crown, no duty, no danger—only two people who had found love despite all the obstacles put in their way.

A polite knock rattled the door, breaking the spell. Charity loosened her hold and stepped back, already missing his touch. But she could not remain there forever in his embrace. They had things to do, and quickly.

Perry smoothed a wayward curl from her face and then called for the footman to enter.

"Her Majesty asked me to bring you paper and ink," he said, motioning for another footman to follow, carrying in a small travel desk.

Charity hurried over to the desk, already mentally composing the notes. "We must send for Selina and Ravenscroft. Would it be foolish to ask Sir Nathaniel to come into town?"

"With extra guards there, Lark should be safe enough. I would invite her to come, but..." Peregrine hesitated, and Charity understood. He thought Lark would refuse. "The magpie will still be in town, but I sent him to tell Selina to depart London for her safety."

Charity did not roll her eyes, though it was close. "Selina will no more leave London than I will, Perry. Write an invitation to Lord Ravenscroft. I will take care of the marchioness and Sir Nathaniel."

Perry took the quill and scrap of paper she offered, but paused before moving away. "What of your parents, Charity? Do you wish to include them?"

His question gave her pause, for until he spoke, she had not thought of them at all. How strange was it, that on this happiest day of her life, she no longer had any desire to share it with them?

This is about your future, logic reminded her. *There is no place here for those still mired in the past.*

"I wish only to be with those who love us both," she answered. "Now, write quickly, for we do not know how soon the Archbishop will arrive."

~

As the bells tolled the evening hour, Charity found herself standing at the altar of the Chapel Royal at St James's Palace. The room glowed with candlelight, each flame reflected in polished wood and gilt. Yet to Charity, the space felt hushed, as if all there held their breath while awaiting the start of the ceremony.

Perry's hand was warm in hers, a pillar at her side. Unwavering, wholly committed, his firm grip anchored her in the moment.

The Archbishop's voice rolled through the chamber, solemn and resonant. "Dearly beloved, we are gathered together here..."

Charity's heart surged at those words. It was not a gathering of hundreds, nor even of the dozens who had attended her first farce of a wedding.

Only five souls bore testament. Lord Ravenscroft, Selina, and Sir Nathaniel had all come at their behest. Queen Charlotte and the Prince Regent were also there, lending their gravitas to the occasion. No one would ever be able to question the validity of their vows, not with the royals themselves as witnesses.

It was enough. More than enough to ensure no one would ever tear them apart.

Each word the Archbishop spoke drew Charity and Perry closer together, ever nearer the future they had once believed to be an impossibility. Exaltation filled Charity's body, blocking out the fears of the past and the threat still looming on the horizon, until nothing was left but her and Perry.

"I require and charge you both, as ye will answer at the dreadful day of judgement, when the secrets of all hearts shall be disclosed, that if either of you know any impediment, why ye may not be lawfully joined together in matrimony, ye do now confess it…"

The pause rang loud in her ears. For an instant she imagined the shadows rising, the spectre of a woman's voice crying out against them. Her breath caught, but Perry's thumb brushed the back of her hand. None would stand in their way.

When the Archbishop moved on to their vows, Perry did not hesitate to give his answer. He spoke clearly, as if willing even fate itself to accept it had been defeated.

His lips curled in a smile as he stared deep into her eyes, exposed and unguarded. "I will."

Charity did not move her gaze from Perry as the Archbishop posed the question to her.

"And wilt thou have this man to thy wedded husband…?"

Now was the time to embrace the future she craved. "I will," she promised, imbuing the words with all the love she had.

Their commitments followed, familiar phrases unfolding like music. "…for better, for worse, for richer, for poorer, in sickness and in health…"

Each promise bound them more tightly together, yet it was Perry's voice—deep, steady, reverent—that lifted them beyond ritual. She heard the man beneath the words. Steadfast and now entirely hers. He stood taller, his eyes clear and sparkling, as though the wounds of his body and spirit had all been healed.

When it was her turn, Charity softened her gaze, letting both her expression and her words convey her love. They had already seen the worst and had come through to where they now stood. When she reached the end of her vows, she strengthened her voice and squeezed Perry's hands. "From this day forward, I promise to love, cherish, and obey, till death us do part."

At the Archbishop's behest, Peregrine pulled a small velvet bag from his jacket pocket, untying it to spill a gold band into his palm. The ring was simple, but it clearly wasn't new. Its surface was worn with age. There was a story to this ring, but Charity didn't know what it was other than that Perry must have asked Thorne to bring it over from the estate.

The golden surface glinted as he slid it onto her finger. "With this ring I thee wed, with my body I thee worship, and with all my worldly goods I thee endow." His voice caught faintly on worship, and Charity's breath hitched, her cheeks warming.

The Archbishop carried on, lifting his hands as his words echoed through the chapel. "Those whom God hath joined together let no man put asunder."

A stillness followed, a moment suspended in time. Charity felt Perry's heated gaze on her and saw the wonder shining there. This moment was real. She was real. This was not some dream from which he would awake.

Charity turned her gaze up to Perry, and she saw not only the man she loved but the life they would forge together—hard won, but theirs. Perry's arm circled her, drawing her close. For one shining moment, the Chapel Royal was no royal sanctum but a sacred space where only two hearts existed.

When at last they turned to face their witnesses, the Queen and Prinny inclined their heads in silent approval. Ravenscroft muttered something suspiciously like "about time." Selina's gaze softened, just for an instant, while Thorne's friendly gaze lingered on them both.

But all of it faded. The candlelight, the chapel, even the presence of sovereign and friends. For Charity, there was only Perry at her side, solid and sure.

Husband and wife, forevermore.

They celebrated the occasion all together, enjoying fine champagne from the royal cellars. A footman worked the cork with a practised twist until it gave a sharp pop. Charity startled at the sound, then laughed softly, pressing her hand against Perry's arm as the golden liquid fizzed into shallow crystal glasses.

Glasses were distributed, and it was Prinny who raised his first. "I cannot imagine why any man would willingly race into matrimony," he declared with mock solemnity, his eyes glittering. "Most of my family have spent their lives avoiding it, and those of us who have succumbed—" he gave a theatrical shudder— "have regretted it ever since. Yet, since you two seem determined to defy my understanding, I am glad enough to have been here to see it done. To the bride and groom."

Ravenscroft gave a dry bark of laughter and raised his glass after him. "Well said. And Fitzroy, your labours to prove your worth have just begun. Her Grace deserves perfection. You, alas, are merely… you. May she never grow tired of whipping you into a finer form."

Peregrine chuckled, not offended.

"It is 'my lady' now," Charity reminded Prinny's magpie tartly. "Not 'Your Grace.' It seems I will have to keep both of you in line."

Selina coughed to cover her laugh at Charity's friendly reprimand. "You have challenges enough without taking on the burden of Lord Ravenscroft. Come, let us leave the men to their talk. Her Majesty and I would like a word."

The Queen had moved away from the group to rest upon a padded chair. She motioned for Charity and Selina to join her.

Queen Charlotte turned to Charity then, her lined face testifying to her years as monarch. "It seems that it falls to me to provide you with a mother's blessing. So this I shall say. The world will demand duty of you until your bones are weary. Take your happiness where you may, and guard it jealously. You may have already learned this lesson, but do not forget it."

Charity's throat grew tight as she recognised the kindness of the Queen's words when her own mother was absent. "I will forever treasure your sage advice, Your Majesty."

"When you make your departure, you will be in the company of palace guards. They will escort you to where you will stay for the night."

"My lodge," Selina added. "It is on a quiet lane in Richmond. Easily protected and very private."

"Come now," the Queen said, rising from her chair. "Prinny and I are expected at our next event. But enjoy one last drink with the others before you go on your way."

The royal family left, and Charity gripped Selina's hand in quiet thanks for her generosity before she floated across the chamber to where Perry stood. With just the five of them there, he let his arm settle at her waist, drawing her close to him.

It felt right. It felt like family, as they bickered fondly and laughed and exchanged small gestures of affection.

Finally, Thorne cleared his throat. He still looked faintly uncomfortable to be the centre of attention, even in their close-knit group, but he lifted his glass. "I've no polish to my words, but I'll say this. On the field of battle, fights are not won by strength alone, but by trust. And for over ten years of my life, my brother showed me that love is the bravest kind of trust. It makes all obstacles less impossible, because you never have to face things alone. We are all in this battle together; if you find yourself in need, never forget to lean on one another, and on us."

"Hear, hear," they all said in reply, and clinked their glasses together. Then Peregrine reached over and gripped Thorne's shoulder in silent thanks.

A hush followed, more profound than any sermon. Charity

blinked back tears, wrapping her hand around her waist, seeking Perry's where he kept her close. When their fingers twined, the warmth of his touch was the sweetest toast of all.

The inside of Selina's lodge was simple and well-kept. Once they alighted from the carriage and entered, they found a narrow hall, wood-panelled walls, and the sound of a fire crackling somewhere within. Peregrine dismissed the pair of servants inside immediately, telling them they would not be needed until the next day. The footman nodded knowingly, but the maid looked a trifle put out until Charity added her agreement.

Finally they were alone, and Perry caught her hand and pulled her close, burying his nose in the scent of orange at her neck. "You wear the perfume still. Are you filled with joy, Sparkles?"

She adored that he remembered those words. That orange blossom stood for that sweet, innocent jubilance. Though her cheeks already hurt from smiling so much tonight, her grin grew wider. "Joyful, yes—but my clever husband would not be content with that. Surely you mean to prove how much happier you can make me."

Peregrine let out a low growl against her neck, pulling her close. "Say that again."

She knew what he wanted to hear. Warmth suffused every part of her body, making her as likely to catch fire as the fuel in the hearth. "*My husband*," she murmured throatily into his ear, stroking her cheek against his.

A table in the drawing room stood ready with wine and fruit. But Peregrine ignored it, scooping her into his arms and carrying her past it all, across the threshold to the bedroom where through the open door Charity saw the edge of a bed draped in pale hangings.

Her heart beat faster as Peregrine deposited her on the edge of the tall bed, leaning his forehead against hers. "My lady wife," he whispered, his voice as smooth as his silken touch on her skin as he rained kisses on her face. "My heart," he added, setting his hand over the flutter in her chest. "*My* joy."

She laid her hand over his chest as well, letting the quiet of the little lodge wrap around them. Whatever storms lay ahead, tonight they belonged only to each other.

Charity toyed with the knot of his cravat, using it to pull his mouth to hers. He obliged her, and then deepened the kiss, stealing the air from her lungs and scattering her wits as his hands began to wander. It wasn't until he had her first stocking pulled from her foot that he gave her a moment to breathe. And that was only because it took that long for him to press his lips reverently to her ankle, making her shiver.

"Wait," she said faintly, after he repeated the action to her other foot. "I want to undress you, too."

Peregrine paused, amused, since removing her stockings had pushed her skirts to an indecent point around her knees. But he waited in front of her, his hands resting on her thighs, staring into her eyes as she began to unwind his cravat. He looked at her with such love that it made her throat hurt, and feeling raw and impatient with it, Charity slipped off the edge of the bed, rapidly undoing the buttons of his coat and yanking free the tail of his shirt.

He nipped at her ear playfully as she gathered the hem, pulling it over his head, and then stood there waiting as she looked and touched her fill, letting her fingers trail over the planes of his shoulders and down the muscles of his stomach. His bare chest caught the glow of the firelight, broad and solid, each breath lifting beneath her hand.

Reluctantly, her fingers stroked over the ragged red scar of the wound that had nearly taken his life. The new scratch beside it reminded her that their trials were not finished. That he might be stolen from her still.

It wasn't until her head was tipped up and Peregrine's lips caught the tear forming at the corner of her eye that she noticed she was crying. "I can wear the shirt," he said softly, as if the ugliness of the scar was what upset her.

"No," she said quickly, meeting his gaze so that he would understand. She let her fingertips trace the roughened shape of it lightly. "It is only reminding me how precious life is. It looks like it is finally healing well. Does it hurt?"

His nose was pressed against hers, and they spent a long moment living, breathing each other's air. "No," he finally answered her. "But if you keep tickling me like that, Sparkles, I might be pressed to *do unto others* as they're currently doing to me."

A giggle slipped from her lips, and grinning, Peregrine spun her, drawing off her gown and making short work of the laces of her stays. He picked her up and tossed her gently into the centre of the bed, sending up the faint trace of lavender that clung to the sheets.

It was as if all of time was suspended for that night. There was not even a clock in Selina's lodge to strike the hour, which suited her just fine. Charity had no intention of rushing things. Tonight would be about more than the consummation of their marriage. She was determined to celebrate their triumph over the forces that had tried to part them. It was a night for healing all their remaining wounds.

When he joined her in the bed, she revelled in his warm skin, the light down of hair that covered his arms and chest, the quiet strength of a man she never thought she could keep. They curled together, mouths and hands tracing each other's shapes as if they truly had all the time in the world to indulge in such explorations.

"I love you," she whispered, holding his head to her chest, feeling the way his breath feathered against her sternum.

He lifted his face, cupping her jaw with such tenderness that he didn't even need to say it aloud. Peregrine's love for her was writ in his gaze, the curve of his lips as he smiled for her, the touch of his fingers threading through her hair. And she could sense it in the way their hearts spoke together, breast to breast, as they finally joined together as man and wife.

He was the other half of her soul. Every part of them fit together as if it had been made to.

And so she knew that he loved her with his whole being, because it was impossible to think otherwise. Even if he never uttered the words again, even if she was blind and deaf, she would never doubt it.

19

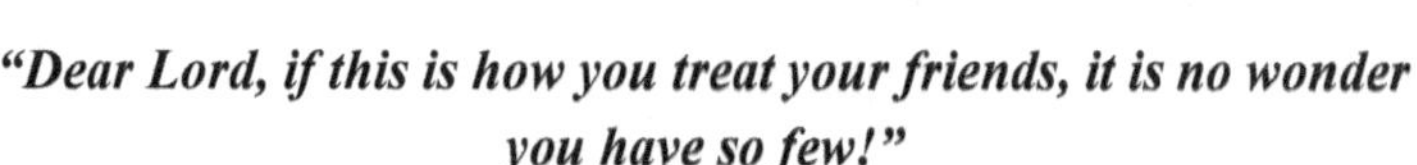

*"Dear Lord, if this is how you treat your friends, it is no wonder
you have so few!"*
— **Santa Teresa de Jesús**

Charity sat tall in the Atholl family barouche the next day, for once happy for the world to take notice of her. Did she look different, she wondered? Her white gloves hid the plain gold band on her finger from view. Yet she felt strongly that if someone studied her closely enough, they would see a change.

The Queen's reprieve was over and needs must. Perry had to see his solicitor. She was to make her way to the Pulteney to pay a call on the Grand Duchess of Oldenburg.

Begrudgingly, the lovers had said their goodbyes with promises to meet as soon as they could both get free. In the company of the palace guards, Charity had returned home long enough to change clothes before leaving for the Pulteney.

That morning, she had taken her butler Pritchard and Miller into her confidence, only of necessity. Announcing their nuptials to the wider world must wait until all the legal matters had settled. And perhaps with time, their friends would grow easier with the idea of calling her Lady Fitzroy. She had not missed how carefully even the Queen and Prince Regent had sidestepped addressing her by the title, as if it was something stained.

Perhaps cursed.

Though she had not voiced her request to Perry, she dearly hoped they would be able to make the announcement of their marriage while his mother was still in London. She wanted to witness the expression on Marian's face when she discovered there was someone else usurping her title.

The hotel was within sight when the carriage rocked to a halt in the middle of the road, rousing Charity from her reverie. "Sorry, Your Grace," her driver said, turning around in his seat. "There's some kind of hold-up in front of the hotel."

Charity hid her wince at the old title. Even though now she felt like a pretender, she would not be able to correct everyone. Not yet. "Has something happened?" Charity leaned sideways, attempting to see around him. Her stomach tightened, her mind envisioning the worst—and that Marian Fitzroy was somehow involved.

"Make way!" The mounted guard accompanying her moved ahead to free space for her to pass. He waved his arm to urge the carriage onward.

The driver clicked his tongue at the horses and shook the reins, ordering them back into motion. The carriage rolled forward until they arrived in the free space in front of the hotel entrance.

"No stopping!" a voice barked, the words bitten off in a harsh, guttural accent that grated against English ears.

A Cossack stepped into view, boots planted wide across the cobbles. He wore a long dark coat belted at the waist, with a fur cap pulled low over sharp eyes. One hand rested on the hilt of his curved sabre, the other raised in warning. His expression was as hard as flint, his teeth bared in a grimace that made it clear he would brook no disobedience.

Behind him, more Cossacks formed a loose cordon before the doorway. Their heavy coats and fierce stares set them apart from London's polished guardsmen. They looked as though they belonged on some distant steppe, not on the pavement of Piccadilly on a warm summer day.

"What is the meaning of this?" the royal guard demanded from his saddle, his scarlet coat blazing in the sun.

"She does not enter," the Cossack snapped, his English thick and broken. "Orders for Tsar's protection. None pass."

"This is English soil," the guard shot back, his voice carrying the clipped edge of command. "By order of the Crown, you may not bar my way."

The Cossack stepped closer, his boots grinding against the cobblestones. "No one passes. Russian guard—Russian Tsar—Russian rules."

Steel rasped faintly as hands shifted to sword hilts. Horses snorted and stamped, the smell of sweat rising from their flanks. A thin ring of onlookers had gathered, holding their breath as the two men glared across the narrow space.

The mounted guard leaned forward in his saddle, pointing down with his gloved hand. "You forget yourself, sir. This is not Russia, but England. Out of courtesy, we have allowed you to bear your weapons. Should you raise them against me, that welcome will be rescinded. Who, then, will guard your ruler? Now, stand aside."

The Cossack squared his shoulders, knuckles white on the hilt of his sabre. His chest heaved with sharp breaths, his voice low and dangerous. "We stand until Tsar says no."

The air was tight, every sound magnified—the creak of

leather tack, the scrape of a boot, the hiss of a drawn breath. It would take only a spark.

The sharp clatter of hooves echoed in the air. A rider pushed through the crowd, his tall frame straight in the saddle. The Propagandist was there, watching the tableau.

Von Gentz's voice carried easily, amused rather than alarmed. "Warriors, surely you do not mean to quarrel over a paving stone in London? If so, I regret to inform you, the spectators have not paid their admission, and I have yet to print the broadsides."

Neither guard answered. Their grips stayed tight on their weapons, though their postures relaxed a fraction. It seemed they both recognised the Austrian.

He let his eyes slide over the guard and the Cossack both, with a smile that was almost kindly. "Russia stands until the Tsar says no, England stands until the Regent says go. Meanwhile, the pavement grows weary of bearing so much pride. Allow it a little rest, eh?"

The Cossack's knuckles relaxed, letting go of his weapon, but he still blocked passage with his body.

"Do you know who this is?" The Propagandist said to him, his voice finally betraying a trace of irritation. "She is the Queen's counsellor in all but name, and confidante of Princess Charlotte. If one wants to grease the wheels of diplomacy, one must not obstruct the road."

With a flourish of his gloved hand toward Charity's carriage, he stared hard at the Cossack. "What say you, brave soldier? As a fellow guest here, I may enter at will. Shall I escort the duchess across the puzzle you cannot seem to solve?"

The mounted guard jerked his chin toward the Cossack, refusing to yield first. The Cossack's lips curled, but he shifted back a pace, the scrape of his boots loud in the hush.

Only when both sides had stepped away did von Gentz nudge his horse forward, smiling as though the whole thing had been a parlour game. "There. The knot untied, without a drop of blood. Come, Your Grace."

He leapt down from the saddle and handed the reins over to a waiting footman. Then, he opened Charity's carriage door and offered her his hand to descend. The clash had ended without violence, but nerves were still taut. Baron von Gentz flourished his hand again, encouraging her to be brave. Or perhaps it was in challenge, testing her mettle.

She took the Baron's hand and gathered her skirts with her other, then carefully made her way to the ground. The Cossacks loomed over her, though they did clear a path to the entrance.

"Mind your step," the Baron said as she tucked her arm through his. He patted her hand in reassurance and then glanced down at her gloved left hand on his arm in surprise.

He had felt her hidden ring.

Her hands had been visible at the Frogmore House dinner, and surely he had noticed the lack of any wedding band then. Gentz studied her face covertly, his lips curling, and suddenly Charity regretted her earlier musings. She did not want Gentz to notice this. But he had, and he forbore to mention anything further about it. Being privy to the secret seemed to please him greatly.

"Where will Duchess Atholl cut her path today?" he asked, eyebrow arching at her title as though the words were a jest.

"I am grateful for your assistance, but I do not want to further impose on your time, sir," she replied. She also did not want to find herself subjected to his sly questions.

"You wound me. I would think a friend of Lady Normanby would know that clever women do not impose—they collect. Influence, secrets, stray allies. You will find me a willing coin in your purse, so long as you spend me with wit."

That drew her attention to the older man sharply. Only Selina had ever referred to secrets as currency in Charity's company. He was offering to smooth her path in exchange for whatever he could gather along the way. Charity could not find a means to extract herself without a scene, so she told him she was there to see the Grand Duchess.

"Ah, dear Ekaterina. Then it seems you do have enough sense to play at a higher table."

Charity ignored his barb. Gentz was like a bird pecking at whatever crumbs of information she would carelessly drop. "I do as the Crown wills. When did the Cossacks decide to stake a claim to the hotel as Russian territory?"

"A few hours after the promenade in Hyde Park. And you should know it is not just there; they are sending the Cossacks everywhere they go for precautions, including to the next destination at Oxford. I did not have the pleasure of seeing you at Hyde Park, *Your Grace*, but I spoke with Lords Fitzroy and Ravenscroft. I thought they might offer to introduce us properly, but it seems you were… otherwise occupied?"

Careful, Peregrine's voice warned her.

"I left early," Charity said, forcing herself to take the steps slowly. "A megrim."

"Is that so?" he asked politely. "I have never tried a touch of royal company as a cure for one."

Fortunately, they arrived at the door to the Grand Duchess's suite before she had to respond. Charity extracted her arm from his and gave her name to the footman.

"I will see if the Grand Duchess is receiving guests," the footman said, leaving.

When Charity finally turned to The Propagandist, he gave her a wicked grin, showing far too many teeth. "The Grand Duchess does not turn away diamonds, no matter their form. Good luck, Your Grace." The baron bowed over her hand and departed without a backward glance.

The suite door opened then, the footman allowing her entry to the Grand Duchess's rooms. The Tsar's sister was alone, for which Charity gave silent thanks. She had timed her arrival to be somewhat earlier than normal visiting hours, hoping she would be received.

The Grand Duchess inclined her head, the movement precise, her eyes glimmering with private amusement. "Your Grace. How very bold of you to appear here, of all places. One might almost call it bravery."

Her tone was smooth, graceful, but still had sly undercurrents. There was a deliberate weight to the pause—a test for Charity to show how she meant to carry herself in light of Marian Fitzroy's accusations.

Charity sank into a deep curtsy, proper to rank, and rose with an untroubled smile. "I hope it is a pleasant surprise, Your Imperial Highness. We had too little time for pleasantries at Hyde Park, and I lamented it to the Queen. She assured me you would not mind my calling, so I trust we have not presumed upon your kindness."

Catherine Pavlovna tilted her head, eyes gleaming. "The Queen is generous in her assurances. Still, one must be careful; those she sends to me usually come carrying more than pleasantries. I trust you have been with Her Majesty recently?"

"I attended Her Majesty yesterday, with the princess. We spent a most delightful afternoon listening to the princess's accounts of Hyde Park, and of you, Your Highness. She spoke of you with such warmth that I thought any friend of hers must surely be one of mine. And so, here I am." Charity inclined her head toward the nearest chair, a gentle reminder she had not yet been invited to sit.

"The princess is dear to me. We should not remain strangers," the Tsar's sister said, her smile cunning. She gestured languidly toward a chair. "Sit, Duchess. We shall drink tea and see whether we are friends… or merely allies."

She rang for the service, and their talk meandered through

pleasantries, each word measured like a move across a chessboard. The weather, they agreed, had cooperated. The races at Ascot had been most invigorating. Eventually, they moved on to the dinner at Frogmore.

"An enlightening evening, was it not?" Catherine drawled, her gaze lingering on Charity from beneath heavy lids. "Young William failed to display his charms to best effect. Prince Paul's merriment was rather too infectious. I made a point of speaking with him at Hyde Park, lest he imagine himself the cause of our dear princess's... altered inclinations. I assured him no lasting harm was done."

Charity knew her response to this remark would set the tone for the rest of their conversation. If she got it wrong, or seemed defensive, the Grand Duchess would shy away from discussing anything deeper. "Sometimes it is only when a man is pressed beyond the bounds of comfort that his true character is revealed."

"Indeed." The Grand Duchess sipped her tea, though not so quickly that Charity missed the fleeting approval. "Who can say where the princess will turn next? Hopefully, her heart is granted some voice in the matter. You English keep the oddest customs— to sever marriage from love, as though duty alone were fit to warm a bed."

As if the Russians were any different about arranging marriages. "You and I have both followed the dutiful path, have we not?" Charity countered, keeping her voice neutral.

"Yes, but should we not wish for better?" the Grand Duchess countered. "When I look at her, I cannot help but think of my brother, Nicholas."

Charity held her breath. "Oh?"

"Yes, my brother Nicholas. He is young, spirited, and not without charm. He too deserves to find a good match."

She paused as if trying to decide what to say. Catherine took her bait, sensing a chance to gossip. "What is on your mind, Duchess?"

"I should not say," Charity dissembled, and had to bite back a smile when the Grand Duchess leaned forward, curiosity sparkling in her eyes.

"We are alone here, and friends, Your Grace."

"I heard a story about Prince Nicholas that I could not credit —" Charity hesitated to gain the other woman's full attention. "Rumour is that he has gained an appreciation for England's roses. Perhaps even the pride of our garden."

The Grand Duchess tossed back her head and laughed. "Oh, how that would vex both Prinny and my brother! Do you know, I almost hope this is true. On a personal level, I would love nothing more than to see them enjoy a flirtation, just to give the princess's father an apoplexy."

"Then you do not believe the rumour?" Charity asked her.

The Grand Duchess flicked her fingers dismissively. "The failure to negotiate a marriage between the Duke of Clarence and my sister proved the impossibility of any match between the English and Russian royal families. The differences between our countries are too great. I see no cause for concern; they will never marry."

Charity stifled annoyance. "But a flirtation?"

"Of course, I would *never* publicly encourage such a thing," Catherine Pavlovna replied so slowly that private encouragement, especially where it might cause chaos, was all but implicit.

But Charity could not even privately encourage such a thing. She could not countenance an unavailable young prince breaking the princess's heart. The Queen was going to be livid when she learned of this conversation, and part of Charity longed to wipe the smirk off the Grand Duchess's face for being so callous about the feelings of a girl who clearly idolised her.

But she reined in the impulse. She could not afford to make

the Tsar's sister her enemy, especially not if doing so sent the Grand Duchess running to Marian Fitzroy's side.

Charity had been lost in thought for too long. The Grand Duchess poured herself a fresh cup of tea and stirred in two lumps of sugar. Casually, she turned them onto a new topic. "Speaking of this year's debutantes, how fares young Lady Lark? I assume you have seen her."

"Not since we spoke briefly at Hyde Park. As far as I know, she is resting comfortably in her home," Charity lied without a qualm. "Lord Fitzroy must be grateful to be able to spend time with her after her long and unexpected absence."

"Pity her mother cannot say the same. She is most distraught, Your Grace. As a mother myself, I can empathise with her. Others may as well."

There it was: a subtle reminder that Russia was not going to let the matter of Lark's kidnapping drop entirely. Charity found herself on a precipice. She could turn the conversation again onto safer ground and let the Grand Duchess's remark stand.

Or you could point out the obvious, the voice of logic suggested.

Charity lifted her napkin and dotted the sides of her lips. Then she set it beside her cup. But before she rose from her chair and made her excuses, she voiced a parting remark.

"I find it most interesting, Your Highness, that not a single highly placed individual in England shares your empathy. Any friends Marian Fitzroy had here are… well, gone. Some more permanently than others." Charity rose then. "I should not overstay my welcome. Before I go, I hope you will permit me to make a suggestion. A friendly one."

"Oh?" The Grand Duchess sat up straighter.

"It might behove you to take a wider view of the world with regard to certain individuals. You may discover that those she sets her sights upon are actually innocent." With that advice ringing in the Grand Duchess's ears, Charity took her leave.

Across town, Perry's solicitor appeared to be doing well in business. His office in Marylebone was in a stately Georgian townhouse, and the letters on the black sign with his name had been gilded. Lincoln Frank was expensive as a solicitor, but given the work he had done to help Peregrine track the last of Marian Fitzroy's accounts and investments, the man had earned every penny.

Fortunately, Peregrine's current request for the man was relatively mundane.

"How can I help you, my lord?" he asked after they were settled in his office.

"I need a Last Will and Testament."

Mr Frank straightened in his chair. "I hope nothing is amiss, my lord."

"Other than my mother returning to London?" Perry tossed back. "You are cognisant enough of the situation to understand the implications of her presence. I want you to draw up a document that appoints a succession of guardians for my sister."

"Very well—"

"I also want to specify the bequests of my assets so that they will be used to protect Lark, and explicitly disinherit my mother." Peregrine forced his hands to unclench. "The document must be ironclad, for my mother will certainly challenge it."

"This can be done, but much of it will hinge on whom you wish to appoint as your sister's guardian. The next in line for your title is a cousin."

"Where the title goes is irrelevant. My wife will take on this responsibility."

Perry's announcement shocked the solicitor so much that the man jerked his hand and nearly knocked over a bottle of ink on his desk.

"Yesterday, in a very private ceremony at St James's, witnessed by Her Majesty and His Highness, I married the Duchess of Atholl—she is now Lady Fitzroy. We are withholding the public announcement for the moment, but you may be assured that the marriage is valid and incontestable."

The other man blinked a few times as this news settled in, but once it did, he returned his focus to his assignment. "In this case, it is best that we update all the documents relating to the estate, and have multiple witnesses attest to your signature on them. It will take me a week or so—"

"I must see it all signed and witnessed today," Peregrine said. "I will stay here as long as is needed, so that any questions can be resolved immediately. Can you make this happen?"

"Yes, my lord," the solicitor agreed after a short moment of consideration. "If you will excuse me, I will call in my assistants and see the rest of my schedule cleared for the day."

Lincoln Frank sat with him for two hours, drilling methodically through everything Peregrine had. When he was satisfied with the list of instructions, he set about dividing the efforts among his team, as efficient as a machine.

Frank finally released him around one in the afternoon with the promise to have the drafted document completed by five. All Perry would have to do then was come sign it, having the clerks serve as witnesses.

Since he had the time to spare, and it was a good time for luncheon, Lincoln Frank had recommended a coffee house down the street.

That's where Hodges came to find him, in a lather.

Perry had ridden down alone that morning so that Hodges could stay with the house. The estate was about fifteen minutes away at a brisk ride, and the road to Marylebone was well travelled. Perry judged that there was a greater risk to the estate than to himself.

It seemed he had judged correctly.

When Peregrine saw the expression on Hodges's face, he threw down more money than his meal was worth and hurried out the door to get his horse. "What happened?" he asked the man tersely.

"Edmunds is dead. Some bastard slipped in after Quinn looked in on him at breakfast—deed was probably done not long after you'd left."

Stunned, Perry stared at his man. "My mother infiltrated the estate? Is Lark—"

Hodges tugged off his hat, raked a hand through his hair, then jammed it back on. "Still there, still safe. Rest of 'em safe too. Thorne an' Quinn are rousin' the Queen's guards, seein' if the bloke's still lurkin' on the grounds."

Peregrine hauled himself up into the saddle, kicking the horse into a canter and leaning forward in his seat. How in the hell had someone managed to invade the house and kill Edmunds with no one the wiser, especially with the guards there?

The moment they cleared enough traffic, both men pushed into a gallop back to the estate. "And what haven't you told me?" Perry shouted over the sound of the pounding hooves, turning his head to look at his general hand.

The man was grimacing, clearly pained. "Sammy!" he growled back. "Boy was in a state. Wouldn't look me in the eye, an' he was twitchin' like a rabbit in a snare."

Perhaps his nephew had encountered Edmunds's killer. The lad was only fourteen. He had been helping Hodges around the estate, defending the house, but he was a long way from grown. Shooting another man, even if it was an intruder, was a hard rite of passage for anyone.

Ten minutes later, they were pulling up to the front door, which was being guarded by a man in blues. They slid out of the saddles, and the guard gave Perry a curt, displeased nod of acknowledgement.

Hodges's mount was lathered from the gallop in both directions, and he checked the beast over quickly, holding his hand to the horse's neck. "Get Dawson to take the horses," Perry suggested. "I want you with me when we go to see Sammy."

Hodges nodded and took Perry's reins, walking the horses around towards the stable. Peregrine went past the guard and through the front door into a scene of madness. It displeased him that none of his servants were attending the door. Where had his footmen and Quinn been relegated? Another guard stood in the hallway outside the nearest parlour and raised voices could be heard within.

Pushing through the door himself, Peregrine found an unexpected trio. A red-faced guard attempted to loom over a gawky boy, shouting at Hodges's nephew, who stood with his head hanging. Thorne was there too, standing like a wall in front of the boy and looking like he was a breath away from striking the Queen's man.

20

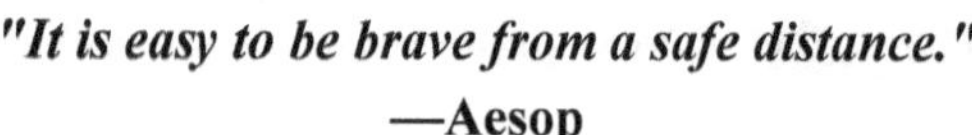

"It is easy to be brave from a safe distance."
—Aesop

"What is happening here?" Peregrine lifted his voice to be heard. "You! Compose yourself!" he hurled at the guard.

Thorne shot a grateful glance at Perry as the guard turned to face him.

"This boy," the guard hissed, "is the reason why a man is dead!"

"Hold your tongue. You shame your colours, speaking to a child so," Thorne snarled at him.

"Let us not forget that *child*, Sir Nathaniel, lured a man away from his post so that an assassin could enter. We are lucky only one man is dead!"

A scuff of boots on the floor heralded Hodges's arrival, but Perry didn't turn. He was watching Sammy, who sniffled miserably behind Thorne's back. The guard's words—however harsh—seemed to be true.

"Leave us," Peregrine commanded the guard. "Finish sweeping the house. I want everyone to be certain beyond doubt that the intruder is not still here." He waited while the sullen guard left the room, and then he turned to Thorne. "Is my sister all right?"

"I left her in a room with your valet in the hallway outside. He said he was capable with a gun," Thorne said softly.

Perry nodded tiredly, pulling his gloves off and stowing them in his pocket before pinching the bridge of his nose between his middle fingers. His breath burned hot against the palms of his hands. "Charity said you are uncommonly skilled at tracking. Can you…?"

"Aye," Thorne murmured. "I'll see if I can find a sign of someone leaving."

"Thank you." Perry said honestly, gripping the man's arm briefly as he passed. "We won't harm Sammy."

"I realise you won't, Fitzroy." Thorne slipped out the door, leaving via the front to circle around the house.

Hodges, however, was a tight coil of frustration. "Sammy," he said finally. "*What did you do?*"

The boy, surprisingly, was staring at Peregrine instead of his uncle. Gauging his reactions. Seeking a new protector now that Thorne was gone, perhaps. Peregrine might be lord of the manor, to be sure, but the boy looking to him instead of the uncle he adored unsettled him.

"It's all right," he told the boy, with no trace of anger in his voice. "Just tell us what happened."

Sammy swallowed a few times, tears dripping down his cheeks. "I'm sorry, m'lord. I didn't want to help him get inside. But he said he'd kill my ma and the babes if I didn't let him in. I still didn't believe him. But he told where she lived, and what they look like."

Hodges jerked as if struck. "He threatened Martha and your siblings?"

"Everyone who might be used as an opening to the household," Perry murmured. "We need to send them away."

His driver looked pained. "Send 'em where? Martha's got no one but me."

"Then we'll bring them here." It wouldn't be as safe as sending them away, but they couldn't be left where they were. "They can't be used as leverage against us if they're here."

His breath left him in a rush as Sammy flung himself against his chest, winding him. "I'm sorry, Lord Fitzroy! I didn't know what else to do," the boy cried. "I didn't see Uncle Will or anybody, and I thought—I thought—"

"It's all right, Sammy," he told the boy, bringing his hands around to the boy's shoulders.

"I thought he was just here to take your sister back," Sammy whimpered. "If I let him in he'd take her and nobody'd get hurt."

Sammy was nearly a boy grown, but he was a boy still. Too young to reckon all the costs of such actions, but old enough to grasp that Edmunds's death had been abetted by him. Peregrine hesitated, drowning in the memory of the last time he had comforted a child. It had been his sister, because Marian didn't believe in showing reassurance or indulging such a weakness.

"Listen to me," Peregrine told him patiently, rubbing the boy's arms. "He was determined to do this foul deed. Even if you had not aided that man, he likely would have hurt someone else to get the job done. The guard. Your uncle. You. That man alone bears the blame for Edmunds death—not you. Do you understand?"

"But maybe if I had—"

"You decided to try to ensure the least amount of harm was done to others and protect your family. There was nothing else you could do. It is a hard truth to learn, Sammy, that sometimes you cannot protect everyone."

The boy swallowed hard, his eyes darting towards Will Hodges, who nodded.

"Did you see the man leave, Sammy?" Hodges asked him. "Can you describe him?"

The boy nodded and told them about a man with a thick, ropy scar beneath one eye who had told him to convince the guard to leave the back entrance. Sammy said he had climbed out from one of the windows on the first floor from the approximate location of Edmunds's room.

Peregrine turned back to Hodges. "We need to finish closing ranks. Ready the big carriage. We will go pick up your sister, her children, and the duchess. And Will—" Perry paused to stress how very important this part was. "Check *everything*. All the tack. The undercarriage. I would not put it past this man to have conducted some other sabotage while he was here."

"Hmph," the man agreed, shifting uneasily. "Give me half an hour to check over everything proper with Dawson."

"Go find Sir Nathaniel and tell him what you told me. All right? I want him to hear what this man looks like. I want you to help him see if he can spot the man's tracks," he told Sammy next, so that the boy could do something helpful. Sammy wiped his eyes with the backs of his sleeves and dashed off.

Perry stood still for a moment, reining in frustrated anger. Then he pushed up the stairs, two at a time, marching towards the room that Edmunds had been put in. The door was closed on the macabre setting it contained, but Peregrine pushed it open, taking it in from the doorway.

Edmunds lay flat on his back on the bed, his legs dangling over one side. The old butler's throat had been cut, forcefully and thoroughly. Judging by the uninterrupted spray of blood on the wall and floor, his killer had held Edmunds upright from behind while he did the deed, likely pushing him back onto the bed as the man died and the flow ebbed.

As if the manner of his death wasn't somehow message enough, the killer had sliced through Edmunds's coat and shirt to expose his chest afterwards, carving the word "TRAITOR" into his flesh.

Perry stared down at the body. His emotions were a confused muddle—mostly anger, frustration and shame.

Some would say Edmunds had earned this death a dozen times over for what he had done for the Fitzroy family over his lifetime. But seeing the old butler cut down like this didn't seem just—not when Perry was alive, not when he had also done so much wrong. It was a hypocrisy.

There was no sadness. Did he need more proof of how tarnished his soul still was if he could stare down at the body of a man he had known his entire life and suffer so little grief? When Hodges had confronted him on the bridge, after the fire, he had told Perry that in protecting Charity, he would find his path towards atonement. This was evidence that he still had a ways to go.

His mother was right. Feelings made everything so damned complicated.

"Blast it," hissed Peregrine through his teeth, stepping over the damp floorboards as he made his way to the window standing open. Sticking his head out, he saw Sir Nathaniel standing below with Sammy, pointing to the torn grass and deep divots left in the ground, and a trail so faint it would be easy to miss leading towards a stand of trees.

Peregrine lifted his face to the ceiling, trying to keep his temper in check. Then he crossed the room again, staring down at Edmunds's face, pale and slack in death. As much anger as he had held towards the man for what he had done to Charity, Edmunds being killed in his house smarted. Another person whom he had promised to protect and failed; one of the last of the dwindling pieces of evidence of his mother's crimes destroyed.

Lark must have told his mother that Edmunds was alive when he had mentioned the butler during their ride last week. It would have taken little effort to deduce *where* he was likely being held.

It didn't surprise him at all that his mother would eliminate Edmunds. What did surprise him, however, was that his sister was, apparently, still here.

Why would the sell-sword decide to infiltrate the house, kill the old butler, and then leave Lark?

He was about to turn and find Quinn and his sister when something half stuck beneath Edmunds' body caught his eye. A battered, smudged, and folded piece of parchment, by the look of it. High-quality paper—the kind that might be at a hotel like the Pulteney.

9 o'clock in the morning, beneath the willow. You may bring the duchess only. We have much to discuss.

The note was in his mother's hand. He'd recognise it anywhere. Was she planning to bargain for Lark? Or something else?

After Hodges ensured that the carriage would be safe, they set out for Atholl House first, taking Owens and Sammy with them.

Perry had left Thorne to mind the guards and set Quinn and Croft to help mind the house and his sister in case Edmunds's killer had planned to stage a second attack now that there were fewer sentries. He would speak with Lark when he returned. First, he wanted to make sure he got to Sammy's mother and Charity before someone else did.

Charity, fortunately, had already been planning on temporarily vacating the house. She listened as Peregrine explained briefly what had happened, gave Miller instructions to ride for the estate with luggage, and suggested that Pritchard send as many of the women servants as he could to stay elsewhere for the next week. Before they departed, she disappeared upstairs and returned with a small cloth bag in her hand.

When they were alone in the carriage, Charity pulled the rest of the story out of him. He didn't have to make any confessions about his feelings; his wife already knew how he still struggled.

"You are working to set things right, and that is worth everything to me," his wife reminded him, whispering in his ear as she pressed her head to his. "I never imagined that the path would be easy, Perry. But that does not mean you aren't worthy of forgiveness. Don't harbour guilt for feeling what you do."

Charity knew Perry still struggled with what he had done, and never wanted him to doubt that she meant those words. That was likely why she had let go of the wrongs Edmunds had done to her the moment Perry had confessed that he had been hiding the old butler.

"You say that because you are stuck with me now," he said with a hint of deprecation aimed at himself. But he smiled softly, because he couldn't be entirely sorry she had chosen him, anyway.

"And you with me. This life and the next." She laid her head against his shoulder, providing the silent comfort of her presence as they made their way through London.

Hodges had put his sister up in a narrow brick front in Somers Town. It was a neighbourhood overflowing with a curious mix of London's working poor and French émigrés living shoulder to shoulder. The street was muddy but filled with a cheerful mix of children and hawkers.

Peregrine turned to Charity as Owens opened the door. "It would be best if you stayed in here with Owens," he told her.

Charity hesitated and then inclined her head, understanding

that she could not stand outside of the carriage, and going inside would attract attention and cause embarrassment to Martha. "All right."

Hodges had gone inside already with Sammy to begin rounding up the family, and Peregrine settled himself at the door to the tenement where he could keep an eye on the carriage and the street. He tried not to listen too closely to the hushed, distressed argument between Hodges and his sister as she protested abandoning the little work she had. Perry would find work for her to do on the estate so she could keep her pride, and he had told Hodges to reassure his sister on that point.

The inside of the house quickly devolved into chaos. Sammy was the eldest of Martha's children at fourteen; the rest appeared to be another boy of roughly eleven, and two girls aged six and three. The youngest was wailing, trying to cling to her mother's leg, and the six-year-old was being more of a distraction than a helper.

Finally, after the smallest was dislodged from Martha's skirts once more, and she sat down on her rump in the middle of the floor to wail, Perry swept in to pick her up before she became an obstacle in someone's path. Bouncing the toddler in his arm to distract her, he reached out a hand to the other girl. "Come on," he cajoled her. "Let us get you both into the carriage so your mama can take care of things. You can help watch your sister, yes?"

Martha flushed scarlet at his intervention, but there was a tinge of relief too. Hodges, knowing that Peregrine was more concerned about expediency than propriety right now, simply nodded his gratitude and set the older two children to work.

He was amused to see his attention immediately intimidated the six-year-old into quiet but endearing compliance. Shyly, she took Peregrine's hand and followed him back out to the front. The child in the crook of his arm was staring at Peregrine like he was painted green.

"This is Owens," Perry told her as the footman saw them coming and hopped down to help. Both children goggled at the size of him and shrank away.

This was the picture Charity was treated to the moment Owens opened the door. Her eyes widened at the spectacle, and then delight lit her face.

"And this is—" Peregrine faltered for a moment, looking at Charity. It felt wrong to introduce her as the Duchess Atholl, even to hide their marriage.

"I am Lady Fitzroy," Charity inserted the words serenely, holding his eyes.

"—my lady wife," he added, turning slightly to the child who was standing behind him with one eye out just far enough that she could watch Charity and Owens. "Can you be very good and sit with her for a bit? Let Owens help you into the carriage."

Nervous, the six-year-old allowed Owens to lift her in. She took the seat opposite Charity, putting her fingertips in her mouth to bite on.

"Well, good afternoon, little miss. Tell me, what is your name?" Charity asked her politely.

"Alice," the girl whispered.

"That is a very pretty name," Charity told her solemnly, and then she turned to Perry, her eyes sparkling in tender mirth to see the babe hiding her face against his shoulder. "And what is your sister's name?"

The girl looked at Perry for a moment, as if she had forgotten he was holding her sister. "She's Sarah."

"Come, little one," Charity murmured, holding out her hands to take the baby. "You may rest with me for a time. You will be perfectly safe."

Peregrine gently dislodged the clinging child, holding her out to Charity. Charity's fingers grazed his as she accepted the toddler without hesitation—despite the child being slightly grubby. She gave him a private smile meant just for him, and then she retrieved the cloth bag, undoing the laces to reveal its contents. A pair of carved wooden elephants, likely taken from a Noah's Ark play set like the one Perry had played with as a child.

That was what she had gone to get. Without any urging, she had thought ahead to how she might keep Hodges's nieces entertained during the ride to the estate.

As the child sat on her lap, making strange coos of delight, Perry found himself to be equally charmed.

In short order, the older children began bringing out things, ignoring their curious neighbours. Between them and Owens, they loaded up rather laboriously well within the hour. That was good, since it was approaching five o'clock, and Peregrine was reminded of his earlier errand that morning.

"Drive by the solicitor's office; it is practically on the way back," Peregrine instructed Hodges as Owens helped Martha in. The boys clambered onto the driver's bench with Hodges, Perry climbed in, and they got underway.

Sitting beside her six-year-old, Martha stared silently at the small bag in her lap for most of the ride, though Charity did try to give her a few reassuring glances. Martha was profoundly embarrassed and uncomfortable as a poor woman riding in such grand company, and had no frame of reference on how she ought to behave—especially since she was knee to knee with Perry.

Peregrine tried to emanate a sense of authority and protection over those inside the carriage. He settled for nodding reassuringly at Martha and then focused on Charity beside him, still holding the babe. Too young to be concerned with matters of social standing, the little one began to blink sleepily, tired out by the excitement, and eventually fell asleep propped against Charity's breast.

Someday, he promised.

One day they would have their own, sometime after all of this was over with his mother. And then they could spend summers in the gardens, enjoying life's idle pleasures. But not now. He could not stand the idea of giving his mother such a precious vulnerability to target.

His stop at Lincoln Frank's office took only a few minutes. Once Perry had confirmed his choices, he signed it quickly, and three of his solicitor's senior clerks served as witnesses. Relief loosened the back of his neck slightly. Now, in that matter, all was official—properly done. But there were still plenty of other headaches to deal with.

For example, the fact that Marian Fitzroy wanted to meet him alone, secretly, and in his own stronghold.

Something set his back up about that, that she appeared to be willing to gamble on her ability to enter and leave the estate. She must have some sort of scheme in place to ensure her safety and ability to leave; otherwise, she would never have taken such a risk.

That she would cede such ground and visit a place his guards were able to watch at a distance meant that she wanted to be close enough to talk with him regarding something. Something important. Calling a truce for negotiation was not an unknown tactic in his mother's arsenal, however, it was one she would employ only in the most unusual of circumstances.

How important was her plan regarding the Prince of Orange? Surely, she must have deduced that he had guessed the scheme involving Lark and the Dutch prince.

Perhaps she imagined that Peregrine might actually allow the scheme to unfold. The engagement between Prince William of Orange and Princess Charlotte, after all, had been ended by his own wife's efforts. So what was the harm? If she were successful in making the match to William, his sister would become a queen.

It was a daring, clever, and audacious plan—he had to give her credit for that much. If his mother had been anybody else, he might even have considered it. But he knew that his mother would not rest on her laurels, satisfied with her daughter's conquest of the Netherlands.

And besides, if his mother had been anybody else, this scheme would never have continued far enough to be considered.

The estate was quiet upon their return, and the guards indicated all was well. Jack came out to help Owens with the full carriage, and if he was surprised to be handed an unfamiliar baby as Charity prepared to step down, he concealed it well.

Charity gave back the sleepy child to Martha once she had descended safely, and Owens led the gaggle to the side entrance. Quinn, who found his way to the front to collect their things, agreed to set Martha up with employment, doing housework.

"How is Lark?" Perry asked his butler.

"Suspicious, my lord. And upset that Edmunds hasn't been sent to her."

"Then no one has told her yet." He would have to break the news gently.

His wife laid her hand on his forearm. "Would you like me to go with you?"

Peregrine hesitated, undecided on whether that would make Lark more disagreeable. "Come with me," he finally told her. "But if things go poorly—"

"If my presence makes things harder, I will leave," Charity said, squeezing his arm.

Giving her a sideways smile in gratitude for her support, he tugged her towards the stairs.

Lark wasn't pleased to see either of them. "Where is Edmunds? What has happened?" were the first words out of her mouth.

Perry let out a slow breath, knowing what he could say was still bound by circumstances. "He is dead, Lark," he said, trying to break the news to her gently.

His sister grew pale, and she swayed slightly. Peregrine didn't think; he simply acted, going to his sister and taking her in his arms, the way he would have before everything had happened. And for a moment, she allowed that too, clinging to him as she stifled a sob against Perry's chest.

"I am so sorry, Sister," he told her honestly, rubbing her back.

At least someone was grieving Edmunds's death. Even if Perry could find no feeling towards their butler, the man had deserved to be mourned by someone.

But after a few moments, Lark shoved herself away from him, her face hardening. "His death was unnatural, wasn't it? Tell me the truth."

"It was. Someone snuck into the house earlier today. That is the fuss you might have heard earlier in the halls. They found Edmunds while I was out and killed him," Peregrine said bluntly.

"Why would someone do such a thing?" She moaned, and then reared back. "Was it you? Did you decide you did not like what he was telling me?"

Perry spread his hands, frustrated, snapping out a question that gnawed nearer to the bone than he previously had had an opportunity for. "Did our mother tell you I was a murderer, Lark?"

Lark deflated slightly, but her eyes still glittered with wariness. "No."

He stepped closer. "Do you truly believe I am capable of such an act? Murdering a servant—even a former one—in cold blood, in my own home? Because I had sent him to speak with my sister and then changed my mind about it?"

She dropped her eyes to the floor, and that was chillingly telling. She did not believe him capable, no. But he had the sense she was beginning to suspect who would be, and she was fighting against it. It was easy to dismiss the small signs of his mother's dark nature, especially if one had the sense it was dangerous to acknowledge it. One of the things Marian Fitzroy had always been good at was ensuring that her children knew prying into their mother's secrets had a price.

"Was Edmunds afraid of me?" Peregrine asked, lifting her chin with his fingertips. His sister wasn't a fool. She surely would have wondered what had happened, that the old servant had willingly returned to the Fitzroy estate and to Peregrine.

When Lark turned her head away, Perry struggled for patience, knowing that she was likely feeling remorse and a share of guilt. She knew she had a hand in the man's death. The same as Sammy.

"He said that many of the things other people had said about you weren't true," she finally murmured.

"After our outing, did you tell our mother that Edmunds knew what happened to Charity?"

Too far. That sparked her temper again. "Mama said you would do something like this—that you would make it seem like she was capable of things like hurting the Duchess Atholl."

Peregrine shot a quick glance at Charity, but he didn't need to worry; she didn't look like she was planning to correct his sister about her name.

"Mama is not who you think she is, Sister," he finally murmured. "It does not matter if you do not believe me, that she orchestrated trouble with the duchess at my ball. Watch her out the window tomorrow, if you want proof that our mother hates her."

21

"We should know what is true before we break our rage."
— **Aeschylus, Agamemnon**

Charity found Perry standing in the breakfast room, staring out the window. He was so lost in thought that he did not turn around at her footsteps. The line of his coat hinted at the tightness in his shoulders, as did his fisted hands at his side. As she neared, he flexed his fingers wide and drew in a deep breath.

Outside, the grounds of the estate spread before them, the bucolic setting bathed in the light of the morning sun. A faint haze gave the scene an almost ethereal glow. It was a shame that the imminent appearance of Marian Fitzroy prevented both Charity and Perry from finding any peace in the view.

Not wanting to startle him, she grazed her fingertips along his arm, gently attracting his attention, before sliding her fingers through his and squeezing his hand. She took her place at his side and rested her head on his shoulder.

"Did your sister come down for breakfast?" Charity asked in a quiet voice.

"No, but I know she is awake," Perry replied. "Quinn said she asked for a table to be set in front of her bedroom window."

"It seems she has taken your words seriously enough to want to watch from her room. That is more than she would have done a few days ago. Your mother misstepped when she ordered Edmunds killed."

Peregrine looked uncertain. "Or she reckoned the risk to her control over Lark was low. Is this where we are now, where the death of a man can be described as a miscalculation rather than an utter travesty? Lark still questions my motives. I almost wish I had not told her about this meeting."

The way he phrased that—that Marian still had control over his sister, nagged at her, but she set it aside. She had felt Perry tossing and turning during the night, his sleep as troubled as his waking hours.

"Do you regret accepting this meeting?" she asked him.

"No. We need to talk to my mother. Still, it makes me uneasy. I am second-guessing whether we should have hidden Thorne or Hodges nearby."

Perry had strategically positioned their guards and allies to prevent a possible kidnapping of Lark while they were distracted. His mother would not be able to leave if she committed any treachery.

Instead, Charity raised their latched hands to her mouth and pressed a kiss atop his knuckles. "I think you have chosen correctly. She needs Lark. It was better to make sure that the grounds were secure."

She cast her gaze upon the weeping willow that stood beside the pond. Its arms trailed down to the grassy carpet, standing sentinel like a widow beside a grave. It was a fitting choice for a meeting proposed by a note left beside a cooling body.

"She will attempt to provoke us today," Perry said, drawing her mind back inside. "Remember that she will use your emotions as a weapon against you. Even her choice of meeting point is a knife between my ribs."

"The willow? Because it is a symbol of mourning?"

"Because that is where she had my dog buried." Perry murmured, looking over his shoulder at her. "You asked me about happy memories here. My father gave me Argus for my fifth birthday. Never did a boy have a more faithful friend. But he despised my mother and was always barking at her."

"Your hound was a good judge of character," Charity said lightly.

Perry gave a wintry smile. "Sometimes I wonder if he sensed her evil, even before she had attempted to have him banished to the stables."

The rough edge of his voice hinted that there was still more to the story. "What happened to him?" Charity asked.

"She wrote to me a week after I left for school. Said he went slavering mad, and that he had to be put down. But for Argus to have been infected by such a thing, he would have had to have been bitten by some other sick creature." Peregrine shifted on his feet. "Argus was nearly as attached to my father as he was to me, and my father would have kept him close after I went to school."

"You said your father also began to take ill after you went to school," Charity said, fitting the pieces together. Perry nodded, and Charity understood that Marian Fitzroy would have considered a protector of any sort—even a hound—to be an obstacle to be dealt with.

What kind of mother would murder her child's beloved pet, Charity wondered. She did not realise she had voiced the words until Perry answered her question.

"The kind of mother who teaches her children to learn to love nothing, for everything one loves can be taken away." Perry shifted around to pull her against him, clutching her tight as if to reassure himself she was real. "But not all of us find it an easy lesson to learn."

"Not anymore," Charity vowed. She rested her head on his chest, listening to the rise and fall of the air in his lungs. They stayed that way until the clock on the mantel began to chime the hour.

Perry allowed Charity to step away, but he kept hold of her hand. When she tried to meet his gaze, he turned his head aside and stared again outside.

"Forgive me for what you will have to see, Sparkles."

For who he would become. Brick by brick, before Charity's eyes, he was walling himself off from all emotion, shifting into the cold-hearted monster strong enough to take on his mother. Just because he was hardening himself now did not mean he wouldn't pay the price of it later.

She reached up to touch his chin, guiding his attention back to her. "I see a man doing whatever is required to protect those he loves. Do not apologise for that. Not now. Not ever."

He nodded his head, but Charity had the sense that he did not believe her. It was one more legacy of the abuse he had suffered at his mother's hand.

Marian Fitzroy strolled slowly out from beneath the branches of the willows. Like her daughter, she was wearing a morning gown that had a hint of foreign influence, though she had opted for less bold colouring choices. But Charity's attention was immediately pulled away from a comparison of the differences in fashion, instead fixing on the expression on Marian's face.

Or rather, her lack of one.

The basilisk was plainly visible in her eyes, and her

expression was not cold… not exactly. It was more that it was somehow inhumanly empty. Like something else was animating Perry's mother, living inside of her skin. And those pupils in her slatey eyes swept back and forth between her and Peregrine, coolly assessing. Watching. Waiting.

When Charity lowered her eyes in return, Marian dismissed her from all consideration. She turned the whole of her attention to her son.

Charity shivered, suffering a chill despite the unusually hot weather they were experiencing in London, staying a step behind Peregrine, as he asked her to. Perry did not want her close to his mother. He did not believe his mother would show up armed, but he was not willing to risk it.

"Peregrine," Marian Fitzroy said, simply. It seemed a strange way to greet her only son, but given everything that transpired over the last year, perhaps this neutrality was the best situation one could hope for. "I see you got my message requesting this meeting."

Perry was stock-still and outwardly calm, betraying not a breath of the anger he was surely feeling. Despite everything that Marian had done to Perry, Charity could not believe the woman's pluck, that she could so cavalierly treat the death of a man who had worked for her for thirty years this way.

"It was difficult to miss," was Peregrine's dry response. "Even Edmunds, mother?"

Marian Fitzroy looked, if anything, bored. She stopped paying attention to Charity, dismissing her, almost, from consideration. Peregrine had warned Charity not to draw more attention to herself than necessary, and she understood why he had asked it of her. She hadn't forgotten the lesson that Selina and Bellrose had taught her—sometimes it was safer to be nearly invisible.

"Do not blame me for your failure to protect you and yours, Peregrine. A few guards, a fifteen-year-old boy, a butler, a valet, a stable hand, a driver, and two footmen. Is that the best you can muster, my son?" Marian asked instead, dusting a speck from her sleeve. "Here I was, given the impression that your loyalty had somehow purchased you an impenetrable defence."

Marian's eyes flicked ever so slightly to Charity, but Charity dropped her eyes again, even though her skin was crawling. Marian's man had managed to tally the complement of Peregrine's household before killing Edmunds. How long had he been on the property?

The basilisk stare again returned to Peregrine. "Is this all the duchess can offer you, Peregrine? You could not have cleaved yourself to someone who can bring you protection? The duchess is damaged goods, used and cast off by the Duke of Northumberland. Tell me, would those royal guards still darken your door if she weren't in your bed? Imagine being propped up by a duchess whose only worth is what she brings you from another man's name."

Charity couldn't see much from the angle she stood, but Peregrine's stance became almost relaxed. His head tipped just enough towards his right that Charity could see he was giving his mother a reproving look, letting her know that her barb had failed to strike.

"You wanted this meeting badly enough to threaten a child's mother. I trust you had a reason," he said, crossing his arms over his chest. "What was so important to discuss that it needed to be delivered with the body of a man who served you for three decades?"

Marian smiled then, and it was like watching someone don a change of clothing. "Well, I needed to be certain I had your attention. As for that young boy, you know how boys can be, my darling. He did not even believe Moxley was a threat. Sometimes they do not understand the situations that they so blithely wander into."

"Mother," Peregrine snapped. "If you have a point, make it. What do you want?"

The older woman pressed her fingertips together in front of herself calmly. "I want to move back into Fitzroy Manor."

Peregrine laughed disbelievingly. "After you hired a man to steal onto the property and have your butler murdered? You *are* a lunatic. Absolutely not."

"Perry, be sensible. We must present a united front to the *ton* and maintain this farce of being a happy family. I would much prefer not to have to air our grievances at the moment. Do not fuss over Edmunds. I could hardly do all that work cloaking the past to leave the matter of him unsettled."

Charity's stomach churned. Perry's warning that his mother would attempt to provoke faded from Charity's memory, lost under the rising tide of fury at the woman's cold disdain. She gritted her teeth to hold back the retort burning at the back of her throat.

Perry, too, seemed unable to remain silent. "He was the only former household member I had left, and he was providing comfort to your daughter."

Marian shrugged one shoulder dismissively. "I have taught you both better than to rely on such things."

"He was no threat to you. He was a broken man. What could he prove?" Peregrine hurled at his mother.

"*You* strive to school me on what does or does not constitute a threat, my son?" she said, her lips curving with amusement. "When you have constantly failed to understand what a real threat looks like? When everything you know now, you learned from me?"

"Clearly, I learned well enough to stay alive," he said lightly.

Marian let her gaze run up and down her son's figure. "I grant you that much, my love. But it bears repeating. You are so much *less* than you ought to have been. Now that you have had your temper tantrum over Edmunds, are you ready to strike a bargain so that I may return to the household?"

Hearing those words of endearment on Marian Fitzroy's lips made Charity see red. "No, he is not ready," she hissed at Marian Fitzroy. "He already told you no."

"Your Grace," Peregrine warned her, turning his head slightly in Charity's direction, and Charity's stomach dipped, to hear him address her by her former title. Even in denying his mother entry to their house, he did not want to confess that he and Charity were married. That she was now the lady of the household.

"Someone taught it to speak," Marian murmured pointedly without looking in Charity's direction, but a broad smile stretched across the woman's face.

It was too much for Charity.

"We know what you are about, you catty witch," Charity growled, pushing forward against Peregrine's suddenly outstretched arm holding her back. "How you are desperately trying to buy back your respectability. That was the only reason you gave back the dagger, was it not? The satisfaction it must have given you to watch both the Regent and the Queen accept your lies! What could be more priceless than to stand at their feet and watch them eat crow? Am I right, *Marian Fitzroy*?"

His mother's head swivelled abruptly in Charity's direction. The woman grabbed Charity by the wrists, yanking her so close that Charity's entire world was nothing but the madness flickering in Marian's eyes.

Caught off guard, Charity gasped at the pain of Marian's pincer-like grip on her hands. Her hands were unexpectedly strong, grinding the small bones of Charity's wrists together.

And just as quickly as Marian grabbed Charity, Peregrine's hand wrapped itself around his mother's throat, his fingers sinking into the flesh behind his mother's jawbones. But Marian didn't pay her son or his hand on her throat much attention—

Perry's grip wasn't tight enough to impair her ability to draw air.

"Do you think you can simply march into this house and take my place?" Marian Fitzroy asked Charity, the black pupils of her eyes swallowing all but the barest ring of blue iris. Her face was a parody of life, with no light of a soul showing within. "You are a child, and *you* understand *nothing* of this world that I have built. Nor what I have planned next."

"*Let her* go, *mother*," Peregrine intoned in a voice that would have been utterly terrifying if it had been directed her way.

Charity dared to break eye contact with Marian long enough to glance upwards at Peregrine, and she saw a hint of the same madness in his eyes. But his gaze was fixed upon his mother, and Charity sensed he was standing on the edge of a precipice.

If Marian didn't let her go, Charity knew he would kill his mother with his bare hands. Not that Marian Fitzroy didn't deserve to die—but she did not want Peregrine to suffer for it. And he would.

For a moment, everyone held still.

Charity's eyes dropped briefly to Marian's bare hands wrapped around her wrists. The skin on the back of her hands began to grow ruddy as the rings on Marian's fingers pinched her flesh painfully against bone and tendon.

"Do I not understand?" Charity breathed into the space between her and Peregrine's mother. "Does it not, perchance, involve your daughter marrying a certain Dutch prince?"

Marian's head tilted only a fraction as she regarded Charity, before Peregrine's fingers tightened enough to make his mother choke slightly, but she did not stop or pay him any other mind.

"That is why you want to move back in with Peregrine, to provide the image of a happy family, isn't it?" Charity pushed, ignoring the ache growing in her forearms. "With Perry still alive and able to control Lark's prospects, you need to convince him to let Lark marry William of Orange. You need to keep the scent of any scandal away from your daughter."

Like a candle being lit, the woman's face suddenly transformed from its terrifying blankness back into amusement. But Peregrine's hand tightened again, and Marian's lips parted, looking for air. Her grip on Charity's wrists finally began to slacken.

"Perry, don't strangle her," Charity said urgently, trying to call him back from the brink of his rage. "She's only holding my wrists."

"I will let her go when she lets you go," Peregrine told her through gritted teeth.

Finally, Marian let her hands drop from Charity's wrists. Charity immediately stepped back, away from the madwoman's ability to reach her, and rubbed her aching wrists. Peregrine released his mother once Charity was out of reach.

Marian staggered slightly on her feet, but she recovered her footing quickly. More disturbingly, she held Charity's gaze the entire time.

"You are nothing," the woman repeated to Charity, her face still twisted in a black sort of delight. "And you have no idea what is happening here. If you doubt me, then I will tell you plainly. I will not have to kill or coerce my son to enact my plans—nor to utterly destroy him, Duchess Atholl."

Marian collected herself so quickly that only the pale marks of Peregrine's fingertips showing on the skin of her throat gave any evidence that anything untoward had occurred. "Trust that I will achieve my aims."

Finished with her message to Charity, Marian drew herself up primly and pointedly turned to her son again. Peregrine's chest was rising and falling quickly, his breathing quickened in ire. "You have overstayed your welcome and need to leave," he told her. "Now."

"You should reconsider my request, dear son," his mother told him. "The next time I ask you to do something for me, it may involve a price you are not willing to pay."

"The hells shall freeze solid before I give you Lark or let you set foot inside this house again," he gritted. "You plighted your troth to the Russians. Perhaps you should go home with them, Mother."

His mother gave him the faintest smile. "The decision regarding that will be up to the Tsar. I shall not consider your answer final, Perry. Not just yet. But if you decide you wish to talk to me again later today, you shall find me at the Pulteney."

"I will never look for you. Not for any reason," he hissed, his shoulders rising as he began to lose his grip on his anger.

"Never say never, my dear." Marian pressed two fingers to her lips, blowing him a kiss. Then she turned smartly to walk the path that led around toward the front of the house.

Peregrine silently and slowly trailed his mother to be sure that she left without trouble. All Marian did was get into her carriage and drive away again. Once she had left, he took Charity's arm and tugged her along, fury speeding his steps.

Charity nearly had to trot to keep pace beside him, but she did not complain or beg him to slow. And when he got them inside the door again, he turned on Charity, his expression tense between the anger and fear coursing through him. "Did she harm you?" he asked her, reaching for her hands.

"It is fine, Perry." She folded her arms over her chest, not wanting him to see or to admit to the bruising Marian surely left behind. Peregrine would lose what was left of his mind over it.

Restless, Peregrine walked deeper into the house, not stopping until he reached the sideboard in his study. He tipped a finger of whiskey into his glass and tossed it back before offering some to her.

"It is harsh, but after that, I think we both deserve fortification."

Charity accepted the proffered glass and gulped a draught, nearly choking at the fire it chased down her throat. But it worked as promised. A second sip, much smaller, allowed Charity to taste the smoky flavour of the drink—Thorne's preferred beverage, she recalled. She took a seat on the leather sofa, tugging the sleeves of her gown down to cover her wrists.

Perry remained standing, rubbing his temple as he stared sightlessly at the shelf-lined wall. "I cannot make sense of this. Why would she ask to return here? It was a fool's errand."

"I thought for sure she would demand Lark's return," Charity added, equally perplexed. But Marian had not so much as even asked after her daughter's health.

"We are missing something," Perry muttered. "Asking to return to the house feels like she is playing for time, and that goes against the idea that she is pressed for it."

He rocked back and forth, unspent anger robbing him of any hope of peace. He set his glass aside and began pacing the length of the room.

Charity tried to help form a new theory, but she was finding it difficult to concentrate. She grew dizzy, her stomach was churning, and a lethargy was creeping up her arms and down her spine. Fatigue pulled her deeper against the seat, and she let herself lean against the back. It seemed like the strong spirits, so early in the morning, were exacting a toll.

Maybe it was a combination of that and the warmth that was making her sleepy. She fought against the tug of her eyelids, biting the inside of her cheek to rouse herself.

But the exhaustion grew worse, not better. A curious cold numbness followed the sense of weight, but despite the sensation of cold, she could see sweat beading on her arms. The numbness climbed up her arms, and black sparkles began to dance around the edges of her vision, obscuring her view of her beloved.

What was happening? No sip of spirits, no matter how strong, should steal her wits so thoroughly. Confusion reigned in her thoughts, and it took too long for the fear to rise.

By the time she caught on to the seriousness of her condition, it was too late. She pursed her lips and whispered his name.

"Perry—?" But nothing came after that. No word. No thought. All the light in her world extinguished, leaving behind complete darkness.

22

"No man ever threw away life while it was worth keeping."
— **David Hume**

The moment his name tumbled off her lips, fear sparked along Peregrine's spine.

Something was wrong. Charity's voice was breathy and faint, and even as he whirled to her, her eyes were rolling back in her head. He leapt towards her, but before he crossed the room, she had fallen against the back of the sofa, her head lolling.

"No! Charity!" he shouted. He cupped her face in his hands, but she was boneless and unaware of his words. His touch. "No, no, no…" he whispered, his heart stuttering painfully. Perry attempted to rouse her by patting her cheeks and jostling her lightly. But those efforts were in vain, even when he grew rougher, his hands shaking as he tried to stimulate her to some response.

Peregrine tried to convince himself she had only fainted, but her skin was clammy and too cool. "Don't do this to me, Charity," he ordered her, his voice trembling as he tried to keep himself from falling to pieces. "Wake. Wake, damn you!"

Some sudden illness? It was possible. But Charity had collapsed less than an hour after his mother left the property, and that was surely no coincidence. A terrible suspicion began to build within the pit of his belly, and he had to cover his mouth briefly, wrestling with the urge to be sick.

"Quinn!" Peregrine bellowed at the top of his lungs once he swallowed back the contents of his stomach. Quickly lifting her feet up onto the couch, he laid Charity out flat. Outside the study door, the household exploded into action at his shout of alarm, and footfalls rang down the stairs and hallways.

He barely registered the thunder of boots on the stairs; his world was narrowing down to the slight wheeze of her breath. Cursing, he sat her up again, tearing the back of her dress and stays open so that nothing could impair her breathing more than it already was.

Quinn came at a run as Perry began to examine Charity. His mother was surely somehow responsible for this, but he did not understand how.

Peregrine checked her skin, her fingernails, her mouth, and her eyes, looking for unusual signs. The colour of her nails was still normal. Charity, however, was pale to the point of being grey, and her pupils were constricted into pinpricks, not widening when he shielded them from the light.

Peregrine quietly panicked for a few seconds, trying to consider his options and what had happened. *Please not this,* he begged God and Fate. He could not fail her, too. He would have nothing left in this world worth fighting for.

His butler's presence finally penetrated the haze of his thoughts. "Quinn, did my wife eat or drink anything today that I did not partake of?" he rasped as the man stood stock still beside him, looking down at Charity's still form.

His butler took a few seconds to consider what Perry was really asking. "No, Lord Fitzroy," he answered. "She had no appetite this morning. You drank from the same teapot."

"Get the red box from the shelf in my mother's dispensary. Please."

"Should I send for a physician?" Quinn asked him.

"The box first. Hurry," Peregrine urged him. "Bring it with some water. I'll take her upstairs."

The dispensary was a small, cool room below stairs that his mother had kept locked. It had been one of the few places that Peregrine had insisted be left alone by Quinn and the housemaids. Many of the plants around the estate and the substances kept in the dispensary were dangerous to the unwary. The red box held the only treatments that most of those poisons had.

Even then, it wasn't much—purgatives and binding substances, for the most part. Haste, prayer, and minor miracles were still required to save someone's life if they consumed the toxic plants in Marian's gardens.

Thorne knocked hard on the doorframe of the open study door, stopping dead when he saw Charity's torn dress and her limbs dangling loosely from the cradle of Peregrine's arms. "Saints preserve us," the knight breathed. "What happened?"

"I don't know," Peregrine said through gritted teeth, carrying her out into the hallway. "Help me. I need the assistance of my sister's maid. And get Hodges. Please."

Sir Nathaniel hurried off, and Peregrine struggled to keep her from slipping from his grip as he made his way up the stairs with her in his arms. The utter limpness of Charity's body terrified him; even when she had swooned after escaping Bellrose, the tone of her arms and legs had not been so lax.

It was a bad sign. Her prostration suggested that it might be something attacking the muscles and nerves of her body.

Something like aconite, which could paralyse her heart or the mechanisms of breathing.

He carried her directly to the mattress in her bedroom, laying her down again and pressing his ear to her chest. A sob of relief escaped him as he heard a steady rhythm, even though it was much slower than it ought to be in repose. Likewise, her breath was slow, but regular.

While he waited for Quinn to return with the box and water, he pressed his trembling palms together, lips resting against his forefingers in silent supplication as he prayed to anyone who might be listening, to give Charity the strength to stay alive and keep fighting whatever toxin ran in her veins until her body could defeat it.

If it could.

Please, please, please, his thoughts whispered, hoping against hope that he was wrong. That this wasn't poison.

His sister's maid helped him remove the remains of Charity's dress and put her into a loose robe. They helped arrange her comfortably in bed, propped up on pillows to keep her respiration easy. Thorne sent Hodges looking for a physician and any other woman with herbal lore in the area.

It was the thinnest of hopes. When it came to poisons, Peregrine doubted any in the area knew even half as much as he did. But he would turn up his nose at no quarter right now.

When Quinn returned from his mother's locked room with the box, Perry found the bottle of fine black powder marked *Carbo Ligni Purificata*. The maid helped him measure out and mix the slurry that could bind itself to many poisons that had been ingested, just in case he and Quinn had been mistaken about what she had eaten.

"Come on, Sparkles," he murmured to her as he leaned her back against his chest, feeding her the charcoal in careful sips to keep her from choking and inhaling it. As he stroked her throat to encourage her to swallow each one, he observed how weak each was. Abruptly she sputtered, the black fluid dripping from the corner of her mouth, and he could feed her no more.

Peregrine rifled through the few notes on symptoms and poisons tucked into the box, looking for answers he might have forgotten. But there was nothing.

He was at a loss.

He looked up from Charity's shoulder to see his butler and Thorne standing there. What more could they do?

Thorne seemed to understand he needed steadying. "As long as she's alive, there's hope, yes?" he murmured to Peregrine, standing beside him as they looked down at Charity, pale and still against her pillows.

"I do not know what this is. Or even if she'll survive it."

Now that he had stopped moving—stopped acting—doubt and despair began to gnaw at his guts. Was there hope? His mother had somehow poisoned Charity. To prove that he was helpless. So that he would grasp without doubt that he would never be clever enough or ruthless enough to stop her.

And as added insult to injury, she had poisoned Charity right beside the grave of his hound. The poor beast that had served as his mother's lesson about the foolishness of allowing himself to care for something.

He should have strangled the life out of the woman who had done so much evil. Peregrine had held her by the neck, and he had let her go. Now his hands itched to right that wrong. He should go right now to the Pulteney and deal with her once and for all.

But… if he harmed his mother now, he would never get any answers. Marian would happily take any hope for Charity with her, to hell.

He couldn't do *anything*. Not for his wife, or against his mother. He had never felt so powerless to act in all his life.

Peregrine then went a bit mad. Or so he gathered later.

There was a horrible blankness, and when he came back to himself, he found himself standing among the ruins of some of the bedroom furniture and shattered vases and *objects d'art*. All items were ones his mother had chosen for the room.

His throat was raw and his bleeding hands were lacerated with splinters of glass. Thorne, Owens and Jack were holding him pinned against the dented wall. Thorne had planted himself squarely in front of his face, holding his head while his footmen immobilised his wrists and shoulders.

"*Fitzroy*," Thorne murmured, his blue eyes fixed upon Peregrine's. "Are you back to yourself?"

Not hardly. Peregrine was unmoored. If he simply released himself to the wind, his spirit might be blown loose from his cage of bones, floating away.

"She poisoned Charity," Perry repeated aloud in despair, numb in the face of his greatest fear. "And I don't know how to save my wife."

Thorne's eyes were full of grief and guilt as he waved off the footmen and circled his palm around the back of Perry's neck. The weight was the only thing fixing him to the earth.

"Steady on, Fitzroy," the man's baritone voice ordered him. "She's still alive. Do not borrow more trouble before it comes to claim us."

Shivering, Peregrine finally nodded. Thorne was right; he needed to cling to this thought. While his wife lived, she needed him. He let them wash the blood and glass from his hands and held still while Thorne bandaged the cuts.

"Did your mother do anything else to Charity?" Thorne asked him while studying a deep gash. "Are there plants that are poisonous to the touch?"

Peregrine inhaled swiftly and rose from his chair. He hurried to his wife's side to pull back the sleeves on Charity's gown as he remembered his mother holding Charity's wrists. The faintest blue tinge of developing bruises circled both wrists.

There were indeed several plants poisonous to the touch—aconite was among them. But his mother's hands had been bare. Any poison on her skin should, in theory, have sickened her, too.

Unless…

He recalled the hazy thought that had flitted through his brain before he had lost his wits. That his mother couldn't die—because she still held the answers he needed. Perhaps Charity's poison had an antidote. Or some other treatment. He knew of no such sureties for the poisons he was familiar with, but just because he was not familiar with any did not mean they did not exist.

His mother had told him where to find her, as if she had known Peregrine would have been willing to strike a bargain. Eventually.

If you decide you wish to talk to me again later today, you will find me at the Pulteney.

"I have to see my mother," he said dully, the anger rising in him.

23

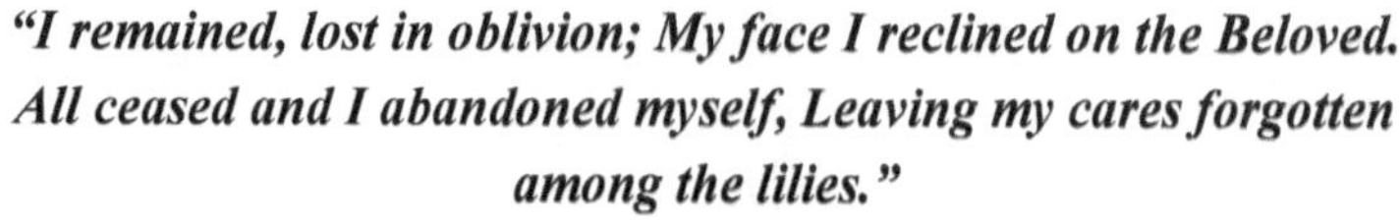

"I remained, lost in oblivion; My face I reclined on the Beloved. All ceased and I abandoned myself, Leaving my cares forgotten among the lilies."
—John of the Cross

I*f our days are numbered, then we must make every moment count for all it can. I love you, Perry, with all that I have,* Charity's voice whispered in his thoughts.

Pain and nausea spiked through Peregrine like a fever. He was wraith-ridden by the sound of a woman in his head who might never wake. Now his wits scattered in a hundred directions as he and Hodges rode for the Pulteney like the devil himself was at their heels.

It had been difficult to tear himself from Charity's side, but for the moment, she seemed stable. It lent credence to the idea that his mother might be trying to force his hand. To blackmail him and make him do something against his will.

So he had left Charity in the care of Sir Nathaniel and his

butler, ordering them to keep watch over both her and the physician who had arrived while they were saddling the horses. He had given Thorne a list of treatments that Peregrine wouldn't permit. Bleeding and antimony would simply weaken Charity more.

His mother—damn the woman—was waiting for him in the lobby of the hotel with a cat's paw smile. "My son," she murmured, inclining her head and turning to walk up the stairs, not even looking to see if he followed.

He followed, soul deadened, in his mother's wake as she brought him back to her private chambers. Swanning into the room without a backward glance, she left the door ajar.

A dare. Would Peregrine enter her lair alone?

He would, because he knew her mind. There was a game afoot, and while Charity's life was at stake, his own was safe. Killing him now would ruin her sport.

Peregrine shut the door behind him, straightening in front of it now that it was just the two of them. Marian turned, then, the ravening beast staring from behind her eyes as she dropped all her pretensions, shedding them like one would drop a cloak upon the floor.

"I am sorry you decided not to bring the duchess with you. Is she not feeling well?" his mother asked, her eyes glittering with madness.

"You know very well how she is. Was that your only reason for coming to the estate this morning?" Perry's hands curled into fists of their own accord. "To punish me by harming Charity?"

The corners of his mother's lips twisted. "Why could it not be about the duchess herself? You are so very wrapped up in yourself, Perry."

"I wonder why!" he hissed. "It seems that defying your will was what put us on this path to begin with. Well, here I am. You have my undivided attention, Mother."

Peregrine spread his arms, inviting his mother to move. To strike him down. But Marian calmly observed her son as if he were nothing more than an irritation, tugging at the edges of a pair of gloves she had not been wearing earlier.

"Well? What will you?" he goaded her. "You threaten the lives of my friends. You have poisoned a woman whom I care for. And now here I stand before you. Unarmed. Alone. You can do anything you like. Stab me, why don't you? Feed me some poison. *Punish* me, Mother. This war is between the two of us; leave the others alone."

Perry did not realise tears were streaking his cheeks until his mother swept towards him, her face a strange caricature of fury and curiosity as she roughly drew a finger through the moisture. If she hadn't been wearing gloves, Peregrine would have been scored by her fingernails.

"What do you want of me, Marian Fitzroy?" he asked her, ignoring his stinging cheek. "What must I trade for the duchess's life?"

His mother's eyes flicked up to his. "So certain there is a treatment, are you?"

"Of course I am. You would not have told me where to find you again if you did not expect I would come here to bargain. You cannot dangle her life as bait if Charity will die."

His suffering gratified her. Peregrine could see the satisfaction in her, that he was humbled and desolate. She would abuse that, forcing him to debase himself. But he would do it without hesitation if it restored Charity to him. He would give up his wealth and title. Exile himself from England. Crawl on his knees.

He might even give her Lark. Lark would be a Queen, after all; she didn't need his protection.

"You're right, of course. This particular poison does have a treatment." Calmly, Marian paced in a small circle around Peregrine.

"I have to thank you, really. If it hadn't been for the necessity of leaving England, I would never have gone to Russia and met Lizaveta," his mother continued. "She is quite brilliant, actually. Most poisons have to achieve only a single aim—kill the person who consumes it. No subtlety is required whatsoever. But Lizaveta made some fascinating mixtures that could achieve other effects. Her personal favourite paralyses and then rots the limbs, leaving one's mind free to contemplate its demise. I cannot help but think about how I could have made a fortune blackmailing people if I had half of Liza's acumen. Ah well, that is all in the past now."

Leave it to his mother to form an acquaintance with someone more vicious and mad than she was. "But that's not what this one is," he said, certain of his deduction.

"No. The rotting poison requires the victim to be dosed at regular intervals," Marian agreed. "But Liza's sleeping sickness—the one I gave to your duchess—requires only one. Duchess Atholl will not die of it. Not right away, at any rate."

Peregrine's thoughts were a perfect, white-hot cauldron of rage. "What do you want?" he gritted out. "My life? I would gladly make that trade."

His mother contemplated his expression, reading him with uncanny thoroughness. "Of course you would, my son. Which is why I would not accept that bargain."

"Then what!" he barked harshly.

Marian stepped closer into his space. "We should trade a life for a life, Peregrine. I have a thought. You should tell the Lord-Chancellor about Lord Ravenscroft's unnatural acts with his valet."

Perry froze, ice tracing a path down his spine. He had been afraid that Ravenscroft would rise to the top of his mother's black list if the magpie delivered his note. It seemed that he was right.

"You would have me condemn a man in exchange for Charity's life? Sodomy is a crime that would see him hanged."

"*Two* men. Guilty ones, at that," his mother murmured, smirking. "You care for the duchess, do you not? This should be a simple choice, to discard men like Ravenscroft for a woman you would devote yourself to. *The law would be on your side.*"

It would be. But regardless of what the law said, their crimes were borne of love. He would not treat Ravenscroft and Antoine like currency, and he would not send them to the gallows for their love.

If he crossed this line, then he would be no better than his mother.

"I will not trade their lives for hers," he growled, ignoring the panic crawling up his throat.

His choice was an illusion. Charity would never forgive him for sacrificing the two men. And the alternative was to do nothing, letting Charity lie in a sleep like death, hoping her body would be able to fight the poison itself, given time.

Some flicker of his thoughts must have passed over his face, because his mother shook her head knowingly. "Stall for time, if you like. The duchess will not suffocate or expire in the meantime. But she will also not overcome the poison. That is not the way this one works, Peregrine. She will die when you find yourself unable to sustain her needs.

Marian ran her finger down his cheek again, lighter this time, her face mocking. "She may choke to death if you try to feed her. Or inhale it and drown. Of course, that may be a kindness, because any little sustenance you might be able to force into her body will only prolong her death. If you do nothing, she will linger long enough to die of thirst and starvation. I understand it is a terrible way to die."

Perry's breath sawed painfully past the lump in his throat, his mind spinning in tight, useless circles.

"Not that I care how Ravenscroft whiles away his private hours, but since he saw fit to meddle in my affairs, turnabout is fair play. So show me that you are in earnest, Peregrine. Lay information with the justices and denounce him. See that done, and I will give you the panacea for the sleeping poison. The Duchess Atholl will despise you for your decision... but at least she will live to do so, my love."

Peregrine was struck by the last time he had seen madness dancing in her eyes this way. *Peregrine's love—his loyalty—his life. It is mine to break or burn, as I see fit,* she had told Charity.

And his mother was doing exactly that. Punishing Ravenscroft was an afterthought. His mother was punishing him for giving away what she considered hers. Marian intended to force him to sacrifice his friendship with the magpie, and Charity's love for him. One way or another.

She was determined to extinguish the light in his darkness, so he would have nothing left. Nothing, except her.

I understand what it's like to live this haunted life, the ghost of his wife whispered in his ear, curling her hand around his heart. *It hurts to keep fighting, to keep believing that we can persevere when it seems like everything is against us. Sometimes I wonder if we will ever have peace.*

Charity would be disappointed. There would never be peace.

Peregrine blinked and found himself abruptly in the daylight, outside of the Pulteney, astride his own horse, and with no real memory of how he had got there. Hodges was staring at him as if uncertain he was fit to ride, and he couldn't even blame the man. The world was greying at the edges.

"What happened?" Hodges asked him. "I assume the harpy's still breathin'."

If only he were sure of that. But his hands were clean, and he was unrumpled. "My mother offered me the cure for Charity if I agreed to denounce Ravenscroft," he said shortly, unable to dredge up any memory of what had happened in those last minutes of horror.

Hodges gave him a wary, uncertain look. "And will ye?"

Peregrine did not even have to consider the answer as he kicked the horse into motion. "No."

The man who had endured the Nive with him had no reply to that one. Some conundrums had no answer. Not beyond doing what was necessary to survive.

"You all right?" Hodges hesitated, clearly groping for the words. "You don't seem yourself, Lord Fitzroy. Your ma could poison two as easily as one."

"She didn't poison me," he said flatly.

"And how d'you know that, then?"

That was easy to understand, if one understood how his mother acted. So he told Hodges what he had heard his mother tell Charity a year ago. "Because I cannot suffer if I'm dead."

He fell silent for the ride back to the manor, lost in thought. Lost in memory. Simply lost.

His mother had won. It was really as simple as that. Killing his mother wouldn't save Charity's life. All it could do now would be to rob him of whatever short time they had left together.

People waited at the door for him. Quinn and Croft. Jack too. But in a haze, Peregrine went straight past them all, climbing the stairs to reach his wife's bedroom. He had nothing helpful to say, so he said nothing. All he wanted to do was find Charity and reassure himself that, for now, she was still alive.

The maid must have gone back to his sister straightaway, because it was Sir Nathaniel sitting at Charity's bedside, and Charity's hair was still pinned up.

Thorne quickly vacated the bedside chair for Peregrine, but Perry ignored it. He gently rolled his wife onto her side, pulling the pins holding up her hair one by one, laying them in a small pile and loosening her hair so she would be comfortable.

"Fitzroy." The way Sir Nathaniel said his name said everything. He saw Perry and knew there was little hope.

"If you do not mind, Sir Nathaniel," Peregrine said quietly to him as he finished taking her hair down, "I would like to spend some time alone with my wife."

Thorne said something—Peregrine did not have the focus to make sense of the words. But he retreated, as Perry had requested.

Once her golden locks lay in a loose mass behind her, he retrieved his comb and sat on the mattress beside her, combing it into a straight, shining cable. It filled his hand with its weight, and brought the scent of sunshine, the sweet citrus of her perfume, and beneath it, the fainter fragrance of her skin.

He tried not to remember that first time he had done this for her, focusing on keeping his hands steady. And slowly he wove the strands into a simple braid.

This was his doing. His fault. Charity had been right. He invited calamity into the lives of everyone around him. Endangered all those who bothered to befriend him.

"Charity," he whispered shakily as he tucked the last few strands behind her ear. "I am not sure if you can hear me, but I am so very sorry, my love. Wait for me? Please."

He curled himself around her as he finally broke completely. Just as his mother had promised Charity he would.

24

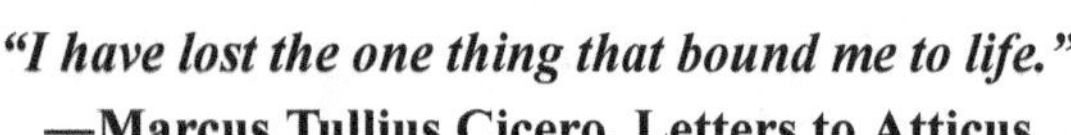

"I have lost the one thing that bound me to life."
—Marcus Tullius Cicero, Letters to Atticus

Thorne paced through the lower hallways of Fitzroy Manor. The entire house was silent as the grave. It had been two hours since Fitzroy's return. Two long hours since Thorne had banished himself from the scene of such heartbreaking tragedy and sent Hodges to contact the others.

Quinn had tried settling him in either the library or morning room, but Thorne was as tight as a bowstring. Too on edge to simply sit, waiting.

For the thousandth time, he wished Roland were here.

He wanted his brother's assistance almost as desperately as Lord Fitzroy had needed Thorne's that terrible evening he had tracked Lady Normanby. But it was better, he reasoned, that Roland stayed away.

He did not want his sister-in-law Grace to be a widow, or his godchildren to grow up without ever knowing their father. Yes, better Roland stayed away from London, as far as possible. Especially since his brother might also be outmatched by this task. Never, in all his years with Roland on the battlefield, had either man encountered an opponent he would call *evil*. But this was surely it.

It was a relief when the guard at the front door indicated he heard a carriage coming up the drive. Thorne beat the footman to the hall. The footman gave him a slight look of reproof, but it was not enough to prevent Thorne from opening the door, nor the guard from peering over his shoulder.

With marked relief, he recognised Lady Normanby. She was alone and looked unusually subdued as she came inside.

"Let me help you," Thorne offered, assisting her out of her coat.

As her right hand slid out of the sleeve, she turned towards him and settled her palm on the hand holding her coat. "Thank you for sending word, Sir Nathaniel," she told him with a small, sympathetic smile. "It is good of you to help the household restore itself to order."

Thorne dipped his chin towards his chest. "Order? I admit, Lady Normanby, it feels like there is so much more I should have done. I was here during both attacks on the household, and never have I been so good-for-nothing."

"Do not be so hard on yourself. Should it help any, I felt much the same in the Pulteney's coffee room. And also when I found myself locked in that wretched basement." Her mouth twisted wryly.

The hard line of his mouth softened into a crooked smile. He hid it, giving her coat to the footman to put away. Since they had left that squalid little basement behind, Selina had avoided mentioning Bellrose and anything about her capture, preferring to forget it all together.

He could hardly blame her. That basement had been a place of nightmares.

"How is Perry?" she asked gently, turning the subject.

"Not well," Thorne admitted, checking to make sure the hallway was empty. "He went to meet his mother, an angry man with a mission, and he returned like one who had lost the will to go on."

The marchioness sighed. "It has been a terrible day. Do not lose faith, Sir Nathaniel. He has had a terrible shock, and he is grieving. But we will rally him."

"I hope that you are right, Lady Normanby." His voice soured on the words. He could hear it, and he regretted that he had not hidden his feelings better, because she would hear it too. Knowing there were other ears about, he led her away to the library.

"A penny for your thoughts?" she asked him as he went to shut the door.

"The nature of justice," he said shortly, mindful of whom he was speaking to. "It is nothing to speak of."

"Because I am a woman?" Selina guessed.

"Because you are titled." He crossed his arms over his chest. "Are you familiar with the story of how I ended up going to war with Duke Percy on the continent, my lady? He was saving me from his father—our father. Thaddius Percy was going to tell the magistrate I was stealing from him, to see me dead or transported. A lie, of course. But who would have cared about the life of a poor servant's bastard son enough to defy the duke's heir?"

He closed his lips on the rest, appalled that he had aired that shameful part of his past so casually to a woman who was practically a stranger.

But she was as clever as Lord Fitzroy, and he had said enough. She easily picked up the thread of his thoughts. "I see. If Marian Fitzroy had been anywhere less highly placed in society, an accusation alone would have been enough to imprison her. But the lady is wealthy and noble, and the law overlooks so much when one is."

Thorne looked away, uncomfortable with the way Lady Normanby was studying him.

She clasped her hands together, moving to stand beside him so that they did not have to look at one another. "I must confess something, Sir Nathaniel. Despite the fact that I owe you a great deal, I have never thanked you properly."

"You do not owe me any thanks, my lady."

"Nevertheless," she said sternly, not letting him turn the conversation, "I did not, and I do not like to think about all the reasons I avoided the topic with you. But the worst is because… I feared you would at some point expose my secret. A lot of people would pay dearly to learn about what transpired in Bellrose's basement."

"No," he barked, insulted. "To betray one's trust at a moment someone is so vulnerable, when the events are not even their fault? I would never do such a thing."

"I believe this—now." The marchioness tilted her head slightly, looking at him from the corner of her eye. "Now that you have offered your own vulnerable piece of yourself to me. Do not be angry with me for harbouring fears, Sir Knight."

He shifted uneasily, but his pride was still prickly. "I am not angry with *you*, Lady Normanby."

"Perhaps not." She turned to him, standing too close, watching him with those green eyes that saw too much. "Still, if the world were less bound by rank, you might not make yourself look away from me so quickly."

Thorne ran his hand through his forelock, his cheeks warming. "Unfortunately, the world is as it is. And there is more to worry about than how fair my lot is."

"Well spoken," she said softly. "Still, these days I am reminded not to leave important things unsaid. Sir Nathaniel, that was the darkest hour of my life. You were the one who found me and brought me home. I do not like to imagine what might have happened if you had not, my knight. So… I shall fix my error and thank you now. I am truly in your debt."

Lady Normanby's beauty was as bright as sunshine along the edge of a blade, and her wits were twice as sharp. She was more than that, even. Bold, brave, and she had a sensibility worthy of a soldier. A man like him had no business admiring her; he might as well pine for the moon, she was so far above his standing.

But she was right; it was better not to leave important things unsaid. He let himself meet her gaze. "My lady, there is no debt between us. Any man of conscience should have done it. But to be the one who did it for you… to be worthy of your trust in such a moment, that is my privilege."

The marchioness's green eyes sifted through the nooks and crannies of his soul. Respect. Knowing. A hint of regret, and a whisper of curiosity. But curiosity would be all it ever was. They stood a world apart, and on a battlefield no less.

Multiple footfalls approaching interrupted their thoughts. The footman, Jack, had Lord Ravenscroft and Hodges in tow. All three looked as grim as Thorne felt.

"Forgive me for taking the liberty, but I asked Hodges to come. If ever we needed another pair of steady hands, it is now." The magpie adjusted his cuffs with a distracted air. "Tell me, how bad is the situation?"

Thorne shook his head. "He talked me in circles at first, but I finally got the physician to speak plain. A handful of days, perhaps as long as a week—she will weaken and pass if she does not wake."

"What did Perry say after he met his mother?" Selina pressed Hodges.

Hodges harrumphed, looking ill at ease. "Practically naught at all. Lord Fitzroy came out o' the Pulteney looking like a man plagued by war nerves. All I know is that his mother offered a bargain for the lady's cure—but my lord would have none of it."

Ravenscroft blinked. "He rejected his mother's offer? And why ever did you not lead with this information?"

Fitzroy's driver, who seemed to care little about the difference in their stations, stared flatly at Ravenscroft. "'Cause her price was too dear. She told him to name you and your valet for unnatural crimes if he wanted the cure, Magpie."

"Oh." The dandy swallowed visibly. There was a long moment of silence as they all digested that information. "Not that I wish to appear ungrateful, but… should a man not choose his wife's life over a friendly foe's?"

"Ain't the matter who's pulled in, is it?" the old mercenary sucked on his teeth. "There's no clean hand in such a bargain. The damage is in the choosin', not the choice. His dam set the board so my lord had to name who lives an' who dies. Playin' God like that'll blacken a man's soul. So he's made his choice—not to play at all."

"But… it need not blacken my soul if I offer myself up instead." Ravenscroft turned, a ghost of a smile flickering as his eyes met Lady Normanby's. "And who knows? It might not even demand our deaths. I could pen a confession for Prinny and be on a boat for France before the ink dries."

He gave a brittle little laugh. "After the year we have had, exile might be a holiday."

"No." The word spilled from Thorne's lips before Selina could take a breath. "Lord Ravenscroft, you cannot know that Marian Fitzroy would honour that bargain. You might throw your lives away for nothing."

The marchioness nodded her agreement, but absently, her eyes distant as she used her thumb to stroke her lower lip. She was thinking hard. "Sir Nathaniel is correct. And what is more… we should make no rash decisions. Marian's actions must have an aim besides just punishing her son."

"Stripping Fitzroy of his allies?" Thorne asked her softly, remembering how Lady Normanby's scandal had bound her hands.

"That too," she murmured. "If we are busy reacting to what she is doing to us, we cannot meddle with her plans. Think. She could have easily given Charity a more certain poison. What would Perry have done if Charity had died?"

Hodges scoffed. "He'd have hunted her down an' done for her like a mad cur. Let the consequences go hang."

"You are suggesting that she may be buying time. Bind her son with grief, so he cannot try to stop her, because he would have to abandon his sick wife to do so. The suffering she causes is naught but an added pleasure," the dandy said, growing angry.

"And if some of us are forced to go into hiding for our lives or our reputations… then so much the better, as far as Marian Fitzroy's concerned. Fewer hands to pry into her business, fewer eyes to watch for her work," added Lady Normanby.

"I hate that woman," Ravenscroft growled.

Thorne was rather certain that opinion was generally held. "She is a devil. Even when we know what she is about, she is leading us by the nose. We have to be cruel enough to ask Fitzroy to make a choice to set Charity aside until we deal with his mother, or we take the reins ourselves and face the hazards that come with it," he said, tilting his head in the marchioness's direction unconsciously. "And pray that we are equal to the task without him."

"Uncertain of my skills, are you, Sir Knight?"

His attention stopped wandering and as his eyes focused, he startled, realising he was staring directly at Lady Normanby. Her green eyes twinkled in challenge rather than offence.

"I shall remind you that you were the one to tell Fitzroy that we were all in this battle together, and to never forget to lean on us. Let him lean," she said serenely. "But… I need to put at least a few questions to Perry. We need to learn as much as we can about what happened. I gather you did not want to invade his privacy."

Thorne's shoulders dropped. "No, Lady Normanby. It was not my place to impose. Not at that moment."

"It is all right," she told him, shifting to leave. "I will do the intruding."

She headed back towards the stair, her footsteps purposeful, and Thorne looked at the two men beside him. Both were looking to Thorne with the expressions of someone hoping he would take command.

He scratched his eyebrow thoughtfully. "Ravenscroft, after Fitzroy, you stand to lose the most right now. It'd be folly to throw yourself on the sword, aye, but just as great a folly to think Marian Fitzroy would not turn that weapon against you herself if you stay. There'd be no reproach from me if you put your own safety first and leave. What will you do?"

"I am no swordsman, but neither am I such a craven," the magpie said sharply, fingers raking through his silvering hair. "Of course I will stay. Still… Antoine deserves the chance to choose his own course, even if it means withdrawing."

Thorne looked to Hodges, who shrugged with one shoulder. "I'm already bound for hell, Sir Nathaniel. Least I won't be lackin' for company on the road."

"So we are forced to ask now… where is Marian Fitzroy trying to keep us from looking?" Ravenscroft muttered, looking harassed. "Or where we might be able to pick up the threads of what she is up to now?"

"The man who killed Edmunds is still a threat we should keep watch for," Thorne remarked. "I tracked him to the edge of the woods, where he had his horse."

Hodges blew out a weary breath. "Near forgot that in the

midst o' all the devil's din. Best I pay a call to Red Hand tonight. Sammy said that one was marked by a scar. Might be Red knows who we're facin'. An' with luck, it'll be the sort we can grease with coin to leave us alone."

"With our luck?" Ravenscroft muttered, his expression dour. "I must speak with Antoine, of course. We would be fools not to place this before the Crown. For once, I think it wiser to petition Her Majesty than Prinny and inform her of what has transpired. She at least may be moved to sympathy. Or failing that, sufficiently alarmed to act."

"Will you be able to speak with her today?" Thorne asked him.

"Tomorrow, early," he said, lifting a hand in caution. "I want to make sure Antoine has sufficient time to leave London."

The mood was grim as the three men stood in a circle, contemplating. And after long minutes, they heard the sounds of Lady Normanby returning from upstairs. Thorne realised then that everyone had been waiting to see what she had to say about the situation.

Her eyes were shadowed, and she went to the sideboard where Fitzroy kept his liquor, doling out four glasses of whisky and passing them out.

"How is Lord Fitzroy now?" Thorne asked delicately, running his fingers around the bottom of the glass.

"Overset entirely," she said shortly. "It was better not to ask him for much. I limited myself to whether his mother had said anything about the poison itself. He said only that his mother learned it from another poisoner she met while in Russia."

She lifted the glass, pressing its chill to her cheek with a brief closing of her eyes. "I have to tell Sidmouth what has happened. Between my disgrace and the loss of Perry and Charity, we lack the means to easily approach any of the members of the Russian delegation. And perhaps… perhaps Xavier might know something about such an exotic poison. It is worth asking at any rate."

Hodges nodded sharply. "I'll put it to Red Hand an' all as well. Plenty o' killers keep a taste for poison."

"Then we have a course." Thorne inhaled through his nose. "Warn Antoine and the Queen," he said, meeting Ravenscroft's eyes before flicking his gaze to Hodges. "See if we can track Edmunds's killer. And see if there is any way to speak to the Russians. About poison, if nothing else."

"And you… guard the house and its people, Galahad," Ravenscroft added. "We have to protect those unable to protect themselves."

The marchioness raised her glass in a toast "To Charity's recovery. May she not be so easily undone. Especially by the likes of Marian Fitzroy."

The men murmured their agreement, tossing the whisky back.

"Martha, wait," Hodges said, following his sister down the servant's corridor.

Martha's shoulders hunched in as she stopped, but she waited, head down. She held a basket of dirty linens to her stomach like a shield. "What is it, Will?" she asked, her voice tired.

Hodges settled his palm on her shoulder. "You all right?"

"Ye certain the master won't blame Sammy for this?" she asked softly.

"Lord Fitzroy won't. Sammy had no part in what happened to her ladyship."

His sister turned to him, her lip caught between her teeth. "What've we been caught up in here, Will?"

"Somethin' bigger than us, but you keep to your work an'

leave the rest to me." He looked down at the basket. "You've been set to laundry?"

Her mouth tightened, and she shifted the basket against her hip. "I asked for work. Wanted to be useful."

He nodded absently, taking in his sister's face. The lines of worry, and the grey hair curling at her temples. "All right. I'll let ye get back to it then."

He did not say goodbye.

She hurried away, and Hodges lingered a moment in the dim corridor. Martha hadn't commented on the weaponry he carried as he prepared to leave the house. That was just as well.

The air was thick with the air of a storm not yet spent. He'd experienced such before, every eve before the next battle. Every time he loaded the carbine. It was as if the world had inhaled and held its breath, waiting.

Quinn was walking towards him from behind. He recognised the butler's gait without even looking. Before Fitzroy's butler could ask if something was amiss, Hodges turned towards the other former soldier.

"Quinn, I'd ask a favour of ye, one man to another."

The butler lifted one eyebrow, waiting. "Yes?"

"Don't reckon on trouble, but I'd be grateful if ye'd see to Martha an' the babes, should I not come back through that door. Got a bit o' coin set by to help her."

The butler paused for a moment and inclined his head. "Of course. I'll see it done—should the need arise. But I expect you'll come back."

Hodges huffed in agreement, leaving through the servants' door and heading to the stables.

Night was fully settled by the time he got back into London, and he made his way from Marylebone into the poorer areas, looking for Red Hand's haunts. He was weary himself.

The last time Hodges had seen Red Hand, Fitzroy had been

desperately seeking information about the Maker and Goldbourne's counterfeit press. The duchess had been kidnapped, and Fitzroy himself had been like a man possessed, all but throwing money at the bludgeoner to gain his assistance.

This time, Hodges had nothing. And Red Hand was not a friend.

The bar was raucous, but the volume dropped considerably when Hodges entered alone, still armed to the teeth. He lifted his empty hands, squaring off against the hostile faces turned his way. "Not here for a fight."

Red Hand stood up, his chair scraping loudly on the floor. "If it isn't our friend Two-faced Will. Come without his master. No fight? Then you've come beggin', or lyin'. Which is it?"

Hodges kept his hands open and his voice even. "Neither. An' you'll shut your jaw about the extra coin. That wasn't kept to cross Fitzroy. It kept him alive. Now. I've questions that touch you, same as me."

A ripple of laughter stirred among the men at the tables. Red Hand cocked his head. "You? With nothin' in your pocket but air? What makes you think I've a mind to talk?"

"You sent word once that Fitzroy's folk were marked. And now a cutthroat's spilled his old butler's blood. A man wi' a scar." He drew his finger in a half-moon below his eye. "An' a knack for carvin' messages in flesh."

"Moxley." Red Hand leaned over and spat on the floor. "That bloody nicker."

"You know him then, do you?"

"Oh, aye. No subtlety in that mad gallows-bird."

"Don't suppose you know who hired him?" Hodges said casually. "Threatened me sister an' her lad. I've half a mind to go pay the bastard a visit."

"Don't, so I don't," Red Hand said with a curl of his lip. "But I have a suspicion. Some foreign cove was playin' at bein'

Austrian while he was askin' around for a killer. Poor play, too. There was laughin' about it. As if we're soft heads what can't tell one tongue from another."

"Man?" Hodges barked, and Red nodded. "Russian?"

"Don't know what he was. Only what he weren't." Red Hand set his elbows on the table and folded his arms.

"An' why d'ye reckon it's that man?"

Red Hand evaded the question. "Where's yer master, Will? Strange sight, you steppin' in here wi'out his shadow. Or is Fitzroy frettin' o'er the debt he keeps pilin' at me door?"

"Believe me, Red, your debt's the last thing on Fitzroy's mind." Hodges looked around to be certain none of Red Hand's men were too close. "His dam poisoned his lady yester morn."

"The duchess? Poisoned?" Red's eyebrows crawled up his forehead.

"Aye. An' I'll thank ye to keep that information close. But if ye've any knowledge o' Russian poisons, we'd take it kindly."

"I'll nose about," Red Hand said with a grunt. "But poison's women's work, sure enough."

Hodges was not surprised that the Irishman didn't have ready information on poison. That Red Hand seemed to have a bit of a soft spot for Fitzroy, and his lady's plight, was not an opportunity to miss. "So then—this foreign cove," he prompted again.

"I told him no," Red Hand said harshly.

"What'd he ask for?" Hodges asked, frowning.

The Irishman cast another glance about, wary of ears too near. Then he leaned in close. "The blackguard was lookin' for someone fool enough to take on a job at one o' the Sovereigns' doin's. Even thinkin' on it's a death-warrant."

25

"If you press me to say why I loved him, I can say no more than because he was he, and I was I."
—Michel de Montaigne, The Complete Essays

L ord Ravenscroft's cravat was crooked. Again.

Antoine had tied it twice already, if his attempts could be described as such. More accurately, he had turned the carefully starched fabric into a wadded mess no self-respecting courtier would wear.

Any other aristocrat would have immediately sent their valet packing after such a poor performance, but not Lord Ravenscroft. Of course, other men of his social class did not usually love their valets as he did.

Other trysts and paramours came and went, but Antoine was the one he kept coming home to. Antoine was the one who made him whole. The one he could never acknowledge publicly.

When his valet made to undo the series of intricate knots for a third time, Ravenscroft reached up and grasped the man's trembling hands. Not that his hands were trembling less. Ravenscroft had spent an evening begging his lover to leave for his own safety, and Antoine had refused to go.

"*Mon cœur, ça suffiit.*" The magpie softened his words by pressing a kiss onto his lover's knuckles. "That is enough," he repeated.

He had never seen Antoine so out of sorts. Stubble darkened Antoine's cheeks, and his hair was still mussed. Ravenscroft forced himself to say again, "I wish you would not stay in London, *mon amour.*"

Antoine pulled his hands free and tugged on the linen knot of the cravat harder than was warranted. "And *I* wish you would not keep trying to send me away."

"We should not be arguing—"

"I will not leave you here on your own!" the man shouted in his face, and shocked, Ravenscroft stared at his lover. "How could you ask me to do this?"

The magpie blinked moist eyes. "Because I love you, you simpleton. Is that not reason enough?"

Antoine grabbed the ruins of the cravat in his fist like he was ready to strangle his lord. "I will not go without you. We both go, or not at all."

Fitzroy forgive him. "If you ask me to go—"

"No," Antoine said with resignation, though the shadow of fear did not leave his eyes. "You should not abandon your duties or your friends. So you will stay. And I will stay with you. You great, stupid, loyal lummox."

The magpie let out a stuttering laugh, a little pained because Antoine was still throttling him. But his lover's anger also stemmed from knowing he would have done the same. Even now —if the choice were his alone, the soft-hearted Antoine would not abandon Fitzroy in this hour of need.

Ravenscroft studied the other man's face. He had memorised

every inch of it. It was exactly because of this man—this tender, caring soul—that Ravenscroft understood a tenth of Fitzroy's sorrow. If Antoine had been the one lying gravely still in a sickbed, the magpie would burn the world down.

Still, his heart was tearing in two. Their lives now depended only on the silence of the most vile person he had ever had the misfortune of meeting, and that was no guarantee at all. He still wanted Antoine to go. To be safe.

"Then we will stay. But be sure, darling. I can refuse you nothing, especially when you speak to me this way."

"I know, *mon ange noir*," Antoine's eyes glittered. "We will stay. We will stay for us. For our right to be happy. I will not cede control over our lives—our future—into the hands of Marian Fitzroy."

The man's bravado filled Ravenscroft with a desperate need. He lifted his hands and cupped Antoine's cheeks, savouring the stubble that scraped against his palms. It grounded him in the moment.

"*Je t'aimerai jusqu'à la mort,*" Antoine breathed, their lips inches apart.

"Let us hope that is no time soon," the magpie said dryly, pulling Antoine's mouth to his.

His valet finally stopped strangling him with his cravat, sinking his fingers roughly instead into Ravenscroft's hair. It hurt in the best sort of way—a trace of pain and wild pleasure commingling, making everything sharper and more vivid. Need. Want. Passion, and tenderness.

It made Ravenscroft come alive.

He needed to go, and was, in fact, due at the palace within the half hour. However, seeing the Queen was the last thing on his mind at that moment. He held Antoine's face captive as he brushed his lips over the man's mouth in a chaste kiss that promised more later. Once. Twice.

As if that would ever be enough.

But then, Antoine loosed his hold and slid his hands down until they rested on Ravenscroft's chest. He pressed against it, halting them there. "Let me tie your cravat properly so you can go see the Queen. You will be late."

He well knew it, but the magpie still grumbled, unsatisfied.

His valet gave him a wicked, languid gaze and added, "Tying *you* up properly will have to wait."

Ravenscroft sucked in air, his interest piqued. "Do not make promises you do not intend to keep."

Antoine lifted his nose, dangling the ruined cravat on his finger. "Perhaps I shall keep this as proof of my word then."

Ravenscroft was, after all, late to arrive at the palace.

In his defence, he did not expect to be waylaid by Hodges, waiting just outside of Carlton House, who also looked like he hadn't slept in a week. Hodges had come to find him after seeking the counsel of the marchioness, following his meeting in the slums.

Only Lady Fitzroy and her henchmen surely would be so daring as to stage an attack at one of the handful of remaining events. Clearly her son was not the target—not if he was at Charity's bedside and unable to intervene.

That meant an attack on someone else. Someone noble or higher. Perhaps even on a member of the royal family.

When the royal guard waved him through the door, Ravenscroft was once again cool and collected.

"Your Majesty," he said, bowing in obeisance. "You are as radiant as you are wise this morning."

She gave him a look. "Wise enough to question why you would bother gilding my ears with your glib tongue, rather than speak with my son," the Queen replied, her tone cold and deliberate. "Your request for a private audience gives me cause for concern, Lord Ravenscroft. Rise and account for yourself."

With a deep breath to steady himself, Ravenscroft explained what had happened at the Fitzroy estate. The Queen's expression grew ever more grim, the blood draining from her face as Charity's plight became clear.

When the magpie finished telling her about the attack on the house and Fitzroy's later meeting with his mother, she was silent for a long time.

"This touches not only one household, but the Crown itself," she said at last, her voice low but ringing. "If the Duchess Atholl lies poisoned in her own rooms, and there is no proof that cannot be excused as accusations in a private family squabble, then no subject high or low is secure. You have done right to bring this to me, though the telling chills me to the marrow."

"You are right about not being secure," he said unhappily, couching his words carefully. "For my part in the kidnapping of Lark, my head may be the next to fall. Marian Fitzroy offered to sell her son the duchess's cure if... he pronounced a slander so vile it cannot be named in polite company."

The Queen cocked her head curiously, but her eyes were keen and knowing. "Did he accept?"

"No, ma'am. His man said that Lord Fitzroy refused. He would not pretend to be God, choosing who lives and dies." Ravenscroft let his shoulders drop as a complicated feeling of guilt pulled through him. "Not even to save his love."

Charlotte leaned on her fist. "I cannot help but think your situation is not unlike what happened to Lady Normanby."

"If Your Majesty means to say Marian Fitzroy has set out to have the lot of us blindfolded, deafened, gagged, and trussed like fowls, we have reached much the same conclusion. Fitzroy's mama is buying time. But I believe we have begun to smell the plot."

The Queen sat straighter. "Go on."

"Marian Fitzroy, through one of her charming accomplices, no doubt, may be scheming an attack at one of the few entertainments left before the Sovereigns flee our shores. And knowing the lady's tastes as we do, it is the princess who likely sits most squarely in her sights."

He explained, the bile burning the back of his throat. Though Red Hand had not known who the target was, it was not hard to form a short list of the most vulnerable and likely. The Queen was too well guarded at St James's and Buckingham House. The loss of Prinny—though Ravenscroft was loyal to the man—would hardly be a blow to England, even he had to admit.

The marchioness had felt certain Marian's target had to be the princess. The future Queen of England. Ravenscroft, unfortunately, agreed. But what was truly terrifying was the idea that an assassin might be attempting to pose as one of the allies to do so.

Charlotte's knuckles whitened as she paused again, considering. "There are not many remaining events. It is just as well that we ended the engagement. I will not need to offer explanations to anyone for closeting the princess. Someone might be trying to spark another war by posing as an enemy."

"Before Your Majesty consigns her to her rooms, might we have a word?" Ravenscroft ventured. "Lady Fitzroy has already managed at least one private audience with your granddaughter since her arrival. If the Princess knows anything of her schemes, now would be the moment to press her for it."

The Queen rapped her cane on the floor. The door swung open, and a retainer hurried in.

"Fetch my granddaughter," she ordered. "And my physician."

"Yes, Your Majesty," the retainer said, though not without first studying the Queen for any signs she was unwell. When she banged her cane again threateningly, he leapt into action and darted out the door.

The physician was the first to arrive. The man hesitated in the doorway when he found the Queen looking well and Lord Ravenscroft sitting at her side. "You will go to the Fitzroy manor," Charlotte informed him. "Do all that you can for the household. If there is any chance you can help my diamond recover from whatever poison she was given, I want you to do so."

He was waved off, and a knock on the door heralded the arrival of her granddaughter shortly after. The Queen indicated a chair, bidding the young woman to take a seat, and dismissed the servants who had followed the princess into the room.

"Charlotte Augusta," the Queen intoned, her voice grave, "we are to speak of matters so grave that you must first give me your solemn word that these confidences will not pass beyond this room."

The princess's eyes widened. "Of course."

"Do you consider the Duchess Atholl a friend?" the Queen asked.

The princess's expression grew wary. "I value her counsel, yes."

The Queen huffed. "I forgave the Frogmore incident days ago. Lord Ravenscroft can reassure you on that."

He nodded when the princess turned his way.

"Then yes, Her Grace is my friend. Why are you asking me this question?"

"Because the duchess is ill and may be dying. I want to be certain that you will give me the truth for any questions I ask next."

The princess blanched. "Charity is ill?"

"She was poisoned, Princess," Ravenscroft said, taking pity

on the young woman. He retrieved his handkerchief from his pocket and passed it to her. "Lady Fitzroy is responsible. We also believe that is not the end of her schemes to cause harm."

"We need to know," the Queen interrupted cuttingly, "whether Marian Fitzroy, or her daughter, Lady Lark, have said anything seditious in your company. Any word—any hint—that they may have indicated the nature of what treasonous plot is afoot."

Princess Charlotte inhaled sharply, her eyelids flickering. "Including the matter of Prince William?"

When both the Queen and Ravenscroft looked at her sharply, the princess shook her head. "Charity told me that Lady Fitzroy —" she cut her words short, looking at Ravenscroft doubtfully. No doubt she was uncertain whether he knew about her involvement in William's poisoning, and Ravenscroft lauded her caution.

"Lady Fitzroy was the one who schemed to put the henbane in your hands," Ravenscroft finished. "Your father told me later."

The princess accepted that. "I cannot think of a single thing either one said that suggested an act of treason," she said softly. "I have done nothing more than exchange a polite word when necessary, Grandmama. I promise I would not lie to you about this."

"What of your prospects?" the Queen countered. "Marian Fitzroy has been playing her game for months now, and has found you to be a willing pawn at least once. Has she encouraged your affections for anyone other than William? Perhaps Prince Nicholas?"

Ravenscroft peered closely at the princess, but she betrayed no startlement at Nicholas's name, or any telltales of a woman about to lie.

"She has neither encouraged nor discouraged me at all," the princess stammered.

"The Russians? The Grand Duchess?" he prompted. "Have

they said anything suspicious in your company? Encouraged you to make an unsuitable match?"

The princess's cheeks coloured. "Her Imperial Highness thought Prince William unsuitable," she admitted, "but she hardly encouraged me to make an unsuitable match. Unless you count being introduced to half the eligible men she thought handsome encouragement." The princess's eyes rolled slightly.

The Queen probed again and again, not letting up. For Ravenscroft, it was clear that the Russians were taking an active hand in guiding the princess's mind toward alliances that fit their needs, but perhaps not that of England.

But then, so had the Austrians and Prussia. Attempting to influence the young heir towards a positive relationship was hardly an indication of something subversive or untoward. Marian Fitzroy's intervention in the princess's future, at best, might be part of a Russian plot.

But if Marian truly had designs on the Princess's life, meddling in her marital plans past blocking an engagement to William did not seem to make any sense at all.

"What will happen now?" the princess asked when it was clear they had no further questions. "Is there any treatment the physician can give to the duchess?"

"Not unless he knows something about esoteric Russian poisons," Ravenscroft muttered under his breath. But not quietly enough, because the princess heard him clearly.

"You think Lady Fitzroy used a Russian poison?" she asked sharply.

"Lady Fitzroy told her son she learned it from a woman there," he clarified.

"Perhaps then a Russian would have the cure. Surely, we could ask them for assistance, then," the princess said stoutly to her grandmother. "It is the least we can do for Her Grace."

Queen Charlotte clearly regretted that Ravenscroft had ever

opened his mouth about the poison. "Charlotte Augusta," she began warningly, "think for a moment about the questions that would arise from such an inquiry. They are already upset that Lord Fitzroy claimed the guardianship of his sister from under their noses. The Tsar might take it as an affront. I cannot see a way to ask delicately without suggesting that either Lady Fitzroy or a countryman is responsible for the duchess's current state."

"The Tsar may, but his sister might not," the princess countered. "If I sent a note to the Grand Duchess, I think she would consider assisting us. She liked Charity. Might it help, Grandmama?"

It was a good suggestion, one that Ravenscroft felt he should have thought of himself. But the events of the last few weeks were clearly taking a toll on all of their minds.

The Queen bowed her head, considering her granddaughter's suggestion seriously. "Pen your note here. I will ask Lord Sidmouth to deliver it on your behalf. We cannot risk sending you anywhere near the Pulteney."

The princess looked positively thrilled to be useful, and she hurried off to write the note. Lord Ravenscroft went to make his own departure, but the Queen had one last thing to say.

"Do not pin your hopes on the Grand Duchess," she advised. "The woman already has too much control over my granddaughter. I will instruct Sidmouth not to send along this note until we are certain it is our last resort."

Though she berated herself for it, Selina fussed with imagined dirt on her skirts the entire trip to the Fitzroy manor in the early afternoon. They were clean; she knew they were. But sometimes it felt as though the grime of Bellrose's house seemed to have permanently stained her.

As the carriage rolled to a stop, she caught herself searching the windows of the front drawing room for any signs of someone looking out. It would have been nice to spot Charity's familiar golden blonde hair gleaming in the streaming sunlight. Deep inside, however, she acknowledged the truth.

She was hoping to see someone else.

Someone, specifically, who might be looking for her as well.

But that would be wrong for so many reasons, not least of which was that she was the daughter of a duke and a widowed marchioness with a reputation for intrigue. Ravenscroft's nickname of 'Galahad' was far too appropriate for the unblemished soul that seemed to be Sir Nathaniel.

Selina should leave him alone.

She wrenched her mind away from the direction of her thoughts. She was there for Perry and for Charity. If she was grateful for anything about his presence, it should be that Sir Nathaniel was willing to fight the current battle at their side.

Still, her heart beat faster in her breast when she found him waiting for her in the front entrance hallway.

"Is there any improvement in Charity's condition today?" she asked him as she handed her hat and gloves off to the waiting footman.

"No. But at least, neither has she worsened. Enough time has passed that the physician has ruled out the worst of the known poisons," Thorne answered.

"And Perry?"

The knight hesitated, unwilling to put an answer to it. "Come. Lord Ravenscroft is waiting in the drawing room for us."

Ravenscroft, still in his court wear, looked too weary to bother trying to hide his own concern. "I hope you had better luck in your endeavours than I, Lady Normanby. The possibility of an assassination attempt on the royal family was taken poorly by the Queen, to say the least."

"Yes, well, you may just imagine how well Sidmouth took the same news," she retorted, availing herself of the settee across from Ravenscroft. "He warned us again to avoid provoking the Russians. Xavier was happy to provide any assistance he might, but exotic poisons are not his usual fare. He will send word here if he has any luck."

The magpie grunted tiredly. "The Queen also warned me against approaching the Russians. It seems that the Tsar's sensibilities must take priority over our safety and saving Charity's life. At least she let the princess write a letter to the Grand Duchess requesting aid—though the Queen wishes to hold off on sending it as long as possible."

Sir Nathaniel remained silent, but from his expression, it was clear that little they had to say was unexpected.

"I hate to admit it, but the Queen is right. The Grand Duchess plays the power games well. Without a clear incentive for her, she cannot be counted on to go out of her way to save Charity, no matter who asks her to get involved," said Selina.

She clasped her hands in her lap, thinking. "Did Perry eat at least?" she asked softly.

Thorne gave his head the barest shake.

Where to go from here? There was no use in asking Perry for his opinion. From what Sir Nathaniel had said, even coaxing him to eat a few bites was a challenge. Lord Ravenscroft and Sir Nathaniel were both looking to her for a decision.

Selina pressed her fingertips to the bridge of her nose and then gathered her skirts and rose from her seat.

"Where are you going?" Ravenscroft asked.

"To play the role of intruder again. I shall throw propriety out of the window and speak with Perry's sister. *Something* must shake loose."

"Should it be me?" he countered. "She likely still resents both you and Sir Nathaniel for her kidnapping."

"I am counting on the fact that she despises me, Ravenscroft. Her anger will be a useful tool."

Hers certainly was. Just as she had told Charity while they had been trapped in Bellrose's basement, Selina began to spindle her own white-hot rage, bundling it within her breast until she could easily imagine herself a dragon.

Lark was standing at her window when Selina entered. She turned around at the creak of the door opening, her eyes wide with surprise. But her mouth settled into a mulish scowl when she saw who it was.

"I did not give you leave to enter," Lark stated baldly, sharpening her glare.

"I did not ask for your permission," Selina countered. "Come with me. There is something I must show you."

"Why should I?"

"Because I think you know far, far more than you are pretending to, and you are hiding your head like an ostrich. Your butler was killed, yes?"

She nodded slowly.

"Did you watch the meeting between Perry and your mother?"

Lark's lowered eyes were answer enough.

"I assume you also have not been stricken deaf," Selina spat. "You look out the window now because you can tell something is wrong. Badly so."

Lark sniffed, but she did not disagree. Selina seized the girl by the wrist and yanked her past her maid, dragging her back into the carpeted hallway and a few doors down. Selina entered the empty master bedroom and kept going until she reached the connecting door to the next suite.

She did not tell Lark to keep quiet. There was no need. She pushed the adjoining door open on its carefully oiled hinges and shoved Lark bodily into the doorway. "Look," she said simply.

The room was so quiet she could hear Lark's hard swallow.

That, she expected. But the involuntary half-step forward was more telling. Lark still cared for her brother.

She was not as cruel and twisted as Marian.

Selina caught Lark's hand to stop her, trying to avoid even looking in on that scene of such private despair. "Leave him be," she warned. "But look your fill, Lark. *This* is what your mother does to the people who defy her. She is violent, cruel, and evil. *This* is why you were spirited away. He did not want you burdened with such sorry knowledge that your mother is a murderer. So because he loved you enough to keep you safe, your mother punished him by doing this."

Lark swayed slightly, setting one hand to the doorframe.

"Do you see it now? Without a cure, Charity will not survive the week. Your brother will go, as well. He will not want to go on without her. And you—you have not been surprised by a single thing I have told you about your mother. Admit it," Selina hurled at her.

"I knew my mother was ambitious," she said shakily. "I didn't *know* precisely how far she would go… but… perhaps a part of me was aware. That part of me has always been terrified of crossing my mother. Of getting her attention in the wrong way."

"Do you believe me yet that your mother is up to no good? Because you are the only hope I have left of figuring out your mother's little scheme in time to prevent an attack on the Crown that *could* spark war."

Selina's bosom heaved as she struggled with the surprising *anger* flooding her limbs and making her hands shake. When Lark cowered away from her, she tried to gentle her voice. "You are the only hope of bringing your brother to his senses. And possibly saving his wife."

Lark's lips parted in genuine shock. "Perry… he married the duchess?"

"Three days ago," Selina murmured, finally glancing into the bedroom. Peregrine sat in a chair pulled up beside Charity. His head was turned away, resting on his arms where they lay folded on the mattress top beside her. He gave no sign of noticing their presence at all.

Or perhaps he simply did not care.

"That is the new Lady Fitzroy, lying there. And you can change the ending of this tale," Selina said, shaking Lark by the shoulder roughly. "What does your mother want to achieve?"

Lark closed her eyes and went perfectly still. "She has already achieved her aim."

"Which was—?" Selina asked, frustration cutting through her last strand of patience.

"To see me wed. To Nicholas—the Tsar's youngest brother."

26

"The only thing that should surprise us is that there are still some things that can surprise us."
—François de La Rochefoucauld

Lark Fitzroy had married Prince Nicholas of Russia? Selina would have been less shocked had someone announced they had seen the Archbishop waltzing at Almack's.

"Well," Selina said flatly. "That is the most astonishing nonsense I have ever been asked to credit."

"It is the truth. I bear his token." Lark's hand went to the chain at her throat. From beneath the folds of her neckline, she drew out a small golden locket, its polish so bright it was clearly newly made. She flicked it open, revealing the twin portraits inside—Nicholas on one side, her own face opposite. The paint was still so fresh it seemed to gleam.

Her chin lifted. "He carries the mate to this. Commissioned as soon as we arrived in London, and gifted to me on our wedding day."

Selina's tongue failed her utterly. She prided herself on keeping abreast of every major activity in London. Or—if not aware, at least having predicted the possibility.

But in all of her speculations with the others, not a single one of them had once considered that Nicholas's English love was *Lark*. There had been no rumours of a wedding, no word of sitting for portraits. Nothing.

Likely, just as Marian Fitzroy had intended.

Marrying Lark to Prince William of Orange had made a certain sense. It would have put Lark on the Dutch throne, and Lady Fitzroy one step behind. But Nicholas… was not the Tsar. Not even the heir. There was another brother, Constantine, between them. And that was only the beginning of the issues with this marriage that made no sense.

But… then, the pieces of the conspiracy slotted together in a way that the Marchioness of Normanby did not like. Not one bit.

She pushed past Lark, hurrying to the bed. "Perry. Perry!" Selina said urgently, laying her hands on his shoulders. "Please. I need you to pay attention, if only for just a moment."

For a long moment there was nothing. Then, Perry roused himself slowly, his movements stilted from the long hours of sitting so uncomfortably by the bed. He lifted his gaze to Selina, unshaven, rumpled. Eyes empty, dark circles of fatigue beneath.

"What is it?" he asked flatly, his voice rusty.

"I know what your mother is doing with your sister. With Lady Lark," she said again to him, trying to get him to attend. "Finally… I have enough to figure out what her true plan is."

Except—there were still parts that made no sense. To figure out the rest, she needed him. His knowledge of his mother's thoughts. And to get his help to manage his sister, who might grow reluctant to aid them if she believed there would be trouble.

There would be trouble, if she had even a fraction of this right.

Peregrine stared through her. "Why? It does not matter what my mother does anymore."

"Do not say such things. Of course it matters," she said fiercely. "If you give up now, you hand her the victory. We are days away from something dire. We finally may have enough information to stop her, and I need you to pay attention to this, Perry. Other people's lives are at risk."

"Other people's lives are at risk because of me." His voice was hollow. "Because I keep fighting her. Perhaps I should stop before more people are hurt."

She needed to get him out of this room. Away from where he could be reminded of Charity. Where, perhaps, she could slap some sense into him without feeling too badly about it.

"You do not mean that. Your mother will hurt people regardless of whether you fight her. Please. Come out to the sitting room for a bit so we don't disturb Charity," Selina ordered him.

"No," he grunted. "I should not leave her alone."

"She will not be alone. Please, Perry. I will get the maid to sit beside her. I promise."

He shook his head stubbornly, making to lay his head down on the bed again, but Selina grabbed him around his upper arm, pulling him upright. "Does it matter more what your mother does," she said, forcing a note of cruelty into her voice, "if I tell you that your sister may very well be in danger from your mother's scheme?"

That made him hesitate, and he looked up again blearily.

"*All* your friends are in danger," Lark added her voice to Selina's. "She did this to Charity. Surely you do not expect her to leave Lady Normanby, Lord Ravenscroft, and Sir Nathaniel alone. They need you to come back to them."

It was her voice that broke through the fog in his mind. He

blinked a few times to clear his vision and then set his red-rimmed eyes on his sister's face.

"Lark?" he asked, as though he disbelieved his sore eyes. "I—" He turned back to stare at Charity's far too still form, and then again looked at his sister. "I have failed people so many times," he said brokenly. "You should not put such faith in me."

"Then we are a merry band of failures together. We have our guilt for what we have not stopped on our own," Selina said tartly, holding a hand out to Perry. "But I refuse to let your mother go unchallenged. Will you? I think that together, with what we know now, we can yet thwart her."

His face fell into lines of worry, and he looked down at Charity again. That he considered the request at all was progress, but taking him any great distance from Charity was going to be an impossibility.

Selina added, "Only to the sitting room, Perry. We can leave the door open."

Lark seemed to intuit that only touch had any real power to reason with him. She bent over and clasped his hand in hers, drawing him up from his seat. Stiffly, he rose from the wooden chair into which he had consigned himself. His grimace betrayed the ache in his bones.

As he stood upright, Selina rushed from the room to call for Charity's maid, and then for the two men downstairs. When she got back, she stopped still, finding Perry and Lark locked in an embrace, each one clinging to the other as they finally reconciled their quarrel in this shared moment of grief.

Peregrine moved like a man half-asleep. But at least he *was* moving. Lark pulled him towards the sitting room in careful steps, her arm wrapped around his waist, and Selina took his other arm.

Suddenly, the sitting room was full to brimming. Lord Ravenscroft and Sir Nathaniel were there, helping to rearrange the disordered pieces of furniture into a conversational setting.

Nathaniel helped Lark settle Perry in the middle of a sofa. Quinn was only minutes behind, bearing tea and sandwiches.

Lark sat to one side of Perry, and Selina looked over the group, settling herself in one of the armchairs, between Lark and Ravenscroft. Commandeering the teapot, she gave herself time to order her thoughts, pouring cups for everyone.

"Make him eat," she told Lark in a low tone when Peregrine pushed away the offers of food. And while Lark coaxed him into finally eating two bites of sandwich, Selina looked at Ravenscroft and Thorne. "Lady Lark is married to Prince Nicholas."

Perry was listening well enough that he choked on a bite of sandwich, and Thorne, sitting on his other side, rushed to pat him on the back.

"What? When? *How?*" Peregrine finally sputtered, disbelief and outrage bringing more colour to his cheeks than the food. He was staring at Selina, but she turned her gaze to Lady Lark, encouraging her to answer the question.

"Six days ago, Prince Nicholas and I wed in a private ceremony at the von Lievens' residence," Lark told him.

Understanding lit through Selina. One of the pieces that hadn't made sense finally did. "The Russian Orthodox Church in London. It is in their home."

Ravenscroft, one hand over his gaping mouth, let out a slightly hysterical titter. "Well, we certainly didn't predict this. To think, we believed Nicholas was courting the princess!"

Betrayal glinted dangerously on Peregrine's face, but his pallor worsened. "I *trusted* the Lievens. You mean to tell me they permitted such a thing to happen under the Tsar's nose? After they told me it was their *duty* to maintain the relationship between our two countries? That is a violation of their laws!"

"Perry, they didn't know," Lark murmured. "They weren't there. Just Mama, the Russian priest, and the witnesses—"

"Selina was right," he said, horrified. "You are in danger.

What you and Nicholas have done violates the laws of succession. Alexander might consider all these actions *treason*. You will be accused of seducing the prince. You could be arrested."

This time, Lark was the one to pale to the shade of parchment. "Treason?" she breathed, her voice almost a squeak. "But... I didn't know."

"Why the rushed ceremony? And why keep this a secret?" he asked. "Has he—are you—" Peregrine wavered slightly in his seat, and Sir Nathaniel steadied him.

She covered her face, her cheeks scalding to be discussing this in front of people who were practically strangers to her. "I am not expecting," she mumbled.

"Did our mother force him to marry you somehow?" Perry asked, clearly hopeful that it was only a manipulation of Marian's. "Who knows what nonsense she might have filled his head with—"

"No!" Lark said, twisting to face him. "He truly loves me. He told me it all the time when we were together... and he told me he'd find a way for us to marry... but he didn't want to wait. We exchanged our first vows to one another in Russia, to be married in the sight of Heaven. And then we married in the church here."

Peregrine sputtered. "And how did you come to be married as an Anglican in a Russian church, anyway?"

Lark stared down at her hands in her lap. "Mama had me convert."

"This was why Marian targeted only Edmunds. Your sister was already married; she had only to wait long enough to reveal it." Selina rubbed her thumb against her lip idly.

"Be easy," the knight murmured to the both of them as Lark and Perry grew distraught. "We will solve this muddle somehow. How did Nicholas think he was going to get around the Tsar's permission? How long did you two think you were going to keep this secret?"

"We were waiting until the right moment to make the announcement and begin our married life. I was told I had to keep the news to myself. I knew that if it was discovered we had married before he got his brother's permission, the Tsar would annul it. But Nicholas and my mother both said that it would be all right. She was certain she could help Nicholas find some way to convince Alexander. We would not have to keep the secret long." Lark stared at her brother, willing him to understand.

"And you believed your mama?" Ravenscroft said, his voice dryly incredulous.

"I did," Lark fired back. "Nicholas is a prince, but he is not the heir. Why should the Tsar care if he marries me?"

"What do you suppose the odds are that Marian would even bother attempting to convince the Tsar?" Ravenscroft drawled. His thoughts were clearly already moving ahead with Selina's. But not everyone else was caught up yet.

"I do not understand why Marian chose this course," Thorne said predictably, brows furrowed. "Marrying Lark to William seemed like a reasonable path to power. And a simpler one. Nicholas is a prince, but he is third in line. Even if Marian killed Tsar Alexander to clear the way towards succession, Constantine is safe in Russia, and he would also annul the wedding."

"The second brother might not be a consideration," Selina said idly. "Xavier—years ago, and in his capacity as the Order's spymaster, mind you—heard rumours that Constantine might be too unstable to sit on the throne. There was talk of him being passed over."

Ravenscroft snorted softly. "That may explain the gossip I overheard. Constantine is a loyal dog to Alexander, but the whispers say he had to be left behind because he was apt to bite the guests. So, Nicholas might actually be the heir after all. And if Constantine still ascends despite that… well, one dead Tsar might easily become two."

Lark's mouth became an O of horror. It was painfully clear Marian Fitzroy had kept her daughter mostly in the dark about her plans. "I know what she did to Charity and Edmunds... but... could it possibly be true she would *kill* Alexander? My husband's own brother? And possibly Constantine too?"

Perry wrapped an arm around her shoulders and pulled her against him, whispering too softly for Selina to hear.

"But... why would she do such a thing?" Lark said plaintively.

"Because if her plan worked, it would put you and your husband on the throne," Thorne told her, not unkindly. "You would have a hand on the largest empire and most powerful military in the world. And your mother, I'm sorry to say, lass, would have her hand on *you*."

He swept his forelock back from his face again, joining Selina and Ravenscroft with a slightly disbelieving laugh on his lips. "Aye, Russia *would* be a far greater prize to your mother than the Netherlands. I will give her that. The woman's audacity could shame the devil."

But Perry wasn't laughing with them. He was fuming. *Good*, Selina thought. She needed him back in the land of the living. And if this protective anger at his sister's situation helped keep him present in the moment, she would take it.

"So much of what we assumed is wrong," Selina murmured, her eyes unseeing as she swept the whole riddle to the floor in her mind and reassembled the pieces anew. "There remain questions about what would be required to render their marriage legitimate. The Tsar's permission, and her conversion, are not the only pieces. But that is not the most pressing issue.

"What is dire for now is the piece that Hodges was able to discover—that someone was trying to strike a noble target at one of the events. We warned the Queen because I assumed that person was aimed at the Crown."

Thorne's face lit in understanding. "You think that is when Marian plans to move against Alexander. In front of the sovereigns, here on English soil. That is why she was stalling for time. And why she—" his face turned to Peregrine.

"It is why she poisoned my wife with a lingering poison instead of something sure," Perry said, his voice growing hollow. "So that I would be too distraught to help. I did exactly as she expected me to."

Sir Nathaniel rested his hand on Peregrine's shoulder, gripping it firmly. "No one here blames you. Your mother created an iron paradox to make you bleed at every possible turn. It should tell you something that she was so concerned you would break free. And you did. We have not lost too much time."

Anguish filled Peregrine's face as he looked through the open doorway to Charity.

"We are not giving up on Charity, Canary," Ravenscroft told him. "She is not in any pressing danger just yet. But we need to make haste. Comfort yourself by imagining how satisfying it will be to *force* your mother to concede. And perhaps then we will take Charity's cure from her."

Wise to keep appealing to his rage, Magpie, Selina thought, as she continued laying out in her head what they knew. She touched on that other curious piece.

"Red Hand's warning about the man he said hired Moxley," Selina murmured. "He was pretending to be Austrian. Because the Austrians are a lucrative target and a friendly foe… or because the man who hired Moxley was trying to hide the fact that he was Russian?"

"Darling, why not both? How many times have we observed already that Marian Fitzroy will never do something for one reason alone?" Ravenscroft said drolly. "If she builds the event correctly, and God knows the woman is a fiend at doing such, accusations that an Austrian hired an assassin could destroy

Russia's relations with Austria. Give them an excuse to go to war, at the worst. And for such a thing to happen on *British* soil?"

He held a hand to his chest, rendered speechless at the idea. "Besides, every assassination needs a scapegoat."

Selina suddenly felt filthy. As though even discussing this terrible act was getting dirt smudged all over her. "We need to find a way to warn the Russians. We must alert Lord Sidmouth," she said, her fingers creeping to her skirts.

"And have him do what? March into the Tsar's quarters and announce he is to die?" Lord Ravenscroft asked. "They might not take kindly to such news."

"Worse than the Tsar dying here?" Selina spat back. She pressed her lips together to stop frustration from making her say something else. Ravenscroft was correct, and she was smarter than this.

"Have him reach out to the Grand Duchess," came an unexpected voice.

All of their heads turned as if on a swivel, to Lark. Her head was bowed, and she was staring at her hands in her lap as if contemplating the absolute ruin her life was shortly about to become.

27

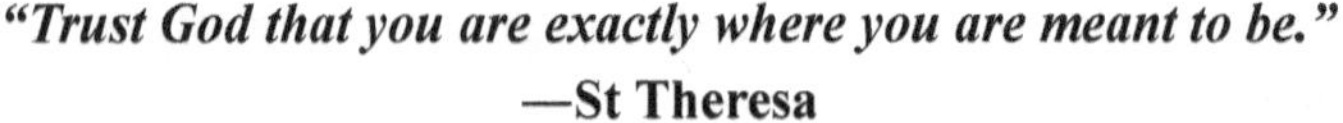

S ince he had reached the age of majority, Peregrine had disliked having people fawn over him. But the people in his house kept touching him now. Steering him. Distracting him.

The contact of his odd little family was grounding him. Helping him emerge from the fog. When his words faltered, or his thoughts drifted back into a darker place, they brought him back to task. He needed their touch. They needed him, so he found he didn't really mind.

Charity's lady's maid was enough of a battle-axe to actually refuse to leave the chair beside Charity. At least, she pointed out with a sniff, until he had a chance to freshen himself up.

Her defiance was so surprising that he couldn't find it within himself to be offended. Especially when he had to concede she was correct. He needed a shave. And a change of clothes, he supposed.

By the time Croft—and the magpie, who invited himself in— had finished with him, he was turning back into something much more… human. Ravenscroft kept himself from being ejected by being useful. Not only did he fill Perry in on every single scrap of information they had collected, no matter how seemingly irrelevant, he also pulled more from Peregrine about both confrontations with his mother.

Peregrine agreed it was important that every detail be shared equally. After all, should something happen to one of them, the others would need it to carry on. With his mother's plans nearly to their critical points, things were growing exceptionally dangerous for all of them.

"Will Prinny give you enough of an opportunity to leave, should the worst happen?" Perry asked the magpie discreetly. "Perhaps you should bring Antoine here."

Ravenscroft patted his cheek. "I appreciate your mothering, Fitzroy, but I have things in hand. Still, the offer of shelter in the worst case is appreciated."

With a finger, the magpie poked the sachet Charity had made for Perry's birthday deeper into Perry's pocket. It was his third attempt to hide the little bag away. Perry's fingers kept drifting toward it, pulling it back into view.

"There. You are a fit presence for the Grand Duchess. If we can get her to show," Ravenscroft grumbled, checking his watch.

The calling hours were long over now. But Peregrine was certain that Sidmouth would turn up, especially if Catherine Pavlovna did not. When Selina had written to him, she told him about the note from the Princess, should he need help convincing the Grand Duchess to come.

The afternoon waxed and waned into the evening by the time an unmarked carriage pulled into the Fitzroy estate's drive. Selina had directed the others into a receiving line in the front hallway, with her at Peregrine's side.

Viscount Sidmouth emerged first, immediately turning to offer his gloved hand to the Grand Duchess to assist her descent.

"Your Imperial Highness," Perry greeted her, bowing his head appropriately. "Welcome to my home."

Catherine smiled neutrally at him, and then turned her head to Lady Normanby, who gave her an appropriate curtsey. The Grand Duchess's expression as she surveyed the disgraced Lady Normanby was… not pleasant.

"Well. I was given to understand that the Duchess Atholl was ill. But I must say, Lady Normanby, finding you playing hostess here in her absence is… peculiar," the Grand Duchess's words were biting. But at least she was not cutting Selina. Yet.

"Give me time to explain, Your Highness. And a bit of grace for the irregularity. There is a great deal of 'peculiarity' in what we are about to tell you," Peregrine said calmly.

Catherine Pavlovna's eyes flickered. "I should say so, given that Sidmouth convinced me to fabricate an excuse to leave my lady-in-waiting behind. He said that time—and discretion—was of the essence."

She allowed herself to be led inside to meet the others, and they all moved into the drawing room. Peregrine and Selina wasted no time in explaining the situation about Lark's unexpected marriage. Suddenly Lark found she had replaced Selina as the persona non grata in the room, withering under the Grand Duchess's open-mouthed glare.

Viscount Sidmouth looked equally horrified, but at least his attention was split between Perry and Selina. Selina had been unwilling to couch any of the truth in her letter, so he was as flummoxed in the learning of it as the Grand Duchess.

Really, all they needed to make this debacle complete would be Castlereagh tearing his hair out in the corner, bemoaning what this would mean for the talks in Vienna.

"Your Imperial Highness," Perry said insistently, pulling

Catherine's hostility away from Lark. "I give you my word. My sister harbours no ill intent towards either Prince Nicholas or the Tsar. Any malice is on my mother's part alone. Lark and Nicholas are young. Lark says he professes to love her, and he believed he could successfully plead his case to your brother.

"Whatever offence has arisen was born of fear and confusion, not design. We have asked you here hoping to set matters right, not to deepen the wrong. If this tangle is to be undone with the least amount of harm to two innocents and the relationship between our two nations, we sorely need your help and understanding."

The Grand Duchess turned to him. "You wish me to accept in your sister's innocence, Lord Fitzroy, but given that your sister spent the last months with your mother instead of you, perhaps you may see why I have difficulty believing it."

"Ask Nicholas," Lark said, tears streaming down her face.

"To be sure, I will," the Grand Duchess said coldly. "Because unfortunately, Lord Fitzroy, you have possession of information that sounds of truth. Constantine had resolved to renounce his claim in favour of Nicholas. It is a fact known to very few. Not even Nicholas himself is yet aware of it. I must inform my brother at once, so that he may annul the marriage."

"Wait—" Sidmouth held up a hand to keep her from standing. "Marrying Lady Lark to Nicholas is not enough to put her on the throne, and that would surely be Lady Fitzroy's aim. There is more to this."

Perry agreed. "She needed to convert Lark to Orthodoxy at the very least, which means my mother did not do this alone. And that means the Tsar has an enemy in his court."

That certainly caught Catherine's fierce attention. "Lady Lark," she purred, pinning the girl with a fierce glare, "who is your *krestnyy roditel*? Your godparent."

"Countess Yelena Orlova," Lark said softly. "She was there for both my conversion and our wedding."

When he felt Selina's eyes boring a hole into him, he remembered. That was the woman who had helped orchestrate his mother's scandal of Selina in the coffee shop. It seemed there would be a line forming of women who had a bone to pick with the countess.

"But the person who approached Red Hand was a man," Peregrine added. "There is more than one traitor. He will likely be working to ensure the Tsar meets his end before the delegation leaves."

"If I had to wager," Sidmouth said, teeth gritted, "the attack will happen at the GuildHall Banquet. The Tsar will be seated at the Prince Regent's side. Perfect for an assassination."

"My brother will not allow such treachery to pass unpunished," the Grand Duchess said. "Lady Fitzroy will be sent away at once, and I shall advise His Imperial Majesty against attending the Guildhall Banquet. It is no longer safe."

"That will tip our hand that we have found the plot," Selina warned. "Hyde Park's military review has the benefit of chaos for the assassin, but your mother will want a captive audience paying attention to her efforts. We could lay a trap to take advantage of such hubris. Besides," she said, turning to the Grand Duchess, "surely you do not wish to let your traitor escape to try again another day?"

Catherine's bosom heaved once in pique. But she inclined her head. "I cannot presume to decide for my brother," she said evenly, "yet I concede there is sense in your proposal. I shall take my leave."

Peregrine nodded, his chin dropping as he tried to force his mind to keep to the task. Discussing his mother's future victims kept pulling his attention away from this room. To a past victim. In defiance of all protocols and gentlemanly behaviour and the guests in his house, all he wanted was for everyone to leave so he was free to return upstairs.

"Wait, Your Imperial Highness," a baritone voice cut in, snagging his faltering attention.

The Grand Duchess met Sir Nathaniel's blue eyes, inclining her head politely as she waited for Thorne to say his piece.

"Forgive me, ma'am, for any rudeness of my words," he explained, his cheeks flushing with embarrassment to speak with the sister of the Tsar. "I intend no offence in asking you this, and I ask only as a mission of mercy. Her Grace is not merely ill; she is dying. Lady Fitzroy told Lord Fitzroy that she had made the acquaintance of another skilled herb woman while she was in Russia. One who excelled in making poisons. If any doctor in the Russian entourage knows about the poisons of the east... for Lord Fitzroy and Her Grace's sake."

"And possibly the Tsar's too," Ravenscroft added. "We do not know how Lady Fitzroy was planning on killing the Tsar."

The Grand Duchess's lips parted. "Do you know the name of that poisoner?"

"Lizaveta," Perry mumbled, his throat growing achingly tight.

Catherine's face darkened with... something. A complex series of expressions flitted across her face. "Direct me to the duchess. Please," she ordered Selina, rising from her seat.

Peregrine sat dumbfounded for an instant, looking at the people who had remained behind. And then he hurried after them. By the time he got upstairs, he found Catherine sitting beside his wife, examining Charity's bruised wrists.

"Here," she said, bending Charity's arm so that they could see the bottom edge of her wrist clearly. Along the outermost edge, against the bone, was a small reddened cut. "Your mother wore a poisoner's ring. If one squeezes hard enough, they fail to feel the cut."

She let Charity's arm fall limply back to the bed. "And you

can see that the mark is easy to overlook. But this poison would be useless against the Tsar. It is known to us."

Known? Peregrine's heart was beating painfully inside his ribs, and he couldn't catch enough air. "My mother tried to extort me for the cure—I assumed it was a lie."

"No, Lord Fitzroy, it is no falsehood," she replied. "But it has been more than a day since she was poisoned. I must caution, the longer it is in her blood, the smaller her chance of recovering her senses."

Any chance was better than none at all. "Please," he whispered. "Whatever you can do."

"If I lend you my aid, you must give me your word that you will assist us in discovering the other traitor to my brother. There will be no retiring to a country seat out of reach while Her Grace lies recovering."

"Your Imperial Highness," Perry said, trying to suppress wild yearning. "If Charity wakes, that will be the easiest bargain I will ever make."

Catherine Palovna smiled grimly, her eyes falling on the discarded apothecary box near the floor. She rooted through the bottles it contained, setting a few aside. "There are a few other samples I need for the compound."

Peregrine laughed bitterly. "Perhaps you would like to look at the gardens."

The Grand Duchess found all she needed and helped Perry prepare the formula before leaving with Sidmouth. "If she does not regain consciousness by morning, Lord Fitzroy," she told him, setting her hand upon his arm, "then know I will be sorry for your loss. I liked Her Grace a great deal."

He swallowed the lump forming in his throat again. "Thank you for what you have done, nonetheless."

The others offered to spell him, but Perry sent the maid and the others away again. He could sit this last vigil alone.

Peregrine toed off his boots and stripped off his jacket and waistcoat slowly, setting them on the back of the chair. He was desperately trying to keep his thoughts cordoned on the narrow path that rode between unwarranted optimism and heartsickness. He could not afford to have confidence in the treatment. He did not want to be uplifted, only to have his heart shattered by disappointment again.

No matter what the outcome with Charity, God or Fate had brought him here—to this moment—for a purpose. This was a task that was greater than he. To help end his mother's reign of terror upon London and the others.

Fishing Charity's sachet out of his waistcoat pocket, he set it next to her on the pillow, letting the scent linger in the air. And then he lay beside her on the bed, atop the covers. He threaded the fingers of his right hand through her left, spinning her wedding ring on her finger with his knuckles.

"I didn't have the chance to tell you the story about your ring, Sparkles," he told her. "It was my grandmother's. She was one of the kindest people I ever knew. It was because of her I learned anything at all about compassion. I suppose… I wanted to show you that not every member of the Fitzroy lineage was a terrible person."

He talked to her about everything and nothing for hours until his voice grew hoarse sometime well after midnight. And then he curled his arm around her hips, weariness sinking into his very bones as the hours went on and his hope flagged again.

His fitful dreams were cruel. He dreamt of her fingers running through his hair. Her breath on his face. A whisper of her voice, so faint he couldn't make out the words.

And then something tugged his scalp sharply, ripping him so

abruptly from sleep that he sat up in the weak morning light, disoriented.

Blinking sleep from his eyes, he looked down to see Charity's eyes were open, and her expression was… well, it was quite petulant. "I'm thirsty," she informed him with a scowl, her throat rasping to prove the words. But then her lips twitched, badly suppressing a smile.

Perry's heart leapt into his throat. Could this possibly be real? Or had stress broken his mind? He reached out with shaking fingers, almost too afraid to touch her for fear that he would find he was only dreaming. But his palm found her skin. It was warm to the touch, soft, like her lip against the pad of his thumb. Still in disbelief, only his hand moved, curving along her jaw, brushing across the flutter of her pulse in her throat. And she turned her head, leaning into his touch.

His vision blurred with tears, but then he laughed. "There you are," he gasped, the words nearly lodging in his throat. He let both hands frame her face then, cupping her cheeks while he brought his nose to hers. "Oh, darling. There you are, my love."

Her mouth was bone dry, and her head still ached. But mostly, Charity did not know what to make of Perry's haunted eyes. She lifted a hand to his cheek to comfort him. "Where else should I be?"

That was when she saw her wrist, and the dark bruises fading to a greenish yellow. A vague memory swam to the surface, of his mother's enraged face with malice-filled eyes, and pain blossoming at her wrists.

"Your mother—" Her voice caught, her throat too tight and too dry to finish the rest. Perry straightened and then hurried to help her sit up. After stacking a mountain of pillows behind her back, he fetched a glass of water. Only after she had taken several sips did he settle back down in the chair beside the bed.

"She poisoned you," Perry said, his eyes flashing with anger before shifting into pools of sadness. "I thought I'd lost you, Sparkles."

The realisation of how close she had come to dying, how easily her life might have been snuffed out, made her head pound and stomach roil. She had only to take a glance at her husband to grasp how her death would have destroyed him.

Charity pulled him closer, letting him lay his head upon her chest. "How long?" she asked after a long moment.

His breath hitched. "Two days and two nights, the longest of my life. If we hadn't got the antidote—"

How desperate would he have been by then? She combed her fingers through his hair, forcing herself to ask the next question, bracing for the answer. "The antidote. How did you get it?"

"In the end... the Grand Duchess." He sat up again, looking away. "But the day she poisoned you, my mother offered to trade it for my denunciation of Ravenscroft and Antoine."

Horror replaced the uncertainty.

"I refused." He dragged in a ragged breath. "I refused to trade their lives for yours. And all I could think was that I had condemned you to die. But I knew you also would not want me to make the other choice."

She stopped him there and begged him to take her into his arms. He was so careful as he pulled her into an embrace. But when her hands slid up his back, urging him closer, his hold tightened.

There was a catharsis in this, she realised—in trusting a partner to hold you safe during a moment so raw. Peregrine's tears made warm patterns on her shoulder as he wept, and hers gathered along the collarbone of his shirt. But there was healing for both of them in it. Against the odds, they were still here. Together. Able to find another chance at happiness.

"You were right. That was what I would have chosen. I would not have blamed you, love," she assured him eventually, stroking her hand along his neck. "But... how did the Grand Duchess come to be involved?"

And so he told her in whispers about how the others had persevered when he had lost hope. That the others had cared for them both caused her heart to swell with gratitude.

"But," he paused briefly, "you will never believe what they discovered after Selina lost her temper with Lark."

Perry was right; it was truly unbelievable. Charity listened, open-mouthed, while he explained Lark had married Nicholas, that the Tsar was going to be murdered, and the Grand Duchess had been summoned to find a way for them to solve this disaster as privately as they could.

That, by whatever grace of God or Fate or random chance, the Grand Duchess had been able to provide Perry with the cure that his mother had tried to force Perry to trade for.

Charity desperately needed to see all their friends just then. She grabbed Perry's hand and urged him to stand.

"Everyone must be so worried. Ring the bell, Perry. You must send word that I am better. More importantly, I want to thank them for all they've done."

He gave her a wry smile. "Easy enough to do. The Magpie and Selina refused to leave the estate last night. They are all here, staying in the guest wing."

"Then call them here," she demanded, excitement filling her with newfound energy.

"Here and now?" he asked, arching an eyebrow. He gestured around. "In your bed chamber?"

Charity was not to be stopped. "Propriety and the early hour be damned. No one who is here will judge me for this decision."

Perry shook his head as he laughed, but did not raise any further arguments against her request. His eyes never left her; he did not even turn his back as he pulled the cord for the servants. Charity's maid Miller rushed in, her face pale, and stopped in her tracks when she saw Charity's smiling face.

Within a scant few minutes, they were all there, laughing at each other with their hair mussed and in various states of dishabille. Selina wore a borrowed wrapper, its too-long belt trailing down her side. Ravenscroft's shirt was half-tucked. Only Thorne was in any semblance of order. His years on the battlefield had apparently trained him in how to dress at a moment's notice.

Ravenscroft hurried across the rug and bumped Perry aside, taking up her hands to kiss her knuckles. "*Mon Dieu*, it is a miracle," he declared. "Say something, anything, so that I know this isn't a dream."

Selina pinched his arm. "There, now you know you are awake. Move over so I can see for myself that Charity is improved."

Laughter bubbled out of Charity at the sight of her friends acting, well, like themselves. Or perhaps it was more appropriate to say that Ravenscroft and Selina were like siblings tussling over a favourite toy. She could not find it in herself to begrudge them their enthusiasm.

Thorne stayed well behind them, either unwilling to wade in, or uncomfortable with the unusual setting. When Charity met his gaze over their heads, he inclined his head in a bow. He had come; they had all come running once again at her call.

Yet, someone was still missing. Lark.

She was the last to arrive. She kept her distance, unsure of her welcome, until Charity invited her to come near.

"I am so sorry," Lark whispered in a hoarse voice. "If you hadn't rescued me, Mama might not have—"

"I would do it again in a heartbeat," Charity vowed, silencing the woman's apology. "We are sisters now, are we not?"

Lark sniffed back tears and held tight to her tremulous smile. "Sisters, and friends."

The sun was well up when Quinn came in and announced that breakfast was being served in the dining room. He offered to bring Charity a tray, but she would hear nothing of it. She sent everyone off so she could get dressed, telling Perry he was allowed to come back and carry her to the table. Anything, so long as it meant she wouldn't have to stay abed while the others talked.

At the last moment, she asked Lark to remain.

The Tsar will annul Lark's marriage, Perry had told her. Had anyone asked Lark how she felt about this news?

"I am sorry for what will come of your marriage, that the Tsar will not let it go ahead." Charity said when they were alone. "Are you in love with him?"

"I care for him," Lark said, answering vaguely.

"I cared for Lord Roland," Charity confessed. "He is a fine man, and he has made Grace a most excellent husband."

Lark tilted her head to the side and studied Charity's face. "I… I do not understand."

"Lord Roland, even the Duke of Atholl, God rest his soul, were both decent, good men. I could have been content with them, just as you might have been with Prince Nicholas. But I will tell you what I have learned in these past days."

Lark leaned forward, curiosity keeping her silent.

"I deserve more than that. You deserve more than mere contentment. The annulment might pain you now, but you must think of it as a gift. You have a choice now, and a chance to find love. Love and respect, and a deep, abiding bond that will carry you through the darkest and lightest of days."

"Like you have with Perry?"

"Exactly. And we will be here, by your side, until you find it."

28

Perry did indeed carry her to the breakfast table, but right now, she could deny him nothing. It was hard to mind when he was so truly happy, and besides, her arms and legs still felt a little unsteady—either nerves, lingering traces of the poison, or the result of lying abed for two days. Surrendering to the inevitable with grace, she wrapped her arms around his neck and laughed as he swept her up and dashed down the stairs.

She did not even command him to put her down once they reached the bottom. She decided that even if the servants saw him fussing over her, she did not care. He had earned the right, that and more.

Perry settled her onto a chair next to his, smoothing her skirts before tucking her close. Then satisfied, he took his place at the head of the table while the others joined them, taking seats on either side.

"My usual cup of chocolate," Charity requested when Quinn asked what she wanted to drink.

Peregrine frowned. "Perhaps a cup of bone broth would be better."

"Perry, I was only asleep for two days," she whispered in pique.

Quinn gave a sage nod, but his gaze slid toward Charity. The corners of his mouth quirked, assuring her he would not ignore her preference.

Perry saw her plate filled with heaping servings of eggs, kippers, roasted tomatoes, and slices of golden toast. He kept her under watchful eye while she did the same.

"You eat," she insisted when he spent too much time watching her instead of his own plate. "Do not try to convince me you took care of yourself."

"He did not," Thorne volunteered from the far end of the table.

Perry set down his fork. "Is there no code of honour among fighting men?"

"There is no honour in concealing such obvious truths from your *wife*," Charity replied testily, saving Thorne from answering. But when Peregrine smiled at her—she would have to remember that he loved hearing that word, wife—she smiled back. "Promise me you will stop fretting if I agree to remain here today?"

"It amuses me you believe that staying was a choice." He smirked. "We cannot let my mother learn that you have recovered yet, Charity. She might change her plans if she finds out, and then we would end up squandering whatever advantage we hold."

"He's right," Selina said lightly from across the table. "Since I remain a social disgrace, I shall stay behind to keep you and Lark company. Let Marian believe she has swept us off the board while we plot her ruin from the comfort of her former home. There's something deliciously poetic about that, is there not?"

Charity had not imagined herself such a spiteful person, but where Marian was concerned, she could warm to the idea of being petty. Charity was the new lady of the manor, a title she had no intention of relinquishing. "Indeed."

"Then let us return to the only question that matters," Peregrine said evenly. "Does anyone here still doubt that the Tsar's death is my mother's aim?"

No one argued.

"I am more convinced she will choose the Guildhall now." Ravenscroft pushed food around with his fork. "Our dear Tsar has such a charming habit of wandering away from where he is expected. Unless she plans to shoot from every balcony in London, I cannot imagine how she would plan around such unpredictable behaviour. Your mother will choose a stage she can control—and the Guildhall offers a lovely proscenium."

"He's right. Mama does not like dealing with the unexpected," Lark murmured. "More than anything, she despises things she cannot control."

Like her children? "You do not have to worry about such things anymore," Charity assured her.

Perry agreed. "My mother's strengths are also her flaws. She's grown so accustomed to planning her way to success— regardless of how convoluted the scheme—that she won't expect us to be this far ahead in understanding the plot. Before the Crown summons us, let's try to plan for the order of events."

Ravenscroft spoke first, offering what he knew. "Like most Guildhall events, the seated dinner will be only for the men. The sovereigns and those of highest status will be at the head table, the other tables filled out by social rank. They have erected great, draperied balconies above for the women to sit and observe during the main course, and after the meal is done, they will join for dessert and dancing."

"Then if the objective is to catch the Tsar sitting still, the attempt will take place during the dinner," Thorne deduced.

Charity had little trouble imagining how it might go based on Ravenscroft's descriptions. With the right disguise, someone might easily sneak in and hide among the skirting or the servants.

"Protecting the Tsar in that circus will be difficult, but not impossible," Ravenscroft drawled. "Prinny can be persuaded to summon a small army of royal guards, especially if one flatters his sense of occasion."

Perry drummed his fingers on the table beside his plate, deep in thought.

"What is it?" Charity asked quietly.

"A single assassin is too large a gamble. Too uncertain. Too easy to stop. We are missing something in her plan, and I cannot help but think it relates to the ring she used on you."

"On me? Why?"

"I think my mother tipped her hand, but whether that was because she was forced to improvise, or because it amused her to poison you so deliberately in front of me, I'm not certain. The Grand Duchess pointed out the punctures on your wrists we missed. If she hadn't done so, I think we all would have missed it. It is a clever way to poison someone. She could easily do it again."

"But not herself," Selina mused. "She will be in the balcony."

Lark had been listening, mostly silent. "Countess Orlova introduced us to the court, but Mama spent a great deal of time talking to many of the men who will be at the front of the room."

"So there is more than just a second traitor in his court, that traitor might also be a second assassin." Thorne shifted in his chair. "Would it matter to Marian whose hand the Tsar dies by, so long as he dies?"

"No. One assassin could serve as a distraction for the other," Selina said into her cup of coffee. "If there is a panic over a man attempting to attack the Tsar—perhaps he brandishes a weapon and attracts the guards—"

"No one would question one of Alexander's men approaching and touching the Tsar. Yes," Peregrine said absently, his gaze distant as he envisioned how such an attack might happen. "That does make sense. Moxley will be obvious, not discreet. But if all he needs to do is cause a distraction, it gives the other assassin the chance to do the deed. Everyone will be looking the wrong way. No one may notice the mark, and then no one will suspect the loyal man."

"But if Moxley doesn't succeed with his attack and the Tsar still dies, will people not question what happened?" Thorne's brow furrowed.

Peregrine waved that off. "There are many poisons that will cause a heart to fail quickly. If there is a panic, and the Tsar clutches his chest, what are people likely to assume? A fit of apoplexy or a seizure of the heart, brought on by fear."

"That is diabolical," Charity said. Beside her, Lark closed her eyes in horror.

"You have met my mother." Perry pushed his plate away, appetite lost. "We will need to watch out for someone waiting for his chance to attack Alexander."

Quinn was called away by a guard, and after checking the situation, he requested Perry too. Everyone looked up expectantly when Peregrine returned after several long minutes.

"The summons came from Sidmouth," he explained, passing the letter to Ravenscroft. "It appears the Tsar and the Grand Duchess are ready to talk."

"At the Pulteney?" Ravenscroft peered at the message as if it had personally insulted him. "Well, that's not where I intended to be indispensable today. I take it you would like me to go with you."

Perry nodded. "Quinn, ask Dawson to drive us in the unmarked carriage. Ravenscroft and I will travel incognito."

Sidmouth's note instructed them to arrive at the tradesmen's entrance to the hotel. By that alone, Peregrine deduced that this was to be a clandestine where secrecy was the first order. Given that he expected at least one member of the Crown present, it spoke volumes that they were willing to cede territory for this meeting to the Russians.

Peregrine took some precautions of his own. Hodges and Thorne did a sweep of the edges of the property before they departed, looking for watchers. It wouldn't do to let a spy get word about his movements back to his mother.

Sidmouth met them at that entrance, ushering the two cloaked men quickly through the basement area and servants' passages into an area blocked off by Cossacks. Only then did the Home Secretary stop and turn to Peregrine, raking Perry's appearance with his gaze. "You look... better. I assume that there is good news at home."

When Perry gave just a curt nod, Sidmouth let out a puff of breath. "Good. That is good. If the Grand Duchess helped you honestly, then perhaps we have a prayer of getting out of this incident with Nicholas without bloodshed. At least between the Tsar and the Crown." He continued dryly, "Castlereagh will be spoiling for a fight when he discovers he was left out."

"Who else is here?" Perry asked.

"The three of us, the Tsar, the Grand Duchess, the Queen, and Prinny," he answered. "The Queen came in earlier to meet with the Grand Duchess for tea. Prinny had to be brought up in a most laborious manner. We had to make sure the pathway I just brought you up was entirely clear of anyone who might identify him. Us… well, we are less important." He gave a brief, feral grin.

"And you left them *alone* with the Tsar? Without supervision of any kind?" Ravenscroft said, aghast.

"Magpie, at this point in time, the Tsar and the Queen killing one another is the thing I am least concerned will happen."

The Cossack standing at the Grand Duchess's servant's entrance opened the door to… chaos.

"—Her Ladyship fled England, it is true. But surely you were aware of the accusations that she had committed theft and had been accused of treason. We cannot be blamed if Russia regrets its decision to choose to make a pet of a viper!" the Queen informed the Tsar coolly, her eyes glinting.

The Tsar gave the Queen his customary Sphinx-like look. "I was well aware that betrayal is her only allegiance," he remarked. "Nevertheless, I would have been the greater fool to overlook the ripe gift of so many of your government's secrets for the plucking."

And the Grand Duchess was having her own argument with the Regent. "England should be careful about casting stones." She looked down her nose at the Regent. "At least our line of succession has more heirs than scandalous affairs."

"And yet, Your Imperial Highness," Prinny barked, "I require no fingers to count the number of traitors who have married into my line."

Ravenscroft turned a look on Sidmouth that so clearly said *I told you so* that Perry could practically hear it in the magpie's voice.

Irritated at the Regent's implications that his sister was a traitor, Perry coughed loudly into his fist, drawing the attention of the bickering sovereigns.

"You." The Tsar's attention speared Peregrine, fixing sharply on his hair. "I question the value of bringing Lord Fitzroy into these discussions, given his relationship to the accused."

The Grand Duchess leaned over to her brother, whispering something, and the Tsar held up his hand to her after a moment, silencing her. "I cannot take such a thing on faith. The alleged poisoning of his paramour does not mean it is not a trick to make Fitzroy appear to be on our side."

"The woman your sister speaks of is not my *paramour*," Peregrine said, bristling. "She is my *wife*. And never would I have risked her life in that manner."

That gave the Tsar pause. He glanced at Catherine, who shook her head. She did not know they were married. Then he looked at the Queen and Regent, who nodded.

When no one said anything, Ravenscroft ventured, "If you are worried about the possibility Lord Fitzroy may be playing a deeper game, Your Imperial Majesty, I was present when Fitzroy was stabbed by his mother's man last month." The magpie paused for emphasis, adding dryly, "Some deceptions are not worth the effort."

The Queen nodded in agreement. "The only reason you are aware of your younger brother's actions is because of Lord Fitzroy and his allies."

The Tsar gave a small wave of his fingers, accepting the point.

"Perhaps it would benefit us to assume that everyone present has a vested interest in seeing Marian Fitzroy captured and punished," Sidmouth said as neutrally as possible. "We believe an attempt is to be made on your life, Your Imperial Highness—"

"Yes, so my sister informed me already," Alexander interrupted, getting to his feet and pacing the room restlessly. "She informed me that you think it will occur at the banquet tomorrow. And that my death will be aided by traitors from my own court."

The Tsar stopped in front of a painting on the wall, his shoulders stiff while he contemplated betrayal and his own death.

"*Sasha.*" Catherine got up from her chair and went to stand behind Alexander, standing close. "Nikolai adores you. This is not the same as what happened with Papa."

"No?" he asked her softly. "It is *always* the same, Katya. I let them whisper in my father's halls. Does the ignorance of my youth lessen my guilt? My father trusted too deeply. I, not enough. Both of us were fools in our own way. Perhaps this is God's punishment for me. It would be fitting."

Catherine lifted her chin, clearly deciding that if the people in this room couldn't be trusted to hold their tongues, then no one could. "There is no sin here. Our father was dangerous, Sasha. To the people and our empire. You are not him, and you made the choice to protect that. *Not* our name."

Peregrine nodded to himself, relating to the Tsar's private shame. He had never believed that Alexander had conspired with the rebels who had murdered his father. But that Alexander had looked the other way while other men talked of sedition, hoping that his father might be forced to step down or see reason? That he would believe.

"Sire, guilt is one of the easiest tools to turn against a man. How well I know this, and oh— my mother is an expert in using it!" Perry uttered, feeling keenly in sympathy.

The Tsar slowly turned to Peregrine, a wary, heavy curiosity shadowing his eyes.

"Do not let my mother's favourite kind of weapon poison your soul," Peregrine told him. "She wants you as isolated and alone, afraid to trust others, just as she wanted me to be. Your sister is right. Do not simply assume Prince Nicholas covets your throne. My mother lied to my sister, telling her they could convince you. She would not hesitate to whisper lies to Nicholas about the possibilities of love."

"That simply makes doing what I must more tragic, Lord Fitzroy," the Tsar said solemnly. "For I could easily picture such a thing. Nicholai is a lonely lad. But I cannot sanction their marriage, even if it posed no threat to my life."

"Nor would I ask you to, Sire," Peregrine murmured. "The only thing I ask for is compassion. For both of them, though you may wish to consider the matter longer. Can we agree we must stop my mother and the traitors in your court?"

The Tsar's eyes flickered slightly as the barest traces of emotions surfaced and were buried again. "We can. I am willing to put myself at the centre of whatever trap you feel is necessary."

Queen Charlotte didn't like the idea of Alexander playing bait, but she couldn't argue against the need. "Lord Sidmouth, I charge you with safeguarding the Tsar's welfare as though it were our own. The Princess and I will not attend, to lighten the effort and protect the succession."

"And we will not bring Nicholai," agreed the Tsar. "Ekaterina, you also should not attend."

Catherine shook her head. "No, I must. The Dowager Lady Fitzroy knows I am going to be there. If I change my plans, she may grow suspicious as to why."

The Tsar looked unsatisfied, but eventually he nodded. "And the assassin?"

"Lord Fitzroy's allies have given us a description," said Sidmouth. "We should be able to identify the man—this Moxley. Given the scar on his face, I am confident the guards can catch him before he sets foot inside."

Perry rubbed his temple. "If the assassin is stopped too soon, we have the same problem. We will tip our hand to my mother and the Tsar's traitor. If Moxley does not show, the traitor may not make his move at the dinner, and we will not find out who it is."

"Then what do you propose?" Alexander asked, sarcasm

edging his voice. "To let this Moxley enter the banquet with a weapon in hand?"

"Nothing of the sort. The timing will be difficult, but if we can catch Moxley outside and question him as to his part of the plan, we can possibly arrange for one of ours to stand in his place. As long as it seems all is proceeding as expected, the traitor should rise to do his part—whatever that part is," Peregrine finished.

"It is difficult to believe that one of my men will betray me like that, Lord Fitzroy. But I confess, I am in no position to disbelieve," the Tsar hissed through his teeth, finally showing some passion. "When I find out who it is, he will regret his own birth."

"Fitzroy's man told you the person attempting to hire a sellsword was pretending to be Austrian, Lord Ravenscroft?" Sidmouth asked. "Should we warn the Austrians that someone is attempting to frame them for this crime? I mislike the idea of involving more people…"

"He did," drawled the magpie. "I know you would prefer not to warn the Austrians formally, but what about an informal warning?"

Perry chuckled, knowing immediately who the dandy had in mind. "The Propagandist."

"The Propagandist," agreed Ravenscroft.

The Tsar looked from one man to the other. "Do you *actually* mean to trust Baron von Gentz with this information?"

"The trickster is sly as a fox, to be sure. But he likes Lord Fitzroy, and I believe he would be a useful ally. More importantly, he is no friend of Marian Fitzroy. I will be positioned near the table, on the Regent's side. But we have no one except guards on the Tsar's other side."

Peregrine closed his eyes, envisioning the table. He wondered if anything had ever come of Gentz's request for England's support at Vienna, but now was not the time to ask—not in front of the Russians.

"Von Gentz will be further along at the head table, past the Tsar. I agree, Ravenscroft. I think we should approach him."

29

"Act well your part; there all the honour lies."
— Alexander Pope, An Essay on Man

Sidmouth did not get his wish to avoid involving more people. But he was correct that they needed to be careful about who they recruited to the cause.

The Propagandist, unsurprisingly, accepted his role immediately. "All I must do is pay close attention to the men at the table? What a terrible inconvenience," he said with amusement, the irony in his voice heavy. "What other task might earn me the gratitude of a Tsar and the Prince Regent both, and a debt that no one would dare put in writing?"

Thinking of debts had reminded Perry of Croft and the fact that General Rowland Hill owed him a rather large favour for employing his former batman. 'Daddy Hill' was tickled to be part of such a secret endeavour and had promised a veritable platoon of trustworthy former military men to help augment the guards on duty.

Some would be positioned in a loose ring around the GuildHall, and would be given a description of Moxley, in the hopes of catching him before he ever entered the building. As soon as the assassin was in hand, Hodges and Red Hand would be there to do whatever was necessary to get information from Moxley about the identity of his target.

The rest of Hill's men would don the uniforms of the footmen. Those would remain near the head table to assist with capturing the traitor, in case the Propagandist was not enough.

Everyone agreed this seemed a wise precaution.

Perry knew several of the men circulating in the room, allowing him to communicate discreetly. It was imperative that he remain well out of his mother's sight, given she expected him to be at the estate mourning Charity's illness.

During the first part of the banquet, his mother would be up in the balcony to the left of the head table, together with the Grand Duchess, Countess Orlova, and the other Russian women. Peregrine would remain behind the curtains, below them on the same side, where he could watch without risk of being seen from above.

The Grand Duchess remained determined to keep a close eye on Marian while they were together. It fell to Perry to caution her. His mother might attempt to poison or enact some other form of sabotage against her. Particularly since she was the most likely to question the circumstances of the Tsar's death.

As for the others… the royal women would retire to separate residences. The Princess would be under guard at Carlton House, kept company by Lark. The Tsar, as a show of faith in the British guards, sent Prince Nicholas to Carlton House as well, trusting his and the Grand Duchess's safety to the Cossacks.

The Queen would be secured at Buckingham House with her own private guards. The Marchioness of Normanby elected to stay with the Queen. But that came about, mostly, because Charity had refused to be there with her.

It was the closest thing to a real fight they'd had in weeks. Perry had wanted her nowhere near the Guildhall, but Charity, in all her infuriating resolve, seemed hell-bent on proving she was strong enough to go with him and sit in the gallery, somewhere his mother would not spot her.

Ever the peacemaker, Thorne volunteered to keep his eyes on her. He was less conspicuous than Perry, and could move more freely if necessary.

And that was the extent of the plans that could be made at such a remove. Like the gears of a giant machine, every wheel had spun purposefully towards one common goal. Dealing with any unexpected actions? That would be an exercise of trust in each other.

Now, it was time to see if their planning would be enough. Concealed in the deep shadow of the drapery, sweat trickled along Perry's spine.

Already, the Guildhall was unbearably hot and noisy, even standing down here on the floor. Above, in the balconies, the heat must be stifling. The women there had been ushered in and seated well ahead of the official procession into the hall. Marian had been among them, Thorne told him, chatting to the Grand Duchess and Countess Orlova with an insouciance difficult to believe.

The final guests were taking their seats now, and with the room so full and bustling, Perry felt safe to leave the narrow corridor made for the servants between the hanging drapery and the stone walls.

His building rage was adding to his temperature.

The first thing he did was peer upwards in search of Charity, where he knew she would be. But she was well hidden. Ironically, he did spot Lady Cresswell—Charity's mother—seated with lower-ranked ladies, and mostly ignored.

And then he surveyed the room.

At the large head table, Prinny and the Tsar sat in the centre. Arrayed around them were all the expected faces. The Prussian monarch. Metternich. The lesser monarchs. And then other important faces as well, like Sidmouth and Castlereagh, the Propagandist, and other highest-ranking men.

"Everyone is here," murmured Thorne, joining Peregrine in his spot near the wall. "Nothing so far seems out of place."

Peregrine's gut disagreed, but he could not immediately put his finger upon a reason. Nervous, he swept the room with his eyes again. "You have seen Charity?" he asked the man quietly.

"I looked for her right before I came back here," he assured Perry. "She is on the upper level of the balcony, sitting behind a woman with ostrich plumes in her hair. She is difficult to see even knowing exactly where to find her."

Perry resisted the urge to go looking, trusting Sir Nathaniel to take no risks with Charity's life. "You say nothing is out of place, Sir Nathaniel," he murmured, "but—"

"My instincts say otherwise," the knight murmured. "I have this sense something isn't quite right. Or that we have missed something important."

That was all the confirmation that Peregrine needed to question what they knew. Again.

A guard—one of Hill's—stepped into his alcove. "News, Lord Fitzroy. We caught Moxley outside, and your man Hodges put him to questioning. We were wrong about the target. Moxley was after the sister. He was moving toward a side entrance, where he intended to climb up to the balcony."

Brows drawing together, Peregrine thanked the guard and sent him on his way.

"So Moxley was sent for the Grand Duchess." Thorne shifted

restlessly, crossing his arms over his chest. "Not the Tsar. You were right to warn her that your mother might strike."

"Catherine Pavlovna is no fool. She has a lady-in-waiting and her personal guard with her." Hopefully, that would be enough.

"I suppose Moxley attacking the Grand Duchess would serve just as well as a distraction." But Thorne still looked uncomfortable. "I dislike how smug your mother was when I saw her earlier."

Perry agreed. Something still felt… amiss.

You are so certain of yourself, Mother, he thought at her angrily. *So calm as you wait for plans to unfurl. Never mind that your ambitions have such a cost. You are an abomination. I will see you fall for your crimes tonight, and I will pay the price to end your villainy, if that is required.*

If he were mistaken about her plans, he would find a way to counter them, nonetheless. They would not fail. He refused to.

Enjoy your evening, you vile harpy, he shot at his mother. *Your reckoning is at hand.*

"Perhaps we are thinking too narrowly," Thorne murmured in his low voice after a long moment. "Clearly, your mother does not shirk away from the idea of serving her revenge for every slight, no matter how small. The moment we kidnapped Lark, she threatened all of us, right down to Antoine and the boy. Would she employ some other attack on the building to strike a wider range of enemies?"

Perry turned to the knight, finding him grim and pale.

"Would she set the building on fire?" Thorne asked him with as quiet a voice as he could manage.

"Surely not with herself in it, Sir Nathaniel," Peregrine said in negation. But Thorne's nervousness was catching. "But if she leaves…"

Thorne shrugged his shoulders, trying to relieve the tension building in them. "If your wife wasn't bloodthirsty before, she is certainly developing a taste for it. Charity is watching Marian as if her very life depends on it. She would flag our attention if it was needed."

"I don't doubt she'd throw a slipper at one of our heads from the balcony if she thought the situation required it," Perry said dryly, thinking about Charity's litany of threats when he suggested leaving her with the Queen.

But Peregrine turned again, forcing his mind to work as he considered the knight's words. He tallied a list in his head of everyone dangerous to his mother, who had either earned a place on his mother's black books, or who needed to be eliminated.

She had threatened their cohort, yes. But she had already worked schemes to keep them from being here—at least, for everyone except for Ravenscroft. Charity was supposed to be dying, and Perry prostrated with grief.

The Queen had surely earned a spot, but she wasn't here. The Grand Duchess, targeted by Moxley, was above. The Tsar, of course, was known. But... Prinny and Sidmouth would also be likely targets for his mother's wrath, if for no other reason than because they had helped keep Peregrine alive. Castlereagh too, if one considered the ambition of a hungry empire.

And then, of course, there was the possibility of her co-conspirator. A man who would surely need to die once he had outlived his usefulness.

Peregrine's pulse quickened as he looked at the head table.

"Thorne," he breathed, his lungs growing too tight. "Besides us, nearly every person my mother wants dead is sitting at that table tonight. All of them. Except for the Queen and the Grand Duchess."

"God's blood," Sir Nathaniel swore softly. "All she would need is something to fall on their heads, or some sort of infernal machine, like they tried to use on Napoleon."

Perry set his hand on the man's arm. "We have to warn

Ravenscroft or one of the servants. Get his attention so he will come over here."

Lord Ravenscroft stood near the wall, feigning indifference to the scene before him. Another day, another royal banquet, or so he would have everyone think. In truth, his hooded gaze missed not a single movement within spitting distance of the Tsar.

The only thing remarkable about the Tsar's behaviour was that he was staying put, for once, though that was taking a toll. His fingers drummed against the tablecloth, then stilled when he caught himself.

Ravenscroft did not envy the man playing bait for Marian Fitzroy's scheme. He dragged his gaze away and returned to watching those in motion. He straightened when Thorne stepped out of the shadows, two alcoves down, blue eyes meeting his inquiring gaze.

Trouble, the magpie thought. *Already?*

Not wanting to arouse suspicion, Ravenscroft took the long way around, circling the entire dining area before approaching Galahad. Thorne led behind a curtain into one of the alcoves, where Fitzroy awaited them.

"We have news," the canary stated grimly. "Both good and bad. Which would you prefer first?"

Ravenscroft jerked around, his eyes searching out the Tsar, then Prinny. Both men were still in good form. "I've been standing watch for the last hour without even a drop of wine to dull my wits. Please start with the good."

"Moxley has been captured."

That was excellent news indeed, worthy of a toast if a passing footman would hand him a glass. "And the bad?"

"We were wrong about his objective. He was not there for

him." Fitzroy tilted his head at the Tsar. Then he shifted his gaze to the balcony where the Grand Duchess sat in the front row of the Russian delegation. "Moxley was sent for Catherine."

Ravenscroft chewed his lip. "But—the Tsar? The ring?"

"That's the worse news," Thorne rumbled.

Fitzroy let out a strangled laugh. "Look at the high table, Maggie. What do you see?"

Ravenscroft resisted the urge to throttle Fitzroy, for he was in no mood for games.

"I see all of Marian Fitzroy's enemies and obstacles. Seated at one table," Perry murmured.

Ravenscroft reeled, understanding his meaning. *"How?"*

"Napoleon almost met his end in 1800, when his carriage drove past a wagon on a narrow street," Thorne said shortly. "It was loaded with a barrel full of gunpowder, stone, and musket balls. The only reason he lived was because the weapon missed its mark."

"And you think such a thing is here?" The dandy clutched his chest dramatically.

"Perhaps," Perry told him. "Beneath the table, well positioned to strike the most. You must go look."

"And how, precisely, am I meant to do that without arousing suspicion?" the man's voice rose an octave.

"Drop a handkerchief. Stumble. Think quickly; we have no time to waste."

Ravenscroft gave Fitzroy a baleful look before turning his back and crossing the room. He went straight to the long table where the allied sovereigns wined and dined. In a performance worthy of a West End stage, Ravenscroft waited until he stood behind The Propagandist's chair before stumbling over his own two feet.

The Baron twisted around and glanced down at him, a raised eyebrow posing a world of questions.

"Dear me, I must have had too much to drink!" he muttered the words sarcastically, lifting the tablecloth to peer underneath with a flail of his arm.

A line of booted heels stretched before him, divided only by wooden table legs. No boxes or bags anywhere in sight. He dropped the cloth and got to his feet, ignoring that The Propagandist's brows had settled into a heavy furrow.

"Do you suppose there are fireworks planned for this evening?" he asked Gentz genially. And when Thorne glanced his way, he gave a brief shake of his head.

The Baron affected nonchalance, leaning hard on the arm of his chair. "I do not know, Lord Ravenscroft. But are not such things best viewed from outdoors? Perhaps we should excuse ourselves for some air?"

"*Tsk.* And risk being held responsible for ruining the show?" Ravenscroft put a hand on the Baron's chair to stop him from sliding it back. "Someone here knows the starting hour. If we are to find the location of the supplies, we need extra eyes watching to see who is checking the time."

Sweat beaded on Gentz's brow. "I will give this to the English—you certainly know how to keep an evening lively." And with that, Baron von Gentz raised his glass and drank it dry.

Thorne had watched Ravenscroft peer beneath the table with no subtlety whatsoever. Hopefully, it had not set Marian's back up.

Beside him, Fitzroy stared up at the ceiling, but there was no chandelier directly above the table, or anything heavy that might fall upon their heads. Not short of the entire end of the Guildhall collapsing.

"This drapery goes all the way around," he finally remarked.

"It seems unlikely, but perhaps there is something hidden behind it."

"I'll ask one of the guards to help me check the length of it," Thorne assured him. "If you can catch her eye, perhaps warn Charity that something's wrong."

Perry nodded, and Thorne quickly found one of Rowland Hill's hand-picked men. Before he could specify which direction the man should go, the soldier slipped behind the curtain and started moving in the direction of the head table.

Well, Thorne supposed it didn't matter; the man could find trouble that way as well as Thorne could. Thorne set off in the opposite direction, walking the narrow corridor towards the distant end of the Guildhall.

Working his way around the periphery, Thorne came out from the edge of the curtain, passing the door that the procession had entered through. He turned his head briefly to glance over the full Guildhall and then continued on behind the curtain on the other side. He came across a second door hidden entirely behind the curtain.

Thorne almost passed it by. He would come back after he finished this circuit, along with the Hall Keeper so he could inquire about what was behind the door. But something made him hesitate, and as he looked down at the stone floor, a faint black mark on the floor gave him pause.

Crouching down, Thorne pulled off his glove, licked his fingertip and ran it through the mark to lift some from the stone. He brought it to his nose, inhaling deeply. It smelled of dust and minerals of the earth, with just the faintest hint of sulphur.

"Black powder," he breathed, getting to his feet again. Thorne let his hand settle on the latch. Locked.

Seized with a sense of foreboding, Thorne exited the curtains, looking around desperately for one of the Guildhall's true servants.

"You," he said when he finally found a serving-man approaching one of the back tables. "Where does the door over there lead?" he asked, waving his hand at the curtained area that hid it.

Puzzled, the serving-man looked over his shoulder. "The crypts, sir."

When Thorne turned in Fitzroy's direction, he found the man's sharp, hawk-like regard suggesting he already understood. There was trouble beneath their feet.

Thorne lifted his finger, the black spot on the tip plainly visible, and Fitzroy's eyes widened before narrowing in anger.

Shakily, Thorne turned back to the serving-man. "I need to find the Hall Keeper, or anyone else with a key to that door. Now."

Charity sank lower in her seat, taking care to stay in the shadows. With any luck, no one would notice her sitting there in the middle of the balcony area. Not that anyone was looking her way. Between the carousing of the titled men at the dinner and the women whispering gossip in one another's ears, there was plenty to entertain.

Charity, however, had eyes for one woman only. Marian Fitzroy sat on the balcony across the room with an anticipatory gleam in her eyes.

You could stand up now and denounce her before all, her mother whispered. A mad suggestion. She had not heard her mother's voice in ages, but seeing Lady Cresswell sitting in the back row of the balcony had caused it to flare back to life.

Hush, Mama. Charity banished the spectre.

Her mother was blithely unaware of her proximity to her

daughter, too busy glaring daggers at Marian Fitzroy. Far too focused to notice the child she hadn't spoken with in days nearby.

Charity leaned sideways to get a clearer view of Perry's mother. Marian was not paying any attention to Lady Cresswell. Instead, she was checking something in her hand.

Then Marian leaned forward, scanning the scene below. A hint of a smile crossed her face when Lord Ravenscroft stumbled, and she turned to comment something to Countess Orlova. Charity grew concerned when the magpie was slow to rise, but then she realised he was speaking with Baron von Gentz.

Charity shifted her gaze, searching the alcoves for any hint of Perry's pale blond head. As if sensing her looking for him, he stepped forward, his face tilted upward. He raised a fist to his mouth and then unfurled his fingers in a wave.

Almost like an explosion, Charity thought, her stomach dropping.

30

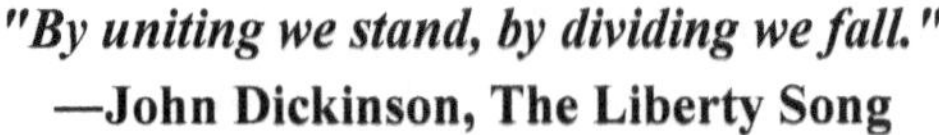

"By uniting we stand, by dividing we fall."
—John Dickinson, The Liberty Song

itzroy caught up with Thorne just as the distraught Hall Keeper stuck his jangling keys in the lock.

"When did you enter this room last?" Thorne asked him.

"Yestermorn," the man murmured. "It is only the crypts down here. Nothing of vital importance."

"Did anyone ask to enter the crypts after that?" Fitzroy barked, making the man's hands jerk. The keyring fell to the ground with a clatter.

"N-no, my lord. But there were plenty of Russian men here yesterday, inspecting preparations and ensuring that everything was in good order for His Imperial Highness's well-being."

Thorne picked up the keyring, examining the end of the heavy key that opened the crypts. "Easy enough to pick a lock like this." And then he shoved the key home, turning it in the lock before thrusting the ring back at the Keeper.

With no further consideration for Fitzroy or the stammering servant Thorne took the lantern hanging on the inside wall and descended the stair. Fitzroy followed quickly, crowding up behind him to see the way in the dim light.

Finally, they reached the dusty floor of the crypt, and Thorne inhaled deeply, the first true stirrings of fear weakening his knees.

Behind him, Fitzroy also took a breath through his nose, picking up the reek of black powder. A lot of it. "Hell and damnation," Perry muttered, his voice failing him.

Thorne moved forward, feeling queer, lifting the lantern high to see. And see, he did. At the far end of the crypts, approximately below where the dais would be, was a small mountain of barrels. More than a dozen, stacked around the pillar reaching towards the ceiling.

"It's the bloody Gunpowder Plot, all over again. I—" Thorne started, and stopped, a hopeless terror crawling through his innards. "You shouldn't be here, Fitzroy. I'll look for whatever fuse or mechanism she intended to use to detonate it. Get the sovereigns out."

"Don't be a lunatic," he muttered. "I'd rather face this and stop it here than explain to Castlereagh why we need to evacuate the Guildhall. Can you imagine me trying to get them off the dais without causing a riot? Tell me what we are looking for."

Swallowing, Thorne cast his eyes over the pile of barrels. "I see no fuse. Or a long-burning candle. Those would be the easiest..."

"Let us assume my mother would never give us the benefit of doing things the easy way."

Thorne barked a short laugh. "Then we're looking for a clockwork timer. Somewhere. Possibly inside a barrel."

"A... what? I know nothing of clocks," Fitzroy admitted, gritting his teeth.

"A spring-loaded mechanism set to strike flint to steel.

Affixed to a timing wheel, gears, and a mainspring." Thorne set the lantern down carefully, tugged off his gloves and wiped his sweating palms. Then he pulled his belt knife out of his pocket. "I've never seen one, but I know the theory of such a thing. If that is what I'm looking for, we are literally in a race against time."

Fitzroy cursed long and loud. "A damned clockwork. McGrath must be laughing at me from his grave."

Thorne didn't have time to argue with a lord who knew far too much about poisons and nothing at all about machinery or explosives. He set his knife blade into the rim of the first barrel, carefully prying the lid up to peer inside without jostling it, but there was nothing except for powder.

"Most of these can't be opened easily," Perry said, pointing to one with a screw, before he moved toward another. Thorne reached over and grabbed his hand before he could rock the barrel.

"Don't shake those," Thorne snarled at him. "The device won't be small enough to stick through a screw hole. If you're going to be foolish enough to make your wife a widow only a day after you saved her from the grave, then I'll thank you kindly not to ensure I'm blown to Kingdom Come along with you and the sovereigns!"

"That delicate, is it?" Fitzroy's voice was dry, but he didn't argue with Thorne further. He simply took his hand away gently and used more care when he took out his knife and prodded the lid of another barrel.

"So I've heard. It wasn't practical for use in the war. Too easy to set off by accident. But here… where the powder's just sitting—"

"Understood."

There was nothing but the harsh rasp of their breath as they slowly opened one after another. Sweat dripped down Thorne's face as he thought about the dense, earthy smell of powder in his lungs and the flickering flame of the lamp. Could gunpowder be heavy enough in the air to ignite? Thorne didn't know, but he hoped he wasn't about to discover the answer.

"Thorne." Lord Fitzroy uttered his name like a plea. He held the lid of his barrel aloft, staring down like a man looking into his own grave.

Abandoning his search, Thorne looked over, seeing a coiled spring and moving gears. It was truly terrifying to behold. "Well," he said, words failing him.

"People ask a man at the gallows if he has any last *words*, Galahad," Fitzroy rasped. "That means you need at least one more."

Thorne didn't lift his eyes from the device. "I've got not one but two more for you, then. Get. Out."

"You can't be serious—"

"You should *leave*, Fitzroy!" Thorne roared at him, putting ten years of the military behind the command. "You cannot help me do this, and if I'm about to blow myself to hell, I'd prefer not to take a friend with me. Go. And do not approach the head table, whatever you do."

Realising what Thorne implied with those words, Fitzroy swallowed hard and tried one last time. "Sir Nathaniel—"

"Give my regards to Lady Normanby. And for God's sake, make sure your mother doesn't weasel out of this."

"Tell Selina your bloody self," Fitzroy retorted, turning to leave. "Be warned, Sir Nathaniel—if you don't survive this I'll make sure to put 'Well' on your headstone."

But at least he didn't argue any longer. Leaving Thorne the lantern, Fitzroy sprinted for the stairs. Now alone, Thorne rested his hands lightly on the lip of the barrel as he looked down into it. The timing wheel was rotating slowly, but the stop pin—the one that would trigger the release of the hammer that would strike the flint—was about to slide into the notch on the next gear.

A minute? Perhaps two. There was no time to think too hard about how to go about this, and no chance Peregrine would be able to do much more than get upstairs to safety.

Thorne positioned his hands over the device, and he uttered the shortest prayer he hoped might reach the Almighty's ears.

"Let this work," he prayed, moving as swiftly as he dared.

The minutes ticked by. First five. Then ten. She had seen no sign of Perry or Thorne since his signal to her. Charity was fighting off an attack of nerves. Was something dangerous in the building? Should they not warn everyone to leave? Had Charity misunderstood what Perry was trying to tell her?

Her position on the temporary wooden balcony felt all too precarious. The only thing that kept her in place was seeing Marian still there across the way. Surely nothing concerning would happen yet, if Perry's mother still sat waiting.

Down below, the footmen stepped forward to clear the latest course. Charity almost looked away, but something made her eyes train on Lord Ravenscroft. The dandy was watching someone with avid attention, but he raised his fist to his mouth as if he were coughing. It was such a peculiar action that she glanced down to see where he was looking.

There at the table below the head, one of the lower-ranked men was in motion. Beyond his purposeful direction towards the head table, it looked like nothing out of the ordinary, except—

Charity shifted her gaze in time to see Marian rise from her seat. She murmured something, sliding along the narrow row until she reached the aisleway. At the top, she turned in the direction of the far staircase.

She is leaving, her own thoughts insisted. *You cannot let her get away.*

But neither could she shout, causing panic. Marian's path along the crowded balcony was slow. As if she were attempting to avoid arousing suspicion. Charity risked movement, rising on her toes to see over the heads of the others.

Below, Lord Ravenscroft was gone—as was the man who had been walking towards the table. And Perry was still nowhere in sight.

Charity had to alert the guards of Marian's intentions. She prayed she got to them in time to prevent Marian from finding her way out of the building.

In retrospect, Ravenscroft thought, they should have told the footmen to limit the wine. The aristocrats were sliding deeper into their cups and abandoning their decorum along the way. Waiting for something to happen was pulling him as taut as catgut. Gentz too, if the man's shoulders were any indication.

Amid such revelry, a man sitting a short distance from the head table, his courses going untouched, finally caught Ravenscroft's eye.

It took him a moment to recall the diplomat's name. Malenkov. One of the younger members of the delegation, if Ravenscroft was not mistaken. The only reason the magpie recalled his name at all was because the man had been at Carlton House on the day that Perry was attacked behind the stable.

Now, Malenkov was stone-faced, his attention fixed on the Tsar. Twice in the span of five minutes, he pulled a watch from his pocket and checked the time. The second time... he raised his hand high enough for Ravenscroft to note the ring on his right hand.

Ravenscroft then knew without a doubt. Especially when he folded his napkin and set it beside his full plate. This was

Alexander's traitor. Ravenscroft coughed into a fist, once, twice, until von Gentz glanced his way. The Propagandist caught on quickly, his eyes scanning the room.

Malenkov rose from his chair to make his way around the table. Ravenscroft shifted into motion, moving to stand closer to the Tsar, and signalled one of Hill's soldiers-turned-footmen.

When Gentz's sharp gaze landed upon Malenkov, he understood. Without a word, he shoved back his chair and rose to intercept. The Propagandist got to Malenkov first, stopping him near the end of the royal table. "Ah, Malenkov—just the man I hoped to consult," he said urbanely.

Malenkov, however, did not want to speak to Gentz. "Pardon, Baron Gentz," he muttered. "Might we speak later?"

"Why wait? I need only a moment." The Baron closed his hand around Malenkov's wrist while Hill's man crossed the room in front of the table. Ravenscroft edged closer so he could support Gentz while keeping his body between Malenkov and the Tsar.

"Your ring is remarkable!" Gentz's grip tightened as he pretended to examine the ring. "Such an unusual choice of jewellery. Was it a gift?"

Near the centre of the table, the Tsar was staring at them, a red flush creeping up his neck. He made to stand, but Prinny intervened, resting a friendly hand on his shoulder to keep him there.

Malenkov's arm trembled visibly with the effort to free himself. He swayed from side to side, searching for an opening, and instead saw the Tsar looking his way and the footman approaching. He was caught and knew it of a surety. His life was forfeit.

A terrible presentiment filled Ravenscroft. "Gentz—don't let him—"

But it was too late. Malenkov's hand, trapped in Gentz's grip, made a tight fist. When Malenkov let go, he gave Gentz a glare of triumph and hatred. And then his pallor changed.

Ravenscroft realised that if he did not act fast, the man was going to die in full view of the aristocracy. "The man's swooning!" he blurted. "Let's take him over there to rest."

He threw his arm around the Russian diplomat's waist and half-rushed, half-dragged the man into the nearest alcove. The footman lent a hand, making sure the poison ring came nowhere near either of them. Rarely had Ravenscroft been happier than when they surrendered the man's dying form into the custody of the other guards.

Baron von Gentz pulled a handkerchief from his pocket and wiped his hands, and then let it fall to the ground, abandoned. He gave a wistful sigh. "I shall have to send a note of condolence." He gave Ravenscroft a devilish look. "Should I send it to the Tsar or to Lord Fitzroy's mother?"

Perry wasn't the most devout of fellows, but a steady chant of prayer followed the rhythm of his feet as he ran. *Let Thorne stop the infernal device,* he thought. *Not for my or Charity's sake. For everyone else's. Please.*

If it blew, half of Europe would be in mourning. And possibly go to war again.

And Galahad was... not an odious person to know. He might even be growing rather fond of him. A little bit, at any rate.

He certainly wouldn't want to tell the Duke of Northumberland, Roland Percy, that he had got Sir Nathaniel killed. Percy's heavily muscled build was the same as his half-brother's, and given his pugilistic prowess, His Grace would be apt to lay him out flat on the lawn.

But if that idiot did get himself killed, Perry was most

definitely putting that stupid word, 'Well,' on his tombstone. It would serve the bastard right. And at least that would make a soiree between Percy's right fist and his face worth it.

He burst out of the door at the top of the stairs, more by feel than sight. For a moment he blinked in the light, trying to orient himself. Peregrine peered out of a gap in the drapery, trying to get a sense of what was happening at the head table, and saw a small skirmish. Ravenscroft and the Propagandist were moving the Russian attaché, Pyotr Andreyevich Malenkov, to the side of the room.

Had he been the traitor working with his mother all along? Malenkov had been the young attaché with Lieven at Carlton House, bringing the accusations of Perry's kidnapping of Lark.

Peregrine's gaze jerked upwards, seeking the spot his mother should be seated. His mother was no longer there.

A chill gnawed down his spine, and trying to muster a casual saunter so as not to attract attention from the banquet, Peregrine crossed to the middle of the room so he could see the other balcony. Charity must have seen something.

But Charity… Charity wasn't in the balcony either.

The icy dread creeping along his back grew teeth and sank its fangs painfully deep. With his heart climbing its way into his throat, he again turned to look at the Russian section of the balcony. The Grand Duchess was still there.

Catherine Pavlovna was looking directly at him, impatiently waiting for his attention. And when Perry's eyes met hers, she pointed most dramatically to the end of the balcony. Where the second staircase down was hidden.

He jerked a curt nod of comprehension. His mother had gone that way. It would lead down into the narrow corridor walled off by the drapery.

His mother was attempting to make her escape. Charity had likely seen, left her seat, and was now trying to prevent it.

Unfortunately for Charity—though he would argue it was somewhat fortunate for him—Charity would have to work her way around the outer edge of the Guildhall.

She would be unlikely to run into his mother before she reached the vestibule and slipped out.

Peregrine hurried to the vestibule door, wasting no time in being discreet. There had been two guards positioned there to prevent his mother from leaving. She had managed to kill one guard, leaving him slumped against the wall, while the other was on the floor, clearly dying. Both had deep scratches on their hands.

It seemed she had a second ring; this one loaded with a lethal poison.

Heartless though it was, he ignored the dying man. Perry couldn't do anything to help him except ensure that his killer was brought to justice. He threw open the door to the outside and jogged out into the night.

Far ahead of him, the silhouette of a woman's skirts, illuminated from the front by gaslight, hurried away. Around her head was a halo of bright blonde hair.

"Mother!" he shouted, breaking into a run.

She slowed briefly, and then stopped, spinning to face Peregrine as he stopped a handful of paces away. Her face was creased with worry. As if she were overburdened with regret and now, faced with the consequences, afraid.

"Perry," she choked out, as if she were about to break into tears. "You must understand. Everything I ever did—I did it all for us. Always for us."

Liar.

What a liar she was, ready to play upon his emotions like one might play an instrument. He knew her too well now. How her vile mind worked. She would say whatever she needed to say. Act however she needed to act.

His mother did not suffer fear—none whatsoever. And a creature who experienced no fear would not worry about death or divine retribution. So his mother wouldn't take the easy way out by surrendering. She would kill, deceive, and hurt anyone who stood between her and her escape.

Peregrine's anger snapped taut, and a roar of denial left his lips. "The hell you did. Lark and I never asked you to kill for us, Mother. We were children. We wanted your *love*. The one thing that never was, nor ever will it be, within your power to give."

Marian Fitzroy's eyes flickered briefly. "How dare you say such a thing to me? You had no idea who your father really was. The beast he was behind closed doors. The way he learned to strike me where the bruises would never show. You were his boy. Someone to be cherished. But your sister had no such protection. In nature, a mother's job is to protect and kill for her offspring, Perry. What is love," she spat with contempt, "if not that?"

But even if that was how it had begun, as something vaguely noble, it had quickly twisted and broken as his mother lost her way. As her soul had, if she had ever had one.

"I wasn't deaf, Mother. I knew what my father did to you. But your ends never justified the means," Perry said sternly. "You do not have the right to decide who lives and dies."

Marian cocked her head, pretending to listen. She took a step closer, still carefully circling outside of his reach.

"Nor do you have the right to determine who loves whom," he said, softer. "Not Ravenscroft. Not Charity. Not I. Just because it is beyond your comprehension does not mean you have the right to destroy something so precious.

"I hate you," he hissed, a tear slipping down his cheek. "But more than anything, I pity you, Mother. Because love is... the most beautiful thing I have ever experienced. I cannot imagine living the way you do. Being denied this gift. What must it be like to not be able to balance the terrible feelings in my life—envy, anger, bitterness—with the things that give me hope, and comfort, and ecstasy?"

He took another step towards the streetlight behind her, and she turned to face him. They were only feet apart now, and the way the shadows pooled on her cheeks was eerie. "I think, in your place, I would have become exactly the same. Sick with resentment and devoid of any purpose except ambition. And perhaps that's not even your fault. But you are mad, and ill, and you cannot be saved. I *will not* let you escape." He dropped the words with finality.

His mother's mask slipped, and any remaining trace of something human, something Peregrine could feel sympathy for, vanished entirely. "You may be right, my son. But for your entire lifetime and more, I have existed without the burden of such weakness. For more than thirty years, I understood better than any how to pull the strings that govern a man's heart.

"But I did not predict that, even had you somehow managed to break your sister, you would find it within yourself to abandon the duchess to be here tonight," she sneered at him. "Do you think you have won? I have the satisfaction of knowing it cost you everything to bring me down. *Everything.* Including providing comfort to your dying *love.*"

Peregrine took one taunting step closer to his mother, smiling sadly at her. "No, Mother," he murmured. "You—your hate—and this duty to stop you... you are the reason I have absolutely everything."

It happened quickly, though time seemed to slow. Marian's hand lifted, as if to dash her palm across his face. But his eye seized upon the glint of metal. The shine of gaslight on the ring on her bare hand. He waited, hands at his side, while her arm began its arc.

And right at its apex, it stopped short, her wrist caught in the heavy glove of the man who had approached Marian from behind.

"You've dealt enough death for one night, I reckon. But this—" Hodges callously broke her wrist, disarming her—"this's also for what you did to my nephew. And what you threatened to do to my family."

Marian's scream of surprise and pain rang through the air, her knees buckling. Peregrine closed his eyes and turned away. It was difficult to breathe. To harden his heart. Knowing this was the right thing—the necessary thing—was so different than living it.

Movement caught the corner of his eye.

Charity, with her pale skirts flowing around her, strode forward like an angel of vengeance. She led a small army of guards in her wake.

Her light had found him. He was not alone in the dark.

Perry's chest tightened. He reached for her, letting his gaze, his fingers, and his very soul tangle together with hers, tracing the line of the ring upon her finger with the edge of his own.

He turned back to his mother, pulling Charity against his chest. "Who could have imagined this feud between you and Lady Cresswell would be what gave me my wife?"

Never had he seen his mother's face like this. Black rage and insanity lurked just beneath the surface.

"Things are not finished between us, Peregrine." The basilisk peered through his mother's eyes, unnervingly steady.

"Perhaps, Mother. But for tonight, I am done with you."

31

"It is easier to find men who will volunteer to die, than to find those who are willing to endure pain with patience."
—Julius Caesar

Peregrine said little as he pulled Charity with him, heading back towards the Guildhall and leaving his mother with the guards and Hodges. Charity had to step quickly to keep up with him.

"Did you see Thorne?" he asked her, worry threading through his voice. "Ravenscroft I saw was fine, but—"

Charity blinked, thinking. "I did not, but I was looking for the guards. Where did you last see him?"

Perry laughed briefly, the sound a little ragged. "I left him with a thousand pounds of gunpowder in the crypts and the ticking clock due to ignite it."

She stumbled a little bit, and Peregrine slowed to steady her. No wonder he was in such a hurry. "The building is still whole," she pointed out, uncertain whether she was reassuring herself or her husband. "He must have stopped it."

They entered through the vestibule, finding the men Marian had killed had already been taken away. New guards had replaced them, giving Charity and Perry a keen look as they came in from the outside. But they recognised Peregrine and stood down.

Inside, the banquet had finished, and the women had descended from the balconies to join the men for dessert. Not a single soul seemed to be the wiser about the calamity that had almost been visited upon their heads tonight. The raucous talking and smiling of hundreds of people seemed oddly inappropriate.

"There's Ravenscroft," she pointed the magpie out in the centre of the room. Ravenscroft must have been on the lookout, for he detached himself from the Regent and began working through the crowd toward them.

"There you are!" the dandy said, with an audible note of relief in his voice. "Did you—is she—?"

"My mother is in the hands of a dozen guards and one very angry Will Hodges. Did you catch the Tsar's traitor? Malenkov?"

"He's dead," Lord Ravenscroft said sourly. "Took the coward's way out with the ring when he realised he was surrounded, before we thought to prevent him from being able to do so. Sidmouth is dealing with that, if you have need of him."

Charity could practically sense the weariness emanating from Peregrine's bones. "Lord Sidmouth is more than capable of handling matters here for the rest of this evening. If he needs help, he can call upon Lord Castlereagh," she murmured.

Perry nodded slightly. "I do not have the patience for politics tonight, Ravenscroft. My only priority now is ensuring that everyone I love is safe, and then bringing them home." He looked the dandy up and down. "I am glad that Malenkov turned his ring upon himself instead of you."

The magpie smirked. "The Propagandist was quite taken with

his role. For what it is worth, I am also glad you and Charity are whole, Canary. And that you found… whatever it was you had me looking for."

"A mountain of powder barrels, with Thorne left standing over them. Can you ensure that a guard bars the way to the crypts? It would be vexing to have prevented the explosion of so much gunpowder just to have an unwary servant set it alight now," Perry told him dryly. "On that note, I have a knight to check in on."

Ravenscroft's eyes widened slowly in horror—though Charity wasn't sure if that was at the idea of the explosion or Thorne's absence. "Well, go then!"

Peregrine turned to Charity, but she lifted her hand. "Do not try to leave me here."

"Are you sure? There might be spiders down there." The corner of his mouth quirked, the faintest sign of humour beginning to restore itself. It relieved Charity more than words could say.

"I trust you to protect me," she said dryly, as he held the drape back enough for her to slip behind.

They found the door and went down more by feel than sight. Charity left her hand on Perry's shoulder as he descended before her. "Sir Nathaniel!" he called out. "Are you still here?"

"Aye," came a pained baritone voice from a distance. "Don't worry, Fitzroy, you don't have to bury me yet. But did you get her?"

"We did."

They reached the ground, and as they turned into the crypt, the dim light from the single lantern near Thorne began to show the way. He was sitting on the floor, propped against a large barrel, a contraption of brass gears and springs beside him.

Perry hurried to Thorne's side, crouching down. "Are you well?"

"Took ten years off my life, this did." Thorne raked his right hand through his forelock. "I needed… a moment."

He sounded like he needed more than reassurance. Now that she was closer, she saw he was shaking slightly. And he was hiding his left hand inside his coat. "You're hurt!" she disagreed. "What happened?"

Thorne looked down at the contraption. "It was meant to make a spark to ignite the powder once the wheel turned enough. I couldn't let the hammer strike the flint."

Gently, Peregrine extracted Thorne's arm from the inside of his coat, and Charity winced in sympathy. His left hand was a bloody mess. That was all she made out before Perry quickly hid it from her sight.

"You saved a lot of men's lives," Perry told him, wrapping his handkerchief around it loosely. And then her husband's voice turned slightly teasing. "But could you think of nothing better to put in the machine than a piece of yourself?"

Thorne grunted. "In the time I had left, and while I was trying to pull it out of the barrel at the same time? None so sure. My hand or my life? Seemed an easy choice then."

"Let us hope it does not cost you either," Perry said as he stood slowly, helping pull the larger man to his feet. When Thorne was somewhat steady, he clasped Thorne by the shoulders. "I can see why Roland is happy to call you brother. You earned that title and more. Let's get you looked after. Charity—take the lantern and lead the way."

Peregrine threw Thorne's arm across his shoulders to steady the man, their steps following behind her.

"Thank you for coming back for me," she heard Thorne say quietly.

"I think Charity will agree with me. You're one of ours, in the only way that matters," Peregrine told him, echoing his words from the night of the fire back. "Our family is small—and perhaps it's rather odd—but it seems that someone once told me that protecting those that belong to it is proper. You did fine work. Let us take care of you now, Galahad."

When they reached the brighter lit main floor without further incident, Charity breathed a much-needed sigh of relief. Yet, it stuck in her throat as she saw Thorne's ashen face. Perry left her with Thorne, ducking past the line of drapery to find Ravenscroft.

"*Mon Dieu!*" Ravenscroft remarked, giving the knight a comprehensive examination. Thorne wisely said nothing, recognising that he was in no condition to fight off the Frenchman.

Ravenscroft produced a handkerchief of his own and added it to the impromptu bandaging, covering where blood began to seep through. "The left arm, again? You have got to stop leading with your good side, Galahad. That side has got more history now than my tailor's ledger."

"I assure you, I do not mean to make a habit of it." Thorne said, rubbing his forehead with his good hand. "But for most tasks, my right arm is the more useful one."

"Which just goes to prove that you are putting some thought into things when you heroically throw yourself into trouble," Ravenscroft grumbled. "But not so much that you stay *out* of it. You are in desperate need of supervision. Fortunately, I know a valet who will be delighted to take you on. He thrives on lost causes and bloodstains."

Leaving Thorne safely in Ravenscroft's hands was a relief. The magpie would make sure that Sir Nathaniel got the attention of a good surgeon quickly. The mechanism Thorne had stopped so bluntly might have broken bones in the man's hand. Hopefully, Thorne wouldn't lose use of it.

Time would tell.

Either way, Peregrine would ensure that he kept his promise. Thorne would be looked after, even if he had to blackmail the Prince Regent himself to do it.

Charity took his arm lightly. "We should tell the Queen what happened here tonight."

"Yes," he agreed distantly, glad for her suggestion. Now that the burden of this duty was falling from his shoulders, he was almost... lost in the crowd of people here. It was a curious, muddled sensation—this swamp of emotions where the anger and pain began to fade away, leaving behind... mostly an overwhelming sense of relief, a sense of hope, and a trace of unease.

It was over. They could finally look forward. But at this moment, he was not quite ready to do so. No more than he was ready to stare into the sun as it rose on their new dawn.

Instead, he looked down at his wife. She was all the brilliance he needed in this moment. And as if she divined the thoughts in his head, she gave him a small, serene smile that brought his remaining restless thoughts peace.

Everything would be all right.

But Charity was correct; there was still some unfinished business to tend to tonight.

"It is late, but I think she will welcome this news even if she is already abed," Perry told his wife. "Let's go see the Queen and Selina. It will put their minds at ease."

"And Lark?" Charity asked him softly.

He shook his head. "I will send a note to let everyone at Carlton House know that all is well. Let her sleep soundly where she is."

"Do you know, there is a real benefit to not officially attending an event," Charity murmured to him with a laugh as they exited the building again. When he turned his gaze her way, she grinned at him impishly. "There is no scandal or need to fret about the impropriety of leaving early."

Perry chuckled. "There is that. But we might need all that extra time to trace where Hodges ended up."

Hodges, however, was relatively easy to find. His footman, Owens, who had been waiting in the staging area with the other carriage attendants, pointed to a trio of men standing well away from the door. "I'll go get Dawson and the carriage, my lord," he added, hurrying off.

Peregrine recognised the outlines of Hodges, Lord Sidmouth, and… Red Hand standing together. It was an odd group, to be certain, but all of their postures were at ease.

"Your Grace. Fitzroy," Sidmouth greeted them, his face looking far less furrowed with strain than it had since before the sovereigns had arrived. "It is finished, then. Lady Fitzroy is secured, the threat contained. You have both my thanks and the Regent's. I was just extending my gratitude to your man and…" he peered at Red Hand, who gave him a shark-like grin, "your other ally."

"While Malenkov was approaching the head table, there were twelve barrels of black powder sitting in the crypts, ready to detonate," Perry informed Sidmouth. "You will want to secure the area until the event is over, I imagine. Twelve hundred pounds of gunpowder suggests another lackey accomplice paid to turn the other way while it was moved in. I trust you will want to inquire about who at the Guildhall might have helped them get there."

The Home Secretary blinked in disbelief, and even Hodges and Red Hand looked suitably awed. "Twelve *barrels*?"

It was likely more than sufficient to shatter the stone ribs and columns, punching a hole through the floor. More than sufficient to kill the people at the table.

Sidmouth frowned fiercely at the other two men. "I trust I do not have to tell you two to hold your tongue about this." Both men shook their heads. "Well then, I thank you again for stopping the explosion, Fitzroy. On behalf of all the sovereigns who were seated at that table."

"I was not the one who stopped my mother's infernal device, Sidmouth. The Regent can thank Sir Nathaniel Thorne for that service."

The viscount's lips pressed together as he recalled the name. "The same man he knighted at Brighton last year?" When Perry nodded, Sidmouth bobbed his head in understanding. "I will make sure the Regent is aware. Excuse me."

He hurried off—presumably to ensure no one accidentally brought down the Guildhall—and Peregrine turned his attention to Hodges and the Irish bludgeoner, who was taking a keen interest in his wife. A respectful one.

"Your Grace. Didn't reckon I'd ever meet the lady who could make Fitzroy turn London inside out on her account," the Irishman said, taking his hat in his hands. He gave her a cheeky grin. "Now that I have, I see why he did."

"You're a brave man sayin' that in front of Fitzroy. Braver than I'd be," Hodges told him.

"So you are Red Hand. I confess, I had imagined someone taller—though perhaps that was simply the stature of your reputation after all I heard from Lord Fitzroy." She gave him a wide smile so he would know she was jesting, and Red Hand blinked, looking... suitably dazzled by her splendour.

"Ah now, Your Grace, you'll have me forgettin' me own name if you smile like that," he coughed into his hand, embarrassed. "But Fitzroy—I had a thought on our... debt."

The bludgeoner leaned over to whisper in Perry's ear. Peregrine, who had stiffened at the mention of the large unnamed favour that he had promised to Red Hand at the end of May, abruptly relaxed as the man's words filtered through his ear.

"I can only promise what is in my power to deliver," Perry told him. "But... I will ask."

Red Hand nodded with a faint grin. "Fair's fair. If he says no, we'll work out somethin' different."

By that point, Owens had returned with Dawson and the carriage from where it had been parked. Hodges took his leave of Red Hand, joining Dawson on the driver's bench as Owens helped Charity and Perry climb inside.

Closing the curtains, Peregrine pulled Charity close to him for the twenty-minute ride to Buckingham House, letting everything outside of the carriage fade away. All he wanted was to let a moment's peace filter through him, soothing the jagged edges of the past few days.

Pleasantly, they didn't even have to argue with the Queen's aide-de-camp when they arrived. "Her Majesty is still entertaining in her private drawing room," the man informed them, leading the way. "You were expected."

A footman swung the door open, and the oddest sounds trickled out into the hallway before two sets of eyes stared back at them.

Was that laughter? From *Queen Charlotte?*

The Queen of England and the Marchioness of Normanby sat together, a deck of cards and bowls of strawberries and cream on the table before them, with glasses of some cordial or liqueur. But the conversation between them was lively, and from here, they appeared to have become the best of friends.

"The strain was too great. They've taken leave of their senses," breathed Charity in an undertone to him.

Peregrine felt a laugh in response rise in his throat. But then he spotted the clear glass cordial bottle sitting on the sideboard, bedecked with a ribbon. The wax seal was broken; the bottle was open. And beside it sat a glass with an inch of liquid in the bottom —a brilliant, bright red, like that of plums.

Abruptly, the warmth in his chest froze, and he rushed forward, ignoring the exclamations of the women. He seized the bottle from the table, lifting it to the light to peer at the colour.

A pleasant, spicy smell met his nose. Abruptly, Peregrine was thrown back six years into the past, into Grenville's office where he had watched the man find his death at the bottom of just such a bottle.

Charity's hand settled on his arm, and the present world snapped back into place.

Selina and the Queen were both silent in their chairs, watching him. Selina, with a hint of sadness. Queen Charlotte with sober, unshakable composure that could bring a court to a standstill.

"Lord and Lady Fitzroy." Her lips twitched into a moue of distaste as Charity's title left her lips, but she carried on. "Lord Fitzroy, you seem rather… unnerved."

Things are not finished between us, Peregrine, his mother's voice lingered in his ear, like the hiss of a reptile.

He had not imagined that his mother's final plans tonight might be so extensive they would involve a strike at everyone on her black books. Or—was it worse? Was Selina the one who brought this poison to the Queen's table? For a moment, he felt faint.

"Fitzroy," Selina said, standing from the table as though she was about to hurry to his side.

He ignored her. "Your Majesty," Peregrine's voice was faint. "I beg you. Tell me you did not drink this cordial."

The Queen stared at him. "Of course, I did not."

"Nor did I," said the marchioness, taking the bottle out of his hands. And then her voice became gentler. More compassionate. "Perry, I knew about what happened to Grenville."

"Sit, Lord Fitzroy, before you fall over," Charlotte suggested wryly.

Charity helped steer him towards the pair of chairs on the other side of the table, and Selina set both the partially filled glass and cordial bottle on the sideboard, looking chagrined. "I am sorry to have given you such a shock, Perry," she said. "I wanted you to *see* the bottle. Not assume the Queen had drunk it."

Both these women, Peregrine realised abruptly, were tipsy. And that was almost as stupefying to comprehend as the fact that his mother had got a poisoned bottle of cordial into Buckingham House.

"Branson brought it in. Do you remember him? The rude little footman? No? Well, never mind him, anyway," Selina said with an airy wave of her hand.

The Queen agreed blithely. "He is sitting in a dungeon waiting to be questioned by Lord Sidmouth."

"A dungeon! Do you even *have* a dungeon here?" retorted Selina.

"Semantics," Charlotte said with a reproving glance that intimidated Lady Normanby not at all. "The marchioness rather strongly suggested that I not trust this gift. Based on your expression, I assume you concurred with her advice and that she may have saved my life."

She laughed. The Queen *laughed*, her eyes sparkling with challenge. "I would not have drunk it, anyway. I abhor plum cordial. But if you had not sent me Lady Normanby, we would not have caught the footman."

Selina's lips curved, the hint of amusement glinting beneath her composure. "We had expected your arrival somewhat earlier," she said lightly, "but one must allow heroes their dramatic timing."

32

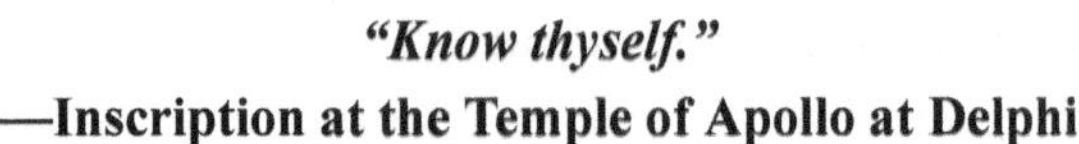

—Inscription at the Temple of Apollo at Delphi

They had two days' grace before the summons from Sidmouth came. Two days of retreat from the social scene, and the sovereigns. And everything that would have to come before the Russians departed England's shores.

Peregrine had little interest in facing the *ton*, knowing that his mother was in the Tower, waiting while two nations argued about her fate.

The first morning, when Lark had yet to return from Carlton House, he retreated even from Charity so he could brood. She found him anyway, sitting beneath a tree in his mother's poisonous garden, staring at the greenery and shredding blades of grass between his fingers. His wife joined him, letting him have his silence until he shifted restlessly, self-conscious.

Charity turned to him. "It is all right, I think," she said, pressing her shoulder to his. "You do not have to don sackcloth and ashes."

"Oh?" he asked her, faintly amused. "What do you suppose I would don those for, Sparkles?"

She gave him a knowing look. "For feeling what you do. Everything is complicated. This last year… how well have I learned, life is not always so simple. I have been thinking a great deal about my own complications. My parents."

She plucked her own blade of grass, peeling it as he did. "What *is* simple is knowing that we will work through what is complicated together."

Peregrine let the grass fall and reached over to take her hand, shifting closer to her. He spun the ring on her finger absently, dropping a kiss on the span of bare flesh between her neck and the edge of the dress. "Who might have guessed that loving you would be the simplest part?"

Charity met his eyes, and her lips curved slowly into that radiant smile just for him. But she said nothing more, content to curl up with him and simply… be for a little while. She took his hand and rested it on her lower belly, and he knew she was letting go of the darker thoughts.

Looking towards their future.

Even though things were still convoluted now, he had faith they would be all right. Someday soon.

Over the rest of that day, and into the next, the others gravitated back to the house, and found a reason to stay awhile. Perry was not alone in needing the solace of family. The kind of family one named by choice, not necessarily only from blood. Lark returned first. Then, Antoine and Ravenscroft brought back the injured Thorne. Thorne likely wouldn't lose his hand or the use of fingers, but the bruising and fractures were severe and uncomfortable. Laudanum was helping him sleep that pain away.

And finally, Selina crept in, saying her house was too empty.

When Sidmouth's summons finally came, the day before the Russians were scheduled to depart, only Lark and Peregrine were invited to attend. Charity offered to come with them, but Peregrine shook his head, and she acquiesced.

Brother and sister entered the outer walls through the gate in the middle tower, making their way to the Tower Green together. Lark leaned heavily on Peregrine's arm, shivering slightly with fear and dismay at the thought of facing the Tsar now he had learned everything.

The grassy space of Tower Green had seen several women's executions. Today, it would see another. Peregrine led his sister through the gap in the closed scaffolding that would keep the affair private.

Behind the scaffold stood the Home Secretary, the Tsar, and Nicholas. The Tsar looked weary, but he approached Peregrine and clasped his hand. "Fitzroy," Alexander said honestly. "Saying merely 'thank you' for what you have done for all of us feels like an insult. And yet, no more can be said without everyone knowing what so very nearly happened."

Peregrine gripped the Tsar's hand firmly in return. "Thanks is enough, Your Imperial Highness. If I had any wish beyond that, I would ask for mercy on behalf of my sister. For her part in my mother's schemes."

"You have certainly earned that much." Alexander looked at him keenly, but then he released Perry's hand and turned to Lark, tilting his head as he considered the young woman.

Lark's lower lip trembled briefly, but she stood tall under the Tsar's fierce appraisal.

"Tell me, Lady Lark. Your brother says you were unaware. Is it true? Do you swear you intended no harm to me?"

Lark dropped her chin briefly, but she did not shy away from meeting the Tsar's curious gaze again. "I swear it. I knew nothing of the plans to assassinate you, Your Highness. I thought—I thought being married to a prince was enough to satisfy my mother's ambition." Lark's lashes fell, her eyes dulling. "It was foolish of me not to have grasped she would crave more."

"And what of Nicholas?" he asked her next. "What do you feel for my brother?"

She jerked her head in Prince Nicholas's direction, shaking her head slightly. Nicholas looked heartbroken—in the way only such a young man who had barely tasted adulthood could. "I am so sorry, Nicholas," she whispered. "I could have been happy with you. I wish—I wish things had been different," she finally said in defeat, extending her hand to him with his locket in it. "But what begins with a lie is not meant to be."

Nicholas took the token, looked at his brother, and then down at his shoes.

"Nikolai, do you also swear the same? You did not conspire to see me dead?" Alexander asked him bluntly, and Nicholas's shocked look was almost answer enough.

He rattled out his response in rapid French, his English not up to the task. *"Brother, how could you even ask me that?"* he asked brokenly. *"I love you as I love—as I loved her."*

Ashamed, he turned away.

Alexander rested his hand upon his brother's turned back, but he glanced at Lark, and then he looked at Peregrine. "The priest who performed the marriage without permission, and Countess Orlova, who served as your sister's godmother, are being dealt with. When I am through, it will be as though your marriage never was.

"I believe you did not want my death," he continued to Lark and Nicholas. "Because of Lord Fitzroy, I am content to let the rest be forgotten."

Sidmouth, who had been watching this exchange, nodded his head. "Lady Marian Fitzroy has been determined guilty of the charges of High Treason against both our Crown and the person of His Imperial Majesty. The penalty is death.

"Given the gravity of the charges, and in the interest of maintaining peaceful relations, she is conveyed forthwith into the charge of the Russian delegation, to suffer the penalty in the manner her treachery towards them demands. We have asked for the execution to be done here, where her death may be witnessed by the agents of the Crown and Parliament." He touched his hand to his chest.

Then he lifted his voice. "Bring forward the prisoner."

Two guards escorted his mother into the enclosure, in chains. Her head was unbowed. Unrepentant. And she almost appeared bored.

She looked from the Tsar to Sidmouth, and then to her children. Her expression barely flickered as she looked over Lark. But the basilisk flared briefly in her eyes when they settled on Peregrine.

"Do you have any final words for your mother?" Sidmouth asked them, not unkindly.

Peregrine had spent enough time as the traitor's son. He searched his heart for what he was feeling, unable to come up with anything more than pity for his sister, and a desire to go home to his wife. For his mother… he had nothing left to give. He had said everything he needed to say.

He shook his head and looked at his sister. She, at least, might want to say something.

Lark's face was a study, every bit as complicated as Charity had said such feelings could be. Though Marian was waiting for her words, she did not look at her daughter.

"I hope everyone forgets your very name," Lark finally told her. "You do not deserve to be remembered, even in such infamy."

And then his sister turned on her heel, marching out of the enclosure.

The guards pushed his mother down to her knees, and Peregrine closed his eyes briefly, waiting for the deed to be done as Russia's chosen executioner strode into the enclosure, holding a heavy axe.

But Sidmouth held up a hand, staying the man's movements for a moment. "Fitzroy," the Home Secretary told him, "you are excused."

The Tsar nodded his agreement.

And grateful for that small mercy, Peregrine followed his sister out.

"The House was informed this morning that Lady Marian Fitzroy has been tried and convicted of High Treason. Sentence was carried into effect. The House declines to publish particulars."
—House of Lords, 23 June 1814

The notice went out in the papers the morning after the allied sovereigns departed. Sparse in details, the proclamation left the members of high society to fill the gaps about Marian's crimes with their best guesses. Selina, having some insight into the matter, went from persona non grata to the top of everyone's guest list.

Charity and Perry ignored it all, choosing to focus on the next day, when Prinny and the Queen would announce their marriage to the *ton*. Before that happened, Charity had one thing she had to do.

It seemed strange to find herself there, in front of her parents' London home, for the first time in nearly a year. Somehow, it felt like both forever and yesterday since she had arrived in London for her debut. She could still recall the nights spent curled in her bed, with Grace at her side, the two of them considering her list of candidates for husband.

She squeezed Perry's hand, and he responded by raising it to his mouth and pressing a kiss to her knuckles.

"Everything we endured was all worth it. *You* are worth it," she told him.

He pulled her closer, his mouth claiming hers with a heat that cared nothing for who might see through the carriage window. But eventually, reason asserted itself. Perry loosened his hold so he could look her in the eye. "Are you certain you want to speak with your parents? You don't owe them any explanations."

This she knew. She was not there to make any explanations.

It was too much to hope anything she said would make her parents accept her decision so quickly. All she could do was tell them herself, before they heard it elsewhere. Hoping that, in time, royal approval of Peregrine might soften their old hatred.

"I will not have the announcement at St James's marred by surprise or scandal," she said. "So, yes. I'm certain. I would rather they hear it from me tonight."

Her parents were expecting her. Alone, but only because she had failed to specify otherwise.

Bennett, her parents' butler, opened the door when she rang the bell. He welcomed her inside, keeping his expression free of all opinion when Perry followed behind. After he closed the door, he bowed low.

"Well met, Your Grace. It is nice to see you looking so lovely after all this time."

"It is 'my lady' now," she corrected him in a soft voice. She flashed him a smile and patted Perry's arm. "The official announcement will come tomorrow."

Bennett, the dear man, followed her cues and offered them both his heartfelt congratulations before showing them into the drawing room where her parents awaited.

As before, Charity entered first. Her father stood near the mantel, gazing into the empty hearth as though he might find the answers to life's greatest questions lying there. Her mother already had a scowl on her lips, and she opened her mouth to no doubt harangue Charity for taking so long to present herself to them.

But those words died before they made it out, burned into ashes when Perry entered the room.

"He is not welcome here," her mother said, leaping to her feet. She pointed at the butler. "Escort the traitor's son out immediately."

Peregrine stiffened, but his face was blank. Anger burned through Charity. "This man you keep showing such disrespect to is *my husband*," she informed her mother. "That is what I wished to tell you in private."

"You *married* him?" Lady Cresswell squeaked and then swayed.

"If it has not been announced, it can be undone," her father said, catching his wife by the shoulders. It was as though he was saying it as much to himself as to keep Lady Cresswell from swooning.

"This is not a conversation fit to have in front of… that man. What will everyone think of us? Send him away!" Lady Cresswell complained to her husband. "Bennett! Remove him from this house!"

To his credit, Bennett did not do as her ladyship ordered. Instead, he feigned deafness and backed out of the room, closing the door on his way out.

Lord Cresswell glanced between his wife and his child, sizing up his choice, and then turned a frown on Peregrine.

That, more than any words could say, snuffed out whatever hope remained in Charity's breast for reconciliation. They were not even willing to listen to what she had to say before turning their backs on Perry. They were too concerned with how the *ton* would perceive them to stand up for him. Just as they had refused to stand up for their daughter.

Nothing, not even a royal command, would make her parents admit they were wrong.

"Sit down, Mama!" she commanded. She, who had never once raised her voice in this home, stunned both her parents into complete silence. "Sit, the both of you. We do not intend to stay long, but you will hear me before I go."

Charity drew in a deep breath and willed her pounding heart to slow. She could do this. She had to, for the sake of their future family. She would not allow the hate from the previous generation to spread into the next.

"Mama, Papa, I have not come here to offer you any explanations or apologies for my behaviour. I am here out of courtesy, nothing more. Tomorrow at St James's, the Prince Regent and the Queen will announce that Lord Fitzroy and I are married, having witnessed the ceremony themselves."

She paused then to offer Perry her hand. He slid his fingers through hers, lending her his support. "I married the Duke of Atholl. As his widow, I earned the right to make my own choices. And I choose him." She held up their joined hands. "*He* is more important to me than the opinion of whoever disapproves. We will *not* be separated."

"You will ruin us," her mother spat. "As soon as you see the *ton's* reaction to this news, you will regret this. You will see."

"The only thing I regret is listening to you in the first place.

You two tried your best to poison me against Perry, for no crime other than his name."

"He did not search for you when you disappeared," her mother reminded them hatefully. "He did not denounce his mother."

"*You* did not search for me either," Charity said in a pointed tone. "I will forever wonder whether you understood, somewhere deep inside, that it was Marian enacting her revenge." She swallowed as another thought occurred to her. "That you didn't look because it was better if I eloped and was never seen again. Or better if I had died, because then you would not have to deal with the damage to your status."

The expressions on her parents' faces… told her everything.

Charity summoned all the poise of the duchess. "You have forfeited the right to have any say over my life, and your place in my future."

Lord Cresswell stuttered, but it was her mother who Charity watched. Lady Cresswell's face drained of all colour, even her lips bloodless. She made to rise from her seat.

"No, Charity, you cannot—"

"But what of your title?" her father asked. "Your hard-won place in society? He lowers you, Charity."

"He lifts me up." Charity tightened her hold on Perry's hand, making clear her allegiance.

Lady Cresswell trembled, but the flush staining her neck and cheeks proclaimed it as fury and not fear. "There is no turning back from such a choice, Charity. We will cut you off, disavow you to all who ask—"

"I do not care, Mama. Do whatever you want. If you cannot accept this man, who risked his life to save mine, and now holds my heart, then consider the blood ties between us to be cut. My loyalty is to the family he and I will make together."

Her words finally roused Lord Cresswell from his silent

stupor. He rose from his seat and marched over to point his finger in Perry's face. "Have you nothing to say about this? Are you going to allow her to keep our future grandchildren from us?"

"You care about my opinion *now*?" he asked, looking amused. "My wife is more than capable of making her own decisions. I support her in all things, including this." Then, dismissing the man entirely, he turned to Charity and asked, "Have you anything else to say, my darling?"

"No," she answered, letting her final word ring in the air.

"Shall we take our leave then? Good day, Lord and Lady Cresswell."

33

"I believe I forgot to tell you I was made a Duke."
—Arthur Wellesley, Duke of Wellington, in a postscript to his brother

Nobles packed the throne room of St James's until they stood near shoulder to shoulder. It was to be one of the last Courts of the season, but that was not why so many had turned out. Everyone was interested in finding out just how deep Marian Fitzroy's treachery went, and no one wanted to miss the chance to pose a well-placed question to those in the know.

When Charity arrived with Perry and Lark, the crowd parted to make space for them. It irked Charity that it was not out of any respect so much as fear. Marian Fitzroy's name was on everyone's lips, and many were speculating they had been convened to see the Crown pass judgement on Lord Fitzroy's head.

Perry was wearing his armour again to protect himself. She noted the expression of boredom and slight superciliousness that others would interpret as cold disinterest. It was the one that allowed him to pretend he was not affected by their words. However, she was not fooled by the façade.

Selina, Lord Ravenscroft, and Sir Nathaniel were among the very few to offer them a welcome smile, Lord and Lady Barbour being the others. Lord Castlereagh appeared to still be holding a grudge over being left in the dark about the events at the Guildhall. Lord Sidmouth limited himself to a warm nod of acknowledgment.

Charity kept a tight hold on Perry's arm and her head held high as they made their way to the front of the room. Lark split off when they reached the base of the raised dais where the empty thrones sat waiting, positioning herself just off to the side.

As if by plan, Selina, Ravenscroft, and Sir Nathaniel slid into place behind the couple, lending them their silent support. The rap of a staff on the wooden floor put a stop to all the murmurs.

"Their Royal Highnesses the Prince Regent, Queen Charlotte, and Princess Charlotte Augusta," the footman announced in ringing tones. The crowd bowed and curtseyed as the monarchs entered.

The Prince Regent strode in first, his countenance free of the lines that had creased his brow and his back unbent of the weight of the days of entertaining.

"The departure of a certain Grand Duchess has taken years off Prinny's face," Ravenscroft whispered just loud enough for their little group to hear. Charity barely stifled a laugh.

Indeed, Her Imperial Highness had claimed a desire to spend more time with her family, and had set off with the Russian entourage for the continent. Prinny had every reason to be relieved, for there was now no one left in England daring enough to demand the orchestra play a tune other than the one he selected.

Well, no one other than his dear mother, Queen Charlotte, but the Queen had far better ways to spend her time than on such trivialities. Her discerning eye scanned the faces in the room, and a slight frown marred her features, as if she were silently judging her subjects and finding them wanting.

The Princess entered last, with a serene smile on her face. As her father and grandmother ascended to their thrones, she chose to stand at Lady Lark's side.

Prinny waited for his mother to sit and then raised his arms to address the gathered crowd. "Another Season approaches its end, this one more eventful than most—"

"That is an understatement…" Selina murmured.

"After spending so many hours entertaining our allies and friends, we shall all soon depart London for a well-deserved break. Before we go," His Highness continued, "there remain a few outstanding official matters."

Charity shifted even closer to Perry, and he gave her hand on his arm a fond pat. This was it, the moment they had both dreamed of.

"In the privacy of the Chapel Royal, my mother the Queen and I played host and witness to a most intimate of ceremonies. A marriage."

A flurry of whispers ran through the room, and Charity noted many gazes shift from Prinny's face to over where the princess stood.

"It is my pleasure to introduce to this court, Lord Fitzroy and —" the Regent stumbled briefly, "and his lady wife, the former Duchess of Atholl. Please join me in wishing the newlyweds many years of happiness."

His announcement reverberated through the room, stunning the attendees into silence. Whatever they had expected, this news was not it, and no one knew how to react.

It was the Queen who broke the hush, raising her gloved hands into the air for a muffled applause. Selina and Lord Ravenscroft followed, offering their hearty congrats. Sir

Nathaniel laid his right hand on Perry's shoulder, and soon others chimed in with their well wishes.

If Lord and Lady Cresswell sulked in the far corner of the room, Charity chose not to see them. There was no space in her life for ill will.

The footman banged his staff again, restoring order to the room.

Prinny took a deep breath and carried on. "My lords, ladies, and gentlemen, it is not often that I have the happy task of rewarding true service to the Crown. Far too many perform their duties because they must; too few because they ought.

"On this day, let it be known by all that Lord Peregrine Fitzroy has done both, with honour, with courage, and with such maddening discretion that even *I* was the last to learn the full measure of his deeds!"

He moved then, leaving the dais behind to descend the few steps to the floor, accepting a bright blue sash from the footman.

"By command of His Majesty," His Highness said, his voice solemn, "you are invested with the Most Noble Order of the Garter."

For an instant, Perry seemed carved from stone, his whole body tensing as every line of him held in rigid disbelief. Charity's breath caught, her heart stumbling as the words sank in. The Order of the Garter, the highest honour awarded by the Crown. For a heartbeat, she could not move.

Then, as the meaning struck home, Perry let go of Charity's arm and stepped forward to receive the unexpected reward.

Before all, Prinny lifted the sash and draped it across Perry's shoulder, the silver star glinting against Perry's black superfine coat. Then, taking the velvet garter from the herald's hands, he touched it lightly to Perry's knee. It was a gesture more symbolic than practical, yet one that carried the weight of centuries.

When the blue sash fell across Perry's shoulder, he bowed his head lower, not so much to the Regent, but to the memory of all that had brought him to this moment.

Then, he knelt in a bow of profound obeisance, showing the Prince Regent the deepest of respect, and Charity's heart went with him.

Prinny rested a hand on Perry's bowed head. "Let it be remembered that loyalty such as his strengthens not only the throne, but England herself."

When Perry rose, the blue of the sash gleaming against his coat, the applause swelled, polite at first, then real. She pressed her fingers together to stop them trembling, the ache in her throat both joy and relief.

Prinny, it seemed, was not done. "From this day forward, you shall bear the title Duke of Fitzroy, a name that shall stand for loyalty, courage, and the quiet strength that England herself esteems."

None was more stunned than Perry himself, and his mouth dropped open in shock. For her part, Charity's mind reeled. Her stunned gaze shifted right to the throne where the Queen was sitting. Her Majesty's mouth twisted into a very satisfied smile, all but telling Charity exactly who was responsible for saving her from being known as the new Lady Fitzroy.

Charity would remain Her Grace—but this time as Duchess of Fitzroy.

The Prince Regent returned to his place and finally sat on the throne. "Mother, I believe you have something else to add?"

Charity could not even hazard a guess what the Queen might say next. Already, she was well past the limits of her imagination.

The Queen cleared her throat. "I would be remiss if I did not recognise Her Grace, for she too has shown to be the most honourable of subjects. Therefore, we are granting her a private warrant. She might attend court only when she wishes. Her loyalty has been proven beyond question."

With those few words, the Queen released Charity from all obligations, present and future. When Charity had stood her ground at Frogmore, not shying away from defending the action that was morally right, Charlotte had been incensed. But she appeared to be acknowledging her respect for that courage now.

It was trust she was giving—and freedom to stand apart.

Perry wrapped an arm around Charity's waist and pulled her against him. They propped one another up as the sheer volume of disbelief made them both weak in the knees.

Charity heard little of what came next, her mind awhirl with the implications. She was freer than any other Englishwoman had been. Honoured and relieved of the burden of rushing to Court at every royal's whim. She and Perry could live as they chose, travel where they wanted, without needing to seek any sort of royal permission.

She had no idea how they would spend the rest of their lives, but that did not matter. There was time enough to dream together.

Lord Ravenscroft and Sir Nathaniel each received medals of valour, and Selina was also recognised, though in her case, it was a gift very much with strings attached. She was named a lady-in-waiting, a title that neatly tied her to the Queen.

Strangely, Selina did not seem overwrought to find herself in such a position.

With the ceremony at an end, the footman invited all to move to the nearby Assembly Room for celebratory glasses of champagne. The royals filed out, with Lark staying close to the Princess's side.

And finally, it was the five of them standing together, glasses in hand. Thorne, whose left arm was tucked in a sling beneath his coat, kept finishing his glass and setting it aside so he would have his only useful hand free. But both Ravenscroft and Selina were partaking in a friendly competition of some sort. Charity wasn't certain whether it was to annoy Nathaniel by keeping his hand full, or to see if they could successfully get the knight three sheets to the wind.

Finally, when Thorne held onto his last glass—a full one—giving them both a darkling look, Ravenscroft turned his attention to Perry.

"What am I to call you now?" he moaned to Perry theatrically. Ravenscroft had unwisely been trying to match drinks with Sir Nathaniel. "'Canary' is now too undignified. But to call you 'Your Grace?'" The dandy made a brief, rude noise, scowling. "The Duke of Drama? No, I have to think hard on this."

"I suppose 'Fitzroy' is out of the question," Peregrine remarked dryly.

"*Yes*, of course it is out of the question," the older man said testily. "It isn't *fair* for you to continue to call me 'Maggie' and not have a sobriquet of your own."

Charity smothered a grin, turning her attention away from the two bickering men. Selina and Thorne were turned slightly towards one another. The knight's face was flushed slightly with embarrassment as Selina adjusted his medal on his lapel, taking care to avoid jostling the sling holding his heavily bandaged hand. Then she took the full glass from his hand, drinking from it herself.

Oh, goodness. Charity had to bite back a laugh at the stunned expression on his face. Quickly she turned away, pretending she hadn't seen it. Thorne might be entirely too honourable for the flirtations of someone as titled and devious-minded as Selina, but… he was a man grown.

And stranger relationships had blossomed.

They all moved next door, where they were enveloped by a sea of well-wishers. All those who had kept them at arm's length were suddenly desperate to rectify their mistake. Peregrine was courteous to all the court vipers, his old charm and cunning reasserting itself. But the set of his shoulders was easy. Charity no longer saw a man who was currying favour and a stockpile of secrets to have weapons at hand with which to protect himself.

He was safe enough now to let that go, too.

It took Prinny approaching to chase people away long enough for Charity to catch her breath.

"I trust you are pleased with your reward, *Your Grace*?" the Regent grinned briefly like a troublesome boy. "My aide will be in touch regarding the formal induction at Windsor into the Order."

"I am indeed honoured, Your Highness," Perry replied. "The Crown has been remarkably generous in its recognition. But there remains one debt unpaid. Someone who lent their assistance that night, who lacks the social polish and invitation to appear at court."

"Oh?" Prinny shifted forward, curiosity driving his brows up. And then, looking at Sir Nathaniel, he leaned in conspiratorially. "Are you suggesting I need to knight another man?"

Peregrine smirked, also leaning in. "No. But… he has asked if he might have the opportunity to see the infamous 'Regent's closet' and meet you in the flesh. I have already warned him you may decline."

"Colour me intrigued, Fitzroy. Who is this mysterious man with so bold a request?"

Perry finally looked a touch uncomfortable, and he rubbed the back of his neck. "Red Hand."

The Regent's eyes rounded. "The bludgeoner?" he whispered. "The one who helped us find Goldbourne's counterfeit press?"

"Among other things," Peregrine hedged. "If you would rather not—or if you deem it unsafe—"

Charity assumed that the Regent was going to sputter with indignation, but instead the man laughed as if this was the most fun he had had in ages.

"A visit to *my closet*, you say?" Prinny lit up. "*Delightful.*

Lady Vivienne will be *outraged*, which suits me well. I am tired of her, anyway. I daresay I could use the company—no one appreciates fine brocade like a notorious outlaw. I shall send a personal invitation. Monogrammed." He flagged down a passing footman with a flamboyant flick.

Then, swiping a fresh glass of champagne, he turned with glee. "Come. Let us go provoke Lord Castlereagh. It'll be tremendous fun watching him try to scold us through clenched teeth."

Charity assured Perry she would be fine and then went off for a private word of her own. Her gaze was set on the Queen, who stood near the window, as though waiting for Charity's approach.

"Your Grace," the Queen said, a glint of amusement in her eyes. "The set of your mama's mouth suggests that humble pie does not sit well with her."

Charity turned to find her mother across the room, cheeks flushed scarlet as she reckoned with the consequences of her own schemes. It was not her reaction that surprised Charity, but that the Queen had noticed it at all. When she turned to face Charlotte again, she found that Her Majesty's expression had already settled into its usual, serene composure.

"Come, Your Grace," the Queen continued, her tone soft but firm. "I would not have reigned this long without learning to read the hearts and ambitions of my court. Your mama ever pursued glory—it took me too long to see she would chase it at any cost. So she shall remain there, cut off from the heights to which you have ascended."

"A duchess again," Charity murmured. "I am sure I have you to thank for the unexpected honour."

"I would not burden you with her stain," the Queen said, her fingers brushing the edge of her sleeve as if to dismiss the matter. "Let 'Lady Fitzroy' die with that woman and fade from memory. The Duchess of Fitzroy will mean what you make of it.

"Now, what do you think of young Leopold there?" the Queen asked, angling her head toward the far end of the room. "He appears quite determined to charm my granddaughter."

Indeed, the princess was deep in conversation with Prince Leopold, with Lark keeping a fond watch over the pair. Charity thought back to the dinner at Frogmore, when only Leopold had cared enough to check on the Princess's state. He had chosen to remain behind when the other royals departed.

"He is certainly worthy of her consideration, Your Majesty."

The Queen nodded, the faintest sigh escaping her. "You are welcome to visit us at Windsor this summer. I am sure the Princess would appreciate your advice as she considers her prospects."

Though the invitation seemed innocent enough, Charity sensed there was a test underneath. Did she truly intend to take advantage of her newfound freedom?

"You are most kind, but Perry and I have arranged to go north, to Northumberland, to be exact. We will fetch the young Duke of Atholl from his school and spend the summer *en famille* with the duke and duchess and their new darlings."

The Queen smiled, and Charity sensed she had passed the test. "Please convey my respects and congratulations." She adjusted her gloves, preparing to move away, but Charity raised a hand to stay her.

"If it pleases Your Majesty, we will return to London in time to join you in celebrating the new year."

"So be it," the Queen replied, her lips curving in approval. "I will see your names added to the guest list. Safe travels, Your Grace. You go with my sincere thanks."

Epilogue

"The greatest thing in the world is to know how to belong to oneself."
— **Michel de Montaigne**

They descended upon Alnwick Castle like an army upon the plains, with carriage after carriage rolling through the castle gates. Charity and Perry rode at the front of the line, followed by Selina and Lark, then Ravenscroft and Antoine. Thorne had weighed all the options and suggested he might ride on Horse. But after that suggestion was roundly shouted down, he had meekly joined Selina and Lark in their carriage.

At Charity's insistence, Hodges had brought his sister and her brood along as well. The young Duke of Atholl had taken an immediate interest in the more streetwise Sammy and had abandoned Charity and Perry to ride with the lower orders—much to Martha's dismay. But it was hard to resist the charm of the young heir.

Charity hardly begrudged her young ward whatever happiness

he could find. Losing his mother and then father had left him an orphan with a title. She would never forget her promise to the old duke that she would watch over him and see him grow into a fine man worthy of the Atholl line.

As the servants flowed out to welcome the guests, their eyes wide in shock at the sheer numbers, Perry cast her a worried glance.

"Do you suppose they have rooms enough to hold all of us?" he asked, leaning sideways to get a better view of the towering facade. "Perhaps you should have been more specific about who you were bringing along when you wrote to Grace."

"It *is* a castle," she reminded him, and then stretched up to kiss him on the tip of his nose. "Thorne assured us we would all be welcome. Open the door and help me down. I have had enough of the confines of this carriage to last me a month."

Her husband did as she bid, leaping down and then holding out a hand while she gathered her skirts. By the time her feet hit the ground, Grace and Roland were on their way out the door.

The women grasped hands and kissed each other on the cheeks, each talking over the other in their excitement at being reunited.

"Your Grace?" Roland asked Peregrine, with a sardonic tilt of his head. "Will you demand all of us address you by your new title?"

"Don't you start," Perry growled. "Lord Ravenscroft has spent the entire trip trying on new names for me, now that he has determined I can no longer be called 'Canary.' Please do not give him any help."

Roland grinned, and the expression was so like Thorne's, it was uncanny. "Prinny's magpie is here as well?" Roland shifted around as though he were just then noticing the line of carriages filling the drive.

"Lord Ravenscroft, his valet, the Marchioness of Normanby, my sister, *your* brother—shall I continue the full list?" Perry told him dryly. "If this circus is too much for you, blame your brother. He had the chance to quell the numbers and insisted there was enough room for everyone."

"I avoided the Season in London, sent my brother instead, and as punishment it seems he brought half of London back to my doorstep." Despite his grumblings, he bore a broad smile on his face. "Truly, I know he was assisting you. But I was hoping he might find time to meet—"

Roland froze, and Perry turned, seeing Thorne giving Lady Normanby a hand down from their carriage. Sina was giving Thorne an arch expression, but Perry recognised that posture. That slightly taunting look.

"Come and meet the twins," Charity called excitedly, interrupting the men.

Perry turned and spotted his gorgeous wife carrying a pink-wrapped bundle in her arms. For a split second, he did not know if he was seeing the present or some future view, but either way, he wanted it desperately.

"Meet Anna," she announced, shifting the blanket to give Perry a view of the baby's rosy cheeks and dark hair. "And the other is Isaac."

With a challenging look, Grace handed her son to Peregrine. But if she expected him to be awkward or flustered, she was going to be disappointed. Perry had only been a boy of eight when his sister had been born, but he had spent plenty of time holding her. He happily accepted Isaac, cradling the boy with ease, and arched his brow at his wife's best friend, daring her to pout about it.

But Grace's lips instead formed a sly, knowing curve.

Motherhood had softened Grace's features and rounded her cheeks, turning her from a pretty waif into a beautiful woman. Roland wrapped a fond arm around his wife's shoulders and stared down at his heir with such pride that Perry's heart warmed.

The wager he had made with Roland Percy last year had worked out for the best for everyone.

Charity lifted her nose from the baby's head, cherishing the indefinable scent and softness of a babe not even three months old. Lord Ravenscroft was standing not far away, seemingly busy brushing the travel dust from his fitted jacket.

She knew better. It was a vain habit likely meant to disguise his discomfort at being in unfamiliar surroundings. To be fair, the north *was* rather a far cry from London or Brighton.

Charity turned to her husband, still holding Isaac. "Would you like to repay the magpie for his torments?" she whispered to him, and Perry's answering, devilish grin made her heart race.

"What do you have in mind, Sparkles?" he asked, eyes twinkling as he took in Antoine helping him fuss with his cravat.

She didn't answer, turning to her best friend. "May we show Lord Ravenscroft the babies? We had best rescue him lest the wrinkles from the travel drive him to distraction," she urged Grace. "He and Antoine were as much in need of a respite from society as the rest of us."

Grace studied the pair closely, clearly sensing mischief, but Roland patted his wife's shoulder. "Go ahead, Fitzroy."

Charity led the way, her husband hurrying to keep up. By the time they reached Ravenscroft, Antoine was standing beside his lover, uncertain what to do about being descended upon by two persons of such rank bearing infants like weapons.

"My lord, you absolutely must see baby Anna!" she gushed

enthusiastically, giving Ravenscroft no time to argue. "Here, hold her so you can see how small she is. Perry, let Antoine hold Isaac."

Gently but firmly, Charity deposited the bundle of Grace's daughter in his arms. Laughing, Peregrine gave Antoine the boy.

Antoine fared far better than Ravenscroft, quickly cooing over his bundle.

Anna, however, started to fuss, and Ravenscroft was instructed on how to lift her up to his shoulder, patting her. She promptly spat up all over the shoulder of his coat, relieved of her upset stomach.

"You may think you are safe now that you no longer have to worry about your mother, Fitzroy," the dandy said in a tone best described as gently murderous, still stroking the baby's back. "But don't worry. I will finish what McGrath started with you."

Perry gave the magpie a sunny smile. "Don't blame me for this. It was entirely my wife's idea. And she was the one who gave you Anna."

Ravenscroft turned to Charity and gave her *the look* that promised retribution.

Alnwick was so... green. And vast.

Peregrine had spent time at the Fitzroy country house, but like Ravenscroft, he was clearly a man of the city. For perhaps the first time ever, he could understand what might possess a man to paint a landscape.

But for the moment, he couldn't envision filling his sketchpad with anything besides his wife.

He watched Roland greet his brother with a careful, one-armed hug. Roland was looking down at Thorne's sling, and he turned to scowl at Perry. But Thorne said something, laughing, to his brother, and Percy's expression eased.

Grace was making the acquaintance of Selina. She looked… intimidated by the marchioness. He could hardly blame her.

Lark had politely greeted their hosts. But when Roland and Grace's attention turned towards Thorne, she slipped away, coming up to Perry's side.

"It is… kind of His Grace to be so close to Sir Nathaniel," she said. "They seem to care a great deal about one another, despite his parentage."

He put his arm around his sister. When she pressed hard against him, he understood she was still a little uncertain about her welcome in their family cluster. And perhaps about her future, but they had all summer to finish healing the marks Marian Fitzroy had left behind on all of them.

"Percy chose who he wanted to make his family," he told her. "Besides, it seems hard not to like Sir Nathaniel."

Lark scoffed a small laugh, and Perry stiffened. "What?" he asked her.

"I was only thinking—Lady Normanby seems to agree with you. Though I think she likes him rather more than she wants to."

"Oh?" Peregrine drawled, leaning in to invite her gossip. "Did something happen in the carriage?"

"No." Lark's face lightened, taking on a sense of mischievous happiness that he hadn't seen in far too long. "But I did force them to sit on the same bench together a few times. It was… the most awkward thing I have ever seen. I nearly perished trying to hold back my laughter."

Perry did laugh.

Alnwick Castle's grassy yard was full of children.

Martha's children and James, the young Duke Atholl, were introduced to Roland's wards, Wes and Willa. And though things were stilted at first—even young, the children recognised the differences in their stations—Wes and Willa coerced Sammy and his siblings into a game of tag.

James stood near Charity, hunched slightly in dejection as the odd child out.

Charity tilted her head towards him. "What is the matter?"

"I wish I could play too," the boy murmured to her.

He clearly felt so isolated and alone that Charity's heart went out to him. "So, why do you not go play with them?" she asked him, touching the tip of his nose playfully with the tip of her finger.

"Because it's not allowed," the boy said stoutly. And then he looked doubtful. "Is it?"

He knew only what he had been taught. Schools and his governess would have emphasised the importance of understanding boundaries. Of keeping himself apart.

She bent down slightly, pressing a kiss to the top of the boy's head. "There is a time for following the rules and minding appearances," she agreed, "but this is a safe place. Go ahead and play!"

The boy hesitated only a moment longer, and then with a whoop, he joined the others.

Grace came over and locked arms with Charity. "I am so glad you brought everyone! I love Alnwick, but really, I am so put out about missing all the excitement! Your letters did not have nearly enough information in them to satisfy my curiosity." She pretended to pout.

Charity leaned against her best friend, resting their heads

together. "You did not miss it as much as you think," she said wryly. "There were so many times this season I was afraid and I would think, 'I wish Grace was here.' You gave me strength—you and Perry both. So you were there for the adventure… in my heart."

Grace's eyes grew shiny, and she threw her arms around Charity. "Oh, but you must tell me *everything.*"

~

Dearest readers,

You may be asking yourselves what is coming next in this Regency world of ours. The short answer is we don't know. We do see a story between Selina and Thorne, but we are not ready to write it yet. To make sure you get notified of future new releases, sign up for my newsletter. You can use this link: https://lynnmorrison.myflodesk.com/bab. You can also find the sign-up form on my website: lynnmorrisonwriter.com.

Writing this trilogy was an incredible amount of work. We don't want to take on another story until we are certain we can do it justice. And let's be honest - Selina won't accept anything less than our best! (And Thorne deserves it too, after everything.)

Happy reading,

Lynn & Anne

Historical Notes

Warning for people who like to read these first: Here will be spoilers!

When Lady Fitzroy departed for unknown shores at the end of The Ruby Dagger (Book 2 in The Crown Jewels Mysteries), we knew she would return. The only question was when and how. To answer those questions, we dove into the historical records for inspiration. Ideally we wanted her return to be at least a year later, so we could give Perry and Charity time to grow and change before taking the big step into main characters.

When we learned of the visit of the Allied Sovereigns in the summer of 1814, we hit the jackpot. Lady Fitzroy could return with an army at her back and a king (or Tsar in this case) on her arm. The Crown would be stymied, requiring Perry and Charity to come up with a master plan to take her down. The summer of 1814 brought along another significant moment—the short-lived betrothal between Princess Charlotte Augusta of Wales and Prince William, hereditary heir of Orange. We overlaid the critical dates and found an exact match. Hooray! And then we started plotting. Cue the madness!

We stayed as close to the historical records as we could, while taking liberties when the plot absolutely required. We also filled in a lot of gaps with our own best guesses (and our imaginations).

The visit of the Allied Sovereigns

Archived copies of The Gentleman's Magazine provided a detailed diary of the visit, and proved to be a critical reference point for our plotting. What day did they go to Ascot? What route did they take? How many people attended the dinner at Frogmore? We found this information as interesting as the original subscribers must have back in 1814.

One key bit we had to fudge was the presence of Prince Nicholas of Russia. By the time we realised he had not come along, we were too far into the book to make a change. And so, he found himself as an unexpected plus one to the event.

The antics of both the Grand Duchess of Oldenburg and her brother the Tsar were well documented. Neither gave one whit about English protocol, finding greater entertainment in thumbing their noses at Prinny's expectations.

The Royal Betrothal

Moving on to the ill-fated Princess Charlotte. The Royal Archive Online of the Royal Collection Trust offered us rare insight into the mind of the young princess. Their digitised archives of the Georgian papers included many of her letters during the week between her seeming acceptance of the engagement and subsequent ending of it. The letters have been fully photographed and are available for view online at no cost, allowing us (and you) to see her words as written by her own hand.

Now, the letters did not mention anything about a Duchess of Atholl, so don't expect to find Charity or Perry in the archives. What is somewhat true is the debaucherous scene at Frogmore House. Prince Paul of Württemberg was very much in attendance and did seem to go out of his way to push Prince

William of Orange deep into his cups. As you can understand, Princess Charlotte was not impressed, especially coming so soon on the heels of her agreeing to marry him. Is it any wonder she dug in her heels and demanded to be freed of the engagement bonds?

Prince Leopold

Prince Leopold, the princess's eventual husband, was in attendance that summer and did meet the princess during one of her visits to see the Grand Duchess at the Pulteney. We don't know if it was a case of love at first sight, or simply the realisation that there were other options available that drove the Princess to call off her wedding. In 1816, she and Leopold married. She died a year and a half later after delivering a stillborn son. Her death set up the path of succession that eventually led to Victoria ascending the throne.

We decided to make Leopold a sympathetic character here as a way to hint at the princess's future (albeit brief) happiness.

Baron Friedrich von Gentz

During our plotting, we needed an independent third-party who could offer some assistance to Perry. We were just about to invent a character when we stumbled upon Baron Friedrich von Gentz, a man who *really was* known as The Propagandist.

The man was, quite simply, even more interesting than anyone we might have imagined. Prussian by birth, his gift with the pen helped him achieve international acclaim. Governments around the continent offered him support and stipends for most of his life, in recognition of the important role he played in defeating Napoleon. It was Austrian Chancellor Klemens von Metternich who kept him close to his side, allowing him to sit in on every diplomatic meeting, no matter how secret. He also sent him to the Congress of Vienna in the autumn of 1814.

Baron von Gentz was exactly the sort of man who would have surveyed the playing field and determined which side was worthy of his support. Given how our story ended, we'd say the fictionalised version chose well!

Marian Fitzroy's Last Scheme

(Hi, Anne here) Marian Fitzroy's last evil scheme took a while to evolve. We kept picking up and discarding ideas as being too small. Simply trying to assassinate the Tsar didn't feel worthy of her genius. But I couldn't think of anything better until I did exactly what Perry did: I made a list of everyone who had crossed Marian or who she would need to eliminate to set Russia—and herself—up to become the next great empire. Once I realised that all of her biggest targets were at the one table, then suddenly I had the idea that all I really needed was a bomb.

At this time in history the definition of a bomb was rather different, and mostly limited to artillery. But the idea of putting a bunch of black powder in a place to blow something up was definitely not a new one. I referenced two notable historical examples: The Gunpowder Plot of 1605 and Napoleon's assassination attempt in 1800 during the plot of the rue Saint-Nicaise, with what the French called 'Machine Infernale.'

But what about the clockwork device that could serve as a remote detonator? Surely that's a piece of fiction? Well, yes, but no. The engineering for such a device all existed well before 1814, as it operated on the same mechanical principles as triggering a clock to chime. Isaac Doolittle invented the first credited attempt at a time bomb for use in the American Revolutionary war of 1776.

But everything Thorne says about such clockwork devices was true. The mechanisms were touchy and easy to spring, which made them poor choices in the theatre of war. For a stationary bomb, however? It would serve. All it had to do was make a spark. Boom.

A Few Final Bits

Anne came up with the idea to have Lord Ravenscroft give

Perry a bottle of so-called 'Comet Vintage' wine for his engagement gift. When a comet passed through the skies prior to harvest, winemakers considered this a good omen for that year's vintage. One of the most famous examples is the wine of 1811 - the year of the Great Comet. That year, the Great Comet remained visible to the naked eye for 260 days. The wine from that year was considered exceptional (though some of that is owed to new technology). It was such an interesting historical tidbit that Anne had to include it.

She also mentioned the Treaty of Tilsit, a pair of peace treaties signed between Napoleon and Tsar Alexander, and Napoleon and King Frederick William III of Prussia in July 1807. The treaties created an alliance between Napoleon and the Russians at great cost to the Prussians, who lost half of their territory. With Napoleon later defeated in 1814 (and again in 1815), King Frederick William once again became an important player on the world stage.

(Hi, Anne again here) I have two last bits, the first of which is a confession about the Pulteney's coffee room scene. We had difficulty finding a place where both men and women of any delegation would be free to congregate together. The room and its political atmosphere would not have been a place where women were welcomed, in reality, but we stretched the truth.

The second involves poison shenanigans. Something I *didn't* use but you might find hilarious is that coffee enemas were a real, honest-to-god documented medical treatment for people in comas and poisonings. I spared Charity the indignity. And all of the rest of us. You're welcome.

Acknowledgments

Long before we dreamed of writing historical fiction, we bonded over our shared love for Jacqueline Carey's Kushiel series. Her intricate plots, regal settings, complex morality, and truly villainous characters had us waxing lyrically. Inspired by her, we set off to write a court intrigue series of our own.

We had no idea what we were getting ourselves into.

It is safe to say that the Diamond of the Ton series would not have seen the light of day in as good a shape as it is without the editorial help of Zoe Burton and Ken Morrison. Brenda Chapman and Lois King provided both moral support and attention to detail, reading early drafts of all three books and giving us detailed feedback.

Kim Killion at The Killion Group understood our vision for the covers and did a fantastic job of showing Perry's and Charity's journey towards their Happily Ever After.

Our husbands and children mostly did their best to stay out of our way when the plot knots threatened our sanity. At all other times, they balanced out the universe with lots and lots of interruptions. Fortunately, we love them, so they are still around. (Reminder - insert poison joke here.) (No. No poison jokes.) (LISTEN, we've spent so much time researching poisons. It feels like a waste NOT to have a poison joke.)

So many thanks to our Discord and Twitch friends for making us laugh and keeping us company while we wrote. This includes Lindsay Sfara (Writerlii), Oz (The_Egg_and_I), and Krista Walsh

(KristaWalshAuthor). Also big thanks to Heather G Harris for sending Lynn long voice notes just when she needed them.

We also want to send a shout-out to Linda's ducks: Perry and Charity. Discovering we had inspired her duck names made our month!

Last, and far far from least, thanks to all of you for coming along with us for the wild ride in 1814 London. For not complaining too much when we had to play fast and loose with the historical record. For loving Perry and Charity as much as we do. And for letting us know it was okay for Marian to finally get her due.

And for our fans who haven't gotten enough love in their life, know that you have ours, too.

About Anne Radcliffe

As an American Expat living in Ontario with a husband and teen son, Anne Radcliffe spends a lot of time editing or writing in order to avoid having to become a Maple Leafs fan. Anne loves a great story no matter the genre or medium - books, graphic novels, TV, movies or video games. You can find out more about Anne on her website at AnneRadcliffe.com.

BB bookbub.com/authors/anne-radcliffe

g goodreads.com/anneradcliffe

a amazon.com/stores/author/B0D1VMVDZ1

About Lynn Morrison

Lynn Morrison lives in Oxford, England and Venice, Italy along with her husband, two daughters and two cats. Born and raised in Mississippi, her wanderlust attitude has led her to live in California, Italy, France, the UK, and the Netherlands. Despite having rubbed shoulders with presidential candidates and members of parliament, night-clubbed in Geneva and Prague, explored Japanese temples and scrambled through Roman ruins, Lynn's real life adventures can't compete with the stories in her mind.

She is as passionate about reading as she is writing, and can almost always be found with a book in hand. You can find out more about her on her website LynnMorrisonWriter.com.

You can chat with her directly in her Facebook group - Lynn Morrison's Not a Book Club - where she talks about books, life and anything else that crosses her mind.

facebook.com/nomadmomdiary

instagram.com/nomadmomdiary

bookbub.com/authors/lynn-morrison

goodreads.com/nomadmomdiary

amazon.com/Lynn-Morrison/e/B00IKC1LVW

Also by Lynn & Anne